Forbidden

Forbidden

CHARLES LIGHTCAP

iUniverse, Inc.
Bloomington

FORBIDDEN

This is a work of fiction. All of the characters, names, incidents, organizations, and dialogue in this novel are either the products of the author's imagination or are used fictitiously.

iUniverse books may be ordered through booksellers or by contacting:

iUniverse
1663 Liberty Drive
Bloomington, IN 47403
www.iuniverse.com
1-800-Authors (1-800-288-4677)

ISBN: 978-1-4759-7712-7 (sc)
ISBN: 978-1-4759-7714-1 (hc)
ISBN: 978-1-4759-7713-4 (e)

Library of Congress Control Number: 2013902840

Printed in the United States of America

iUniverse rev. date: 3/15/2013

Edited by Rachel Hopkins

Dedication

I WANT TO TAKE this opportunity to dedicate this fictional work to mainly one child, and toward the public's awareness of the babies that have cancer. I was fortunate to have met Katie Duffin and her family members while I volunteered at the Oncology Clinic within Saint Christopher's Hospital for Children located in Philadelphia, Pennsylvania.

There are thousands of babies and children diagnosed with cancer every year, but the public's awareness is mainly directed toward adults. Let it be known that once a person is diagnosed with cancer, they have to deal with its effects until the day of their death. Remission is not the end; it is merely a stage of cancer, only the beginning of the ongoing stress related to its ever possible relapse.

I believe that what I was recently told is actually the truth, but I find it difficult to comprehend "Why?" The American Cancer Society allocates less than 1% of the public's donations to the needs of our children, but yet 19% to the paperwork and telephone calls that procure the public's donations.

I retired from my life's work in September 2001, and subsequently found that I had many more hours to myself, which enabled me to put more time into this fictional journey and I was able to volunteer some of my time. Volunteering was always impossible to do during my working years due to the fact that I always worked split shifts with many types of children. During the last year, I continued to write, always attempting to close in on an ending. During 2003, I found the time to volunteer at St. Christopher's Hospital for Children.

Three of my nieces work at St. Christopher's, and Joyce Hathaway told me of Dr. Halligan who heads up the Oncology Clinic; Joyce had compliments for this doctor and his staff. Knowing that I wanted to work with kids that had cancer, she directed me to this doctor. All of the necessary paperwork was completed and then I was notified of my start date.

As of October 2003, I had volunteered on Wednesdays and Thursdays, and eventually worked entirely within the Oncology Department. It was at this time in my life that I experienced mixed emotions, but more often than not, a warm smile appeared upon my face, for I thought of a child named Katie Duffin who I had met back in June.

What a spectacular child; playful, joyful, filled with life and energy, warm and generous, Katie cared enough about others to have her own cancer website. I knew nothing of Katie's history, but for whatever the reason, she chose to reach out and befriend me.

Katie's mother, Terri, accompanied her to the clinic, and after witnessing them together, we gradually became acquainted. I always brought an assortment of puzzles, and games to the clinic, and it was these items that made Katie and many of the other children happy and challenged, despite their debilitating illness.

It was after a couple of months that Terri chose to share something that I forever hold close to my heart; she said that Katie always asked, before coming to the clinic, if Charley was going to be there today.

Until June of 2003, Katie's cancer had been in remission, but then it relapsed with a vengeance; believe it or not, Katie was only experiencing the fourth year of her life. She had already endured enough pain and suffering for an entire lifetime, but more was to come.

This is not to say that her pain and suffering is unique, for it is not; all of the parents, brothers and sisters, and the children diagnosed with cancer: Travis, Ashley, Icelsa, Matthew, Natasha, Felicia, Jordan, Emma, Sean, Lee, Ronesha, and Jonathan have all experienced a similar misery.

I have been fortunate when it comes to understanding the pain that I see at the clinic, for it severely affects the lives of everyone involved. The parents are the ones that have to cope with all of the surgery, and subsequent healing and scarring; the physical changes, the stares from the public, the one-hundred-plus visits to the clinic, the inconvenience and costs, the learned ability to calm their grief stricken and terrified child, the varying blood counts, the mood changes that the therapies cause, the radiation treatments, the remission, the possibility of a relapse and, above all else, the resources to keep their child's hope alive whenever he or she looks to them for support.

I think that it was in June of 2003 when Katie relapsed and subsequently had to struggle mightily to reclaim her health and happiness, but it was not to be! Months of visits, and continuing on with chemotherapy; unbelievable pain and the suffering, and as a last resort, intensive dosages of radiation; but all was in vain.

While the morphine dripped, causing her entire body to itch, Katie found herself agitated, but she continued to fight for her right to life. One week, and then almost two in the ICU; her days were stable while her nights continued to be life threatening.

Certain to die one night, she miraculously overcame what appeared to be inevitable, and was actually thriving the next day; preparing for the challenge. Every hour of every day, night, and subsequent morning, Katie had visitors, but the mainstays were her mother, father, and grandmother.

Katie's father's name is Paul, as is her brother's, and they all did their best to provide loving support. Although the immediate family, relatives, and friends were always warm and gracious, what affected me most were the times that I would visit Katie's room and find Katie and her father alone, snuggled together while sleeping on a chair, or in Katie's hospital bed.

Occasionally, Katie was able to fight off her morphine induced sleep and open her eyes; it was at these times that she searched for someone, said a few words, and in no time, was again fast asleep.

Her prognosis worsened and the nights were completely debilitating; during the evening of August 12th, 2003, Katie finally breathed her last. It was a few weeks before her fifth birthday. After her death, a few people were heard to say, "Katie was this..." or "Katie was that..." To me, *Katie Is, and will always be love!*

$\mathcal{P}$reface

FORBIDDEN IS MY FIRST work in the realm of fiction, and while it has many factual names and locations, it is, for the most part, merely a fantasy.

The inspiration to write Forbidden came as a result of watching a television show, or maybe it was something I heard on the radio many years ago when I was a child. Those were the evenings when listening to the radio vied with a new-fangled contraption, the television; it had no remote control, the picture rolled, and the initial picture tube was horizontally flat.

To view the black and white picture, the lid had to be elevated at a forty-five degree angle, thus permitting the picture to be seen from a distance through an image reflecting mirror attached to the underside of the angled lid.

Well, at that time, there was a daily show and it totally captivated me. I do not remember the title, but it was the lead character that made the show appealing. Radio was very descriptive and convincing; it really did not matter whether the program was actually heard on the radio or seen on television, for the characters were vivid to the audience. The lead character was dressed in all black, had a full-length flowing cape, and a wide-brimmed, black hat. This character lived underground, though he occasionally surfaced to roam the dimly lit, cobble-stone, catacomb-like passageways of the city...perhaps it was Paris?

What caught my attention was the way the man wore and carried his cape; he had a crooked arm, with his forearm held directly in front of his face, and the cape hung from it, thus never revealing his identity.

If you had grown up with me in Germantown and we remained in contact during our lifetimes, it is possible that the creature-like being could be seen as paralleling the life and times of myself.

It was during the year 1999 that I began working on *Forbidden,* and while I labored, I would occasionally find an eager audience listening to what had been written to that point in time. Each time that I had the chance to share this story, it was inevitable that a passerby would stop and eavesdrop, eventually wanting to know if what I was discussing actually had happened. When responding that the work was fictional, the eavesdropper would say that it sounded as if it was reality.

Whether it is reality or fiction, there is the distinct possibility that Doylestown and the town of Edison, both located within the County of Bucks in Pennsylvania, were evident one-hundred and fifty years ago. At that point in time, the majority of the County of Bucks was rich in farmland, and as people walked nearby, the smell of fertilizer permeated the footpaths. To the farmers, this was what drove them to work from very early in the morning, until late in the evening, six days of every week. The farmers owned the land that they worked, and many farms were in excess of one-hundred acres.

Farming in the County of Bucks was good, and the richness of the soil enabled them to supply the demand that was necessary for all to prosper. Year after year, the supply always met the demand; there were vegetables, fruits, corn, and a variety of grains. Gradually, the communities grew; some more significantly than others, but everyone depended upon these crops to sustain themselves and their ever growing families.

Life was better than could be expected, and then change reared its ugly head; initially, the change lacked volatility. For whatever the reason, an unsightly child was born to one of the more influential families within the county. A midwife delivered the baby and was substantially paid to keep quiet; she did so, and during the years that followed, there were other births of this kind; like the first, they remained known only to the immediate family and the midwife.

It was gradual, but over time, these unsightly babies matured, as did the horrific sores that gradually covered most of their bodies. Initially, these sores could be maintained, but in time, they began to secrete a liquid that possessed the foulest of odors.

Eventually, it became more than evident that one family after another, previously seen as active in their community, had all of a sudden become reclusive. When the first family became what was considered as withdrawn, it was seen as an oddity. Ultimately, several of the families stopped attending church and their children stopped attending school; this created a great pause within the entire community.

Very early one morning, a child was on her way to the schoolhouse, but instead of taking the lengthy path, she chose to cut through a neighboring farmer's field. She knew the family and noticed what she thought to be a strange child at a distance. The child was working alone in the field and was seemingly planting seed here and there. All the while, the child laid the seed while the oncoming girl remained unnoticed. As the little girl moved further upon her path, she realized that she did not recognize the little girl planting seed. While watching the child lay the seed, a "hello" escaped her lips. Startled, the children could do nothing but stare at each other; both remained this way for what seemed to be an eternity, and during this period, it became evident that there was something unsightly about this child, or was it a child?

You can imagine how much fear enveloped the teacher and the other kids when it was announced that there was someone, or something, in a farmer's field. When questioned further, it became evident that what was seen in the field was an unknown entity; it was probably a child, but as grotesque as some sort of creature. Further questioning revealed that the unknown entity eventually ran from the field and entered the nearby home, as if it knew where to go.

During one of the ensuing town meetings, it was revealed that the unknown entity was indeed a young child, a child born with leprosy. Of course, there was concern, that is, until it became evident that all of the families that had previously chosen to become reclusive had one or more children born with this disease. Each family attempted to raise their diseased child, or children, but in time, reality caused change. As hard as it was to believe, the hierarchy of each family unit committed themselves to the fact that a separate community had to be constructed, and when ready, all of the diseased would be the ones to live there for the remainder of their lives.

Years passed and every so often, a diseased baby was born, thus becoming unsightly and a member of the leper colony. During the initial stages of the colony, family members would visit, but over time, the grotesque appearances and the adjoining horrific odors caused all but a few to stay away.

Through research, it was realized that the colony had a noncommunicable disease; a disease that could not be passed on to others by any means. The colony's population continued to grow, and as it did, borders widened. This caused it to be secluded, and further away from the nearest of the communities.

There was a growing fear that the colony would somehow, sooner or later, though most probably sooner, negatively impact the supply and demand for the crops that the farmers and their families depended upon for their livelihood. The leper colony grew, and then, for whatever the reason, there were no more leprous babies born outside the confines of the colony. What appeared to be odd was that the community's offspring ceased having the debilitating disease.

One town meeting after another provided no viable solution. Meetings were continually organized, but the attendance gradually became less and less; there seemed to be no answer for the riddance of the dreaded leper colony. Frustration was rampant and then, the answer came; an answer that made sense, but it did not sit well with most within the community, for the diseased were all directly related.

Chapter 1

HEAVY EQUIPMENT WAS BEING brought in on flatbed trucks owned by Dick Geppert of 'Geppert Bro.' and this current flatbed was being driven by John Henry Lightcap, husband to Kathleen and father to Ryan and Grace. John was responsible for securing the equipment onto the elongated flatbed trailer, and then delivering its contents to a specified site. Once the equipment arrived at its destination, the equipment would be driven off the rig. This process continued on throughout the day and into the evening, if necessary.

When all of the equipment had been delivered to the sites, it was then that John would drive back to Geppert's storage yard. John didn't return to these specific construction sites until the job had been completed, unless there was no longer a need for that piece of equipment, or that a piece of heavy equipment had broken down.

The equipment was often loud, and its heavy tracks vibrated the barren earth; as each machine rumbled around a site, one could already visualize an established housing development or mall. The drivers of these powerful mammoths are usually within their own world, often listening to music at full volume on their headphones as they level the land mass to the specifications of the developer. One of these drivers, a fellow by the name of Jeff Fischer, finally recognizes, as he works the land, far away from any of the other equipment operators, that his bulldozer is sinking heavily, more-so to the rear. The bulldozer is also leaning to his left, and this is confusing because the land has been previously surveyed, and is considered to be flat, and solid.

Jeff, until this point in time, had been enjoying his favorite Led Zeppelin song, but luckily notices before it is too late that the bulldozer is slowly sinking; Jeff immediately and forcefully shifts the machine into its lowest gear and the bulldozer responds, climbing steadily out of its descent and onto an area where it sits level. Upon the realization that his mammoth was now on solid ground, he halted the machine, removed his headphones, and sat motionless. As Jeff was regaining his "not a worry in the world" attitude, he still felt a considerable amount of anxiety, and thus he made sure that the machine was in neutral. He climbed down from the bulldozer and approached the hole.

When fairly close to the hole, he recognized a horribly foul and putrid stench emanating from it; acrid enough to make him immediately and violently sick to his stomach. He swiftly turned away, as if hiding his face from a fistic assault, and forcefully vomited until he was experiencing extensive dry heaves. Thinking that this was a previously placed sewage pipe and that the bulldozer had somehow split it open, Jeff struggled to get his thoughts together. Fearing that he might be held accountable and cause the company a possible lawsuit, he straightened his torso and looked around the area, trying to assess if his recent actions had gained the attention of any of the other operators. Fortunately for Jeff, he was in an area all by himself and the closest of the other operators was about eighty-five yards away. From that distance, it was probably assumed that Jeff had gotten off his rig to check something lying on the ground, and when he bent over, that he was merely investigating what he had found. No one appeared to have paid him more than the slightest bit of attention.

Jeff walked back and climbed upon his bulldozer, placed the engine into proper gear, lowered the shovel, and began to hide the damage. With each mound of dirt that was pushed back into the hole, the stench lessened, and eventually the hole was filled. Jeff added more dirt than what appeared necessary because he felt that the hole may not be totally filled. Slowly but surely, he drove the bulldozer around the outskirts of the mound, compacting the earth as he went. As Jeff got closer and closer to the center, he added more dirt and eventually the damaged area held the total weight of the metal monster. With each pass over this area, he felt more and more confident that the damage had been corrected and that no one would ever know that it was he who caused this sewer break.

"Whew!" impulsively gushed from Jeff's mouth as his stress level, and subsequently his blood pressure, lessened; these were replaced by a "get over it" kind of laughter. He drove away from this immediate area feeling so much relief, much like the relief that he felt after encountering a hostile teenager, verbally working through the problem with the youth, and finally after using his learned skills to resolve the issue. You see, Jeff's full time job is as a youth counselor at the Buck County Youth Center. However, he found it necessary to work part time as a heavy equipment operator. This extra work helped pay off his college loans, plus it helped with his newly acquired mortgage payment.

Chapter 2

MYCOBACTERIUM LEPROUS seeks the cool places in the host body, particularly the skin and the surface nerves. This makes it a very visible disease, starting with patches on the skin; it may also damage nerves in the face, arms and legs. No one likes being disabled, let alone having crooked hands, lumpy, swollen faces, or sores on their hands and feet. It is this visible disability or deformity that leads to much of the fear and stigma from which affected people suffer. This lends itself to feelings of fear and shame, which may mean that those who suffer then neglect to come for treatment at the onset of the disease, and only come when they already have nerve damage. Damaged nerves result not only in paralysis, but also in loss of sensation. Multi-drug therapy treatment cannot reverse nerve damage. Loss of sensation in hands, feet and eyes means that everyday activities are fraught with danger; burns go unrecognized, wounds untended, and stones in shoes and grit in the eyes both go undetected and untreated. The end result can be the loss of sight, fingers and feet.

The vast majority of humans that resided in the original Edison community were healthy and tested negative with regards to leprosy, and they were narrowly sighted when asked to be compassionate toward those that had this horrific disease.

Little was known about leprosy some 120 years ago. While most people have a natural immunity to the disease, those that do develop leprosy can be cured with modern treatment modalities. Life-long care of anesthetic limbs is one of the greatest challenges faced by people affected by leprosy, and neglect can cause damage so severe as to cause paralysis, such as clawed fingers or the inability to blink, resulting in corneal ulcers, and if untreated, blindness.

Worldwide, there are millions of people affected by leprosy, with over 800,000 new cases detected each year and over one million are on active treatment. A further two to three million people are estimated to be living with a disability incurred through leprosy.

Within the members of the governing body of the Edison community, judgment appeared to be easy when it came to decisions regarding those that had what they viewed as this diabolical, disabling disease. The governing body, and the townspeople of Edison, often gathered for town meetings, and when those afflicted with leprosy was the topic of conversation, the consensus of opinion was that these lepers would most probably prefer death, rather than a lifetime of pain and suffering. The community continually searched for a way to rid themselves of their leper colony.

The members of the community realized that it was the fault of the leper colony that they were afflicted with this horrible disease. A consideration was given to displace the colony to a desolate location to live out the remainder of their lives; for it was quite evident that none in the colony would purposely procreate the continuance of their pain-filled existence. This decision not to procreate their kind was evidenced by the fact that every one of their unplanned offspring has always been inflicted with this disabling disease, and its horrific appearance. The community of Edison, and their close neighboring areas, were well aware that all within the colony saw procreation as a means of bringing inevitable, unwanted pain and suffering to a newborn.

There was considerable thought given to exiling the colony to a far off wooded area where they could live out the remainder of their lives together; a location, similar to a commune, a concept which was prevalent during the 1960s. The community finally decided to move the leper colony deep into an isolated, remote wooded section of Edison. It was here that the colony lived for many years, though their seclusion continually weighed on the governing body of Edison and Doylestown.

Eventually, the leper colony took its toll on the community members that were not afflicted and an official town meeting was scheduled. At this meeting, the discussion centered upon the projected cost factor relating to the care of those living within the colony; the care that included costly items such as housing with central heating and air, waste management, a water supply, food, clothing, medical coverage, eye and dental maintenance, and other necessities.

Communication came from those living within the town of Edison, and also from others living in the surrounding communities of Bucks County. It was evident that something had to be done, and a decision had to be made during this meeting. Options were considered, but were quickly abandoned, mainly due to the fact that continual care would be a cost that was not affordable; along with the cost for daily care came the fear related to the potential spread of the disease.

These considerations weighed heavily upon the governing body of the community, and the eventual decision to exile the colony. However, not to a wooded area as it had in the past, but exiled to live the remainder of their lives deep within the black bowels of the earth.

Knowing that the lepers would be devastated if given the information that the Edison community had made the final decision to exile them into the deepest recesses of the earth's bowels, it seemed obvious that some means of communication had to be created. Several ideas of how to get the lepers within the earth, without a struggle, brought no viable solution. Considerable time passed and just when the meeting was about to break up, a solution was found, and was agreed upon by the majority. The community began the formal planning of the lepers' demise, that is, their proposed burial site.

Chapter 3

OFF BY ITSELF, FAR away from any resemblance of a community, within a thickly forested area, their search led them to an uninhabited place that appeared to be the answer. Laborers from the area worked at least eight hours per day, digging an extended tunnel that gradually descended, further and further toward the earth's core. Realizing that it was necessary to thoroughly confuse the lepers, once they were manipulated into these depths, the laborers were given plans to construct intersecting passageways to and from the far end of the initial passageway. A week passed, then two, and then a month, and the monumental feat continued.

A tremendous amount of earth was being removed; with each passing day, the passageway extended deeper and deeper, foot by foot, until it became evident that the laborers began to fear for their lives. Some of these laborers were extremely cocky, but the extreme depth also made them fearful of a cave-in. The laborers were assured by the engineers that the depth was safe and that the work could go on. The inability of the engineers to convince the laborers was the reason that precautions were finally taken, and these took on the form of the supports, such as those that had been erected in mine shafts of the Old West.

The pace of the work slowed as wooden beams and planks were installed to prevent a possible collapse. The work was time-consuming and quite rigorous: to fully understand, and to identify with the plight of the laborer, one would only have to use their musculature to the point of exhaustion. One of the laborers would use a pick axe to tear into the earth and another would use a shovel to load the moistened, weighted earth and variety of small rocks into whatever was available at that time. The rocks that were larger, and considered to be boulders, were not moved to the surface, instead they were merely unearthed and hand rolled to the farthest area of construction; the farthest point from the entrance, and completely out of the way. As the passageway gained in length, depth, and height; the rocks that were unearthed and could be lifted were clumsily carried to a location, close to that of the boulders.

Eventually, wheel driven containers were brought to the site and these measured approximately three feet by four feet, and were four feet in depth, with a rounded bottom. At each end of its length, and close the top, there were swivels that allowed its contents to be rotated from one side to the other, discarding it in a designated spot. Initially, these containers were pushed up the tunnel's gradual incline and once upon the surface, they were wheeled about fifty feet and then dumped. This process continued until the work load was too heavy to push it to the earth's surface.

It was at this point that the precautions came into play, where the beams and planks were installed over-head, and on the earthen walls. These precautions were deemed necessary due to the fact that the work was being done so far into the earth. Because of the length of the trek, the wheels were often heavily greased and holes were driven into and through the topmost area of each dumpster. The metal hole was approximately two inches in diameter, and covering the metal surrounding the hole was a constant lubricated material. This material allowed the rope to slide, in and out, without causing it any wear or damage.

One end of the rope was securely attached at the earth's surface and the other end, when extended to its full length, was in excess of 250 feet. This heavy, thickened rope was then laced through the holes and taken to the furthest depth. When the dumpster was three-quarters of the way filled with earth and small rocks, and stones, the laborers found it difficult to understand, "that with each load removed, their workload was increasing." The laborers saw it as, "with each load removed, the end to this dangerous job would come closer to an end." While this mentality made sense, the laborers found the idea, "that with each load removed, the workload was increased," to be ludicrous. However, with a thorough explanation, they realized that with each workload removed, they were gradually going deeper and deeper into the earth. This meant that each time the dumpster was filled; the decline would increase, causing the laborers to use more physical exertion to move each load from its starting position to the surface.

As the days turned into weeks, and the weeks into months, the passage gradually extended, until the construction began on the maze of deliberate, but useless passageways. Eventually, the maze of short, intricate, and complicated walkways was completed, and it exited to a lower area where another passageway extended to the entrance way of the intended burial room.

As the passageway lengthened, the workload became close to unbearable, so more laborers had to be brought in to assist those that pushed, and those that pulled the heavy loads. To lessen the struggle for the laborers known as the pullers, these men remained upon the surface and after knotting a separate length of heavy rope to the front of the dumpster, they would line up, one behind the other, and pull as if in a contested tug of war.

These powerful individuals pulled steadily, hand over fist; being of great help to the laborers below that were pushing. Using the musculature of their shoulders, chest and back, along with their own set of muscular legs, these chosen men used their shoulders, arms and hands to steer the dumpster along the temporarily lit passage. At the farthest area of the tunnel that was below where the dumpster and the pushers were situated, there stood two burly, muscle-bound men that had a firm grip on the farthest section of rope. The rope, also tied securely to a tree upon the earth's surface, extended downward from the surface, through the drilled holes in the dumpster, and then was held securely by the two burly men. This rope, when held quite taut, was used to help guide the path of the dumpster as it ascended the passageway, heading in the direction of the earth's surface.

The lengthy, ever descending passage, which led from the surface to the recent construction, had a crude pathway of soil and rocks. When this passageway began to show indentations from the wheels, it was then that there was a temporary work stoppage. Not knowing how fast the earth would give way to the dumpster's weight, it was decided to lay planks along the entire passageway. Initially, the pullers were only needed when the work began at the extreme depth of the passage; it was their responsibility to get the heavy load into motion. As the passageway lengthened, the pullers responsibility increased to the point where they continually pulled the weight of the loaded dumpster at the same time as the pusher's pushed, until its payload reached the earth's surface.

It should be noted here that when the intricacy of the maze was completed there was thought given to using its passageways rather than creating a bypass because the maze area was more level than the two tunnel sections. The laborers recognized that moving the dumpster throughout the labyrinth's intricate path might be less exhausting than when in the passageways, but this thought was given little merit after initially attempting the course. While it was true that the maze was more level than the passageways, its intricacy made the work much too laborious. Finally, after three and a half months, the initial passageway and maze were completed.

Now that the lowest passageway was being constructed, the fear of getting lost, as one went further and further, became a real concern for the laborers. As a solution, several clotheslines were secured at the earth's entrance and when extended, they reached a length of 275 feet. These lines were replaced every few days to avoid any breakage. When a laborer entered the initial passageway entrance, he would securely attach the line to his belt loop and then journey into the passageway, continually descending until he passed through the maze, and eventually came to a depth where the work was progressing. There was some exultation among the workers because they knew that the work was closing in upon its completion, and that meant they could get the hell out of this dangerous situation.

Further into the recesses of the earth's dank bowels, the second passageway went, and after every fifteen feet, the digging halted and that area was supported against the possibility of a cave-in. The work brought the crew to the point where the burial place was to be constructed. It was to be constructed off to one side of the lowest point of the passageway, and when finished, it would measure thirty square feet, with a height of eight feet. The puller's remained upon the earth's surface, pulling the separate rope that was attached to the front of the dumpster while the others pushed. The dumpster began its assent from the loading area, up the ever extending passageway, and traveled along the path of the rope's alignment, while the puller's and pusher's used their strength to advance the dumpster to the surface.

This work was so excruciatingly hard on the body that occasionally one or two would quit, only to find out later that there had been a pay raise. With each passing day, their bodies seemed to ache more than the previous one, for there was not any getting used to the back breaking work. It was commonplace in their everyday construction work where, with a similarity of each day's workload, a laborer's body would become accustomed to their muscle and joint pain; unfortunately, this was not the case relating to this work. With each workday, the load seemed to get heavier, and the pushing and pulling more pronounced, to the point where the pain was felt all the way to the core of one's being.

With each passing day, the large room, where the lower passageway led, began to take its intended size and shape. Eventually, it was finished and measured the size that was initially planned. It was late in the afternoon and all of the work was done; the laborers gathered their belongings and tools, and gradually removed themselves from the depths using the clothesline as their guide until they were breathing the clean air found upon the earth's surface. Before departing this site, one of the more macho-type laborers grabbed a hold of the thicker and heavier rope and retraced it, all the way to the burial place. Once there, the laborer placed the remaining section of the rope upon the burial chambers surface, and then retraced the rope, until it led him along the intended return route.

Ascending up and along the passageway, the path was eventually blocked, forcing a person to experience the intricate maze. Once through the elaborate and extremely difficult labyrinth, one could ascend another long passageway to the earth's surface. Before any of the laborers departed the area for the final time, each person, one at a time, touched the mobile dumpster, as if paying homage to it. Recognizing that this job was now completed, and that the day was Friday, the entire crew decided to celebrate at Kelly's Tavern in nearby Doylestown

Chapter 4

NOW THAT THE PASSAGEWAYS, the intricacy of the maze, and the burial chamber had been completed, the removal of the leper colony from the earth's surface was addressed--out of sight, out of mind.

It was fortunate for the majority of Edison's population that the lepers had previously organized their own community: The colony was a separate entity a good distance from all that didn't have the debilitating disease. Those without the affliction attempted to find a nonviolent solution for getting the lepers from their compound to the burial place, but the solutions involved too much force. After a while, the answer finally came to one of the more organized and calculating of the community; and this solution was so easy that all wondered why they had not come up with a similar solution.

It was decided to add a colorless, tasteless, sedative type drug to the leper's water supply and then deliver it to them. It was further decided that the water supply would be held back for two days so that the community could feel assured that the drugged water supply would be swiftly ingested by the entire group. This plan was simply intuitive; it was nonviolent and would be so easy to carry out, or so it seemed.

The plan went into effect on a Wednesday evening when the supply of water was not delivered. A messenger came into the leper compound and notified them that the water supply had somehow been contaminated and was causing severe bouts of diarrhea; that there would be no water until Friday evening. It was easy to see the confusion and fear on the faces of those within the compound, for a leper was dependent on its daily water consumption to a much greater degree than someone without the disease. Questions abounded, but the messenger confirmed that the water supply would be delivered early Friday evening. That kind of thing had never happened before, and so there was little suspicion that the messenger was lying. As the more insecure lepers began to feel increased anxiety, the messenger realized that some of these lepers were moving in the direction of his personal space. This movement made the messenger extremely anxious, and thus he swiftly departed the compound. When the messenger arrived within 'his' own community, he recounted his experience.

Friday evening came and the water supply was delivered as promised; it was easy to recognize just how the lepers cherished their daily supply. The hose nozzle was directed into an enlarged drum that had a 500 gallon capacity. At this time, the nozzle was held securely, the water line was opened, and the water came bursting from the nozzle, eventually topping off the drum with the fresh, drugged drinking water.

The leper colony, one and all, filled containers and ravenously drank their fill. They gulped, and swallowed the life sustaining liquid until they could drink no more. Now full, their bellies noticeably swelled, all experienced difficulty when walking. They eventually sat and let the water circulate their inner bodies; some. However, fell asleep while waiting for their comfort level to return.

As the evening wore on, the drug took its intended effect. Some were affected sooner than others, but all were eventually sedated. Watchers were posted on the distant perimeter, and as the hours passed, it became apparent that the lepers were stumbling and losing their balance. It was now night and while the full moon illuminated the sky, the leper colony was experiencing their induced sleep. The drug was expected to impact the entire colony by the early morning and to maintain its firm grip until late that evening. Around noon, the citizens of Edison entered the compound, finding the lepers overwhelmed by the effect of the drug. These citizens assisted the lepers onto their feet and guided their movements until all were seated in a number of school buses. The citizens remained on the buses to prevent the lepers from possible injury while they were en route to the passageway's entrance. Being quite clumsy, the lepers would occasionally nod off, but were quickly awakened so as not to allow the drug to affect them to the point where they became immobile. Eventually, the buses stopped and the lepers were handheld and guided toward the passageway.

Once at the passageway, the heavy rope, the same one that was previously attached to a tree in close proximity of the passageway's entrance, and extended through the labyrinth, until it lay bundled in the burial place, was checked to make doubly sure that it was securely fastened. It was at this point that the descent began toward the deepest, darkest bowels of the earth, descending in the direction of the burial chamber.

With each step, the lepers were led further, occasionally losing their balance, but remaining erect by tightly grabbing, and tugging onto the arm of one of the people that were guiding their descent. Surprisingly, the lepers paid more attention to keeping their balance, than to the reasoning for, or the direction that they were headed. Their guides led them along what appeared to be an everlasting jaunt, in and out, down and through passageways.

There were times when all were forced to stop and rest because the lepers were exhausted by the drug's influence, and their guides were weakened by the hold and weight the lepers had on their shirts, belts and arms. Their guides were greatly assisted by their headlamps because both of their arms were constantly occupied; one for supporting and righting the drug induced lepers, and the other for holding onto the heavy rope.

Initially, the thought was that there was no need for the rope, especially when having access to headlamps. However, that thought changed when the attempt was made to travel through the maze. During its construction, laborers regularly got lost and would eventually be found in one of the maze's pockets, and then were led to safety. Therefore, the rope was introduced for two good reasons; first, for safety, and secondly, so that those ascending the passageways could be guided through the maze, and when experiencing the steepness of the ascent, pulling upon the rope would be quite helpful.

During what seemed to be an endless trek, the guides held fast to the rope as it led them further towards what they considered to be the core of the earth. Finally, the trek culminated with their guides and the lepers finding the burial chamber. Now, with the burial chamber temporarily lit, the guides half carried the lepers into the center of this large room and laid them upon the earthen floor. Within a matter of seconds, as the lepers lay motionless, the drug noticeably induced a heavy sleep. Upon checking the entire colony and finding that all were experiencing their deep sleep, the guides returned to the surface, only to return with approximately a two week supply of food and clean water. This plan was accomplished without the slightest hitch, and once the lepers and supplies were delivered to the chamber, it was then that the guides retraced their route using the rope until they reached the surface. Now, upon the surface, the guides removed the last remaining perceived hope that the lepers would ever witness the surface of the earth. Or would they?

Yard by yard, hand over fist, the weight of the rope was drawn out of the chamber, up the passageway, and then it snaked through the labyrinth. Once out of that intricacy, it ascended, moving closer and closer to the earth's surface. The rope was pulled up the remaining length of passageway to the earth's surface, and there it was laid in a circular position, from its beginning to its end.

Realizing that the tunnel entrance was thoroughly hidden by the roughness of the terrain, and that it was seen to be impossible for the lepers to find their way to the earth's surface, the site engineers found that it was unnecessary to close off the entrance.

Chapter 5

MANY HOURS ELAPSED WHILE the lepers experienced their drug induced sleep, but now they began to stir. One by one, they came out of their heavy stupor, only to find that they had been blinded, or were they? Was each experiencing a kind of dream state?

As the first of the lepers gained consciousness, he attempted to communicate, hoping that he was not alone. At first, there was no response, and so feeling totally alone within this pitch black environment this sole leper remained stationary. Feeling stressed and equally anxious, he found that it was extremely difficult to listen to his immediate surroundings. As this leper's nervous system gradually calmed, he could hear what he believed to be another's breathing. He quieted as much as possible, and then was self-assured that it was, indeed, another's breathing. This leper, in an attempt to communicate once again, found himself exalted upon the realization that others in that area were stirring.

Hopefully, the breathing was coming from the lungs of one of his own kind. Tremendous relief washed over all of this leper's senses as the calm allowed it to pick up the body odor that was equal to no other; this could only be one of his own. Believing that his sense of smell was, indeed accurate, this individual communicated two messages to all that may be in that area. The messages were in the form of a statement, and a question: "That anyone in this immediate area was no longer alone," and "What was happening?"

As one of the other lepers captured its senses, it also felt that it was in the grip of a nightmare. Gradually, all of the lepers regained their conscious state; piecing together whatever they could remember. As the pieces of the puzzle began to take form, it became apparent that no one was clear headed. As they tried to recollect how they had gotten to this site, they continually ran into one mental block after another; the thoughts would appear, but before they concluded, they seemed to break down and disperse.

The last vivid recollection was that they were milling around, within their compound, and then they were at this destination, wherever this pitch black environment was. Fuzzy recollections that eventually came to mind were recounted as these lepers listened to each other's thought patterns. The gist of the memories was that they had somehow lost their composure and will, and found themselves being moved en masse, from their compound. How? Why?

One of the lepers offered, what it communicated as a garbled recollection, about being led to a vehicle and wanting to resist; but didn't! It seemingly lacked all will power! This same leper recollected bouts of losing, and then regaining consciousness, and being driven somewhere. He awakened, only to realize that he was falling, and that with someone's help, he regained his composure. This leper went on to communicate: "I vaguely remember being assisted as I walked down a hallway; and the further I walked, the cooler it got, until I stumbled one last time and lost consciousness." The only added recollection was that, "while stumbling and descending, it appeared as if someone was physically helping me." All of the lepers communicated that this was also the extent of their recollections and that none remembered getting to this present location. "Where were they?" "Why were they here?"

Another of the lepers also wanted to know where they were, but also wanted to know why their colony allowed themselves to be led into what appeared to be such a dismal, damp and cold location. They all realized that the community had recently shown a strong desire to rid themselves of the entire colony, but never dreamed that the community would take their want to this extreme. One day they were at their compound, and the next thing they realize is that they are somewhere unknown; unknown, where it is cold and void of light. Where the hell are we? It was obvious that the setting was absent of light; were they in a room without any windows?

As the lepers searched for the slightest bit of light, they also attempted to acclimate themselves to the dark. They began to get fearful, for no matter how often they tried, they could not see each other, or see their hands when directly in front of their faces. Could it be possible that they were blinded before entering the site where they now found themselves? The conclusion was evident as to why they were led here, and the overall consensus was that they were somehow manipulated during their previous day while in their compound.

Was it in the water? Becoming more and more clear-headed, the lepers recollected that their water supply wasn't delivered as it had always been; in fact, their compound was without its usual supply of water for two full days. The water supply came the following day and was ravenously ingested. It most probably contained some sort of debilitating, tasteless drug, and this allowed the community to remove the lepers, without the least bit of resistance to their present site...drugged!? We should have been prepared! Needless to say, they were not prepared, for here they were, not knowing for sure where, but obviously in an aphotic environment. The more their minds cleared, the clearer was their experience, or better yet, predicament.

Recognizing their inability to walk without great effort; and their weakened physical and mental state, they knew that somehow they had been drugged, en masse, prior to being led to this location. It was now evident to all of these lepers that they had been drugged. It was their recollection that they were led to the tunnel's entrance, and eventually led to this location, where they found themselves more than willing to be escorted. They knew that if they were in their right minds, they would not have followed along without a life or death struggle. These lepers, which included the elders, those that made up the hierarchy of the colony, after much attempted deliberation and mind boggling recollection, decided to set out upon what they hoped was their destiny: To discover the way out of this darkness.

The elders recognized why the community had decided to exile their kind to spend what remained of their lives within the bowels of the earth. These lepers had been drugged and abandoned, but the community's shortsighted leaders had come to this conclusion without enough time given to the circumstances. The community's leaders were of the belief that the lepers were so severely depressed and depleted, and that they visualized their lives in such an apathetic way, that they would all die off within this crudely constructed chamber. The community's leaders could have been correct in their assumption, but this, in no way, was the convincing factor for the leper's to simply lie down and die without some sort of fight.

Calmness somehow had prevailed as thought was given to their immediate surroundings, the colony members got up from where they were and began to investigate; it wasn't long before one of these lepers collided with an earthen wall, and almost simultaneously, other lepers collided with the walls of the chamber. The troubled sounds and sighs were evidence that the ones doing the investigating were experiencing some kind of discomfort.

Others slowed down their movement and after a while, they came to the realization that they were in a fairly large room. The room did not give evidence of light in any direction, but as one of the lepers was searching, she fell over an obstacle. The impact caused her to topple, and when attempting to recollect her thoughts, it became apparent that the object was also toppled. Upon further investigation, this obstacle was found to be a small cache of food and bottled water, enough for a couple of weeks, if rationed properly. After thoroughly checking the food and water supply, the elders gathered and began to coordinate a plan. Rather than die off, the leper colony searched for ways to adapt to this life below the earth's surface They gathered the fruit, bread, a variety of other foods, and the water that were left as supplies; for those that had their wits within their control, the realization that the majority of this food was, indeed, perishable, and that it was practically useless to store was clear.

The supplies were protected by the strongest lepers and were to be distributed equally over the longest period of time. Remember that these lepers were not animals, but were human beings with a debilitating affliction. The rationing of the food and water weakened some of the lepers. The eldest of the lepers, not the elders, did not agree with the schedule of distribution; they argued, but gained no ground, for it made sense that they all had to sustain their life, day to day, as long as possible.

The main reason for this type of rationing was because of the rather small amount of food and water. These supplies had to last over the longest period of time, at least until an alternative food and water source was discovered, and/or a path was found to the earth's surface.

While many of these lepers realized that this room was meant to be the colony's burial ground, the elders, and the majority of the others, remained level headed. A few of the others displayed an abundance of crying and hysterics. The elders accepted the immediate responsibility and began to search the enclosure for an exit. They walked the room's perimeter and gradually became evident that the walls were constructed of dirt and stones. The room wasn't that spacious, so it did not take long before one of the investigators came to an opening. This finding was announced and it immediately brought immense hope to the colony.

A few of the elders went to the area where the communication had come from, and they too recognized the opening. The elders went through the opening, having high hopes, but immediately were let down by the continuation of the darkness. Through the opening they went, purposely staying close to an earthen wall, and soon they found a place where the wall made a hard turn to the right; and then another void. The roughness of the terrain and the ever-present veil of total darkness began to take its toll.

Fear was beginning to dominate, and therefore dampen their spirits. They continued to walk cautiously, using their hands to feel what their eyes could not see. One after another, the elders found the far side of the opening, and thus they continued to move forward. One cautious step after another…and soon they realized that they were ascending what was thought of as a passageway. A few of the elders walked along one side while others walked across from them.

These lepers, still feeling some effect of the drug, found that their bodies were vastly depleted of an energy source. After taking a few more steps, they found it necessary to stop and rest temporarily. The search continued and so did the degree of their exhaustion. After an hour or so, it became apparent that the passageway had a dead end. "Oh No." was clearly understood as it emanated from the mouths of the elders like a continuous echo. What a disappointment.

While clearly distraught, a few were evidenced to be quite angry. These few punched the walls, and one was punching the wall with such force that a slapping thud was easily heard upon impact. He moved along the wall that was considered to be the dead end. Thud! Thud! Thud! Each slapping sound came with more and more force, so forceful that the momentum of his final punch took him into an opening. The momentum caused the elder to lose his balance and begin to tumble forward, bouncing off the flooring and walls. He then forcefully collided with another wall, this time causing a slight concussion. The other elders, in that immediate vicinity, heard the ruckus and seemed to communicate a sense of humor at the elder's predicament. That humor was short-lived because the sounds ceased soon after they began; there was a possibility that the leper could be seriously injured.

The leper quickly regained his consciousness, equilibrium, and the cautiousness of his search continued. He felt for an earthen wall and found it with ease; he steadied himself and found another opening off to one side, about ten feet in one continuous direction. He immediately communicated this finding to the other elders and they all moved to that location. As a group it was easier to search, but after their search took them in several directions, left, right, right, left, right, left, it became evident that they were in some sort of labyrinth. Eventually, these searchers got lost and it took additional hours, and an extreme amount of expended physicality, before they were fortunate enough to return to the location of the other. They put their heads together and realized that venturing into, and through, what was perceived to be a web of shortened passageways could be a very dangerous choice. At that time, they concluded that there just may be no escape route to the earth's surface.

As the supplies dwindled and were almost gone, the lepers understood that they had to find some additional food and water source, or they would inevitably perish from malnutrition and dehydration. It was discussed, and generally agreed upon, that to survive they would have to adjust to a new, and necessary diet; eating live animals and drinking of their blood. All of the lepers voiced that this option would be extremely difficult, but it became evident that this was a life or death decision. For some, this choice was impossible to act upon, and these lepers searched more frantically for a way to the surface. They used the discarded food packaging as a tool, and dug into the earth above and beyond their present location. It didn't take long for these lepers to become physically exhausted and after several more attempts, they recognized that their quest was futile; their bodies and minds could not endure the inevitable, and one after the other, these lepers died.

Chapter 6

SURVIVAL MEANT THAT SEVERAL things had to be embraced. To live meant that they had to adapt to the murksome environment and that they would have to adjust to eating the raw flesh of animals and drinking their blood. As they adjusted to their predicament, they gradually were able to find moles and various other small rodents as they burrowed close by. These burrowing animals didn't stand a chance once their movement could be heard by the investigative lepers. Using whatever they could acquire, from the leftover food containers, these lepers frantically dug into the earth until the burrowing animal was sensed. It was a no-win situation for the animal, for its flesh and blood were the breath of life for the lepers.

It was now time to give their situation some additional, serious thought. The lepers gathered and began to communicate their thoughts to one another. They vented about what had happened to their colony during the past few weeks, and the fact that they were not wanted on the earth's surface. They also recognized that if they returned to the surface, there was a good chance that they would be hunted down and killed. Some of these lepers thought it best to risk this development, but were sternly rebuked by members of the elders.

Using the logic that if one was found upon the surface, then the community would recognize that the lepers had indeed found the earth's surface, and were, in fact, assembled in some nearby location; subsequently, the community would hunt for the leper colony. Once they were found, there was no telling what avenue of death the community would employ to be completely assured that the colony was exterminated. It was also evident that if they decided to return to the surface, that their leprosy would prevent them from blending in with any normal society.

The elders' logic made complete sense to all that were in the area, so now they needed to further their plans to include a safe living space and the necessary sustenance for the colony's survival.

The lepers gradually became acclimated to their new situation and, over time, were eating small animals of every description. It was as if each animal was a true delicacy since none knew when the next meal would become available. There wasn't much that remained once a leper began to eat what the earth offered; even the bones were pulverized, and consumed, as an additional form of nourishment.

Initially, their food staples were insects, worms and grubs, bats, rodents and a variety of roots, and also water that filtered its way through the soil, rocks, and roots. The only items that they could not digest were the skin and the attached hair of the variety of animal life that they consumed; this, they mistakenly consumed and consequently regurgitated, much like domesticated felines do when coughing up a hair ball.

Instinctively, these lepers recognized that they were going to have to find a more substantial food source. The group, en masse, thought of themselves as underground lepers; that they were driven by an insatiable desire for varieties of food, and, to this point in time, flesh and blood was to be their staple. They continually groped for additional kinds of food. The hours gradually passed and became days, then days became a week, and weeks became a month; in no time, months had swiftly gone by, their captivity gradually ushering them into a dismal state and then finally a downward spiraling depression.

While these lepers were trying to find a way out, others, given their situation, kept their minds as stress free as possible. The room was not very large; it was damp and cold, but surprisingly, not freezing. It became evident that they were supposed to die in this setting, but it was their instinct to adapt, *to live!*

These lepers found the dimensions of this burial chamber to be quite restricting; occasionally, they found themselves disoriented, and subsequently collided head-first with one of its bordering walls. Whenever this initially happened, a sound would usually emanate from the damaged leper, bringing increased attention to their plight.

As this disorientation continued, it became commonplace to identify individuals with these distinctive sounds of pain; occasionally, the same leper would haphazardly collide within the enclosure's restrictive walls, and then the sound was more of complete frustration rather than a mistaken movement. With this sound of frustration came a feint sound of what could be recognized as laughter from the identifying lepers.

Once these lepers realized that it did not matter if they were blind or sighted, they became aware that sight was of no use in the labyrinth. They also realized that their disease affected their ability to physically feel, and over the years could cause considerable damage to their eyesight. A hard substance, similar to plaque, could form a crust on their eyelids and in the corners of their eyes. This crusty build-up diminished the leper's ability to blink, thus damaging the eyesight.

Chapter 7

IF THEY WERE DESTINED to live within the earth, as their leprous skin and horrible smell indicated, then they would have to accept the fact that it was almost certain death to return to the earth's surface.

They reluctantly agreed that they would acclimate themselves to this internal environment, and that specific lepers would be created to govern the colony; to make plans, and to be counted on for decisions. This body of lepers was given the title of the elders. The first and foremost item that had to become a reality was that the earth's surface had to be found. The reasoning behind this decree was that there was a need to construct extensive catacombs, or passageways, and a large communal area, far away from the entrance that led to what was conceived to be their present burial ground. It was evident to all present that they needed their safety, presently and in the generations to come. They must become an unknown; thought of as dead within their proposed tomb.

Realizing that their attempt to find the surface had been futile, the lepers attempted to recognize why that attempt bore them no reward. Was it possible that there wasn't enough thought given to that initial attempt? The most important find was that the passageways interlocked, much like the construction of a maze. The elders decided to organize another search.

Finding the earth's surface was paramount, for the catacombs and the birth chamber could not be dug if there was no place, other than the community's proposed tomb, to rid the area of the tons of dirt. The elders attempted to retrace the passageways; along which they had been led, that eventually descended into this tomb. It was evident that they had walked a considerable distance when drugged after entering the initial passageway. It was equally evident that they had spent a considerable amount of time in what was understood to be a maze-like construction, and then descended further, walking for quite a distance more.

The elders ascended the passageway that led them to the entrance of the maze, finding the trek very taxing to their legs, lungs and heart. They plodded along, and when they sensed that they were close to the passageway's end, they reached out, feeling for a wall that could be somewhere directly in front of them. Trudging along with out-stretched arms helped prevent the group from colliding heavily with a passageway's end. Once there, they rested for some time, gradually recognizing that the burn in their lungs was lessening, that breathing was less of a struggle, and that their hearts had stopped thumping within their chest cavity. At this point, the elders continued their trek and entered the intricacy of what was apparently the maze; it forced them to turn immediately to the right and then, after walking what seemed to be about ten feet, to the left.

Each walkway seemed to mimic the previous one, and this only frustrated them. An hour or two passed, and it was believed that they were making progress. There was a heartfelt jubilation when they came to the end of the maze, but this was short-lived; demoralized, once again, upon the realization that this opening descended in the direction of their proposed burial chamber.

Feeling defeated, the elders milled around, shaking their heads, feeling what seemed to be despair. Several hours passed since the elders had left the majority of their colony within the chamber; they descended a passageway, made lefts and rights, and once again were in the company of the others. It was apparent that the surface had eluded them.

The elder's despair entered the mindset of all present; there was no more energy among the entire group and the laziness seemed to indicate defeat. With depression and despair came lengthy periods of sleep. The elders knew that this demoralization could deplete the entire colony's will to live. Something good had to happen, and finally an event changed the lives of these evolving lepers; it was as if they received a gift from the spirit world that would change their lives significantly, and for all time!

A very large animal, unlike any other that they had killed and eaten, was recognized through its omitting scent, produced by its obvious fear. This animal was frantically pounding the corridors of the maze, descending towards the proposed burial chamber, or what the others had called their tomb. Bewildered by its predicament, the animal was now definitely in the lower section of the labyrinth; moving in the direction of the burial chamber. As soon as it departed the maze and came to the chamber, its life came to an abrupt end. Picking up the animal's scent and the sound of its hoofs glancing off the planks, the evolving lepers pounced upon whatever it was, and heavily pummeled it with hand held rocks until certain death greeted the creature. Initially, this animal wasn't recognized for its true worth, but mistakenly was only recognized as a food source.

These evolving lepers realized that the animal had a considerable amount of meat and blood, so they quieted their own frenzy and conceived of a plan before cutting the skin of the animal. The lepers dragged the animal's carcass to the burial chamber, gathered whatever tools that were readily available, and dug a hole into the earthen floor; it was then decided that this was to be a vat for the blood supply. Realizing that the dirt was indeed porous they planned to use the animal's skin to line the vat.

First things first! How could the blood be stored while the skin was in the process of being scraped clean, dried, and then strewn as the vat's lining? These evolving lepers collected the plastic gallon jugs that previously held the water supply; using the now sharpened tops of emptied cans, larger openings were cut in place of the spouts. They now had a way to temporarily store the blood while the vat was lined. The evolving lepers gathered containers from whatever remained; they searched for the largest of other emptied cans, and for jug-type containers. Finding several, they gathered all so each and every container touched. They then gathered the metal tops of the crudely opened cans and further sharpened them by rubbing the metal while holding it angled against the roughness of various rocks. Once these implements were as sharp as they could be, the carcass of this large animal was dragged closer to the vat and the conglomeration of containers.

Checking the animal more closely, it was believed to weigh one-hundred and fifty pounds; its skin had short hair, and the hair covered its entire body. It had a short hairy tail, four long legs, and an elongated neck. Atop its head were the beginning stages of horns, and so the evolving lepers believed the animal was a deer. If this was indeed correct, and from all indications it was, then the blood could be directed into the selected containers without a significant loss.

The plan was for two of the stronger lepers to lift the animal's hind quarters, and while holding them above its lowered neck, a deep slice would be made where the neck met the shoulders. Cutting an artery would allow the blood to flow freely into the group of containers. After the animal was depleted of its blood supply, it would be gutted, paying great attention to saving all of its edible meat; including its heart, kidneys and liver. At that point, the inside of the skin would be scraped as clean as possible, dried somewhat, and placed in and around the walls of the crudely created vat to securely hold and store the entire blood supply. Using the sharpened utensils, the meat was to be cut-up and shared among the lepers; the smaller of the cans would be used to drink the blood. Compared to the amount of meat that came from the burrowing animals, the deer was considered to be a feast. Once satiated by their meat and blood source, they all found themselves in a fetal position, falling into a much needed sleep.

Chapter 8

WITH THE STRAIN AND stress of the recent occurrences weighing heavily upon their minds, the evolving lepers slept fitfully; none the less, they all slept for hours. As the lepers awakened, it was evident that several thought that they had been in a dream. Impulsively, the lepers communicated with one another and the gist of this dealt with the large animal that they had recently killed.

These lepers eventually concluded that this large animal had to have come from the earth's surface. There was great anticipation throughout the room as this theory began to take hold. At this point in time, none of the lepers had been upon the earth's surface since arriving in this room; not since being abandoned to their intended gravesite. The anticipation brought with it a tremendous amount of fear for the leper, or lepers that were projected to be the first upon the surface, and also for the remaining lepers that inhabited the burial chamber.

Being abandoned and left to die was the source for the majority of their anxiety. They recognized that their horrific appearance could make them easily accessible to being caught, and if caught, it could result in certain death.

The deer was the first of that size that the lepers feasted upon and it whet their appetite for more of these larger types. As these thoughts materialized, the lepers found themselves anticipating, with a heightened desire, for larger prey to wander through the labyrinth. This is where it met its vicious death; and subsequently, a needed sustenance for the colony.

The rather large animal, in all likelihood a large deer, had to have come from the earth's surface; realizing this as fact caused a heightened anxiety. A few of the elder's moved toward the maze, attempting to backtrack the individualized, musky scent that this animal had emitted as it frantically moved from the earth's surface to its death. Now, at the lower entrance of the labyrinth, these specific and ever evolving lepers reared their heads upon their necks, continually sniffing for the scent of the deer.

The scent was evident, enabling the lepers to follow the frenzied animal's trek. As they ascended, they found themselves feeling somewhat secure; secure, that is, until the path ended, and then began again in a totally different direction. Recognizing that the path had taken a change in direction, the lepers continued, only to recognize another distinct, directional change, and then another turn, left and then right, and then left again. It seemed monotonous, as if their path was going nowhere, just a bunch of useless turns that could very well return them to the burial room. Mass confusion reigned among the group. Anxiety was rampant! Their abdomens tightened, causing spasms of pain. It was in their recent memory that their previous search caused them to feel considerable confusion; confusion and then desperation, depression. It took considerable effort for them to quiet their nerves, but after time elapsed, that is precisely what happened.

These elders, relying upon their intelligence and sense of smell, recognized that the scent was still musky, but yet it seemed to be strong; enabling them to feel an increased sense of hope. At times, these evolving lepers moved too swiftly and found themselves at a dead end. When this happened, they backtracked and paid more attention to the scent than to their impulsiveness. The scent had them within what seemed to be an extended passageway. Not knowing where they were, they considered abandoning the search, but chose to remain and collect their thoughts.

The lepers considered returning through what they imagined to be a maze so they could rejoin their colony. However, they were fearful that the scent would fade, to the point where it would no longer be helpful. The return was certainly an option, but they chose to continue their trek to the earth's surface, for without that discovery they were doomed to die-off. As they walked up the path they found themselves breathing laboriously, and subsequently, having to stop and bend over at the waist. They all sensed a great need to recuperate from the exertion of their musculature, and almost succumbed to a restful sleep, but one of the more calculating lepers communicated that the animal's scent could further fade from their senses as they slumbered.

This leper went on to say that if the scent would disappear while they slept, then there was a reasonable possibility that they could be forever lost, and would die-off; frightened by this revelation, they pushed onward. Continually exhausted by the incline of the passageway, they stopped more than once. They felt a sense of despair because the incline gave no evidence of a light at the end of the tunnel. The darkness meant that their trek took on little significance; laborious was the best word to describe their trek. Everything that added to their futility, and that hindered the fluidness of their movement made the trek that more exhausting.

All of a sudden something happened. They were facing toward the incline when what seemed to be a wisp of cool air came down the passageway and passed through the group like a ghost. The entire group stood motionless, as if transfixed, mesmerized by the excitement that they felt.

After standing for another ten to fifteen seconds, the entire group got further proof of the reality: another cool wisp of air. The group, believing that the entrance was close, seemed to forget that they were exhausted. Feeling exhilarated after so many setbacks, the evolving lepers began moving in the direction of the surface. It seemed as if each step was bringing them closer and closer to their goal.

After walking for a distance, they stopped, hoping that what they were sensing was the smell of grass and wild flowers. Eventually, they rumbled toward the scents, and their level of excitement grew, along with their anxiety. It was true that pleasant fragrances were indeed emanating from somewhere, and probably close by; they leaned forward, and willed their bodies onward. Placing one foot in front of the other, they plodded upward, and eventually were rewarded by a dim light that seemed to be emanating from somewhere directly in front of them

When all of the elders arrived at the location where the light could be seen and the fragrances were more than evident, they all identified with the apparent jubilation that the leaders must have felt. A pleasing fragrance was flowing towards them, though from how far above and beyond their present location wasn't actually known. What they all recognized was that this fragrant smell was a distinct reality; that there was a definite difference between the variety of putrid smells that were a mainstay in their proposed habitat, and this pleasant surface scent that strongly reduced that significant stench! There was excitement in the air along with the ever-present anxiety. It was understood why the lead leper hadn't attempted to go any further without notifying the others; there was that great fear, anticipation, and anxiety associated with the surface.

The lepers remained where they were until they fully recovered from their exhaustion and were able to raise their heads with ease. They were elated when they felt another stream of cooler, yet fragrant air, and saw, not more than thirty feet to their front, what was believed to be a definite entranceway to the earth's surface.

These lepers realized that they were not to be on the surface, and so they moved with caution. Now, within a few feet of the surface, they huddled together. Luckily the sun was setting, and this enabled one of the lepers to move out of the entranceway and onto the camouflaged surface, crouching there in the dying light.

While surveying the area, the leper realized that the entranceway was camouflaged from any human in the neighboring community, and so it felt more at ease as it continued to survey the area. What it saw, through its damaged and weakened eyes, was truly amazing; was it a special gift from God? There, no more than twenty feet away, securely attached and knotted at one end of a sturdy tree was what appeared to be a thickened, heavy rope. Peering through its blurred vision, this rope seemed to be quite lengthy and it was estimated to be around four-hundred feet long. It was encircled many times, in what appeared to be an eight-foot diameter, and rose approximately five feet above the surface. Knowing that it was too heavy for him alone to move, he returned and got two others to move the bulk of the rope to the entranceway. The two lepers cautiously departed, and zeroing in on the rope, moved in that direction. These two joined up with the leper that was first upon the surface, and together they dragged the rope from the area of the tree to the entrance.

The elders felt quite fortunate that the animal's scent was still lingering, so they unwound the distant end of the rope and readied it for their return trek. After organizing their thoughts into one synchronized plan, the group held tightly to the rope and began to descend that passageway. Two of the group remained in the direct vicinity of the encircled rope, making sure that it unwound without tangling. The weight of the rope was felt as the two continued to unwind and assist it down the passageway. Feint smiles would have been recognized upon their faces if, in fact, there was enough light, for it was much easier to physically descend, rather than ascend, this lengthy passageway.

Other than the two lepers that were at the surface, and were securely camouflaged by the trees and excessive bushes and shrubs, the remainder of the search party all had hold of the rope as they trekked in the direction of the labyrinth. While holding tightly to the rope's lower end, they, without the slightest hitch, arrived at the maze's musky entrance. In and out, and through short intricate walkways they moved, all the time realizing that the length and weight of the rope were being guided from its bulk, and therefore it was able to snake along the passageway, and through the maze that was behind them. With the musky scent evident, the lepers reached the lower end of the labyrinth. It was here that they felt such a great sense of accomplishment and subsequently congratulated one another.

While steadily pulling the rope, the group exited the maze and entered the lowest of the passageways, leading to the large room. Gathering there, they had to use their musculature to pull the lengthy amount of slack out of the rope, so it was now taut from the tree to where they had gathered. While pulling the slack out of the length of the entire rope, it became evident that the encircled rope that was previously at the habitat's entranceway was now being encircled within the proposed burial chamber, but it wasn't as extensive.

After a brief rest, they told the others of their successful journey and of the luck that they had had finding their way through the maze, finding the surface, and the rope. After recounting their successes, the elders told those in the room that they had stumbled over a few boulders while bringing themselves and the rope to that location. The two lepers that were previously upon the earth's surface had since moved to the labyrinth; one at its entrance, and the other at its exit. The plan was to leave the bulk of the rope in the proposed burial room and to follow its lead to the area where it was securely tied to the tree. Since the manageable boulders were within the two ends of the labyrinth, it was possible to roll each to a specific end point. It was part of the proposed plan to take some type of digging instrument with them. Once they found the appropriate sized boulders, they would then be rolled close to each end of the maze. A leper would then dig into the earthen floor, deep enough so each of the boulders could sit securely and permanently within. Now, just before rolling a boulder into the depth of its assigned hole, the rope would be wrapped several times around each boulder, and then that boulder would be rolled one last time, sitting permanently in the hole, with the rope beneath the boulder's weight. It was also part of the plan to leave an abundance of slack within the rope that made up the length between the boulders so that any leper could walk while holding the rope, guiding them in either direction. The evolving lepers felt an amount of elation and their confidence levels somewhat mended.

The animal's scent was all but gone, but this did not matter, for they possessed the intelligence to correctly use the scent and the rope. The leper that they passed remained at his post as the group searched for the initial boulder. After following the maze for a short time, they came across a boulder that met their needs. It was within a shallow indentation, and so it was easy to unearth, and get it rolling towards the lower end of the maze. Slowly but surely, the speed of the boulder was controlled by moving it while following the guidance of the rope, to the left and then to the right, repeatedly, until it was maneuvered to the lower end of the labyrinth. Now, at that end, a deep hole was dug and then the boulder, wrapped with the rope, was rolled and dropped into the hole, with the encircled rope underneath. When in the hole, the boulder was slightly below the surface, and when the dirt was leveled there was no evidence of the boulder, whatsoever. It was now that the group, including the leper that had been at this post, left that area in search of the topmost end of the maze.

The group trekked along, and stumbled over a few boulders along the way, but finally came to the topmost end. It was here that they backtracked, searching for the closest boulder. It was of a good size, though it sat deeper into the earth than the previous one. Extensive digging caused the group to realize that this boulder was quite a bit larger than the first one, but at that time it did not matter, for their recollection was that the previous boulder was moved easily toward its destination. It was soon realized that there was something different about this move. At first, it was thought that the boulder wouldn't move as readily because of its larger size and its weight; the lepers exerted themselves further, but yet there was very little evidence that the boulder would move. At this point, one of the frustrated lepers exclaimed, "What the Hell?" Then another leper verbalized that, although the labyrinth wasn't as inclined as were the passageways, it still had some incline, and this, plus the boulder's excessive weight, was what caused the boulder not to roll. No one disagreed, and a few of the stronger lepers replaced those that couldn't get the boulder rolling. These guys were the real deal, much like Evander Holyfield was in his prime; the difficulty was due to getting this boulder into motion, and to keep it rolling. With their strength responding, they took deep breaths and placed their bulbous shoulders against the bulk of the boulder's weight in unison. This was a completely different story, most likely with a positive ending. Once in motion, it was found to be very important to keep the boulder rolling. Of course, this was much more difficult than along the decline. Every revolution of this boulder was an achievement, as it went this way and that towards the inclined end of the maze; this was muscle fatigue at its utmost! The boulder seemed as if it always wanted to stop, and remain totally still, so its motion was of the utmost importance. In and out, and along straight paths it went, motivated by extremes in strength. Finally, it was evident that the boulder was at rest at the topmost section of the labyrinth. "Hallelujah!" Here the elders gathered with others that had mingled in the lengthy passageways.

Greetings were exchanged and then the rope was given considerable slack before being wrapped around this second boulder. The boulder was rolled within the depth of its hole. This work was finished off by packing the dirt around and on top, until the boulder was thoroughly covered. Checking to make sure, and only after being totally convinced that the boulder securely held the rope, it was only then that the entire group, one by one, hand held the rope, and followed it to the exit of the lower passageway. They then followed the lead of the rope until they were within the room that was intended for their death.

At this point in time, the elders brought all of the lepers gathered and communicated that it was the right time to pay their homage to the deer for its flesh, blood, and skin. It was also proclaimed that the deer had an elevated status; that it was sent by God to guide the colony to the earth's surface and that it became a major source for their sustenance. Time was then taken for all to recognize the deer's spiritual value; heads were lowered and soulful thanks were offered.

Chapter 9

NOW THAT THE PASSAGE to the earth's surface had been found, it was essential to put all of this information to good use. The colony's eldest knew that the younger generation didn't want to spend the remainder of their lives within the depths of the earth, especially now that the route had been found, enabling them to depart their dismal grave.

The oldest lepers, along with the elders, organized a gathering that had, as its end result, the reality that their life was, for all intents and purposes, to be lived within the earth's surface; it was evident that living upon the surface had little, if no reward, for the colony.

Living throughout the four seasons of every year caused such discomfort; especially the hot, humid days of summer and the bitterly cold months of winter. When comparing the dismal temperatures within the bowels of the earth to the temperatures upon its surface, and the factor that the leper colony was presumed to have died off in the community's burial room, there was a greater benefit when remaining within the earth and continuing to construct catacombs, that is, adapting.

At the gathering, it was agreed that abiding by the laws was paramount. It was also agreed that their most important law was that no leper was permitted to surface without the governing body sanctioning that move. To exit the labyrinth without the sanction of the governing body would mean death for the offender, or offenders. There was a good reason for the sternness of the punishment; it was well known throughout the colony that they were not welcome upon the surface, and, in fact, were believed to be dead. If a leper was to enter the surface and be seen, then the community would, no doubt, hunt for the colony, and when found, annihilate them, one by one.

To camouflage the fact that the colony had indeed adapted, they positioned the dead lepers, those that could not change their diet to the raw flesh and blood of animals, to remain exposed upon the floor area of the large room and gradually decompose. They believed that this gradual stench would permeate the room and passageways. If members of the community returned to verify the lepers demise, they would, upon smelling the stench of the rotted and decomposed flesh, believe that the colony had truly perished.

They also believed that the community would not find it necessary to seek out further proof beyond the stench that flowed toward the surface. Trusting that this stench would thwart off the discovery of their survival, they knew that they needed a way to guarantee solidarity among the colony, one and all. This was the reason for the sternness of the decision regarding death for any leper that surfaced without the sanction of the elders.

The elders made it crystal clear that the laws and stipulations were binding for all lepers. All were present at this time, and all took a solemn oath to abide by the guidelines, and in fact, to remain within the earth. It was also understood that the group, known as the food gatherers, would be the hunters and that they would be the only members of the species that had an open invitation to enter the surface. It was an understanding that they could venture upon the surface to hunt for prey, like the deer, that had recently been pummeled to its death.

For many years, the evolving lepers struggled, creating passageways and tunnels; the excavation began where the upper passageway and the entrance to the labyrinth intersected. It began here and traveled away from the intersection because it was the place where the passageway led directly to the surface, and would lessen their workload significantly. They could have used the labyrinth as a security measure, but to haul the dirt and large stones through the maze, and then up the length of the passageway did not justify this type of work.

The lepers found that the remainder of the deer skin could be cut into large sacks, and that each could hold tremendous amounts of weight. Initially, they made use of their clothing to carry the dirt, etc., but soon found that clothing tore easily, and could not hold the weight. There was a great need for more animal skins, and so the diggers and carriers met with the elders. It was at this same meeting that it was decided that the hunters would go out that night and attempt to kill a few of the larger animals; they were aware that several cattle ranches, a multitude of farms, and an abundance of wildlife were in the surrounding area. During the discussion, it became paramount for the hunters to not obtain their prey from one ranch alone, but to spread out the kills so that they would go unnoticed.

The hunters went out that night and did as they were instructed. They killed cattle from various ranches, but had considerable trouble getting the cattle back to the habitat. Once they had finally gotten to their destination, a couple of the hunters went to the chamber and awakened a few of the stronger lepers; they then returned to the surface and all maneuvered the cattle to the tomb-like room.

Chapter 10

THEIR CRUDE DIGGING MATERIALS had been misplaced, or were broken down to the point where they had lost their usefulness. The evolving lepers had to resort to using their teeth, hands and feet, and fingers and toes. Over many months of daily toil, the fingers and toes wore away, changing to nubs; talon-like appendages gradually replaced the fingers, extending first from the nubs of the diggers. As these talons grew, they also thickened at their base, gradually curling inward; and they became, with constant use, razor sharp and pointed at the end. As time went by, these diggers were the first to significantly change, resembling some sort of creature rather than a human being. These diggers found that their sharpened, pointed talons, caked with decayed and rancid food particles, could be trusted to unearth large amounts of dampened earth, especially when seeking any sort of recognizable sustenance; animals that burrowed and scurried to escape the creature's pursuit. Being a source of food for these creatures, the small animals never escaped the wrath of a creature's talons.

As their primary responsibility, the diggers moved soil into dumpsters that had been discovered, along with the rope, upon the surface. Many of the others were pushers, whose responsibility was to mobilize the dumpsters, after each was fully loaded with dampened dirt, along with different sized stones, from the ever increasing length of the catacomb. Subsequently, they would make use of their amazing strength and push the loaded dumpster up the ever ascending passageway toward their destination. Once upon the surface, they would continue to push the load a distance from the entranceway and empty it at a predetermined site; it was then their responsibility to return the dumpster to the site of the ever increasing excavation.

This work was tremendously difficult; it took many, many years for all of the work was back breaking. Inch by inch and then foot by foot, the catacomb took on its length and shape. The dumpster's payload had to be physically moved to a desolate area upon the surface, and then to the site that was out of sight of any member of the community. Initially, the discarded dirt and debris created small mounds upon the earth's surface. However, over time, these mounds became elevated hills, supporting the growth of trees, wild flowers, insects, and small wildlife.

As the strenuous work continued, the singular years became decades, and the diggers, the carriers, and the pusher's bodily appearances steadily transformed. The easiest way to explain this change was to visualize the appearance of one of these evolving lepers that had taken on the change of evolving to that of an adult creature. This became evident when the next generation was fathered by one of the lepers that had experienced bodily changes due to its role as a digger. By the age of six years, the digger's offspring had a bodily appearance that experienced the most dramatic of changes.

The digger types experienced bodily change and through self-exploration discovered this to be factual, and quite disturbing. By the age of six years, a male that was fathered by one of the digger's, or by a carrier, would have grown to be approximately seven feet in height and weighing in at more than six hundred pounds. Through the years of evolution, their skin became leathery, with layer upon layer of protective scales, and a surplus of open, crater-like oozing sores; the liquid that escaped their mouths, ears, nostrils, surface sores, and all other orifices had a putrid, inconceivable stench.

There was a ragged foot long, curved and pointed claw, protruding from each side of their head. These claws curving inwards, resembled the structure of the talons, and had mobility.

Most of the significant changes that their bodies experienced could be logically attributed to their extreme work load, but the claws originated from an unknown source. Possessing superior strength, and resembling pincers, they were primarily used to grasp and hold an adversary's head. Once the head was secure, the lower extremities could be securely held with its razor-sharp talons and the creature could then violently rip the head clean from its host. Once the head was removed, this ever evolving creature would often ingest it, and after ingesting the head, the creature would take its fill of the prey's flesh and blood, thereby sustaining its own life. Imagine, if you can, the strength within its jaw; after killing a formidable prey with a sizeable skull, the creature could use its jaw power to cut through that skull as if it was a lobster's shell.

During their first two decades, this slow, continual evolution was necessary. With their increased size and strength came an exaggerated increase in muscle mass, and these massive creatures needed an increased amount of sustenance to fuel their musculature and extensive workload.

It became quite easy to differentiate the diggers from the pushers. The diggers had massive upper-body size and strength! Their upper appendages were enormous compared to their lower, less muscled appendages and a very noticeable thickness from the waist area up. Their neck area was also extremely thickened with bulging lumps of muscle and tumor growths. This area had become heavily muscled through the usage of the claws for digging and dislodging rocks of various sizes and shapes. The diggers lower appendages, while very powerful and noticeable, were not symmetrical to its monstrous upper body size. Also noticeable was the denseness of the callosity that was to the forefront, and center, of its four limbs.

The pushers were built noticeably different; their lower appendages were unbelievable, truly the envy of any world class super heavy-weight body builder, with their own set of enormously muscled legs. The pusher's muscles appeared to be lumped together and they rippled from the base area of the lower sets of talons to the waist. The upper back and shoulders displayed extreme musculature; these muscles were used to place against the rear area of a fully loaded dumpster until it broke free of ground below. The object was to keep the dumpster in motion, all the way to the end of this level catacomb and to keep it in motion as it entered the beginning stage of the inclined passageway to the surface. To get to the surface was tremendously painful and fatiguing to their musculature, but this muscle pain wasn't comparable to what was endured when pushing the weighted dumpster up the final stages of that passageway. At some point during this arduous task, the pushers usually found their arm and shoulder strength numbing, so while keeping the dumpster in motion, they changed the positioning of their arms and shoulder mass; leaning lower to the ground and primarily using their leg strength to move the dumpster up the remaining incline and onto the surface, one strenuous, deliberate step, after the other.

Chapter 11

AS THESE CREATURES EVOLVED, their instinct and intelligence made them aware of one very important thing, a creature needed a nutritious food source to support its voracious appetite and body mass. No longer would a diet of burrowing animals, grubs and worms, various roots, and the water that dripped through the earth above, be enough to sustain their appetite for any extended period of time.

Deeper and deeper within the earth, moving throughout their tenebrous environment, these creatures learned that they shared their ever lengthening catacomb with bats, and other creatures that eventually found a purchase within the creature's lengthening ceiling. As it continued to lengthen, more and more of these vibrating life forms were recognized to be hanging from the make-shift ceiling; with each passing day, additional numbers also found their purchase. Occasionally, these would be eaten. Over time, the bats became one of the creature's learned staples. The creature's talons would swiftly and spontaneously lash out in the direction of the elevated presence, moving toward a compacted ceiling of the catacomb. They'd extend the talons of their upper appendages, always reaching, so that their razor sharpened extensions could stealthily glide through a clumped grouping. It was then that the talons, with their speared quarry, would be directed toward their mouth, laden with pierced and wriggling, blood dripping life. Each evolving creature learned to maneuver the bats, before swallowing, so that the chewing process left the wings falling to the floor. Before evolving into these hideous creatures, these lepers were outcasts, living within their own colony; then, due to a hideous, repulsive appearance, and a putrid stench, they were banished; exiled from the earth's surface, to die within it.

Upon the completion of their initial catacomb, the diggers turned their attention to a much needed sacred chamber; a site that was to be located at the end of the catacomb, approximately one half mile from its entrance. The intention was for this site to be secure and totally safe from detection; it would be quite large and situated deep within the earth, but at the same time, its ceiling would be the closest area to the earth's surface. It was to be the sacred chamber because it was to be the birthing site for the membranes, the place where all of the flesh and blood would be stored, and it would house all of the bones and skulls that were procured during their lifetimes.

The diggers, carriers and pushers worked feverishly, and as time went by, they realized that the process was much too slow. They had maneuvered their way to the room that lay at the end of the descending passageway, and once there, they searched for and found the discarded section of the deer skin. It was at this point that one of these creatures was fortunate enough to find a jagged lid from one of the discarded cans. This creature moved to the deer's carcass and then positioned itself so as to be able to lay the skin out flat upon the earthen floor. The skin had stiffened somewhat so it was necessary to add softness to it before attempting to cut it into sack-like bags. This was done by pummeling the outstretched skin with rather smooth, handheld rocks, and then the cutting began.

Two sacks were created by visualizing the deer to be in a standing position, and then cutting the area along the under belly, lengthwise, from the front legs to the rear ones, and then up its one side to the top. From this point, the skin was cut toward the deer's shoulder, and once there, it was cut down to the rear of the front leg, and to the under belly. This procedure was duplicated on the other side; leaving two large skin sacks to assist with the ever increasing workload.

A stroke of genius then came into the thought process of the creature. It cut away the majority of the head, leaving the antlers securely attached to the skin that covered the neck cavity, and curved backwards toward the topmost area of each front leg. These antlers had several elongated points, and so the creature, using the rocks, broke away two of the sections that were antler points. The others that were present were confused by what they imagined to be happening, but soon recognized that these sections of curved antler points were to be used to hold the topmost ends of each sack together. Furthermore, the points were to be hooks to grasp as the sack was hefted throughout their extensive trek to the surface. The neck cavity also served its purpose, but was unable to hold as much dirt as the sacks. Now, there were two types of earth movers: the pushers and the carriers; the diggers worked as hard as the other two groups, but were not classified as movers or haulers.

After a week or two; there was a noticeable change in the amount of dirt that had been moved to the surface. Unlike those that qualified as pushers, there were several others that carried the sacks. These skins always came in handy. Upon the completion of the sacred chamber, the workers turned their efforts towards the construction of a tunnel that would lead to lower catacombs, some twenty feet below the initial one, and then even lower. The plan was to have a multitude of catacombs, intersecting tunnels and chambers…and that they'd extend for miles beneath the farms and ranches of Bucks County.

Chapter 12

WHILE LIVING UPON THE earth, the leper's birthing method was as all other humans, but within the habitat, they experienced physical changes, both internally and externally. Something within their environment, whether it was the result of the fecal matter and urine, the pitch black coldness, the grueling work, or the total of all three may have been partially responsible for the leper's grotesque epidermis. The females changed more internally, than externally, and were verbally described as fetus carriers. While experiencing their pregnancy and birthing as a human being, these lepers made full use of their umbilical cord; but now, as an evolved creature, the umbilical cord had lost its significance, and over time disappeared.

Instead of having the use of this cord, the evolving fetus was now born from a membrane, experiencing a cycle similar to that of a reptile. The membrane that housed each fetus had life sustainable nutrients from the fetus carrier's pregnancy regimen. Once this cycle of nutrients was complete, the membrane would then house the fetus and the encircling life sustaining fluid. At this point, the membrane closed, seemingly forever. Still, within the birthing position of the fetus carrier's swollen body, the fetus gained much warmth and nurturing.

Over months, the membrane's weight caused pressure to the fetus carrier's birth canal and gradually it began the gradual decent toward independence. As the membrane descended, and spread the birth canal, it eventually severed itself from the inner wall of its host. It was at that point that there was a popping sound; somewhat like the sound when suction loses its purchase upon glass. While this process happened, the fetus carrier moved to the sacred chamber, and sought a warm spot fairly close to the flesh and blood cache.

In preparation for dropping its membrane, the fetus carrier would have to squat deeply while leaning forward. If the squat was not low enough, then the membrane would most probably fall too great a distance, breaking it, and killing the fetus within. The fetus carrier was always vocal as it strained toward its lowest position, feeling the membrane enter the final stage of the ever spreading birth canal. At that point, the fetus carrier was in severe pain, but knew that the pain would cease momentarily. Still, in great agony and sweating profusely, the fetus carrier would have to lean forward, for balance, and in doing so, deliver the membrane ever so softly upon the earthen floor.

Each membrane had a form similar to that of an egg, and its shell started its cycle with a high degree of elasticity. For many months, the fetus within would remain in its established position, living off its always encircling liquid sustenance. Over months, each male fetus took on the physical attributes of a creature, and when this happened, it was certain to be near the end of its term. Soon after, it was that the fluid lessened, leaving the membrane with less elasticity. As if possessing a memory, each membrane continued to harden, causing stress cracks to appear.

It was inborn within the fetus to add pressure to the surface cracks while it escaped its enclosure. What remained would be ingested during the breakdown of the membrane's composition, and if the creature, at that time, could not escape its shell, then it would have to be patient. Eventually, the nutrients would be gone, and at the same time, the membrane would no longer have elasticity. At that time, the membrane would swiftly break down, leaving the creature with an easy avenue of escape. It was now that the newborn would break through, and instinctively slither toward the cache of nourishment; the coagulated blood and the aging animal flesh.

The newborn would manage to leave the membrane and immediately sensed the steamy, heated environment, of the birth chamber; to say the least, this area was to be considered sacred throughout the creature colony. This spacious chamber had many births, in past generations, and over time all of the membranes decomposed, leaving remnants of a once complete shell.

For every fetus that survived, one would die just prior to, or at the time of their birth, and those that died remained in their membrane for additional months, decomposing. As the remaining nutrients broke down, and gradually vaporized, the membrane hardened, and subsequently cracked, allowing a pent-up gaseous, very putrid stench, to rush into the chamber; strong enough to permeate deep into the chamber's earthen walls.

The underground dwelling lepers lived and sustained their lives below the surface of the earth and ventured to the earth's surface during the nighttime hours to hunt. During the time of the hunt, the majority remained behind and worked in the foul, acrid smelling catacombs. As the diggers, the pushers, and the carriers constructed the various tunnels, the lengthy catacombs continued to extend further beneath the farm land, housing developments, and forested area within the County of Bucks.

Chapter 13

THE UNDERGROUND CREATURE'S SUBGROUP, known as the hunters or the food gatherers, was considered to be the elitists of the colony. Above all, the other attributes they were prized for their intelligence and athletic ability. Although they were usually the largest and strongest of their colony, athleticism was paramount. These hunters had to be able to work as a unit whenever they encountered a food source that was swift and agile, close to their size and strength, or could be seen as a threat to their own lives. Out-maneuvering, subduing, and eventually killing all types of food sources meant that the creature colony could continue to survive and thrive. Killing a food source was therefore recognized as a necessity, valued much more than the life of their own kind.

The hunters were protective of one another, whether they were within their habitat, on the earth's surface, or seeking and killing a food source. Their staples; cattle, horses, sheep, goats, hogs, pigs, and bats required little energy, but when encountering a buck or the majestic elk, this became a challenge and a potential threat to one, or more than one, of the hunter's lives.

Through time and experience, the wildlife was recognized as a death threat because they had extremely sharp hooves that could cut, much the same as a razor; and the extensive, hardened, and pointed material, which extended from the tops of their head's, and could inflict a mortal blow. This is when one's athleticism would come fully into play.

As the generations passed, the hunter's skill became highly adaptable to all types of animals. There wasn't an animal that they could not kill. To observe these adroit hunters as they frustrated, confused, exhausted, and out-maneuvered their prey was mesmerizing!

The hunters continually kept the attention of their prey, parrying and feinting attacks until the selected prey's head began to droop from anticipation and fatigue. The hunters depended upon their reduced vision, but also upon their other senses when attempting to be exact. They sensed exhaustion whenever their prey began breathing laboriously, and by its gradual lack of mobility. Realizing that their prey was fatigued, and subsequently weakened, there was no more feinting. It was now time for the kill.

A few of these hunters had the specific assignment to cause their prey to position itself, unbeknownst, for a swift kill. Once maneuvered into this position, the prey's attention was diverted. Now! The most experienced and deadliest of hunters and the smallest and most agile of the food gatherers displayed a speed that was blurring, and an adeptness to cause a paralyzing, swift kill. At the exact second when the now exhausted prey had its attention diverted, the killing machine moved with extreme speed and purpose, turning its body while in motion, sliding, skillfully positioning itself beneath the under carriage of a steer. Now, it was too late for the prey to take flight, or to maneuver out of harm's way. With the agile creature lying on its back, it used the earth's surface for support. It then used its razor-sharp talons extending from its upper set of appendages. With great force, these talons were forcefully jabbed deep into the upper sides of its prey. With each talon equally penetrating the muscled flesh, the creature simultaneously clenched, ever so tightly, so that the talons held its prey securely while its stronger, lower appendages, with their own razor sharp talons, sliced deeply and cleanly across the underbelly. Before the steer realized what had happened, it would be lying motionless on its side, motionless and lifeless...unbelievable!

The weight of the prey became quite evident by the sound

of the carriers' laborious breathing; these carriers had to move without pause, whenever upon the earth's surface, so as to avoid detection. Hunting was always difficult, but even more so while hefting a kill's weight back to their habitat. They were always keenly aware that if they were ever detected it would mean the certain extinction of their culture and colony. The carriers were more than formidable creatures, and often hauled the heavy weight of the kills, as the food gatherers would urge them on; at times up to a mile. An audible sigh of relief was often heard whenever these carriers got beyond the entranceway of the declining passage. It was here that a carrier could temporarily shift the animal's weight and stop momentarily; rest and feel the security of being within their habitat, undetected and undiscovered. Once again they had gotten back to their home without being detected by the human; their dreaded arch-rival, and enemy.

After adjusting the weight of the kill upon its shoulder, the carrier descended the passageway to the initial catacomb's entrance. Once there, they often had to readjust the weight. Now, continuing their trek to the sacred chamber, they would occasionally lose their balance and have to wrestle, while adjusting their burden, again. Although these elite creatures had an impressive stature, they realized that once they got back to their catacombs, this would be the ultimate test of their status as a food gatherer and hunter.

Occasionally, the hunters had long treks after a kill and when this happened, the carriers often found themselves questioning the need for their designated status. Whether a long or short trek, this was not the real issue; there were times when the trek went from a few hundred yards, to a distance of a half mile or more. The length of the trek and the weight of the kill were real concerns, but the main issue stemmed from the fact that each carrier had the responsibility of carrying the animal from the site of the kill, all of the way to the sacred chamber. At times, this responsibility seemed to be totally unreasonable, especially when the carrier was noticeably exhausted, weary, and weakened; and there was a hunter within the group that had no responsibility other than to trek back to the habitat, unnoticed.

Upon entering the habitat's initial catacomb, the carriers had one additional, very important responsibility. No matter how fatigued or weary they may have been within the habitat, they knew that they could not take the weight from their shoulders until they entered the semi-elevated sacred chamber. With each laborious step came the squishing sound that their feet made as they sunk into the deposited waste and pungent smelling urine. If visualizing their trek, one would be able to see these carriers constantly attempting to maintain their balance and their sanity!

Whenever they lost their balance, they would do everything imaginable to remain in an upright position, holding more tightly to their kill. When feeling a foot slip or their balance waver, they would seek out the security of the catacomb's wall. Digging a set of their talons deeply within the earthen wall, they were always able to find the necessary purchase to keep their body upright. Once satisfied that their feet were secure upon the earthen floor, they'd move onward, one designated step after the other, in the direction of the sacred chamber.

Stopping momentarily from time to time, these weary carriers would use the time to regain their normal breathing and balance. Then, they could continue their trek along the sculpted catacomb until they entered the distant chamber. Their extraordinary musculature, being deeply fatigued and spasmodic, ached from the long, arduous journey. Although saturated with pain, exhaustion, and anguish, the carriers stood motionless, their thoughts focused on where their kill would be placed. Once decided, they unloaded their cargo, still knowledgeable that they had to blood-let the animal, or animals, scrape all of the meat from the skin and properly store it, eventually eat from the kill and fall into a much needed slumber within the semi-warmth of the sacred chamber.

Chapter 14

ADDITIONAL TUNNELS AND CATACOMBS were constructed, interconnected and extending for feet, then yards, and even miles. The chamber was all but complete, and its location was at the farthest end of the topmost catacomb; safely off to the topside of a deep tunnel.

The sacred chamber was constructed primarily to house and protect fetuses while they initially grew and matured; experiencing the many months within their membranes. Besides being the birthing site, the sacred chamber was used as a storage room for food and blood, and was a place that allowed the fetuses to thrive. This sacred chamber was also a place to house the dead, along with their decaying flesh, including the newborns that weren't fortunate enough to experience life beyond their membrane.

The creatures were in agreement that the group called the food gatherers would be the chosen ones and that these creatures would be the only ones that would ever be sanctioned to be upon the earth's surface. All others were strictly forbidden to ever leave the catacombs, unless all were forced to enter the surface, as the colony, en masse.

The hunter's status was clearly stated; they'd be considered the hierarchy; on a level equal to the elders because they were the more intelligent, the largest, the most heavily muscled, strongest, the most agile and cunning, and the most athletic. Two of the distinguished hunters were extremely fast, accurate, and had absolutely no sense of remorse. These were, by far, the swiftest of the creatures, and also the most deadly.

The food gatherers were selected, and as they huddled together in this area that was recognized to be somewhere close to the surface, the others dispersed and spent hours rerouting themselves. Using their keen senses, they walked this way and that, always honing in on the areas that were the most familiar to them.

For the next twenty-four hours, one of these elite remained at the entrance, listening intently in order to find the safest time to experience the earth's surface. This look-out, having adequate vision, used other senses more efficiently, choosing the time when it was the coldest and darkest because this was the time period when there was the least amount of sound and daylight was gone. This creature was also able to hear sounds when its skin felt warmed; creature sounds, unlike its own, but also sounds that were nonthreatening.

In their calculation, the creatures chose only to hunt when there was little or no recognizable sound; when the moon lit the sky, or without the moon's light, when there was darkness similar to that of the catacombs. This time was chosen because the darkness afforded the hunters camouflage when upon the surface.

The food gatherers, also known as the hunters, knew that the time to be upon the earth's surface was during the evening hours, when the sun no longer shined. After forming their group, they left the entranceway and began to familiarize themselves with the surface area that surrounded the entrance to their habitat.

Night after night, they trekked this way and that, each time becoming more and more comfortable, and seemingly more proficient upon the landscape. Each time that they surfaced, they ventured further and further from their habitat, always attempting to seek out a new experience. Included within these experiences was remembering a variety of landmarks to return from their treks to the habitat.

Trek experience taught the creatures the lay of the land; the locations of hills, boulders, trees, and shrubs, and, last but not least, and certainly the most important were the various treks to the ranches that had huge herds of the larger livestock.

During these treks, they also discovered, and remembered, the areas where the deer and the bears were, and where the deer were much more plentiful than any other animal. Gradually, these hunters became familiar with the earth's cycles and were now prepared to proficiently hunt for their sustenance.

The underground creatures used their muscularity and razor sharp talons to propel their heavily muscled and weighted mass up and down tunnels and along what seemed to be the endless passageways, one exhausting trek after the other, eventually surfacing for a hunt. They did this for one exact reason, to kill and collect their sustenance and then take it to the sacred chamber.

The food gatherers were known to assist the colony whenever they deemed that their help was needed throughout the interior of their earth dwelling. If it be the case that they were not preparing for the hunt, they could be heard procreating their kind. Other than procreating, they'd use sleep and their intake of the flesh and blood as a means to rejuvenate their energy.

Although these food gatherers became an organized bunch, it was initially evident when hunting that they hadn't yet become a synchronized team. They worked together to acquire kills, to supplement the colony's daily need, but their want to act independently was evident whenever a large animal escaped their attack. It took a while for the group to lose the need for independency. However, in time, they became noticeably cohesive. The larger and swifter animals were no longer escaping their corralling effect, and the flesh and blood reserve became more than plentiful.

One of the kills was an extremely large bear. This animal was considered to be the highest level of kills and it was a rare and significant occurrence when the scent of the bear's flesh and blood was recognized by the others within the 'habitat.' It was generally felt that the bear was a spiritual gift to the entire colony.

The bear's dense body supplied the colony with a tremendous volume of valuable, nutritious blood, several hundred pounds of flesh and protein, and an extremely large skin. The bear held more value for the colony than any other animal that was known to them.

Seeking it out and hopefully being able to kill a fully grown bear was the greatest challenge for all of the food gatherers. In the past, this scent equated itself with great fear, tremendous anxiety, and the death of one or more of the food gatherers; killing the revered bear was never a certainty.

As generations passed, the hunter's tactics and skills improved. The food gatherers felt that they had gained somewhat of an advantage when encountering a bear. It was genuinely felt that this formidable foe was one of their own because of its fighting skill, super strength, razor sharp talons, rather large size, and ultra-powerful jaw. What completely set it apart from all other types of prey was the rich fiber of its flesh and extraordinary content of its nutritious blood. When the bear's unique scent spread throughout the catacombs, this meant that the food gatherer's had succeeded in outmaneuvering their greatest adversary and were successful in killing it. However, unlike all of the other animals, this kill always came with some sort of price.

As the food gatherers used their instinctive and learned hunting skills to outmaneuver this treacherous animal, they always encountered a great force that could easily outmaneuver them. It was recognized by the food gathers that as the bear became exhausted, and thus vulnerable, that this brought on the greatest sense of anticipation and fear among the hunters. When these experienced hunters got the bear frustrated to the point of total exhaustion, it was at this point that the bear would rear up onto its haunches, standing totally upright with its outstretched arms and teeth ready to strike.

Unlike the food gatherers, the bear was less agile when it stood on its haunches, and thrashed its very sharp claws in aggression. There was little that it could not crush with its sharp, cutting teeth, and the foulest of smells often emanated from its mouth. At that very point, the hunters became aware that the bear was taking a power stance against them and would fight to the death; either its life or that of the hunters would end.

When the almighty bear was at its greatest height, it was standing upright at approximately seven to nine feet and could weigh as much or more than any one of the largest food gatherers.

The food gatherers recognized that this was also the time when this great bear was the most vulnerable; the hunters had a variety of options, but it was inevitable that one or more of the creatures' would have to risk their life when battling with this ferocious and formidable foe. The bloody battle persisted until the bear, or a hunter, was mortally wounded!.

The creatures instinctively knew that this large, equally powerful, and in some cases, dominant animal had a fierceness about it, a fierceness that could end up mortally wounding several of them. When the designated food gatherer felt that it had been propelled close enough, it used all of its powerful limbs to vault, thrusting its body upwards and forward with tremendous, focused power. This course of action had to be very swift, for if the bear recognized it, then it might parry, and possibly gain the upper hand, mortally wounding its attacker.

Knowing the danger of being mortally wounded, the hunter's adrenaline spiked an instant before it swiftly flew at and into the bear's muscled upper torso like a warhead. Its talons on all four appendages protracted, straining for their intended purpose. Within seconds, this individual hunter's powerful thrust had its upper and lower sets of razor sharp talons embedded deeply into the bear's chest and groin areas; its head very close to the bear's mouth and throat. The hunter's force temporarily unnerved the bear and knocked it off balance. It was then that the creature forcefully sank its talons, as deep as possible, into the bear's thickened chest cavity, and utilized its head claws to grasp the skull in its death grip.

As this specialized hunter held the bear's upper torso securely, it then used its leverage, purposely sinking its lower talons as deeply as possible into the groin and hip joints, and had little trouble slicing through the connective tissue that, in turn, seriously disabled the bear.

It was imperative to disable swiftly, before the bear could recoup any of its senses and awareness. For if this happened, before being mortally wounded, the bear could use its own daunting claws to rip and slice the back and sides of the food gatherer. At the point where the bear became totally disabled and mortally wounded, the hunter would move away from the severely weakened, and blood-letting bear and fall heavily to the ground, fully spent.

While laying a distance from the mortally wounded bear, and experiencing the various stages of recuperation, the hunter would allow the other food gatherers to meticulously search for wounds that the bear may have inflicted. It was usually the case, when facing off against such a formidable animal, that a hunter would experience serious cuts and punctures. It was never documented when it actually became a reality, but for some reason, the creature's saliva had healing powers for these types of wounds. If during their meticulous search a wound was discovered, then the hunters would deposit large amounts of their own saliva into the wound. In a matter of days, they'd heal completely, without the slightest indication of scarring.

Chapter 15

AT THAT POINT IN time, the creatures were experiencing a completed life cycle, whereas the older ones were dying off; like all living things, survival of the fittest was what mattered. Physical battles ensued for most types of hierarchy; these personal battles often had, as their point, the fetus carriers, and the freedom to mount these creatures whenever the need arose. A vicious fight, often to the death, could show its ugly face whenever a creature chose to mount a certain fetus carrier. The fetus carriers were not the workers, and experienced the least physical change. They were significantly smaller than the majority of the males, and lacked their extreme musculature and strength.

The fetus carriers most resembled the female lepers that once lived among the community of Doylestown, Bucks County. Their significant difference stemmed from the fact that they no longer had use of an umbilical cord, but rather gave birth with a membrane. These fetus carriers were physically receptive for most of the days of each and every year. Due to their size and strength, a male would have his way with the fetus carriers. When it was sensed that a fetus carrier was in their immediate area, the male would make his presence and intention known. At this point, the fetus carrier would cower and become submissive, readying itself to be mounted. It was then that the male would move directly behind the female, assuming the mounting position, preparing for a powerful forward hop, with an aimed thrust toward the bent over and submissive female. Although the environment was without an ounce of light to guide their bodies, there was no doubt that these males were adroit at their well-honed skill.

The shameful aspect of these sexual encounters was the fact that the fetus carriers were led to believe that this relief was their primary role within the colony. The fetus carriers took pride in relieving the formidable males of their frustrations, but hardly ever experienced the sensation that indicated pleasure, or their own release. The fetus carrier's achievement came when the male shook and collapsed into the wall of a catacomb, or even more so upon the eventual realization that the coupling had resulted in a pregnancy.

Survival of the fittest played a role during the time of coupling. It was at this time that a male creature and a fetus carrier temporarily became one, but this could be seen as problematic for the hierarchy. It was well documented throughout the colony that the food gatherers considered certain fetus carriers to be their coupling partner, and that this fetus carrier was not for servicing another male. If any other creature mounted a food gatherer's coupling partner, then there was sure to be a problem. The food gatherer, also known as its coupling partner's protector, would intercede when realizing a mounting hopeful was attempting to dominate its significant female. It was at this time that the protector was known to heavily swat the hopeful away from his fetus carrier and against a catacomb's wall. Sometimes, the swatted individual would land in fecal matter and urine. This was a very serious decision by the protector because the other creature now had a choice, a slim choice, but a definite one. Either take up the challenge and have little possibility of defeating the fetus carrier's protector, or accept the given fact that this fetus carrier's protector was indeed dominant. A fetus carrier was in an ideal situation if its protector was, indeed, one of the more powerful and vicious creatures, such as a hunter. Lower than the true hierarchy, but still one of the chosen, a carrier, pusher, or digger had specific fetus carriers, all possessing the status of being protected. It was almost unheard of that one of these hierarchies would ever have to keep its fetus carrier from the lustful want of any wandering soul. If, on the other hand, a needy wanderer decided to fight for its need to mount this protected fetus carrier, then the viciousness of a fight would commence.

There were times when the beginning of an altercation would be calculated, but at other times, there wasn't any time spent in parrying. The viciousness of the aggression was evidenced as these two combatants thrashed out at one another, at times using the talons of their upper and lower appendages, and their head claw. Parrying or not, this battle continued until one, or both of the combatants experienced a mortal wound. Some of the battles were short-lived, some lengthy, while a few were epochal.

During these fights, there was always bloodletting, and the taste of an adversary's blood caused great euphoria for the victor; the blood's nutrients had the tendency to throw a power crazed victor into frenzy. It was during one of these altercations that cannibalism first reared its head as a survival option. This cannibalism happened totally by accident, but led to another avenue as a food and blood source. After mortally wounding its adversary, the victor, as previously said, was thrown into a frenzy by the taste of an adversary's blood; before realizing what was happening, the victor's frenzy encapsulated its desire! The victor viciously pounced upon the victim of its aggression, and using its teeth and talons tore into the body, and drank the new blood source. This was a ravenous sound, especially when the taste of the warm, fresh, and nutritious blood threw the victor into what could be best described as a chaotic, ferocious feast.

To those in the immediate area, they were awestruck by the primal sounds that emanated from the victor. After cannibalizing its kill, the protector, as usually was the case, would wander off, and most probably fall into a long, recuperative sleep. This, being the initial cannibalization, was the cause for a gathering of the elders. During this gathering, it was universally recognized that their own blood was far more nutritious than the blood of any other animal they had killed. The focus of this gathering brought about a by-law that was agreed upon, that is, cannibalism must be controlled. It was allowed, but only in a controlled fashion. "At the time of death, either from a mortal wound or from old age, or sickness; then that member of the colony was not to be ravenously consumed, but instead, was to be taken to the sacred chamber by the food gatherers or the carriers." Included was the understanding that the hierarchy would always be given first choice when there was fresh blood and/or flesh, especially the blood of their own!

A newly deceased or killed creature would have their head removed and devoured. Then, the body would be hung upside down, directly above the vat, until all blood was drained, to the very last drop. It was at this point that the hierarchy enacted cannibalism to be a necessary part of their evolutionary process. It was an added surplus to their already stored kills and blood supply.

Chapter 16

AS BIRTHS INCREASED THE population, so was the increased need for additional sustenance; more flesh and nutritious blood. Cannibalism was seen as a way of harvesting the living. The food gatherers, being generally thought of as the hardest workers and at the top of the hierarchy, were given the honor of drinking the freshest blood and consuming the nutritious, bloody flesh. The newly acquired blood was usually kept out of the storage vat and subsequently not mixed with the aged blood until the food gatherers had imbibed, and had eaten the freshest of the meat. Once these food gatherers were satiated, then and only then, were the diggers, carriers, and the pushers permitted to enter the sacred chamber. As far as status was concerned, the diggers and carriers were just a step lower than the food gatherers, and just below all three were the pushers. Fresh, coagulating creature blood, possessing the highest nutrient value, was what these creatures constantly sought, but hardly ever attained. That elixir, and the flesh and blood from a most recent animal kill, had the highest source of body building protein; these being the substance and sustenance for life, superior size, and growth.

Not all of the creatures were of the realization that cannibalism had now become universally acceptable and regulated throughout their colony. Since the initial cannibalization, it took some time for the news to spread throughout the subgroups, which lived at various levels throughout the entire colony. It was then recognized that the number of dead in the chamber had lessened dramatically, and that the blood supply had to be replenished sooner than in past months.

The youngest creatures were growing noticeably stronger and physically superior to those of past generations. It became evident that their dead were not just a source for blood, but were also utilized for food; they were, in fact, being cannibalized, as soon as was possible, sometimes before being added to the flesh pile. This reality caused widespread confusion among the oldest members of each subgroup, and they made a concerted effort to separate themselves from any of the cannibalistic youth. This effort was down-sized, almost immediately, when the young began to dominate all others in any sort of physical confrontation.

Using a crude method of deduction, it became evident that cannibalism was necessary for the survival of the youth and therefore for the continuance of the habitat's construction. Confusion continued to reign because the oldest members did not need to be cannibalistic to survive. They were noticeably smaller and passive, rather than aggressive, but significant change was now being processed.

The majority of the culture gradually accepted cannibalism and found, by doing so, that an increase in size and strength had become the norm and that the cannibals were generally more aggressive. More of these creatures ate what was their own and craved blood. It was further realized that cannibalism had become, and would continue to be, an essential part of their culture, and the colony's life force. This act was no longer taboo. It just hadn't been recognized for its worth until that specific point in time.

Chapter 17

IT WAS EASY TO feel the presence of a food gatherer, their aura of strength and ferocity radiated, even within the absolute darkness. The food gatherers were horrendously large and muscled to the max, possessing a very thick physique and almost no visible neck; similar in size to that of a super heavyweight body builder that utilized both steroids and human growth hormone.

To this point in time, no one upon the earth's surface that lived within the confines of Bucks County's numerous towns and communities had the slightest inclination that these creatures had survived, yet alone were flourishing beneath the earth's surface within that immediate area. Bucks County was, and is considered to be affluent, and is best known for its quaint towns and villages, beautiful housing complexes, a community college, several outstanding high schools, of which a couple are nationally recognized for their football prowess.

Upon the surface, the typical American landscape persists. Central Bucks-West has been a perennial powerhouse in the State of Pennsylvania, and is one of the premier high school football programs within the entire United States; and ranked close behind Central Bucks-West, also within Pennsylvania, are the North Penn Knights. Up until very recently Central Bucks-West was coached by Mike Pettine, while North Penn continued to be coached by Mike Pettine's son, and his knowledgeable staff.

Much like the State of Indiana, and its reputation for high school basketball; Pennsylvania's Central Bucks-West and North Penn's football programs had built reputations as football dynasties. On the outskirts of these towns and villages are rolling hills and large amounts of uninhabited land; land that is camouflaged and thickly populated by trees, shrubs, boulders and high grass. The rare times people are seen in these forested areas are during hunting season, or when children, on a whim, choose to play some sort of game in a wooded area. Gas station chains dot the area, along with restaurants such as the Marabella family chain of fine eateries.

There are numerous distinguished sights in this county, including the towns of New Hope and Peddler's Village. Not too distant is the Valley Forge National Park, with its vast land mass and its multitude of wildlife. If you look hard enough, you just might see George Washington exiting one of the many log cabins. Occasionally, deer collide with a passing automobile; they are abundant and have the freedom to run onto the roadway, unimpeded.

Beautiful, elaborate homes constructed by the Toll Brothers have been built, and continue to be constructed on the land masses that once stood the test of time as farms. Although the farmland is gradually being displaced, farming can still be witnessed. Farming is still the way of life for families, but on a much smaller scale. During the last century, ranchers have lost their livestock here and there, but no one has come up with how or why. During these past one-hundred years, it has been documented from time to time, that horses, pigs and hogs, cows and steers, chickens, and an occasional dog have disappeared, without a trace.

Chapter 18

DEEP WITHIN THE EARTH'S crust, these creatures heard, and learned to tolerate, the disturbance of heavy equipment preparing the soil for planting, and within time, the harvesting of the crops. The vibrations could be, at times, severe. Though, the passageways remained intact, at least to that point in time.

Housing developments and malls were being constructed, causing the catacombs to experience even stronger tremors and fierce vibrations that could damage the supporting walls and ceilings of the habitat. The heavy weight and shear number of these machines became a growing fear among the entire creature colony.

The oversized machinery was being utilized to speed up the preparation for prospective building sites, thus causing varying degrees of damage to the land masses. Oversized bulldozers could be seen from a distance, and one day, as an operator was maneuvering his machine, he realized that the bulldozer was, in fact, slowing sinking into the surface of the land. Unbeknown to the operator, the birth chamber's ceiling was experiencing a collapse, thus letting in a small degree of the brisk cold, and letting out the overheated, putrid stench of the stored flesh and blood. This chamber was the storage place for thousands of pounds of sustenance taken from the various ranches and farms, and the area wildlife. Clumped together, these carcasses added to the acrid smell of death. The large chamber was constructed closer to the surface than the catacombs and tunnels so the sun's rays that warmed the surface of the earth also gave a degree of warmth to the large, open space.

This large room housed the decomposed membranes, afterbirth, rotting animal flesh, dead fetal matter, and the flesh of those creatures that had died as the result of being mortally wounded while fighting or hunting. The remainder of the food cache came from the members of the colony that had died off because they became feeble, and, or were too old to be of any use other than as food. Gradually, this room took on the appearance of an enlarged compost bin; it was very hot and steamy. Due to its warmth, especially during the winter months, the members of the hierarchy used the room for copulation, a birthing site for the membranes, a place for an unimpeded slumber, and a bank of food and blood for the entire colony.

As the bulldozer slowly sank, several of the unborn fetuses that were unfortunately too close to the break in the earth's surface could not cope with the drastic change in temperature and became stillborn. Fortunately, the fetuses that were within their membranes, and were furthest away from the damage, survived the cold blast and were only slightly inconvenienced. Any damage to these membranes was incidental, and subsequently did penetrate the fetuses within.

Weeks turned into months, and the steamy environment tended to quickly mature these fetuses. Eventually, as the fetuses neared the end of their cycle, they were now too large for the sustenance that remained within their enclosure. Now fully formed and feeling somewhat famished, they engulfed the remainder of the slimy ooze that once filled their membrane, but that was still not enough. This clear and thickened liquid, that was dreadful and foul, satiated their need for the majority of their cycle. However, at that point, it was gone. Once the slimy ooze was completely consumed, the creature's encircled membrane would lose its elasticity and stress cracks would appear. Instinctively, the newborn would add pressure to these surface cracks, breaking open the membrane. It was then that the newborn would leave its membrane and slither in the direction of the stockpiled food and blood cache.

Inbred, within these creatures, was the Instinct of how to survive the cold, dark, dismal environment of the catacombs. When a creature was strong enough to move away from its membrane, it instinctively slithered toward the smell of rotting, putrid flesh. It did not pick and choose what it ate. It simply tore into the cache, and fiendishly engulfed whatever it felt was sustenance.

When the newborn was completely satiated, it then abandoned the flesh and upon finding a warm spot, lapsed into a long, deep, restorative sleep. During the initial phase of its life cycle, which lasted approximately three months, these newborns remained within the chamber. Even at birth, the male creature, rather than the females, had horrific sores and orifices from which the foulest of smells would escape.

The creatures had adapted to their smell, but for a human to get any closer than ten yards would cause the most hardened person to spasm, violently vomit, and subsequently experience extensive, pain-filled, dry heaves. The foulest of smells came from the birth chamber of these unknown, underground dwellers.

The community members that had decided to lead the leper colony to its burial site believed that the elaborate maze would prevent the lepers from finding an escape route to the surface. It was further believed that these lepers would consume their two week food and water supply, and then would die off, as was previously planned.

For more than one-hundred and twenty years, these outcasts evolved against all odds, becoming survivors; grotesque at best, even beyond what was envisioned as totally impossible.

Chapter 19

EARLY IN ITS EVOLUTION, one underground creature, since acclimating itself to the bone chilling cold and dampness, began to feel an internal drive to experience what it had not before, the Earth's surface. This Lone Creature instinctively felt an overwhelming want for freedom, and the need to explore.

Whenever the food gatherers assembled and subsequently departed the habitat for the sole purpose of restoring the colony's food cache, the Lone Creature recognized that they would be gone for extensive periods of time. To say the least, the creature was envious, and wanted to experience the Earth's surface, either as a food gatherer, or on its own. There were two givens in this colony: one, to become a food gatherer, a creature had to be physically qualified, and these hunters would only consider adding a qualified creature to their elite ranks if one of their own had been mortally wounded; and two, it was strictly forbidden for any creature, other than a food gatherer, to ever leave the protection of the catacombs.

There was a universal exception to the second of these given rules, however. If the time came that the catacombs were under siege, then to elude capture, and, or death, all of the creatures could move, en masse. They understood that they were to move to the far end of the vast catacombs; beyond the sacred chamber, and to leave their sanctuary, to escape the assault of the human.

Every time these food gatherers returned, laden with the tedious weight of one or two full grown animals, this Lone Creature felt the pang within to join them for the hunt. Knowing that its status would not allow it to venture out of the catacombs, it often felt frustrated, but instinctively knew that leaving the Catacombs, other than on a sanctioned hunt, was strictly forbidden. This law was feared, and therefore had never been tested; still, knowing this, the Lone Creature had a drive that it couldn't deny, and within time, it didn't. It also knew that approaching the elders for an agreeable solution was out of the question!

Could the Lone Creature get to the Earth's surface undetected, experience what it had only fantasized, and return to the habitat without causing suspicion? It knew that forbidden meant exactly that! The underground creature deliberated for lengthy periods and believed, even stronger than any previous time, that it could do what no other creature had done, other than the food gatherers, experience the Earth's surface.

There was one significant problem; it had to plan its departure for a time when there was a surplus of food and blood within the sacred chamber. Presently, there wasn't a surplus, and so it recognized, despite its internal drive, that this was not the time to journey. The ever-increasing want to trek upon the surface continued to gnaw at its every fiber! A couple of months went by, and then one night it became evident that the elders had assembled with the expressed intent to surface for the hunt. Together they departed, leaving the habitat behind. Many hours passed and light began to displace the darkness that was beyond the habitat's entrance. The food gatherer's returned with more than one carrier laden with a weighted kill, fully covering its shoulder mass; their physical make-up strained, and their breathing labored from the tremendous weight of these kills. Euphoria spread throughout the catacombs like wildfire as it became recognized that one of the kills had a tremendous girth. Was it the feared and revered clawed animal?

The sweet smell of the clawed animal's flesh and blood swiftly permeated every creature's senses, throughout every catacomb, and even within the chamber. Two food gatherers shared the responsibility of carrying this clawed animal during their return to the habitat. The elders, or food gatherers, were always shown the highest amount of respect when in the direct vicinity of all others.

The others held the food gatherers in such high esteem because they were the chosen hunters and also because every time they went out of the habitat, these food gatherers risked being seen, or possibly killed by a human, and they chanced being mortally wounded during a kill. It was also recognized that these hunters supplied the food and blood for all, and that the food and blood were the colony's lifeline. Being held in such high esteem was one thing, but the reverence that was shown to the food gatherers was more readily recognized whenever they killed, and subsequently returned, to their habitat with the great clawed animal. Several days thereafter, the fetus carriers were given the opportunity to copulate with these hunters, and hopefully become impregnated. Whenever a food gatherer came into the direct vicinity of a fetus carrier, it was then that the fetus carrier would obediently, and more than willingly, take the position for sexual permissiveness, submission, and now, potential gratification.

A few nights went by, and then the Lone Creature felt that it was time to leave the only home it had ever known. Sixteen long years of living in this habitat and now apprehension and exhilaration were felt. This youthful underground creature moved along the catacombs, and as it moved, it bumped and nudged its way through the multitude of others, young and old alike. It used its senses to recognize when there was a tunnel opening directly to its forefront.

The tunnels were always tested; the creature would claw its way up and through the opening, until it came to an area that was closed overhead. At this point, the creature would hold tightly to the circular wall using the sturdy talons of three of its four appendages, and then would reach out with its available appendage, utilizing its talons. It was in this way that a creature searched for a vertical tunnel's ending, and subsequently for another horizontal catacomb. When within a vertical tunnel, a creature was able to ascend, or descend, bypassing one catacomb after another. When it moved from one horizontal passageway, up or down to the next, it had to make use of the variety of tunnels while having access to passageways. In time, it would eventually find the significance of an over-head blockage. It was common to find tunnels of different lengths, and where some ended above, that ceiling was traversed by a catacomb only a few feet above. The challenge of the tunnels and catacombs, and their conquests caused the Lone Creature new found anxiety and apprehension. Nervousness and fear prevailed beyond its ego, and after trekking through catacombs and ascending several tunnels, the youthful creature recognized that it was getting close to the Earth's surface. Its nervous energy escalated.

As this youthful underground creature moved upward, it recognized that the dirt was becoming softer and mildly warmer, and the fact that it was softer allowed its razor sharp talons to dig deeper, and hold faster, as it moved its heavily muscled, and weighted body, ever-closer to its goal. One tunnel after the other; always ascending, the Creature finally found itself in a pleasant environment, rather than that of its ever present stench.

While this Lone Creature temporarily rested, it recognized change! The creature was now content to fully breathe in the full extent of the change. The soil was cold, but not the damp cold that had previously invaded its bones while living far below the area where it now was situated.

Not known for its dexterity or agility, the Lone Creature had to depend, at times, upon its upper torso's muscular strength. This strength came into play whenever its lower appendages, being heavily muscled, became noticeably fatigued. When these heavily muscled lower appendages got fatigued, they'd violently spasm; this is when the creature dug its upper talons more deeply into the facing of a tunnel, and as the talons sank deeper and deeper into the earth, the creature instinctively pointed the tips of these talons downward. It was at this point that the creature would pull each of its pain filled lower appendages from their purchase, leaving it hanging precariously, calling upon its upper body strength until the pain and spasms were no longer debilitating its body. Being unable to see always caused these creatures to work harder, so as not to overlook an item or issue that could be burdensome or potentially damaging to the colony.

After hours of climbing tunnels and trekking various catacombs, the Lone Creature was closer to the surface than it had ever been; apprehension displaced the want to explore. It felt tremendous anxiety, and because of this, considered returning to the depths. Though now, it realized that it was completely depleted of energy, and fatigued.

The creature's continuous excitement and the extensive use of its physical strength had taken a great toll. The creature found itself too exhausted to return to the depths of the habitat or to climb further towards the surface. Realizing that its system was shutting down, it moved into the security of a nearby passageway. Without knowing what was happening, the Lone Creature shut down completely, and slumped into a contorted, exhaustive sleep. The creature slept uneasily, rolling from side to side, but never woke until many hours had passed. It was as if this underground creature was experiencing anxiety regarding the Earth's surface before it actually got the opportunity to experience that reality.

Awakening from a fitful sleep, the creature could sense that it had rested somewhat and that the surrounding coldness was not as severe. As the creature was getting up, it recognized that its entire body had grown sore from the trek up and through the variety of tunnels and along the catacombs. It slowly stretched its various body parts, and while straining, gained its balance. It was now ready to continue its journey toward the unknown: the Earth's surface. It was also hungry, but by no means famished; this youthful creature moved from the area where it had just recovered. Once in the ascending passageway, it could see a source of light in the distance. As if trying to understand, the creature slowly moved its head in one direction, then the other, and came to the conclusion that it was night when its body had shut down. Upon awakening, it was now seeing what was thought of as light, and this caused it to squint. It gradually got used to the light, but now knew why the food gatherers only surfaced during the darkest hours. This youthful underground creature found that its eyesight was somewhat diminished and stressed when looking in the direction of the light, and therefore knew that it would have to wait until sundown or even later.

The Lone Creature gradually organized its thoughts and was aware that the food cache was at this level of the catacombs. Having hours to wait until darkness, it decided to trek to the sacred chamber for some of its sustenance. Trekking along this catacomb, the creature realized that the distance to the sacred chamber was much farther than it had imagined. The stench of the flesh and the coagulated blood got stronger as the creature closed in on the chamber. Now that the odor was more apparent, the creature realized that it was at the sacred chamber, and subsequently, its appetite increased. Not knowing what exactly lay on the floor of the chamber, the Lone Creature cautiously moved toward the food source. In its attempt to avoid a collision or fall, the creature leaned forward using all four of its appendages. This was a wise decision because no sooner had it gotten down on all fours, when suddenly it stepped over several objects. While maintaining its awkward balance, it soon was directly in front of the large mound of rotting flesh.

If a human observed the creature at this time, as compared to when the drugged lepers were first led to their proposed death, it would realize just how much these creatures had adapted. When the lepers were led from their forested compound upon the earth, they were eating and drinking things that were common among humans. What was now evident, to an observer, was the reality that these creatures had adapted for their survival; they were carnivores, flesh eaters and cannibals.

The Lone Creature ate and drank its fill, and then made the long, return trek, to the precipice of the ascending passageway that led to the earth's surface. With its head leaning backwards, it listened intently, attempting to recognize if others were in his immediate area. Hearing nothing, he thought of entering the passageway that inclined toward the surface. This Lone Creature attempted to remember things that had been passed down over the generations while it had learned to adapt within the darkness of the catacombs; things that were pertinent for the food gatherer's survival when on the earth's surface. This youthful underground creature attempted to visualize the specific information that had been communicated to it, and to the others, by the food gatherers, during its lifetime. It was struggling now, because, until recently, it had little thought of realistically trekking upon the surface.

Fragmented scenes came to its mind as it tried in vain to understand, but could not! The Lone Creature's mind reeled from its visualized thought patterns, and as hard as it tried, this youthful underground dweller knew that it had no actual experience to be able to sort out what was visualized as fact or fiction. Anxiety was apparent, and the question was, would the anxiety lessen once the creature had surfaced?

The Lone Creature, knowing that it didn't have the knowledge or experience of the food gatherers, decided to be cautious and use the survival techniques that it had learned to that point in time. It believed that its instincts and size would protect it against any predator, including, and dominated by, the human. It decided to surface; it dug its talons into the softened earth of the ascending passageway, and, after trekking for a distance, it surfaced and felt exhilarated by the brisk dryness of the air. The youthful creature swelled with pride. It was the first time that any creature, other than a food gatherer, had felt the effects of the fresh, night air.

All of the sudden, and without the slightest bit of warning, the youthful creature lost its balance and fell, out of control, down a rocky, bumpy hill. As if in a learned survival mode, the Lone Creature balled itself into a tightly wound fetal position, and while tumbling, collided with boulders, smaller rocks, and small trees, which its body weight forcefully snapped, until It came to a full stop, approximately forty feet below the habitat's entrance.

Remaining within the fetal position, the Lone Creature believed that this position was what instinctively saved it from serious injury; it was also thankful for its thickened, solid musculature. Once the creature realized that it was finished tumbling, it gradually regained its composure, and then began to check its physical being for cuts, bumps, and bruises. Eventually, this youthful creature felt that it was relatively safe to release itself from the fetal position, and right itself upon its four appendages. As the creature slowly maneuvered its body parts, it found that nothing had been broken, but upon a more thorough investigation, realized that it was in considerable pain. Recognizing that it was safely hidden from the outside world and that its fall had not alerted any of the others, it rested right where it was for a while. While resting, it gave considerable thought to its situation; it was injured, but felt self-assured that there were no broken bones or internal damage. The creature decided to return to its habitat until it was fully healed. It did exactly that.

This underground creature climbed the hilly, rocky terrain, and once at the entrance to the habitat, realized that that immediate area outside of the entrance was flat, and circled around to the rear, behind the entrance. In the creature's mind, it was easy to follow the imbedded tracks that led from the entrance to the rear area. It could be seen that by the depths of the various tracks, how much heavy work had been done in the construction of the colony's homeland.

The Lone Creature spent a considerable amount of time filling in the tracks, and thereby removing those indentations that led to the habitat, and the evidence of the colony's survival. With the evidence removed, the Lone Creature methodically moved from the surface's warmth into the security of the entrance. This was a strange sensation, for the darkness caused the creature to lose its balance once again. Though this time, it merely had to lean against a nearby wall to collect itself. The Lone Creature stabilized itself and then listened for sounds within the habitat; sounds that would be recognized, if present.

There were no sounds, no disturbances. This Lone Creature was positive that it could descend the initial passageway, travel the vastness of the catacombs, and experience the tunnels that dropped toward the interconnected catacombs, until it got to its specific living space. The Lone Creature eventually arrived at its living space, and spent several days and nights recuperating from its many bumps and bruises; fortunately, there were no deep cuts, or apparent broken bones. The creature made a calculated decision to resurface, but first to revisit to the sacred chamber. Feeling powerful, once again, and being able to move about with little discomfort, the creature began its trek to the sacred chamber.

As the Lone Creature trekked along and finally arrived at

the topmost catacomb, it moved closer to the sacred chamber. Eventually, it recognized the scent of rotting animals and human flesh, and the vats of coagulated blood that were interlaced with new and aged quantities.

Upon entering the chamber, the creature recognized that it was alone. It balanced upon its hind quarters and reached with its upper talons and head claw, securing the freshest meat available. The creature ate its fill and then moved to a vat; once there, it knelt onto the joints of its hind quarters, and utilizing its upper appendages for balance, lowered its head and drank deeply from the vat.

The Lone Creature, once again being satiated, re-routed itself until it was ascending the passageway to the surface. No other creature was in the immediate vicinity and thus here, this adventuresome creature sat, leaning its body against a wall and fell asleep. Time slipped by, and eventually the creature awakened, remembering that it was extremely important to familiarize itself with the distinct scents and landmarks that surrounded the entrance, and the immediate vicinity.

When the Lone Creature got to the entrance, its overall pain had lessened; subsequently, its movement was less inhibited, so it went out and onto the surface. Feeling fortunate, rather than simply lucky, as Ed 'Sonny' Kennedy used to say, the creature exited the passageway and was now on the Earth's surface, this time being completely wary of its immediate surroundings. The night had come, and the darkness was a blessing, for the creature's epidermis was camouflaged by the color of the night. The creature moved apprehensively to the precipice of the hill, and had flashbacks of its tumble down, and against rocks and young saplings. It edged to the overhang, and once there, decided to use its skill level to back down the hill, so as to avoid another forward tumble, and the possibility of serious injury.

Tentatively, the 'Lone Creature' lowered itself over and below the boulders and rocks, and around the various trees, feet first until it was at the bottom of the hill. The creature realized that it had to use its intelligence; it had damaged sight from the effects of its leprosy, and during the previous sixteen years of its life, it only knew darkness. Furthermore, not knowing the extent of its damaged sight, it may have to depend upon its other senses to remain safe and secure.

The Lone Creature rocked backwards while keeping its lower appendages separate; backwards until its rear end was solidly against the surface. There it sat, somewhat balanced, and it began to sniff its environment for future awareness and recognition. Seemingly convinced that it was now comfortable, the creature rocked fully forward onto all fours. It was now ready to venture away from the only home that it had ever known.

Initially, the Lone Creature stopped every ten yards or so, for fear it would lose its return route. The further it ventured, the farther the interval became, until the creature traveled fifty yards or so, and then reared its head, sniffing its previous path for a continual recognition. As the creature moved further from the entrance, it seemed to gain an unidentifiable intestinal fortitude, and felt increasingly secure, but still apprehensive of the unknown.

As the underground creature plodded along, it continued to depend upon all four of its appendages for stability. It realized that the surface of the land was going to be a definite deterrent and, at the same time, a constant challenge, far more than walking the slush and rough surface of its habitat's passageways. As it apprehensively moved, it occasionally lost its balance, and occasionally stumbled and fell, its momentum allowing it to roll right into a righted position. Whenever this happened, the creature sat motionless, preparing itself to continue onward.

After a while, the creature gained enough self-confidence, and then slowly moved onward. It continued to stumble here and there, and encountered things under its lower appendages that were snapping beneath the weight of its body. The Lone Creature felt overwhelmed by these occurrences and would stop, becoming absolutely still.

With the youthful creature's motion coming to a full stop, it cowered from the unknown, taking deep, calculated breaths, attempting to recognize any sign of danger. It sniffed anxiously and extensively, leaned its head slowly to the left and then to the right, not recognizing an appropriate reason to be fearful and apprehensively continued its trek. This youthful underground creature found that it was bumping into and tripping over immovable objects that were lying on the surface, that other objects tangled its feet or were taller than its outstretched reach. The hilly, bumpy terrain and the wooded area unsettled the creature to the point where it decided to return to the safety of the habitat. The creature sniffed the area and easily recognized the return route to its habitat.

The underground creature methodically moved towards its home, using memorized scents and various landmarks. Once inside, it realized that no one had been aware of its recent departure. The creature worked its way down the initial passageway and along the route of the initial catacomb until it picked up the unique scent of the chamber. The youthful creature found itself moving faster as it neared the sacred chamber, and once inside, recognized that its hunger and thirst was stronger than it imagined. The Lone Creature charged the large mound of rotting flesh, and tore into it with a famished vengeance. Its thickened claws, which protruded from its head, pierced the flesh; and as the Lone Creature pulled a large chunk of flesh from the huge pile, it lunged forward, purposely ensnaring the meat as it fell toward its cavernous mouth. The Lone Creature's massive and powerful jaws enabled its pointed, boulder-like teeth to menacingly rip the flesh, and consume it, as blood covered and freely dripped from its mouth. The creature moved from the mountain of flesh to the large, steamy vat, and drank extensively from the pit of discolored, viscous blood. It tried desperately to figure out why it had decided to return to the habitat rather than go on, but found itself too spent. It also attempted to recognize the reasoning for its ravenous appetite and thirst, and came to the conclusion that this ferocious need was due to its mental and physical anxiety while upon the earth's surface. It also understood that its recent jaunt had taken a massive toll, causing it to slump onto its side. Possessing the knowledge that it was in a safe environment, the Lone Creature prepared itself for a lengthy period of sleep. Hours went by, and the Lone Creature's stay within the security of the habitat turned into days, then a week or two, and then the Lone Creature found itself yearning for the warmth of the earth's surface.

Realizing that the cache of food and blood had been restored, the Lone Creature moved along the passageway, and was once again at the entrance to the surface. Being ultra-sensitive to the sun that seemed to be on the verge of peeking through the horizon, the Lone Creature moved onto the surface while its comrades slept. Immediately, it encountered a new phenomenon, a cooling liquid was falling onto its body as it moved upon the surface. The Lone Creature threw back its head, deeply sniffed the scent of the area, and attempted to sense a reference point for this falling liquid. No reference came to the creature, but there was the realization that the falling liquid was not a threat. It bravely stuck out its tongue, and felt the coolness of the liquid dropping onto it, and then felt another sensation. Something else was falling from the sky that had a slightly solid feel to it. These weightless objects were noticeably landing on its tongue, and then quickly dissolved to a liquid form. Some of these objects landed on its eyes and the lids, causing a pleasant, cold sensation. The creature remained in this position, seemingly mesmerized, and eventually the liquid and semi-solid matter ceased.

The creature moved forward, paying close attention to the layout of the land, and found itself attempting to sense the location of the wooded area; the same wooded area that it had found just prior to returning to its home environment several weeks ago. Thinking that the wooded area was much closer, the creature wondered if it had taken the wrong course after leaving its habitat. Ultimately, this Lone Creature did find the entrance to the wooded area, and managed not to fall along the way. Prior to entering the wooded area, it stopped its movement, deeply inhaling the immediate area for recognition. Once the creature was comfortable with its return route, and that the immediate environment was indeed safe, it was then that it resumed the trek.

After a distance of what seemed to be longer than in the past, it encountered small, fragile objects that were scattered all over the surface, and the long, thick, immovable objects that it had probably tripped over during its recent trek. The Lone Creature felt a measure of frustration when It bumped into objects that were taller than itself; some thin and others very thick. This frustration eased as the youthful underground creature remembered its trek into, and through, this same wooded area. Showing that it possessed intelligence and instinctual prowess, though also a possible limitation in sight, the creature began to feel its way through the area, depending more upon its upper appendages rather than solely on its encrusted, damaged eyes. Using its upper appendages and their talons to guide its movement, the creature was, at times, unsure, but it was reasonably comfortable because its formidable talons were colliding with the immoveable objects rather than its head, chest and shoulders.

As one would expect, the Lone Creature stopped every now and then, sniffing extensively toward the direction that it had just traveled. Now confident that it could return when it wanted, from its present location back to its habitat, the creature plodded through a variety of obstacles, finding that this forested area was extensive. Having previously ventured into these woods, this youthful creature used its instinctual intelligence for much needed answers, deeply sniffing its immediate surroundings. Not recognizing the slightest hint of a threat, the creature somehow knew that it had to trust its instincts and survival technique, especially if it wanted to continue this random jaunt.

Further and further from the security of the habitat, the creature ventured, finding itself more dependent upon its upper appendages and their talons as guidance mechanisms. It felt that it could rely more on its physical attributes rather than its weakened eyesight; and that it was able to traverse this wooded area, using only its lower appendages for its source of mobility. Eventually, the creature found itself at the far end of the wooded area and within an open space. It recognized that for its own stability, it needed to have all four appendages touching the earth's surface. Its primal intelligence was now being summoned to the forefront as the creature's eyes began to feel as if they had sand for lubrication and both got tired and irritated. This wasn't a problem prior to entering the earth's surface, but due to the unknown environment, the creature found itself having the urge to resort more to its eyesight for safety and direction.

With this limitation, the creature's eyesight now appeared to be an ally because its other senses were in a state of heightened awareness. There was a brisk wind and with it came a flood of fragrances. The Lone Creature could smell the fragrance of wild flowers, moss, grass, and an extremely rich fertilizer. After taking these fragrances fully in through its nostrils, it turned to its sense of hearing. This youthful underground creature was aware of different kinds of animals and it was attempting to place the various sounds into a mental reference index. It sensed life along the passage of the wind and felt things scurrying swiftly here, stopping on a dime, and then running there, just above its head and also upon the surface. Some seemed to be quite small and fast, while others were larger and noticeably slower. It was easier to recognize the presence of the larger, yet slower animals. It appeared as if all of these animals had recognized the Lone Creature's presence during these early morning hours.

The 'Lone Creature,' believing that it hadn't been in the vicinity of this wooded section for any length of time, found itself unnerved by recollections that were now flooding its head. Why this confusion? Memories, from an unknown past, were flooding its head and began to conflict with what the creature recognized as its reality. To say the least, these visions were disturbing. In its mind's eye, it was witnessing pictures, swiftly flashing their brilliance, and then, as fast as they came, they vanished, though periodically coming into view again and again and again. These mental images were concerning the creature because it was evident that the scenes were being witnessed in some semblance of form and order; frames, much like the appearance of the ancient home movies that were shown on reel to reel projectors. Could it be that these were flashbacks of a past life, a reincarnated life, or possibly a glimpse of the present; a present that the food gatherers experienced whenever they came upon the earth's surface to hunt? This youthful underground creature stopped all of its movement and attempted to come up with an answer for its visions. A considerable amount of time and thought was spent, but nothing proved to be substantial.

The Lone Creature, being just within the outlying border of the wooded area, listened intently to the wildlife, and then rocked forward, digging its four groups of talons lightly into the moistened soil. Before moving from this position, the creature slowly moved its head from side to side, attempting to listen to nature and to lock onto any perceived threat to its safety. Satisfied that there wasn't anything present to threaten its safety, the creature moved onward. It found that the uneven surface was difficult to traverse, and therefore it took a while to acclimate itself to the terrain. While moving, it found that by squinting its eyelids that this did two things. The first was positive, although its eyelids were encrusted with a plaque-like material that prevented the eyelids from closing entirely, it was quite evident that the squinting increased the focus of the creature's sight. The second was a less than positive thing. After squinting for any length of time, the lubrication seemed to exhaust itself, and needed time to recapture its essence. If the creature did not rest its eyes when it was deemed necessary, then they would become drier and quite sore. This circumstance had never been an issue while living within its cold, moistened labyrinth.

Once acclimated, the Lone Creature seemed to sense when a mound of earth, a rock, a boulder, or a downed tree was in its designated path. This Lone Creature gradually gained enough confidence to move further from the habitat than it had ever previously been. It traversed the landscape for approximately another mile and at this point, it found itself lying upon the softened, powdery earth. Feeling an increased sense of confidence and somewhat playful, the creature threw caution to the wind and created quite a disturbance, in what could be easily recognized as a wheat field, if indeed this were the growing season.

The creature was vigorously attempting to rid itself of the stress factors that unnerved it since leaving the security of its habitat. This youthful creature began to vigorously roll and tumble within the seemingly soft, powdery earth, and in doing so, created an encircling area of dust and flying particles of dirt. Never before had it experienced such a heightened sense of freedom and fun. It finally succumbed to this vigorous, playful activity, and laying back, remained there for a while. Eventually, the creature righted itself, sniffed the air to get a read on its location, and then prepared to trek back. Almost immediately, and before taking its first step, its instinct told the creature to stop, and to remain perfectly still;

anxiety and a heightened fear rushed to every surface inch of the Lone Creature's rough and abraded skin.

This immediate perception was totally unsettling and its sense of security was severely disturbed. Something, or someone, was close by, and this presence was perceived as a real threat. The Lone Creature was secure within the scope of its own self-preservation, but was now unsettled by this perceived threat. It did not sense this threat to be a bear, and now wondered. Could this disturbance be the greatest threat to its existence and to its survival. The Lone Creature honed in on the immediate area where the threat was perceived, but felt no threat coming from that specific location. In actuality, the location was a school bus stop on a side road just far enough off of Route 611, so any child waiting for their school bus would be safe from the excessive amount of speeding traffic.

Chapter 20

JACK HENGY AND HIS wife Jill lived within the County of Bucks and were friends with John and Kathleen Lightcap; Jack and Jill were often seen on their front deck, sipping their steaming gourmet coffee, making sure that the Lightcap children, Grace and Ryan, remained safe until the school bus came by and transported them from that area. Grace was nine years of age, and Ryan was twelve; they are brother and sister and the best of friends. This morning, Grace and Ryan were at the bus stop, dressed appropriately for this brisk, sunny morning; they both wore a coat and hat, mittens, and shoes, rather than sneakers. Both were comfortable in this attire because prior to moving to Bucks County, they had lived in Maine, where the weather was often damp and cold.

Grace and Ryan were all-American types. To know them was to want them as your children, or as your brother and sister. It was common to see them together, with their smiling faces and concern for each other, and for others. Ryan, being the older child, readily accepted the role of Grace's big brother, and therefore her protector. These children were born in a small, quaint town in Maine, and lived there with their parents until very recently.

While living in Maine, the children often heard folklore relating directly to Bigfoot and as they aged, they both began to discuss this creature, and the way that they each perceived its appearance. They roamed Maine's countryside during their early years, often imagining that they would come across something unique. Both youngsters had a vivid imagination, but Grace believed that Bigfoot was real while Ryan was more skeptical. Grace believed in fairy tales and fantasy, while Ryan was more the realist. During Grace's first six years, she had often heard of Bigfoot, and as the years went by she could visualize its form. She saw Bigfoot as a large creature covered with long, unkempt hair; much like the depictions that were seen in newspaper articles, and she envisioned it to move about upon its legs. Unlike the printed articles, in magazines and newspapers, Grace visualized this creature, at times, using all four appendages for guidance and balance. When playing in the woods, she would occasionally say that she saw Bigfoot and describe this creature to whoever would pay her any attention.

While attending school, Grace often heard stories related to the reality of Bigfoot, and while in Maine, there were shopkeepers who would pique her imagination. Grace was able to visualize Bigfoot's unique appearance and she was often very convincing, when talking to others, regarding the creature's existence.

Folklore was common in that area of the country and Bigfoot, or Sasquatch, was often an intricate part of all folklore. School reports, essays, and an occasional newspaper story centered upon this large, hairy creature that had the ability to walk in an upright position; stories often depicted Bigfoot to be well over seven feet in height.

Since Grace and Ryan both attended school for full days, their parents were able to work full time jobs; John, as a heavy equipment transporter, and Kathleen, as an elementary school teacher. They had spent most of their lives in the Philadelphia area, but after marrying, they decided to raise their children in a much less violent environment. They didn't want to leave their family roots behind, but since Kathleen was now pregnant, they soon relocated to Maine. While this area was indeed less violent, it also had less to offer than a big city, such as Philadelphia. Ryan was born and then three years later Grace. No one could ask for more than these kids offered. They spent their early childhood in Maine, but almost every lengthy vacation was spent in the Philadelphia area, with their relatives, and new found friends. John and Kathleen, and the kids, ached to be with their relatives and friends, so after living in Maine for thirteen years, they decided to relocate once again. John and Kathleen had many discussions and finally decided to relocate somewhere within the affluent area of Bucks County, Pennsylvania.

John had a contact within Bucks County, and wondered if his contact person, who had a thriving business, could be in need of his working expertise; there always seemed to be a need for drivers who could handle, and deliver heavy equipment. Kathleen realized that there were better teacher salaries within the Bucks County school system. John got in contact with the company that he knew of, while growing up in Germantown, and while he drove cross-country for a major hauler. He found out that his driving experience was needed, and so he spoke with Kathleen, who in turn had sent her resume to the Bucks County Elementary School System. Kathleen, not Kath or Kathy, received a favorable response, sooner than anticipated and an interview was set up.

Much to Kathleen's joy, the interview went better than she could have ever expected, and she was now employed in Bucks County. Kathleen returned to Maine and soon after both she and John, and the two children, shared the news with their friends, neighbors, and their present employers. They were leaving Maine and heading back to the area where John and Kathleen were raised, and to the area where their families, and relatives, still resided. After saying their heartfelt goodbyes, and making the necessary plans to relocate, the Lightcaps were making definite plans to return to the Philadelphia, Bucks County area, and the comfort level that they sorely missed. John got in contact with his brother Bob, who had been a moving and storage man for most of his adult life. Bob's experience goes back to when he was a youth and worked at his grandfather's and father's company, Charles W. Lightcap & Sons, Moving & Storage. Like many other businesses that originated in Germantown, this one, after eighty-five years of doing everything honestly, succumbed to a variety of pressures and closed its doors forever. Bob then worked for Hunting Moving and Storage, located in Northeast Philadelphia, and has been there for many years. Bob, like his father, will always do for others as much as he can, and then some. He agreed to borrow one of the owner's trucks and then found an agreeable weekend for the move. Bob hired on two of Hunting's employees, and then drove to John and Kathleen's home in Maine. Together they finished packing whatever still needed to be, and spent several hours placing everything into the truck. Bob's expertise was packing household goods and loading all of those items into a truck, so that the variety of goods would be safe when being transported, and he always did a first rate job. Everything was out of the house by early Saturday evening, and thus Maine was now part of history for John, Kathleen, Ryan and Grace.

While driving back to the Bucks County area, there was happiness for the adults and children, and also some mixed emotions, for they were leaving behind a large part of their history, and friends, to that point in time. What would the future behold for them?

John, Kathleen, and the two children moved into an old stone farmhouse that sat on a half-acre, had several small trees and a narrow free-flowing stream. What Kathleen loved most about this farmhouse was its history, and the fact that it had a gorgeous fireplace, with a wood burning insert. Being inside the house brought back memories of the television series The Little House on the Prairie, for this house, and family, had the same air of wholesomeness. The cost was much higher than they had ever experienced, but they knew with their increased salaries, they could handle this mortgage along with the variety of responsibilities, namely, the ever rising cost of raising two children.

During the next few years, Bigfoot was all but abandoned in the minds of the children. If Grace ever brought the topic up, none of the other children picked up on it as something that was worth discussing. Grace tried to make Bigfoot a topic of conversation at various times, but as the months went passed, no one was even slightly intrigued. Maine and Bucks County had similarities, but the legend of Bigfoot was not one of them.

Grace and Ryan gradually became acclimated and got acquainted with the area and made many new friends. They found that they were constantly amazed by the size of their new school and at the number of students in each of their classes. When living in Maine, the number of students in their classrooms was small compared to the largely populated classes in Bucks County. It further amazed Grace and Ryan that the total number of students in their Maine school could actually fit comfortably into a single Bucks County classroom; what a tremendous culture shock.

Chapter 21

IT WAS NOW LATE in the month of March and the Y2K scare was a major bust. People had prepared diligently so as to avoid the anticipated catastrophe, but it was all in vain. Many theories came to the forefront, of which, being ripped-off by businesses that sold computers, VCRs, generators, and other varieties of electronics. The sudden increase in sales of shelters, bottled water, all types of jerky, canned items, powdered milk and similar products, and health food items resulted in serious attention and complaints from consumers. Investigations followed, along with a lawsuit here and there, but there was little or no compensation paid to any of the complainants. In the year 2000, in fact, during the month of April, there was a story in the business section of a Philadelphia newspaper; the headline stated 'Long-lasting effects seen from Y2K spending'…excerpts from the story are as follows: "Remember Y2K? For most of us, the year 2000 computer glitch was a non-event. But in one respect, cost, it was all too real. The one-hundred largest 'Public' Companies in the Philadelphia area spent an estimated $1.46 billion on preventing Y2K computer problems, according to an analysis of documents filed with the Securities and Exchange Commission. Such problems stemmed from the inability of many computer programs to properly interpret the abbreviated date 00 as the year 2000 instead of as 1900."

"Nationally, the Y2K bill was estimated at between $150 billion and $225 billion by a consulting firm. The Commerce Department put the U.S figure at $100 billion. Since we were anticipating gloom and doom, just as the rest of the world, we did a lot of work to ensure that our business continuity processes were in place in the event of a disaster on Y2K; a spokesman for an insurance company said, "This is something that will live forever."

"The main benefit of all that spending might be the fact that nothing happened. Considering the enormous amount of over-time and the billions in capital that was spent by big business to prevent the Y2K glitch, this fact, when taken into consideration, regarding the various law suits, probably was the main reason why the suits got little validation worldwide."

The winter months were coming to an end and Y2K – The New Millennium, had taken little of its predicted disastrous toll. Wall Street and the world economy were, as always, unpredictable; illegal handguns and automatic assault weapons were flooding America. Children, in their preteens, and teenagers were no longer using their fists, but now resorted to handguns to kill off any perceived threat. What, at one time, would have been no more than an argument, or at most a fist fight, was now a debilitating injury, or death, from gun violence. The youth of America are involved in massacres in our schools, our neighborhoods, and at a variety of scheduled public events. People no longer say hello to peers that are not known as they pass them on the street; the fear is that person may be homeless and, or mentally ill, and could be carrying a loaded weapon. Paranoia continued to spread. It seems absurd, but people now fear mortal injury when walking in their own neighborhood, even during the daylight hours, though more so at night.

Chapter 22

GRACE AND RYAN WERE at the bus stop that was located very close to their home in Bucks County. Grace was aware of her immediate surroundings while waiting for the school bus, and Ryan's attention was totally absorbed by one of his favorite comic book heroes. Unlike most mornings, Jack and Jill Hengy, close friends of the Lightcaps, were not on their deck, sipping their coffee and watching the kids get off safely to school. Jack was in Iowa, on one of his many hunting trips, and while away, Jill usually stayed with her parents in Shamokin, Pennsylvania.

As the creature rolled around and flexed its talons towards the sun, it sensed a comfort level like never before. Dirt and dust were flying in every direction and the area was discolored. This Lone Creature eventually exhausted itself, with all of its stretching and vigorous movement, and now rested. It eventually got onto its two lower appendages and began to move awkwardly away from the dustbowl that it had just created. It didn't venture far when all of a sudden its world and that of Grace's were about to experience significant change. As the Lone Creature came closer and into a clearer focus, Grace noticed that it had come to a full stop. Luckily for Grace and Ryan's sense of smell, the wind was blowing away from them and towards the creature; still Grace felt sick to her stomach. Besides being huge and somewhat hairy, Bigfoot now took on a dimension like never before; no more a fantasy, Bigfoot was real and it actually stunk.

The Lone Creature apprehensively moved toward Grace and Ryan. With each step, it attempted to sense whether or not they were a perceived threat. Eventually, it was close enough to attack, but didn't because this presence was not aggressive, nor did it take flight; this was unnerving! The Lone Creature was completely taken aback by this unknown presence, and it stood motionless, not knowing whether it should attack, or take flight. Within its habitat, the creature depended upon its size, extreme musculature, and physical prowess to overthrow any perceived threat. However, in its present situation, there was so much more involved than merely utilizing its aggression to attack, that is, to survive. Knowing that it was upon the surface, without the elder's sanction and without their guidance, the creature did not want to risk being discovered for what it was. If discovered, the Lone Creature knew that it would be risking its life, and in turn, the discovery and annihilation of the colony and habitat. Forbidden meant exactly that, forbidden, and there was a definitive reason for this all important designation. To this point in time, these underground creatures had lived anonymously, for more than a century beneath the surface of the earth; unknown to the entire human race! And, this is the way the elitist group wanted it and needed it to remain. The leper's plight was a part of history and they were perceived to have died off more than a century ago.

The lepers were hampered by their eyesight, and as history eventually would state, the community members believed that the colony's poor eyesight would keep them deep within the earth's surface, unable to ever find their way through the maze and to the surface. They were considered outcasts when living among the community, and to further support the contention that these lepers had died off, after being placed within the bowels of the earth, human skeletal bones were eventually found in the area where it was presumed that these leper types had been placed. These bones were thoroughly examined, and the findings showed that the bearers of these bones died more than one-hundred years before. Since these bones were found in the immediate vicinity of the leper's burial ground, it was taken for granted that all had perished, and the search for any further leper types ended.

To these kids, this morning seemed to be just like any other, but Grace felt uncomfortable while Ryan continued to be absorbed by his action packed, superhero comic book. Eventually, Grace sensed that something was terribly wrong. Birds, squirrels, and other small animals were a common site, but this morning nothing could be seen or heard. Why?

Grace's attention was now piqued as she smelled what she could only perceive to be as a large number of hogs or pigs. The smell lingered and was debilitating, and quite foul, but there weren't any hogs, or any other type of animal farms that Grace could remember in that vicinity, at least not close enough to give off such a disturbing odor. As she searched further along the horizon, she finally saw something, and knew that the putrid smell was emanating from...Bigfoot!?

Grace was terrified by the sight of this Lone Creature; she found herself spellbound and frozen in place, staring directly at this horrendous site. Grace's intellect told her that this was indeed Bigfoot, but her logic disagreed. This Bigfoot was not full of unkempt hair, in fact it had little recognizable hair and it did not resemble a man. This was a creature that was indeed tall; much like the legendary Bigfoot, but It was unsightly, perverse, and stunk to the high heavens!

Ryan finally looked up from his superhero comic book because he had heard the bus rumbling toward their stop; more than once, he passively attempted to get Grace's attention, but when she didn't respond as usual, he assumed she was daydreaming. Grace finally succumbed to Ryan's jerking on her sleeve, and she looked in his direction. He mentioned that the bus was coming and momentarily her attention wandered to the oncoming bus. She finally blurted out one single, softly spoken word, "Bigfoot," as she reached for, and grabbed hold of Ryan's arm. As her body's nervous system violently shook, Grace looked back in the direction of Bigfoot, and pointed! They both looked but there was nothing strange within their sight. Ryan did see an area, not too far away, that was quite dusty and attributed this to the wind. Again, Grace quietly repeated the word, but this time it was in the form of a question.

The Lone Creature had sensed stillness in the air and its anxiety changed to fear of this unknown presence. Its instinct directed its attention away from the excitement of being outside of the habitat; the exhilaration of experiencing fresh, sweet air, and the sun's warmth that it found while being upon the surface. The creature's attention was on self-preservation; fight or flight became flight!

Using muscles that it had never used before, the Lone Creature found itself balanced on all four appendages, digging every talon deep into the earth, and immediately bounding in the direction from whence it had come. It needed to hide itself from the unknown presence that it feared was possibly its greatest threat, the human.

Being extremely frightened, this creature paid little attention to the direction it was heading; it did, however, recognize that it was heading towards the scent of the wooded area. The creature's heart raced, and forcefully pounded within its chest cavity; its breathing was noticeably labored. Its lungs ached and screamed for some sense of calm, but the Lone Creature could not afford to stop until it reached the security, and therefore the safety of the wooded area.

Experiencing such a high degree of unexpected exertion, it bounded across the terrain, and found itself losing its balance; falling hard, it bruised a shoulder, its back, and appendages. Still, the creature was quickly able to right itself and continued to bound forward, stretching its fore-appendages beyond their normal range, digging its talons deeply into the soil cover, and pulling backwards with such a tremendous amount of force. As the front appendage's talons dug deeper and deeper, and began to hold the earth, its rear appendages swiftly, and with great tenacity, moved forward, throwing clumps of earth behind, propelling the creature forward with greater speed. Once the back appendages were imbedded into the earth and strained to propel the creature, the forward appendages, with talons extended and straining, reached as far forward as possible. The creature felt such a rush upon the realization that its body had such unforeseen power. Before the

Lone Creature recognized that it was within the wooded area, its lower section of front appendages collided with a fallen tree and its momentum, size, and weight caused it to snap a young sapling, as if it was a toothpick! This tree was not enough to slow down its force, but directly beyond this toothpick was an old, healthy tree with a massive trunk. There was a great collision as the creature smashed into it; this time the tree didn't budge and the creature slumped to the ground in obvious agony.

Almost immediately, the Lone Creature experienced an unconscious state. Unaware of its circumstance, it awakened more than a day later, to the chill of the night, and the radiance of a full moon. The Lone Creature tried to recollect how it had gotten to this place, and then its most recent memories flooded its consciousness. Its head, shoulder area, right flank, and right thigh caused the creature excruciating pain, with the slightest bit of movement. These injuries disturbed the creature, but even more so, it was terrified when it recognized that it tasted blood, and that this blood was coming from within. These sensations were dominating the Lone Creature, which had always, to that point in time, carried itself with an air of invincibility.

The amount of anxiety and fear were new felt emotions, emotions the creature recognized that it would prefer to be without; and the amount of pain left the creature disturbed. Using considerable effort and strength, the creature slowly began to unwrap itself from the base of the tree; as it did, memories began to flood its mind. Although having trouble with its sight, the creature was able to mentally visualize clouded and distant images, visions that were somewhat confusing, as it attempted to move its body parts. With each movement, there was great pain. However, after spending several minutes, the creature forced itself to stand partially erect. While standing, the creature tilted its head as far back as possible, so far that its nostrils were high into the air. In this position, the creature slowly and steadily inhaled the environment. Though soon after attempting to inhale, it realized that it must be internally damaged, for the slightest attempt at inhalation brought with it searing, sharp pain. The creature continued to inhale, but due to the pain, inhaled much slower and shorter breaths.

The Lone Creature searched areas of the land for recognition, and subsequently, the return route to its habitat. It searched relentlessly, but nothing reminded it of the return route. Memories eventually returned of its previous choice to take flight, and subsequently of colliding with an object; an object that probably knocked it senseless. These memories were totally confusing, to the point where the thoughts had no order. The creature tried, in vain, to assemble its thoughts, and put them into a reasonable perspective, but due to the enormity of the collision, it didn't know which thoughts were real, and which were not. Questions flooded its bewildered mind. The Lone Creature recognized why it was strictly forbidden for any of the creatures, other than the food gatherers, to venture upon the earth's surface, especially alone.

Feeling disillusioned and extremely anxious, the Lone Creature sank heavily and swiftly recoiled into a fetal position. Experiencing the pain of its anxiety, it remained in this futile position for quite some time, and then began to slowly organize a plan. The creature had recollections that it felt were more realistic, such as its colony and its habitat existing within the surface of the earth; but giving these recollections the necessary amount of thought only created additional confusion and frustration. Frustration became totally dominant; at this present time, there was absolutely no awareness of its habitat's direction or location. The creature ached for home; it was evident that, for the time being, it could no longer take its food supply and its safety from the elements for granted as it once did.

As the creature sauntered around the wooded area, it found that its pain was still severe, though lessening. Actually, it was searching for a large enough land mass with adequate camouflage where It could build its own habitat with a chamber. The creature searched and eventually found a suitable location. Thus, it became the digger and the carrier for the creation of its habitat. This would eventually be the place where it could store its food supply, protect itself from the elements and any perceived threat, that is, especially the human.

The Lone Creature knew that this land mass was of a sufficient height and depth to house itself, and so it began to displace the earth from within. The creature used its upper sets of talons to create the initial opening for its proposed habitat, using these talons to move the earth away. It scooped, and subsequently threw the dirt backwards between its lower appendages, as far to the rear as possible. This type of work continued until the creature had formed the beginning stages of a shaft. Once the shaft's depth was a full body length, the Lone Creature was able to become much more proficient at digging, and removing the earth and rocks, much like a larger canine digs a hole when assuming there is a bone, or something of interest, hidden within the surface cover. The creature held its rear talons purposely together while imbedding its front talons into the dirt; and placed the majority of its body weight upon its rear appendages.

The Lone Creature alternately used its rear appendages, with their lengthy attached talons, to forcefully throw the loosened soil out of the shaft. As the shaft lengthened, the work became more laborious, for the creature had to displace the temporary piles of loosened soil until the majority of it was entirely removed from the shaft. The creature's work brought with it a reward; the shaft gradually became a catacomb of some twenty-five feet. The catacomb continued to lengthen, but its height would only allow the creature to enter, or leave, while assuming the position of being hunched over; hunched over to the point where all four sets of talons were touching the surface. The Creature found that its inability to stand fatigued its muscular lower back. It tried alternative methods to work the soil, but all of these were just as problematic. Eventually, the fatigue dominated, and so the Lone Creature, being at least twenty-five feet within the hill and well beyond the camouflaged entrance, succumbed to exhaustion, and drifted off within a dream state that far surpassed its previous ones.

While in this dream state, the Lone Creature visualized its previous habitat and could actually see that animal skins were being prepared as sacks so that the carriers could remove dirt and stones out of each catacomb. After many hours of a recuperative, depth of sleep, the Lone Creature began to stir. It recognized that it now needed some form of sack. The creature believed that it remembered its part in creating the segment of the exit that was constructed beyond the chamber, the exit that was to be used as an emergency escape route. It remembered the ever continuing construction of those catacombs and how animal skins were prepared, cut, and utilized as sacks.

Still quite sore from its collision with the unnoticed, immovable object, the Lone Creature needed a food source, and at the same time, an animal skin to enable it to drag the dirt and stones from an area that was deeply within the habitat. Recognizing that the air was now considerably colder and that the daylight had all but disappeared, it sensed that it could hunt for an animal to satiate its hunger and thirst, and subsequently use the animal's skin as its much needed sack. This creature moved away from its entrance and proceeded to traverse the wooded area until it came to an area that was silent beneath its appendages. The creature stopped its forward motion, stood as still as possible, and sniffed the area for any prior recognition, all the while trying desperately to pick up the scent of an animal that it might recognize. This necessary animal would be one that the food gatherers had previously carried as they proceeded through the habitat to the storage area, the sacred chamber. It slowly leaned its head backward, and as it did, the creature continually drew in steady, long, but still pain filled breaths.

This ritual paid dividends, for the creature picked up a scent that was familiar. It slowly moved along the outlying perimeter of the wooded area, always in the direction of the familiar scent, and eventually halted its motion. It then moved further away from that land area, but found that course suddenly impeded by some sort of blockage. Realizing that this blockage extended in both directions, as far to its left as it did to its right, and beyond, the creature attempted to adjust by using what sight it had. It squinted upon the blockage, realizing that the resistance was full of large holes, but that each was only large enough for an upper appendage to fit tightly through. After a thorough investigation, the creature found that this sturdy blockage was securely attached to upright standards, measuring approximately five feet in height, and planted deep into the earth.

The Lone Creature realized that its intelligence was paramount at this specific time. It placed both sets of its frontal talons upon the topmost portion of the upright standard, and recognizing that the standard was indeed sturdy, slightly squatted and immediately sprang up and forward, easily jumping over the blockage. It landed upon the opposite side while steadily holding onto the standard for balance. Having done this successfully, the creature felt a tremendous sense of accomplishment. Once upon the other side of the formidable structure, the creature found itself focusing upon its present mission, namely, to seek out the scent of an adequate food source, and to kill it swiftly. The creature could sense that a food source was reasonably close, and that this potential kill was not a threat to itself. While honing in upon the animal's location, the creature moved stealthily forward. Within its eyesight range were several four legged animals grazing in a pasture. Being aware of its need for sustenance, the Lone Creature moved purposely forward, unbeknownst to its prey. It instinctively sensed that it was within striking distance, and thus the Lone Creature stopped all of its motion and purposely slowed its breathing. The animal that was closest and within its eyesight appeared restless, making guttural, snorting sounds. Realizing that its own presence could be seen as a real threat, the Lone Creature remained still, attempting to calm itself further, and at the same time, calm its quarry. It was now that the creature could sense that the animal had resumed its previous demeanor, for the ones that were within its sight had their heads close to the grass, and appeared to be eating. The creature was envious of the animal's situation, simply sauntering around the field, eating their fill whenever their appetite warranted it. Now reassured that these animals were of no threat to itself, and most likely would be a swift and easy kill, the creature, very slowly and deftly, dug its talons deep into the earth, readying its purchase for the great rush toward the closest of these unsuspecting animals. Muscles pushed other muscles into action, and subsequently, the explosion of its entire musculature propelled the creature close enough to pounce upon the targeted animal. The cattle attempted to run and did, but the one immediately felt the extra weight that it was carrying. As the creature had pounced, it simultaneously dug the talons of its upper appendages so very deeply into each flank, and almost simultaneously, the talons of the lower appendages sank into the prey's hind quarters. The creature rode its muscled prey for a very short distance, and then the steer collapsed, mortally wounded: dead.

The creature regained its composure and sniffed the area for any sign of danger. Finding none, it loaded the kill onto its massive, boulder-like shoulders and its powerfully built upper back. Along the way, it encountered the same blockage, but had little trouble getting its kill and then its own body over the object. Once the creature was within sight of its new habitat, it settled down to skinning its kill, gorging itself of the warm bloody meat. It then drank of the warm, nutritious blood. The creature drank until its stomach stretched beyond its normal size, and could not stretch anymore. It used its talons, and the larger bones of its kill, to scrape the inner-skin clean, and then laid the skin out in the open air to dry. The creature then felt its system quickly shutting down, as it had in the past, so it hastily moved within the unfinished catacomb, and succumbed to a very deep, lengthy sleep.

The creature was much more tired and fatigued than it had realized, and slept for many hours. Awakening to the reality of unexpected warmth, the Lone Creature ventured outside the safety of its partially constructed habitat. It retrieved the animal skin and returned to work on the completion of the catacomb, and its own sacred chamber. Now within the catacomb, the creature used the talons of its upper appendages to further the depth, and after digging for a while would then load the skin. Once loaded, the creature jabbed its talons through the overlapping areas of the animal skin, and then dragged the loaded sack out of the catacomb and to the surface beyond. Once outside, the creature would then heft the sack onto its powerful, upper back, and trek a distance, before unloading. After digging and carrying, for an additional depth of ten more feet, the creature rested, lying upon its side, in a fetal position. After resting for a little while, the creature rolled onto its back, placed the talons of its four appendages against the catacomb's low ceiling, and began to slice away, causing the ceiling to heighten. It was in this manner that the creature was able to use its talons to add height to the catacomb. This process continued until the catacomb's heightened ceiling extended for thirty-five feet. Now, the creature felt overly fatigued and slept once again. Upon awakening, warmth was still prevalent. The creature again ventured out of the catacomb and consumed much of what remained of the kill; the sun baked meat, and the blood that still saturated the flesh. Returning to the catacomb, the creature traversed the area and, not paying close enough attention, collided, head first, with the section that was to begin its own chamber. Being stunned, but not severely injured, the creature began its torturous work of digging and carrying. As the chamber began to take form, the creature was now dragging, and at times, carrying these heavy loads further and further, exhausting its every fiber. As the chamber got larger, the creature found itself longing for one of the others to help, but unfortunately there were none. The chamber took on its spacious, yet crude form, but the creature found itself aching more often, due to the enormity of the strain put upon its shoulders, neck, lower back, and thighs and arms. It could no longer be upon its back and work the ceiling because now it was too far above, that is, beyond the creature's reach.

To add height, so as to eventually stand fully upright, the creature was now upon its lower appendages, balancing the best that it could, and subsequently reaching slightly above its head, clearing dirt from the ceiling. In time, this angle of work seriously taxed its shoulders, and carrying the sacks a good distance from the habitat fatigued mostly every joint.

The creature was hungry and thirsty, but much too tired to hunt. It returned to the area where the scraps of the kill lay, consumed this meaningless amount, and even suckled the blood that was found puddled on and within the surrounding grass. The Lone Creature found that these scraps weren't enough to relieve the slightest of its hunger pangs, let alone enough to satiate its ravenous appetite. It returned to the entrance way and maneuvered along the catacomb's length, and now felt achievement and contentment, being within the safety of its cooled chamber; cool compared to the warmth directly outside its habitat. Fatigue turned into sleep, and insignificant dreaming, and eventually the creature awakened, feeling stiffness and pain. It felt fortunate that it had spent the time, and energy, constructing the height of the chamber so that it could stand upright, and then some. Slowly, and instinctively stretching, the creature's body gradually felt a lessened amount of pain.

The creature knew that it had to hunt soon, so as to store food and blood for its sustenance and nutrition. It continually stretched its body parts until it felt somewhat limber, rocked its head from left to right, backward and forward. The chamber had gotten noticeably colder than when the sleep was initiated, so the Lone Creature departed the chamber and walked along the catacomb until it was at the exit. Once at the exit, it was understood that darkness had set in, and that this was its time to hunt. The Lone Creature checked, sensing that there wasn't any threat to its safety, and so it moved out and away from the habitat. Once out of its home area and upon the surface, it stood upright and fully stretched, this time feeling tremendous exhilaration. It fully straightened its upper appendages and extended its talons skyward, as far as possible. With its head tilted backwards, it directed its limited eyesight to the moonlit heavens above. The Lone Creature gave thought to this hunt, and then walked onward. As it sauntered through the area, it finally came upon various standards, and their subsequent enclosure that housed the nonthreatening animals. .

The creature, now falsely believing that it had gained the status of a food gatherer, began to stalk one animal that was perceived to be part of a rather large herd of cattle. Stealthily moving in the direction of the unsuspecting animal, the creature continually prepared for its attack. It stretched its upper appendages and their curved, connecting talons, as far forward of its body as possible, and then dug them deeply into the pasture's soil and grass roots. Doing this caused the rear set of talons to also move forward and take a strong foothold, preparing for a dynamic, quick burst.

The creature set itself in this position for a short time, while giving thought to its plan. Naturally, the cattle were somewhat unnerved by their recognition of the creature's presence, but not yet to the point of scattering. They just may have scattered if the creature did not, instinctively, stop all of its motion. Due to the denseness of the trees and shrubbery, the cattle did not see the creature, but could sense the presence of a completely foreign scent. This was a putrid, disturbing, fecal smell; apparently, the cattle sensed that this disgusting smell was emanating from the matter recently dropped from several of the herd, in the direct vicinity.

Several seconds had transpired, and at this time, the creature felt euphoric, believing that the cattle were at ease. Without the slightest bit of warning, the creature burst, more likely exploded forward in the direction of one of the largest in the herd. The steer sensed the creature's swift approach and attempted to flee; feeling its pursuer close at its hooves, it instinctively kicked to the rear, with great force, attempting to mortally wound its perceived attacker. The steer ran, and intermittently kicked, ran and kicked some more, and then changed direction. This form of escape caught the creature unaware, especially due to its limited eyesight, but the creature had the innate ability to stop, as if on a dime, also changing its direction. The Lone Creature then put its ultimate amount of energy into the chase; the steer seemed to sense that it was not a match for its pursuer, so it slowed, calculated, and put a lot of its weight onto both front legs, simultaneously lifting its hind quarters high into the air. It was at this time that the steer, using all of its pent-up force, shot its hooves backwards at whatever it felt was close behind. Unfortunately, for the frenzied steer, the only thing that the hooves cut into was the trailing wind. The creature was not pursuing the steer from the direct rear, but from an angle. Using this means of attack, the creature found it easy to intercept the animal, swiftly killing it.

Following a short rest, the Lone Creature loaded the large steer upon its shoulders, allowing the main part of the weight to rest upon its massive upper back, while the remainder hung close toward the ground. It was in this fashion that the Lone Creature transported the steer to its habitat, and into its chamber. This time, it had a place to store the flesh, and a vat, lined with the drying skin of a previous kill, so as to store the retrieved blood. The chamber somewhat resembled the sacred chamber of its colony, but it wasn't below the surface of the earth. It did, however, have adequate space to store the flesh and blood of one, or more kills.

The Lone Creature did not consider it sacred because this chamber did not smell of newly created fetus membranes, the stench of rotting animal and creature flesh, the decomposition of membranes after the fetuses perished within, or the blood that had coagulated during its lengthy storage time.

The Lone Creature maneuvered the kill's heavy weight the entire length of the catacomb, and then into its chamber. Feeling a great sense of achievement, and a self-fulfilling air of confidence, the creature hefted the animal's head above its body cavity and sliced into the base of its neck, just above its shoulders. In doing so, the creature purposefully positioned the animal's head close to, though slightly above, the blood vat.

Blood began to come from the sliced arteries, but since the shoulders were elevated above the main portion of the animal's body, the blood flow was minimal. It was at this point that the creature used its ultra-sharpened talons to swiftly sever the animal's head from its neck, at its shoulder level, and then, as if all in one motion, lowered the exposed arteries into the depth of the vat. The blood bubbled as it freely flowed from the steer, and continually overwhelmed the pre-existing levels. Initially, the vat filled swiftly, but as the level neared the top, the blood flow slowed down dramatically and the steer's weight was noticeably lessened. At this point, the creature realized that there was an overflow of blood, but that this wasn't an issue. What was important was that the vat appeared to be leak proof, guaranteeing the supply would last for quite a while.

The creature spent a considerable amount of time dragging the steer's carcass several feet away from the vat, and off to one side of the makeshift chamber. Once relocated, the creature, utilizing its talons, deeply sliced the animal's underbelly, from between its hind legs and then forward, until the slice went between and in front of the anterior legs. The slice continued until the cut separated the two shoulders. The steer's body remained intact, but after a few more slices in the same vicinity, the undercarriage separated, and flopped into two parts. The creature, being in its darkened environment, proficiently used its talons, cutting away the majority of the bloodied flesh, and then piling it into an ever-growing mound.

It was at this point that the Lone Creature removed the wet skin, along with what remained of the intestines and organs, and took these to an area where the skin could dry out in the sun. The creature then returned its weary body to the chamber, feasted upon the mound of the bloodied flesh, and intermittently drank of the nutritious blood. Now completely satiated, and its ego bursting, it felt a heightened sense of pride, it slumped to the chamber's surface and once comfortable, moved its body into a fetal position. It slept more soundly than it had since finding itself lost upon the earth's surface, or possibly more soundly than ever before.

Chapter 23

AS GRACE AND RYAN boarded the school bus, Ryan couldn't help but notice Grace's agitation. He had to use an excessive amount of force to release her grip, and subsequently felt some pain. Ryan reached back as he struggled to release her grip, and simultaneously grabbed her from behind to help her up the steps. As they walked toward a seat, Ryan could hear Grace occasionally mumble the word Bigfoot, softly, but somewhat clearly. The imprint of her hand was felt on his forearm as he took his seat on the bus.

This morning was different; she was sullen and had distanced herself from the immediate environment. She sat, looking straight ahead, and didn't speak. Ryan wondered why Grace was not being her usual, joyful self. He raised his eyes from the comic book and was upset, somewhat cautious, seeing Grace's blank, numbed appearance. Needless to say, he was concerned. He said, "Grace" more than once, and finally his attention was solely upon her. "What's wrong...Grace?"

Grace told Ryan that she had seen Bigfoot when they were at the bus stop and that it frightened her. Ryan knew that his sister was always a down to earth, honest person, and he never felt the need to doubt her word. Whenever Grace had ever talked to him, he always felt that what she was saying was sincere. If anyone else would have told him this thing about seeing Bigfoot, he would have probably been skeptical, but since this was Grace, he looked at her and said, "What did it look like?" Grace said that Bigfoot was Ugly and smelled stinky, like a hog, and she wanted to know if Ryan hadn't smelled it when they were at the bus stop.

Ryan recollected being at the stop, but nothing came to his mind that was different or noticeable. Grace then said that Bigfoot did not look anything like the pictures in newspaper articles depicted him as. She also said that this Bigfoot was so ugly. Grace went on to say that it reminded her of Freddie Kruger. Ryan, not knowing what to make of this description, reassured her that everything would be okay.

Upon their arrival at school, Ryan, not realizing the extent of Grace's disturbance, walked toward the front of the bus. Ryan began a conversation, saying "Grace," but soon recognized that she was not directly behind him. He turned, and realized that she was nowhere to be seen. Ryan quickly returned to their seat and found Grace lying on it, locked in a fetal position, and shivering violently. The bus driver had previously gotten off and had entered the school. Ryan reached down to Grace, coaxed her to a seated position, took off his coat and wrapped it around her. He held her close and soothingly rubbed her back. After a short time, Grace appeared to snap out of her lethargy, and visibly improved. Hearing the school bell signaling the beginning of classes, Ryan asked Grace if she did, indeed, feel okay. Grace said that she was feeling better, and so Ryan encouraged her to get off the bus and go to her class. Once Grace and Ryan were off the bus, they then hugged and said their farewells, reassuring one another that they would see each other later, maybe during lunch. Grace returned Ryan's coat and they both headed into school.

Grace went to her classroom, but found herself, again, withdrawing deeply, riddled with fear and anxiety. Not knowing what to make of Grace's symptoms, her teacher sent Grace, accompanied by one of the other students, to the nurse's office. The student did as was asked, and then left her there with the nurse. Grace was examined and found to be in excellent health, but there was something that was noticeably unnerving her.

The nurse then accompanied Grace to her guidance counselor's office, and once there, fully explained what had happened. Grace was noticeably lethargic while sitting next to the counselor's desk, but attempted to recount her sighting of Bigfoot. She fully described what the counselor understood to be a very large creature, possessing claws coming from its head, and something that had talons for fingers and toes. Understanding that Grace was being totally sincere, but nonetheless traumatized by her experience, the counselor's thoughts centered on Grace's imagination. Feeling somewhat distanced by what was believed to be a very vivid imagination, the counselor attempted to focus upon Grace's story.

The guidance counselor asked Grace if she had recently watched a video or television show that might have frightened her, thinking that she was going to find the source of the little girl's fear. In fact, Grace wasn't allowed to view such things. The conversation switched to a more pleasant topic, and once Grace's attention was on the new topic, she gradually calmed, and in time returned to her classroom. Grace remained somewhat subdued throughout the remainder of that school day, and then rode the bus back to her home area.

Instead of getting off the bus and going directly into the house, as she had always done in the past, Grace found herself exiting the bus and then robotically walking across the landscape, away from her home. She was not headed in the direction of the area where she had noticed Bigfoot, but in a completely different direction. Grace found herself purposely walking towards an area that was dense with high grass, trees, and plenty of shrubbery. Now, a hundred yards or so from the bus stop, she was within the perimeter of a dense, forested area, and sensed a similar, nauseating stench similar to that of her Bigfoot experience. As she further penetrated the forest, the stench got stronger. Before she knew it, she found herself bewildered, noticeably trembling and completely out of control.

Grace could not believe what her eyes were witnessing. Immediately to her forefront on the ground, was the fly infested, bloody remains of what seemed to be a mutilated animal. Grace found herself staring at these remains and began to slowly, but steadily, back away. She wanted to turn and run, but couldn't respond appropriately. She was stunned by what she had seen. Grace backed off a few more steps and then found herself bent over, violently vomiting, shaking, and involuntarily crying. She paused, feeling spasmodic, and then began to clumsily walk in the direction of her home. Grace, while struggling to walk, eventually entered her home and sat heavily onto the nearest chair.

Kathleen, Grace's mother, was already home from her teaching job and was in the kitchen preparing a snack for the children's return from school. Kathleen had heard Grace come in and almost immediately sensed an unsettling smell. Kathleen found Grace in the living room and while observing her, noticed that Grace's coat was speckled with vomit, and her daughter was severely disturbed and twitching. Moving toward Grace, she asked why she was late coming home. Kathleen received no response and said "Grace!" What was usually a bundle of energy and brilliant smiles, was now distant and withdrawn, depressed. Kathleen went directly to Grace, comforted her, removed her coat, and led Grace to her and husband John's bedroom. Once there, Kathleen, without questioning Grace any further, had her remove her shoes and lay on the bed, and once confident that Grace was somewhat calm, she then went to the bathroom and rinsed out a washcloth with cold water. Kathleen rung out the majority of the water and then returned to the bedroom, There, she applied the cold compress to Grace's forehead. The impact of the compress immediately soothed her, and the somewhat intermittent breathing gradually became less labored.

"Oh Grace," her mother said. "You lie here, relax, and I'll be back in a minute." Kathleen then left the room and went to a phone that was in another room. She called the school and asked to be transferred to the guidance counselor's office. Now connected to this office, she spoke directly to Mrs. Lindgren, Grace's assigned counselor. Kathleen had met with Mrs. Lindgren during parent-teacher meetings and had always been impressed with the way this younger woman had presented herself, and by the bond that she and Grace had since Grace entered this elementary school. Mrs. Lindgren, to the majority of the parents, but Nancy to Kathleen; Nancy appeared to be kind, affectionate, and considerate regarding Grace. There were occasions when Kathleen was food shopping and inadvertently would bump into Nancy. When this first happened, it was discovered that they were neighbors. Every now and then, they met outside of the school and occasionally Kathleen had Grace and Ryan with her, while Nancy had her girls, Allison and Rebecca.

Kathleen got right to the point, detailing Grace's symptoms, and after sharing her own anxiety with Nancy, Kathleen received the details of Bigfoot, with the claws coming from its head, and talons instead of fingers and toes. She also was made aware that the school nurse had examined Grace and that there were no signs of fever or any other kind of illness. Kathleen, not knowing what to make of this, thanked Nancy for the information, hung up the phone, and immediately returned to Grace.

Upon entering the bedroom, Kathleen instantly took notice that Grace was twitching intermittently, that her eyes were closed, and she seemed to be sleeping. Kathleen removed the compress, wet it again with cold water, rung it out, and reapplied it to Grace's forehead. Grace moved slightly, but did not open her eyes.

Convinced that Grace was indeed asleep, Kathleen went to the phone and notified John, Grace's father, of the circumstances. She then telephoned the pediatrician, whose advice was to let Grace rest and to bring her in whenever she awakened. Upon hanging up the phone, Kathleen noticed that Ryan had come into the house with his normal greetings. Kathleen had him sit down and as he did, he wondered if, in fact, he had done something wrong. Ryan asked his mother if he had, indeed, done something wrong, and she assured him that he was not in any trouble, and then told him about Grace's situation. At this time, Ryan told his mother about Grace's school day and about her sighting of Bigfoot. Kathleen seemed to be dumbfounded.

John got off work early and drove directly home, not knowing what to expect, but fearing the unknown. He arrived, entered the house, and spoke with both Kathleen and Ryan. John then went into his and Kathleen's bedroom and found that Grace was still sleeping fitfully. John sat lightly onto the bed and laid his hand upon Grace's arm; he then bent over, kissed her cheek, and whispered that everything was going to be okay. Grace stirred, but remained asleep.

John returned to the living room and sat amongst Kathleen and Ryan. For a while there was nothing but quiet, and then Kathleen said that she was going to call the doctor to reschedule the appointment for early the next morning. This was met with some skepticism by John, but Kathleen reassured him, saying that she felt that Grace had gotten somewhat better with the compresses, the rest, and the fact that she was in the immediate company of her family's love. That night, and into the next morning, the mood of the family was that of concern and tender loving care.

Kathleen and John notified their respective employers of their situation and said that they would not be into work that day, then called the appropriate school personnel to let them know that both of their children would be missing school today, but hopefully would attend the following day. The Lightcaps had a light breakfast and then were on their way to the doctor's office, hopefully to receive answers that were not damaging to Grace's psyche. They all went into the waiting room, but after being there for twenty minutes, Grace and her mother were led into the doctor's examination room while John waited with Ryan. A thorough physical exam showed that Grace was, indeed, in very good health, and so she was scheduled for an MRI and a battery of tests as soon as they could get to the hospital. A follow up appointment was scheduled to get a clear understanding of the results. After being seen by several specialists, and experiencing a complete and exhausting battery of tests, Grace was finally through with all the relevant testing and a barrage of medical questions. Not a single doctor found a symptom to cause her to behave the way that she had yesterday.

After a restful weekend, Grace and Ryan returned to their elementary school. The family had stayed close to Grace at all times, and Kathleen checked her several times, during each night, to be self-assured that Grace was indeed sleeping peacefully. On Sunday, they all attended church and then went home rather than to the restaurant where they usually ate following mass. Monday finally came and everyone attempted to return to their normal routine; John and Kathleen were out early while Grace and Ryan walked to their bus stop. Once they were at the bus stop, and had been there for about ten minutes, Grace finally said, "Ryan, there is something out there." Ryan responded with, "You mean out there in that field?" Grace deliberately said "No" as she was slowly shaking her head. "Where then?" Grace then pointed toward the heavily wooded area and said, "There...there!" Grace pointed in the same direction of the wooded area.

It was at that time that the school bus rumbled toward Grace and Ryan, and in doing so, changed the importance of the conversation. They got onto the bus and sat together, with Ryan having his arm across Grace's shoulders and holding her reassuringly. Grace responded by saying, "Thanks Ryan." They got off of the bus and Ryan walked Grace to her classroom. Once there, Ryan lightly kissed her cheek and said that he'd hopefully see her during lunchtime. Grace faintly smiled and said, "See ya."

Monday was an eventful day for all the children that knew Grace, or wanted to. She had seen Bigfoot and none of the children questioned the authenticity of the sighting. Grace now had a celebrity status, and though she was shy, by nature, this recognition seemed to bring her somewhat out of her doldrums. She found herself temporarily forgetting her reality of this creature and gave a variety of kid's images of the Bigfoot that she saw, not very far away from her home. That was okay, and took a lot of pressure off of her throughout the school day. Though once she was home, Grace was turned inside out with fear.

Occasionally, Ryan rode a different bus home than Grace, but today, coincidentally, they were on the same bus. It unnerved Ryan to see the changes that Grace was mentally and physically experiencing, as their bus got closer and closer to their drop off point. When finally at their drop off point, Grace was extremely stressed, but was able to walk and talk. Ryan, feeling protective, got off the bus just prior to Grace, and very slowly began to walk to the right, in the direction of their home.

Grace got off and stood motionless for a few seconds, looking shyly in the direction of the heavily wooded area. Ryan turned and saw that Grace wasn't following so he said, "Grace, come on."

Grace turned her head toward Ryan, but did not walk to him. She said, "Will you come with me? I want to show you something." Again, her voice was barely audible. Ryan then said, "Where?" Grace emphatically pointed to the same wooded area as before. Ryan told Grace to wait one minute, and after saying this, he ran into the house and left a note, "Grace and I are going for a walk, be back soon." To the note he added the time, 3:30 p.m. This little addition was something they had learned from their parent's guidance. Ryan then ran back out of the front door and caught up with Grace, who was already walking towards the designated wooded area. They had played in this area several times and knew it as a fun place. However, on this day, Ryan felt somewhat apprehensive.

As Grace and Ryan approached the outskirts of the woods, Ryan began to feel more at ease and attempted to initiate a conversation. Grace led the way without responding, and now they were within the woods, walking among the trees, shrubs, rocks and grass. Finally, Ryan's sense of smell felt abused, but he noticed that Grace seemed undaunted. Twenty more feet and Ryan walked up on Grace's heels as he wasn't watching where he was going; Grace had previously stopped. Immediately, Ryan bent over and began to vomit, with tremendous force because his sense of smell had been totally victimized. Never had he experienced such a disgusting and putrid stench. The smell caused Ryan to vomit again and while still bent over, his gaze focused in the direction that Grace's eyes were staring. There, not more than five feet in front of Grace, were the remains of some dead and decomposing animal, an animal skin that slightly resembled that of a bull. It had been so savagely ripped apart and almost all of its flesh was missing. Fear completely dominated Grace, and then Ryan, but before either could move, they heard sounds like nothing they had ever heard.

They heard terrifying, chilling sounds, but could not see anything. They were prepared to run, and then Grace put two and two together, and realized that Bigfoot could actually be somewhere in this immediate area. She didn't have to tell Ryan twice that it was now time to go. They retreated slowly, but ever so surely, as not to fall over something in their path. They kept their eyes glued in the specific direction of the decaying flesh, and to the general area where the sound had emanated. When they reached the borderline of the wooded area, they checked one last time for something abnormal, and then, feeling secure, turned and ran about fifty yards, until they were home.

Once inside, they found their mother and were told that she was headed out to do some grocery shopping. Though before departing, their mother inquired as to where they had ventured on their walk, and if they had enjoyed it. Both were quite anxious as they told her that they had been in the wooded area, and were quite descriptive regarding what they had seen and subsequently heard.

After hearing their story, Kathleen, like any other caring mother, found that she was anxious, and couldn't have been more concerned. She made a telephone call to the Doylestown police department, and before the police came up with some sort of plan, the town's newspaper got a hold of the story. Soon after, a policeman was sent to the Lightcap's residence in order to find out if the story was indeed valid. Writers from the Inteligencer, and more than one television reporter, along with his cameraman, parked vehicles and went to Lightcap's front door. Understandably, there was some confusion, but Kathleen invited them. Starting from the beginning, Kathleen told all in the room of Grace's first encounter with this thing; and how that possible encounter led to counseling and a complete battery of tests, including an MRI. Kathleen went on to say that the test results had been evaluated and that Grace had been given a clean bill of health, both physically and mentally. She explained that until today, only Grace had seen or heard this thing. However, during their walk, both children had witnessed the badly mutilated remains of what appeared to be a large animal; probably a bull, of which its skin, its head, legs, and much of its body parts were missing.

It was at this point that the Doylestown police officer gave some serious thought that this could be the site for animal sacrificing, and devil worship. He verbalized this to all that were present, and the consensus of opinion, among the writer and the television reporter, was that devil worship was a definite possibility. All of the people present wanted an interview with Grace and Ryan, and thus Kathleen called both to the area, where these reporters were patiently waiting; pens and notepads at the ready. Grace walked into the living room with Ryan, and it was easy to recognize that she was somewhat dependent upon her older brother. As she entered, Grace looked for a place to sit where there was enough room for Ryan. As she recounted her story, it was evident that she was not lying, but was this her vivid imagination or reality? One of the newspaper journalists excused themselves and went, seemingly, toward the kitchen. Clearly out of sight, the journalist took out his cell phone and punched the speed dial number that connected him to the news desk. That evening, the headlines of the evening edition read: **'ALIEN CREATURE LIVING WITHIN BUCKS COUNTY?'** and Grace's recollection followed, in detail.

The story stunned the newspaper's readership for they recognized that this wasn't a newspaper that sensationalized articles; it was factual reporting, and the expectation of the journalist was that the material, in fact, was truthful. As soon as the paper hit the streets, calls were tying up the newspaper's customer service phone lines. Needless to say, all were concerned with the creature from outer space.

A telephone call came into the Doylestown police department, and the officer answering the phone was told that the creature had gotten the attention of the President's cabinet. The officer was informed that a fax would be following their conversation, but it was of the utmost importance that no one, without written permission from the Pentagon, be within a half-mile radius of the creature site until representatives of the government arrived.

The residents that lived inside of the half-mile radius were notified of this restriction, and each signed papers verifying that they would not interfere, in any way, shape, or form, with an ongoing investigation. Furthermore, these families were "prioritized," and all were on a strict "need to know" basis. Government representatives went to all of these residents, within the specified area, and made these civilians aware of the government action. Each family was given the opportunity to choose; either remain at their home address, or be temporarily relocated to the campus housing of

The Buck County Community College. If the college was their choice, then, at no time, were the families to return to their homes, until they were officially permitted to do so. Furthermore, while at the college housing, each family would be informed that their needs, such as bedrooms, food items and beverages, and use of all campus facilities, would be afforded to them at no charge. The campus was to be their temporary home away from home. This option was tempting, but each family signed the necessary paperwork, choosing, without exception, to remain at their private residence.

Chapter 24

THE UNITED STATES GOVERNMENT stepped up its involvement by contacting NASA, questioning if there had been any possible U.F.O. activity within the last month. The official response was that there had been several reports of possible activity, but that none had been confirmed. A team from NASA's headquarters, along with personnel from other government agencies, was immediately flown to the site.

The Willow Grove Naval Station was put on its highest alert and all civilians were placed on leave with pay until further notice. These civilians worked at a variety of jobs and always exited the base at the end of their stated shift. They were notified that they had one hour to collect all of their personal belongings and to vacate the premises. This was done in an orderly fashion and no answers were given to any of the personnel's questions, whether the questions came from one of the civilians working on the base, or from one of the regular soldiers. When it is said that there were no answers given, this wasn't totally correct because there was one standard answer to every question, that is, *it*'s classified.

The Willow Grove Naval Station became the headquarters for this operation. If there was indeed an alien, then it was the government's intention to sedate it, capture it alive, and then transport it to the federal installation that was located approximately eight miles east of the naval station.

This federal site had been abandoned for more than fifteen years and had been maintained and kept secure by signs that stated: **"This is a Federal Site. Trespassers will be prosecuted to the fullest extent of the law!"** The site is approximately 48,000 square feet and is also enclosed by a tall chain-linked fence with rusted barbed wire, running atop the entire compound.

This situation, as far as the government was concerned, was not going to resemble, in any way, the confusion and cover-up of Roswell, New Mexico, during the year of 1947. This site, within The County of Bucks, is bordered by Bristol Road, and intersects Newtown Road and Orion Road at two of the site's corners. This was a perfect location because the site was vast, totally enclosed, and all of the buildings, including its airplane hangar, were now vacant.

The federal government got right to it, and hurriedly installed state of the art technological equipment within the hangar, in preparation for specialists within their medical field that would soon be arriving. In addition to the technological equipment, there appeared to be other equipment that was the very best; in fact, there was equipment that was so advanced, that no one present could identify it.

The barracks were swiftly brought up to code and another internal fence, this time charged with electrical current and topped off with a heavier, and more menacing razor wire, was erected. This new fence was constructed twenty feet within the length of the original perimeter fence and was noticeably taller than the one that was now rusted and discolored with age. The residents living within this area were getting an official taste of what the "Highest Form of Security" was all about.

Now that the federal site was in complete readiness, the Lightcaps were invited to the compound, to witness first hand where this creature would be kept, if captured alive; it was also the intention of government personnel to have Grace describe the creature in as much detail as possible. In this way, they would clearly know what they were up against, and also more appropriately construct the creature's living space within the hangar.

Eventually, a guarded entourage entered the compound and

for the first time, John, Grace's father, truly realized the intensity that surrounded the security relating to the creature. Every military person had a sidearm, or was carrying a rifle, though there were a few that had both. These soldiers were impressive; they were physically fit, stood upright, and their uniforms were perfectly pressed.

Once the entire entourage was within the compound, all of the vehicles came to a complete stop. Doors were opened and held while the family exited. The first recognizable building was that of the hangar, and everyone was escorted into this building. When looking at the haggard building from the outside, it became mind boggling once a person was inside; it was a true case of night versus day, everything appeared to be brand spanking new, and state of the art.

The family was given a thorough tour, and then was led into one of the hangar's connecting rooms. When questioned, Grace said that she had only seen Bigfoot one time, and that was when she was waiting for the school bus, several days before. She also said that Bigfoot was in a field, initially, and then it began to move slowly in her direction. Now, as she talked, there was a sense of fear in her voice and body language. Tears welled up in her eyes, and her breathing became noticeably labored. All of the sudden, Grace hesitated, acting as if she was actually seeing the creature on that terrifying day. It was as if she was actually seeing the creature moving in her direction, for she became noticeably uncomfortable. She cringed, shook, and as she did, there wasn't a person in the room that doubted the authenticity of her fear. It was then that her mother moved to Grace's side and hugged her tightly, for what seemed to be an eternity.

Kathleen sensed that Grace's anxiety had lessened, so she took her arm away and lightly stroked Grace's hands. Grace, somewhat calmer, began her story once again. She said that the creature continued to walk in her direction. When it was fifty to seventy-five yards away, Bigfoot had stopped. She said that she looked away, in the direction of the oncoming school bus, but when she looked back, Bigfoot was gone. Grace was then told by her mother that what she saw as Bigfoot could actually be an **alien** from another planet, or galaxy. Grace seemed confused because she only knew of one explanation for an unknown creature that was occasionally seen walking upright within the forested lands.

Grace sat quietly for a short while, and then agreed that the creature she saw was most likely not Bigfoot. She then asked her mother if all aliens were as ugly, and stunk as bad as this creature. The artist listened intently to Grace, and doodled, while waiting for the creature's specific characteristics. She said that this creature was Big Shows size, a giant; that it was so ugly, and that it really, really stunk! It was then that the artist hesitated, and eventually asked Grace what she meant when mentioning the Big Show, and her father, John, then commented that Big Show is a wrestler on the professional wrestling circuit; that he is over seven feet in height and weighs in at more than five-hundred pounds. Grace said "yes, Big Show, The Rock and The Hulk, Hulk-a-mania!" Everyone smiled and then the artist, feeling that he was the only one in the room that hadn't recognized these celebrities, asked Grace to continue with her description.

Grace then said that the creature was as big, if not bigger, than a fully grown grizzly, and that some of its body parts were actually similar. She said that it had huge arms and legs, and its fingers and toes appeared to be clawed; they were long, curved, and appeared to be pointed. It also had an enormous head and on each side, there was a very large, thick claw that protruded from its head, circling inward. Grace went on to say that when she first noticed this creature, it was rolling around in a field, like animals do at the zoo, stirring up large clouds of dust. She said that the creature stood on its hind legs, but when it moved from the standing position, it was then on all four, having the likes of a silverback gorilla. Grace went on, saying that when this creature got close, and had come to a full stop, that she could more clearly see the same pointed claws that were where fingers could have been, and that these same claws replaced its toes. She said that it was full of large scales, from the top of its head to the bottom claws, somewhat like an armadillo. Grace hesitated, and then said that the creature had many of what appeared to be holes covering its body. Grace was then asked if she could remember anything further that might help. Grace sat pensively, and then added that it was unmistakable that this creature had a very large mouth and an evident nose, but that she does not remember noticing its eyes. "If the creature had eyes, then they probably weren't open when I saw it."

Grace was fast becoming a celebrity, not just in Bucks County, but throughout the United States, newspaper headlines read **'ALIEN?... CREATURE? FOUND IN BUCKS COUNTY, PENNSYLVANIA?... ALIVE!'**

Local news teams were driving into the Doylestown area; or, if out of the Philadelphia area, were flying in from all over the United States. The Philadelphia International Airport was being over-run by a noticeable increase of commercial flights and private jets. Traffic at the baggage claim area was never seen to be like this in the recent past; in fact, nothing like this **was ever witnessed** by airport employees.

This scene continued throughout the entire day and into the night; flights arriving at an unexpected rate, and reporters from newspapers, television news, and writer's for a variety of national magazines were now paying cab and limousine driver's higher fees to get out of the airport to various hotels and motels in Bucks County. There was chaos at the airport, on Route 95 N, the Schuylkill Expressway, the PA Turnpike, and Route 611, all heading in the direction of Doylestown, some forty miles from Philadelphia's International Airport, and twenty miles from downtown Philadelphia.

The Willow Grove Naval Station was a fortunate destination for those that had the proper clearance and unfortunate for those that didn't. The naval station was approximately four miles from the location of the creature sighting, and eight miles from the federal installation, bordered by Bristol Road. Hotels, motels, and bed and breakfast sites; anyplace that had an empty bed was for rent and was now being allocated and advertised, specifically for those people that were covering this event.

Additional help was temporarily hired, and an enormous surplus of food and drink was being stored in the area's distribution centers, and subsequently, at local eateries. This was fast becoming more than an event; in fact, it had the potential to be historical! This was the first time that a massive amount of people, from all areas of the United States, and many reporters from locales outside of the U.S. may get the opportunity to personally witness a real, live alien.

Chapter 25

GRACE HAD FINISHED HER description and simultaneously the artist was finishing up the likeness of what Grace described. The artist showed Grace the creature and she said that the drawing was similar, but that the creature was, in fact, much larger and that its legs, arms, and neck were much thicker. Changes were gradually made, and then Grace said that the latest drawing was a likeness of the creature that she had seen while she waited, with Ryan, for the school bus.

For security reasons, copies weren't made, but the drawing was shown to all military personnel involved. As a precaution against interference by the media, and as a precaution to keep the creature within its specified limits, the government personnel built an electrically charged perimeter fence that directly encircled the entire wooded area, and placed it approximately fifty feet beyond where the creature was said to be. Guards were given powerful stun guns and were sternly warned not to use these weapons unless the creature had somehow gotten over the enclosure, was escaping, or was a direct threat to their life. These guards were placed at fifteen foot intervals and were each given a pager that was activated by depressing a handheld lever. Whenever the small, red lever would be pressed and subsequently activated, a signal would go directly to a temporary control center, and assistance would arrive within seconds. The lever would remain in this activated position until slightly depressed further; this further depression would automatically release the signal and the alarm would automatically shut off.

The control center was manned and ready twenty-four hours of each day, and there was a control panel that had specific, miniscule, green bulbs for each of the manned locations along the exterior of the fence's perimeter. Whenever one or more of these pagers were tested, the designated bulb would brilliantly light, and an ear piercing, unmistakable sound would emanate from the control panel. This piercing, steady sound would not stop until the soldier that had activated the pager, pressed the button deeper and, in turn, automatically released the button to its original position.

Each guard had a walkie-talkie, just in case he or she had to get into direct contact with the control center for relief, or to notify one's operator that the pager's button had been mistakenly pressed. A large sign was placed intermittently upon the fence's entrance and perimeter that clearly read, **"No deadly weapons are permitted within this specific location."**

It was generally assumed by all media personnel that when the creature was captured, it was to be transported to the Naval Station, but this was not the government's plan; this was a false assumption! Located just off of Bristol Road, where Newtown Road connected with it, was an abandoned federal government site. During the last fifteen years, this site had only limited activity, such as the mowing of the grass. The site had large, distinct areas, full of dense foliage and tall, fully grown trees, surrounded by a massive, grassy, landscape. The civilian neighbors, of which there was only a handful, and the work force of a nearby business, were found to be discussing why there was so much busy work being done, especially to the airplane hangar.

It seemed, as if overnight, another chain linked fence was erected twenty feet within the original one. Two individual sets of gates were plain to see and also something that had never been witnessed at this specific site; spools of razor wire were placed between both lengthy, chain linked fences. Had this site suddenly become what was previously evidenced in 1947, at Roswell, New

Mexico? Within forty-eight hours, this federal installation had been hastily renovated, and now that the work seemed to be complete, it made sense that military personnel became a constant presence

Meanwhile, at the Willow Grove Naval Station, a high priority meeting was scheduled for 0800 hours, and no media types were permitted. The topic of the discussion centered upon the alien being; its living space, if it had one, and how to capture it alive. An investigator, escorted by military personnel, met with Grace at her home, and she then took these people to the location of the mutilated carcass. Once they were approximately twenty-feet from the carnage, Grace stopped and would not go any further.

Recognizing that this was the general location where she and Ryan said that they has seen the mutilated animal, and had heard very strange sounds, the investigator decided to leave one of the personnel with Grace. He then had the remaining person go with him in the direction that Grace pointed; in the direction of what he suspected to be the mutilated carcass. The investigator walked cautiously for another twenty yards beyond Grace's immediate location and then they had a reason to pause. Whew! An unimaginable, lingering stench overwhelmed their senses. Believing that they were close to the mutilated animal, the investigator, and his escort, placed a kind of salve just below their nostrils, seemingly to mask the putrid smell and to make it, at least, tolerable.

It was now that the investigator's movement became noticeably calculated, and both had their formidable stun guns at the ready position as they were certain that they were close to the mutilated carcass, and that they just may encounter the creature. Even with the protective salve applied, the stench gradually worsened, and before they were prepared, they were dominated by swarms of flies.

When looking directly at the ground, it became crystal clear that they had happened upon the remains of stagnating, discolored organs, and a carcass that had become fly-infested. The investigator and his military escort paused and quieted as they surveyed their immediate area, looking and listening for anything additional that could be considered strange. The men eventually appeared to be as calm and stress free as the situation would allow. This was quite difficult to accomplish, but once they had moved away from the infestation, they found that a segment of their previous training was now coming into play; it was now that they listened and looked with extreme purpose.

Initially, the men could only recognize the sound of their own breathing, but in time, they found themselves zeroing in on an area where they could actually hear the distinct sound of breathing that was not their own; breathing coming from somewhere close by. This, undoubtedly, was the heavy nasal breathing of what they assumed to be the alien; the unknown entity that they were seeking, and that they found themselves unnerved by.

While they continued to listen, they realized that they were involuntarily moving in the direction of a guttural sound. Another ten yards and they were within a thicket of bushes, shrubs, and a variety of trees. Just beyond this thicket, it became obvious that a crudely built cave had been recently constructed. The investigator could hear the pronounced, guttural breathing, and so he and the escort backed slowly away, and returned to the area where Grace and her guard had been waiting. All formed one group and then departed the immediate area. Once within her home, Grace was spoken to, at length; the people seemed to be okay with Grace's responses, and then the men returned to the Naval Station.

The military personnel that were in charge of the Alien Entity Operation, or AEO, listened intently to all of the relevant information, and then they put their minds together, coming up with a plan. Highly trained combat soldiers carrying the sophisticated stun guns would enter the compound and would be stationed, periodically, around the entire fenced-in perimeter. Once these combat soldiers were properly situated, it was then that highly sophisticated equipment was to be brought within the enclosed fencing, and subsequently set up where the carcass of the mutilated animal had been discovered. This highly sophisticated equipment would be set up, and then, after being electronically connected, would be used to hone in on the exact location of the creature.

Once located, the creature would have to be physically motivated to leave its habitat or forested area, and move into the open, but at the same time, be encouraged to remain within the electrically charged, perimeter fence. When the creature was manipulated into the open, helicopters would swarm and personnel would expertly drop heavy metal netting upon it, the type of netting used to control the frantic movement of a rogue rhinoceros. Once covered and enclosed with the netting, there would have to be confusion in its mind, and the creature would be targeted and immediately hit with propelled darts, subsequently releasing a potent solution causing a long lasting sedation.

Rather than simply manipulate the creature into the open and shoot it with sedative darts, it was believed that the heavy metal netting was necessary, that is, necessary to prevent the creature from returning to its thicket before collapsing. While attempting to vigorously free itself of the unwanted enclosure, the sedation would activate itself more swiftly within the creature's blood stream, causing it to slumber in the open area. Soon, the sedation would have its full effect and the creature would be fast asleep, not having a care in the world. The personnel would then move into the immediate area of the enclosure, and with the heavy netting still intact, a precaution was to be taken. Around the perimeter of the netting, clawed staples of an enormous length and weight were to be sledge hammered deep into the ground. When the creature was deemed secure, it was then that medical personnel would enter the compound and perform as thorough an evaluation as was possible. This evaluation would be done, considering the circumstances, to assure all present that this creature wasn't damaged or cut, and was, in fact, fit to be transported.

The iron staples that were holding the netting securely in place would then be removed and each would be hefted onto the nearby flatbed. It was at this point that a sizeable crane would be driven through the perimeter's gates and be used to remove the netting. Then, the crane operator would maneuver the creature so that it lay centered, directly above the metal netting; the plan was to then secure the netting, and use it to hoist the enclosed creature off of the surface. When this was done, the creature would be hoisted onto the specially assembled flatbed truck, and the netting would be cautiously removed from beneath it. The creature's body was then to be lowered, centered onto the flatbed, and a titanium steel cage would be assembled, completely enclosing the creature. When the cage was finished and deemed secure, only then would it be completely covered with a breathable, camouflage-type mesh, and the creature world be deemed ready for transport to the renovated airplane hangar.

A back-up plan, which was considered to be less desirable, would be put into order if the creature got out of control within the wooded area, and could not be manipulated into the open space. Then, it would be hit with the propelled sedation. When deemed unconscious, the creature would be first checked for injuries, and once satisfied that it was not in any danger, would remain in place and covered with the weighted netting, and then securely held there with the iron, elongated staples. While sedated and covered with the secured netting, a wide path would be cleared through the trees, boulders, and shrubs, so that the flatbed and crane had enough room to maneuver within the location surrounding the sedated creature. It would then be hoisted, as in the original plan, placed upon the flatbed and the cage enclosure would be immediately assembled. Once the cage was covered with the breathable, camouflaged mesh, then the creature would be transported to the hangar at the federal site. Everyone was anxious to implement the original plan, and so it was scheduled to take place the following day at 0700 hours.

Chapter 26

IT WAS NOW 0700 hours. The plan was initiated; the gates were unlocked and swung open. The ground troops were the first to enter, and they moved into their designated positions throughout the interior, surrounding the site where the creature was believed to be. Each specialized soldier wore camouflaged clothing and had weapons designated to stun and disable the creature rather than mortally wound it.

Next came the surveillance team with their Thermal Imaging Equipment; this specially trained team had been instructed not to activate their equipment until they were told to do so. They moved in the direction of the creature's suspected location, and then remained approximately thirty yards from that designated site. Finally, the coordinating officers entered the enclosed compound; the gates were closed and secured behind all that were within. A designated soldier secured the gates and remained there while the others went about their responsibilities. The officers, moving on foot throughout the compound, checked the positioning of all relevant personnel, and then remained with the team that had the responsibility to pinpoint the exact location of the creature. All military personnel were notified that the operation was now a go and immediately following this clarification, the Thermal Imaging Equipment was activated. Slowly, but with great accuracy, the area was scanned; the handheld equipment depicted trees, large rocks, and eventually came upon a hilly section.

Buzzing was heard when the equipment moved to the center section of one of the hills, and colors appeared to be energized upon the screen. "This can't be..." muttered one of the men that operated the equipment, "...Something must be wrong with this monitor!" The coordinator asked him why he had said that. The operator said that the equipment was picking up two images on the screen, both being at the same location. He then said that only one of the images appeared to have a life force. The location was pinpointed and this location was communicated to the operators of the military helicopters. Also communicated was the location of the gate, and in what specific direction the creature was to be manipulated once it was outside of the location where it presently was in hiding.

Feeling more secure than it had since entering the surface, the youthful underground creature was sleeping fitfully in its crude chamber, but felt safe now that the catacomb and its subsequent chamber had been constructed. It also had a feeling of satisfaction because it had a sufficient supply of food, and part of the animal skin was retaining stored blood. It wondered if this feeling was the way the food gatherers felt on a regular basis. As the creature slept, it experienced a dream of its original habitat; the only real home that it had known prior to finding itself adapting to a life upon the earth's surface. This Lone Creature was lost and it felt great emotional pain, but yet a certain amount of much-needed security.

This youthful creature felt isolated, and without the slightest warning, it felt liquid dropping from its eyes. This feeling continued, and melancholy was starting to dominate. All of a sudden, a loud, earth shaking sound was felt close by. Feeling startled and at the same time threatened, and not knowing what this meant, the Lone Creature found itself physically moving into a protective fetal position. Fear dominated its thought processes; could it be possible that the human had spotted it while hunting, or had it somehow been tracked after coming in contact with one recently. Its nervous system felt shattered, and being totally unnerved, it hadn't the slightest idea of what to do. Again, it felt totally uncomfortable at the prospect of being found by a human; that this discovery could definitely jeopardize the colony that lived within this general area. Anxiety dominated, and this youthful creature began to second guess its need that got it into this precarious situation.

Hoping beyond all hope that the loud sounds were simply a coincidence, the creature huddled in a fetal position upon its chamber's floor. Very slowly, it began to calm. Then, another earth shaking sound was heard, and this one seemed to be much closer to its location. Dirt was now falling in clumps from the ceiling and onto its body. Boom! BOOM! The creature's crudely built dwelling began to cave in. Fretfulness flourished, and now the creature was forced to leave its habitat. Another explosive sound, though coming from a source closer than the others, forced the creature to move away from its dwelling. Boom, then another, and it felt itself moving on all fours, trying desperately to avoid the effects of the volatile pounds and at the same time remain balanced upon the shaking earth. Being consumed by fear, it began to run from the location of one explosion after the other, and as it did, this youthful underground creature collided with saplings. Seemingly bounced from one tree to another, the lower portion of all four appendages collided with large rocks, stumps, and downed trees; using whatever sight that was available the Lone Creature urgently tried to keep its head from colliding with the unforeseen.

At this point, the creature had what it imagined as a vision, it was in a similar predicament, and the vision caused it to slow down. Before its thought processes had finished with the vision, the creature found that its momentum carried its body into a clearing, completely from the forested area, and even further away from its perceived colony

To the amazement of all military personnel periodically stationed around the perimeter's fence, the creature appeared to be even more captivating than the way it had been described by the schoolgirl. It was beyond immense in size, and its smell was of dead, decayed flesh. It did, indeed, have a noticeable claw emanating from each side of its large head, and the creature's body had scales, talons, and a musculature that seemed to have no equal. From whence had it originated was on everyone's mind.

Bewildered, the Lone Creature continued to move, unaware that the booming sounds were forcefully ushering it from the wooded area, out into the open. "A little further, c'mon, a little more!" Without the slightest warning, the helicopters swept in, expertly dropping the heavy metal netting upon the unsuspecting target. One heavy net after the other, dropped, and when the first one came into contact with the creature, it took on a defensive posture; it put all of its weight onto its hind legs and feet, reaching skyward in a defensive posture, as if attempting to protect itself from what was falling from above. Inevitably, the weight of the nets impacted and frightened the creature, knocking it completely off balance and onto one side. Knocked down and covered by the excessive weight, the creature found itself wailing; a sound that was audible for quite a distance and chilling to all in the general area. This sound seemed to be a plea for help and somewhere, not too far away, there was the colony that was startled by the pain filled, heart wrenching and soulful weeping.

Initially, they were eerie sounds that were reminiscent of pleas for help, or maybe the wail signified its inevitable capture. Whatever the reasoning, no one actually knew, but all of the sudden, the creature began to thrash out violently, using its strength, its talons, its jaws and head claws to rip at its weighted covering. Anger and frustration seemed to freely flow and violently pulsate from every movement of the creature. As the creature attempted to free itself, it continually cried out, giving off extensive sounds that seemed to depict a depth of sorrow and despair, along with intensive and aggressive sounds of anger. The creature's bulging muscularity was easily evidenced by all, and most wondered if the netting could remain intact. Anxiety flourished among all that were present, for this Lone Creature appeared to be stronger than any creature known to mankind.

Fortunately, the creature's strength and formidable physical weaponry couldn't damage the metal composition of the netting, or so it appeared. All of the perimeter personnel felt secure as they witnessed the creature's futility, frustration; it continued to thrash about, and violently chew at the linkage. Believing that the creature was beginning to tire, all began to feel a false sense of security; along the netting that was closest to the creature's body, various links began making loud popping sounds, and very soon afterward a large opening appeared.

This realization amazed everyone in the immediate vicinity; the creature's force was utterly terrifying! Realizing the immediate danger of its possible escape, helicopters swooped in and several sedative darts were expertly propelled; their impact predictable. The creature immediately turned its attention from the netting and attempted to remove one dart at a time. Enough of the darts held fast to the creature's body, and subsequently it felt the effects of shutting down. As it had in the past, the creature weakened, became disoriented, and slumped to the ground. Its wail was no longer heard, as it was now experiencing a very deep, drug-induced sleep.

Before preparing to hoist the creature onto the flatbed, its vital signs were thoroughly checked. It appeared to be in good health. Using a powerful crane, the creature, within the damaged netting, was safely hoisted above and slowly rolled from the damaged net onto the flatbed plate. The other undamaged net was placed over the creature and it was securely attached, holding the creature tightly against the flatbed.

Titanium was an added ingredient to toughen the steel bars used for the sides of the creature's flatbed cage. Once all of the bars were fixed and ready, it was then that the plated ceiling would be maneuvered and lowered, allowing all of the perimeter bars to penetrate both the ceiling and flooring plates. With all of the bars in their correct setting, the ceiling and flooring plates were locked in place and the creature was now ready to be transported. Now that the cage was finished, the steel was removed and a breathable, camouflage type cover was used to envelop the entire cage.

The camouflage covering was then secured to the flatbed for the inevitable trip to the federal government site. The flatbed then rumbled along slowly, being led and followed by a cavalcade of policemen, operating their Harley-Davidson motorcycles and cruisers. Along the designated route, all traffic lights were constantly blinking and policemen were on foot so that the flatbed did not have to stop until it was within the federal government site and, in turn, close to the door of the airplane hangar.

Everything went as planned, and once inside the doubled set of entrance gates, close to the entrance of the renovated airplane hangar, the creature's vital signs were checked. The creature was in good condition and completely under the influence of the sedation. As was the case prior to building the cage, the Lone Creature was covered and secured with the metal netting. With the netting in place, the cage was quickly dismantled, leaving the creature lying prone upon the flatbed. The creature was, without a doubt, heavily sedated, and so the netting was removed, and cable extensions were lowered.

The operator gradually persuaded the crane's powerful machinery to lift the creature until it was entirely off the flatbed. At this point, a tightly bound metal mesh was manually placed beneath the creature, so when attached, and lifted at its four corners, it would support the creature, and subsequently slacken the cables that were independently attached to its individual extremities. The cables were then lowered so that the majority of the creature's body weight rested within the mesh, and subsequently upon the flatbed plate. The mesh was stretched tightly and then secured to the four additional cables, so that the mesh could be positioned to hold the weight that had been previously attached to the creature's extremities. Having the mesh connected, as it now was, took the massive weight off its extremities and joints, and placed all upon the mesh. Meanwhile, within the hangar, an elaborate mobile cage had been erected, a sliding metal entrance door was mechanically lifted, and once it was fully open, the mobile cage was brought out of the hangar. The mobile cage was connected to and led by a large four-wheeler until it was placed alongside the flatbed. With its temporary cage dismantled, the creature was now lying upon the open flatbed. Now, the crane operator manipulated the machinery to heft the creature's weight above and completely off the flatbed.

This time, the mesh held the creature's weight while allowing slack to be seen in the beings upper and lower extremities. As a safety precaution, the cable extensions, which had been previously attached to each of the four extremities, at what could be regarded as the wrists and ankles, remained intact. The operator, after locking the crane in place, maneuvered the creature off of and above the flooring of the temporary cage, and slowly maneuvered it so that it was centered above its readied mobile enclosure. The crane's operator slowly lowered the creature until the mesh was approximately a foot above the designated drop off point. Now, once again, the cable extensions were checked to see if they were secure, and once this was confirmed, the creature was lowered the short distance, laying it upon the flooring of the mobile cage. It was then that the creature's entire weight was removed from the mesh's connections; these were then disconnected and subsequently the mesh fell to the flooring below. The crane's operator lifted the creature approximately a foot above the cage and held it there only by the four appendage connections while the mesh was removed from beneath the creature, and laid completely out of the way. The crane's operator then grabbed hold of a certain lever and the creature was, once again, lowered toward the floor plate of the cage.

Slowly, deliberately, gently it was lowered until the creature rested comfortably upon its back; slack, noticeably visible in all four extremities. Then, the military personnel moved onto the floor area and hand-directed the heavy steel bars, one at a time, so that the crane's operator could maneuver each above their designated hole, for which the pole/bar was to be inserted. Using hand and eye coordination, these personnel directed the crane's operator, as each pole/bar was gradually lowered, completely into its designed hole, and then was securely locked in place. Now that all of the poles/bars were inserted into their designated holes and locked in place, the crane's operator swung the unattached cable housing to the area just above the heavy steel plate. This plate had holes that corresponded exactly with the floor plate; the crane's main cable now had an additional set of four cables hanging equally in length, and each had a formidable hook. It was at this point that the hooks were attached to the four corners of the steel plating.

Eventually, all of the poles/bars were locked in their designated holes, and the cage gained its necessary strength and security. Once all of the locks, both top and bottom, had been secured, it was then, and only then, that the cage had its exit, entranceway installed. Again, like the ceiling plate, the steel door had extension holes attached, and once properly in place, it was lifted and balanced so it was close to the place where it was designated to be. The main difference was that the ceiling had a slot cut into it, directly above the one cut into the floor plate; being this way so that bottom of the door housing could be put into place, and then the top area could be placed easily into its corresponding slot. Once this maneuvering was completed, the door was to be locked and secured. When the door was in its proper alignment, there was no doubt that this mobile cage was a solid and secure place to house and study this youthful underground creature.

At this point, military personnel climbed onto the plated flooring and removed the crane attachments from each extremity. As each extremity was freed of its cable extension, these personnel paid special attention to carefully lowering it. At the point where all four extremities had been released and carefully lowered, it was then the creature's vital signs were taken; the creature was found to be experiencing some sort of upheaval.

The powerful four-wheeler was attached to the opposite end of the mobile cage and then both entered the hangar. Once inside, the sliding mechanical door was lowered, and when fully at the bottom, there was a convincing sound; a sound that told all present that that door was indeed closed, formidable! Just inside the hangar, there was an enclosed passageway that connected to the hangar's entrance. All relevant personnel found themselves enclosed within this tubular structure that had a flattened base. What seemed to be an eternity was actually a matter of seconds and then a voice interrupted their anxiety.

Through a speaker came information that what all personnel were sensing was actually a form of a cleansing mist that was necessary while within the large, glass-like enclosure. All were advised that this procedure was completely safe and that its effect would end, without any residual effects, upon one's departure of the hangar. This much needed information helped temper everyone's anxiety level, for what personnel could not see from outside the hangar, and thus could not realize, were medical personnel draped in what appeared to be state of the art spacesuits. The four-wheeler's engine was activated and the machine was placed into the lowest of its forward gears. Ever so slowly, the formidable cage was moved forward, and eventually, when in its designated position, the wheels were locked in place. At that point, the creature was checked again for its wellness. Its irregular heartbeat remained evident, but not to the degree that it was during the previous examination. Now, the waiting began for the sedation to lose its effect.

Chapter 27

AS THE CREATURE HAD been transported to the Bristol Road location, its crudely constructed habitat was thoroughly investigated. Not knowing what they could find, personnel and specialized machinery were brought into the immediate area, and ever so slowly, the cave was unearthed. Initially, the ceiling of the passageway and to a connecting large room was removed, revealing an entrance to what appeared to be a living and storage space. At best, it was crudely built. Within the large living space, there was a small mound of decaying animal flesh, and off to one side, there was a gaping hole. It was now that the specialized team surmised that this mound was what the Thermal Imaging Equipment picked up as the second creature. The hole had been dug and was lined with an animal's skin and was partially filled with blood. Following an in-depth investigation, it was discovered that this enclosure had been built no more than a week or two ago, and that the dark red liquid, was indeed, animal blood. So, where had this creature been living prior to being witnessed by the elementary level schoolgirl? Could it actually be an alien? Had it arrived upon the earth only recently? In no way did this thing resemble a human. If an alien, why was it here?

One of the known tabloid's came out with a questionable article, and as usual, it was a story based on fact, but possibly fiction. It did not seem to matter whether this story was authentic

143

or not, for no sooner had the edition hit the streets, when it was completely sold out at every location.

Not of this Earth? Creature Captured in Bucks County, PA

The government has stepped up its investigation and is in control of the situation. The unsightly creature was first seen by an elementary student in Bucks County, PA. A state of high alert has been associated with this creature since it was discovered living in a crudely constructed, cave-like dwelling within a forested area of Bucks County... If you have seen the creature in the movie Predator, then you have some idea of this creature's appearance. However, unlike the movie character, this creature is the real thing! The alien creature is much larger than the Predator: tall, heavily muscled, and weighs approximately eight-hundred pounds; and extremely ugly!

Adjoining the sensational headline was a picture that crudely resembled the creature. The story went on to say that the Lone Creature supposedly had a claw protruding from each side of its head, and lengthy, curved talons instead of fingers and toes. Evidenced by the instant "sell-out" of this edition, the public was already enamored with the story. Included in the story was the description of the child, Grace Lightcap, who was reportedly the first person to actually see this creature. The story continued beyond the front page and adjoining the story was a picture of Grace, along with a picture of the creature.

Captivating articles followed; they were in every newspaper, magazine, and tabloid. What was captivating the public's eye was the authenticity of the information and the government's reaction.

Chapter 28

THE ELECTRICAL CHARGE WAS disconnected now that the creature had been transported out of the forested area, but the fence bordering the wooded area remained intact. The military personnel continued to guard the perimeter as if the creature was still within. Military personnel stationed at the Willow Grove Naval Station, and at any other location within Bucks County, were on a continued high alert status. The creature was held within the secured site, and subsequently the journalists, various reporters and news media were outside of that location. The area surrounding the federal site was shut off to local traffic and public access. All of the access roads were now guarded by what many civilians described as being much too excessive, but nevertheless, no one without the proper credentials was permitted to venture beyond the location of these perimeter guards.

A specialized medical team with highly sophisticated equipment entered the compound via military helicopter. The helicopter set down on the designated heliport within the site's chain link fencing. There were two perimeter fences, one noticeably old and rusted, and the other was noticeably new; barbed wire sat atop the rusted fence, but in between, and also sitting atop the new fence, was the razor wire.

The medical specialists included neurologists, surgeons, anesthesiologists, DNA specialists, and lab technicians. Inside the hangar, it was easy to take notice of the state of art computers and advanced medical equipment. The people within the acrylic glass structure had no way of knowing just how advanced the medical equipment was, but all had been expertly trained on computers. Here, state of the art took on a new meaning; these PC's had exquisite sound systems and each had a monitor screen that measured approximately twenty-five inches. The keyboards had similarities to a standard one, but there were advanced differences as well. There were many more keys, and each key was raised and noticeably separated from those next to it. This site measured approximately one-hundred and fifty feet in length and was oval in shape, narrow at one end, and when close to the other, it measured seventy-five feet in width. Also, at its widest end, the ceiling was forty feet in height. This enclosure was built especially to house the creature. It was completely sterile and had clear, heavy sections, of bullet-proof glass.

Upon entering, a doctor, or any other professional, had to show their proper credentials, and then would enter a specialized shower stall; allowing a foam solution to cover their entire nakedness. Following the foam cleansing, each person was completely rinsed and then had to enter another room. Now, each person would experience a soothing mist, and then that process ended with varying degrees of warm to heated air. Once completely dry and sterilized, each person would then step into a waiting space suit that was extremely pliable and bacteria free. At this point, the outfitted professional would go through another set of sliding doors and walk through a sterilized tunnel that was directly connected to the oval shaped room. The operating room was strikingly sophisticated. Just beyond the operating table, there was an additional glass door leading to an area where one would be able to remove their space suit.

Soothing music, much like the type played to calm violent inmates in super-max prisons, was continuously heard within the glass enclosure, and now the creature was beginning to stir. It had already been decided that this creature would be permitted to vent any show of force and anger, as long as its enclosing cage-like cell remained intact. If it became the case that the cage-like cell was not strong enough, then the creature would have additional sedative darts propelled into its body.

Upon awakening, the Lone Creature sensed a number of people within its immediate vicinity, but continued to lay motionless. After sensing that it was not in a threatening environment, it began to move. This movement did not go unnoticed, and everyone present appeared to be somewhat anxious. After relaying the fact that the creature was stirring, little communication was evidenced, as all appeared to realize that what they were witnessing was something unique, and likely historical. Everyone had their gaze locked on the creature. This attention was rewarded as the creature was slowly, but surely, moving toward an upright position. While observing, it was easy to see that the creature was still under the influence of its sedation; it swayed and continually lost its balance. After several attempts, it was practically upright, with the majority of its weight on its hind legs. In this stance, the creature had the posture of the great silverback gorilla. Many of the observers seemed to empathize with the creature's plight, and were noticeably saddened at the sight of this huge being, having to be locked in a cage, and unsteady due to its sedation. If this was indeed an interplanetary alien, why had it ventured off its course? Was it intentionally visiting Earth? Would our government allow or perhaps assist it in finding its way home?

Upon unsteady legs, the creature slowly reared its head, and in doing so, appeared to be sniffing, as if attempting to get a sense of its surroundings. Then, it seemed to focus its attention on self-preservation and, as if sensing that its body had been severely weakened, slid down the poles until it returned to a prone and fetal position. Within a matter of seconds, the creature appeared to be fast asleep. While it slept, everyone within the hangar eventually got back to their assigned duties, and the doctors, along with their assigned nurses, went over the medical supplies and equipment, making sure that everything was readied and in good working condition.

Initially, the Lone Creature slept fitfully, as if experiencing a nightmare. However, over time, its body ceased jerking and entered tranquility. As personnel were finishing up their shift, and were planning to take their leave of the glass cubicle, one could take notice that the creature was stirring once again. Before one of these people could place his hand over his mouth, a sound escaped, "Yo!" Subsequently, everyone looked in his direction. Feeling flustered by the attention, and embarrassed by his utterance, he said, "Sorry about that, but the creature is awakening." Immediately, all turned their attention to the caged creature, and indeed, it was moving. As the creature stretched, it became apparent that the majority of the drug had left its system; each movement was exact, and there was no sign of weakness. The creature was moving, as if attempting to stand, but when almost achieving this stature, it bent its lower limbs and lowered its rump into a seated position.

This youthful underground creature balanced upon its rear and appeared as if it was surveying, possibly evaluating, those within its sight. It then leaned slightly forward and took on an aggressive stance upon all four appendages. With its massive weight now shifting partly onto its upper limbs, its talons made a screeching sound, as the tips were brought across the metal flooring. What came next affected everyone, and luckily the videotape was recording. The creature's head went back and once fully to the rear, a wail, similar to that of a huge wolf, emanated from it. This was similar to the previous sound that was heard in the wooded area, when the capture actually took place. This wail was indeed similar, but was evidenced, this time, as more of a plea for help than a display of anger. Extremely loud, yet deliberate, and far reaching, this soulful wail seemed endless, but eventually it tailed off, and what seemed to be tears could be seen streaming from the creature's eye sockets. It was as though this creature was attempting to get into contact with what was suspected to be a distant presence.

The wails were definitely eerie, and some thought that these could be heard for quite a distance, but none checked to find out just how far, because this seemed to be of little consequence. *There was only one of these creatures, so why investigate this as more than a significant happening?* The creature then recognized that there was a thick slab of meat in its enclosed cubicle, along with a container of blood. Anyone within its sight was in awe as they watched it aggressively move in the direction of the flesh. Once in the immediate area of the large slab, the creature spent little time attacking what initially lay on the floor, as if it were a mere snack rather than a massive section of pure meat. As the creature was devouring the meat, it eventually lifted the weight, secured it with the talons of its upper appendages, and began ripping the meat with the boulder-like teeth within and along its massive jaws. Somewhat satiated, with scraps caught between its teeth, and hanging outside of its huge mouth, the Lone Creature moved to the container of blood. It moved toward what it believed to be liquid nourishment; blood that was rich in nutrients, saturated shards of marrow, and a liquid with a thickened consistency. Just prior to the drinking of the blood, the Lone Creature submerged its entire head, as if searching for the saturated marrow, but there was none. It appeared as if the creature was of the realization that there were no bones, so it brought its head from the vat, and shook it vigorously, side to side, spraying droplets of blood every which way. As with the meat, the creature seemed to inhale the blood. The rich, red liquid streamed from its mouth, down its thickened neck, and lay outside of the container, in various sized puddles. Giving the appearance as if it had made this kill, the creature stood upon its lower appendages and sent vibrations throughout the hangar, as if congratulating itself.

Judging by the way the creature had devoured the meat and blood, it was now evident that it had an even larger appetite then envisioned. Again, there was an eerie volume of sound, but this sound was more of recognition rather than confusion and the fear of an unknown. As the shrill tailed off, the creature gradually laid its massive body onto the floor, stretching its various body parts as it had in the past, moving into a fetal position, and drifted off to sleep.

Chapter 29

GRACE WENT FROM A quiet, young person, to a young person with a celebrity status overnight. The producers for The Tonight Show with Jay Leno and those with David Letterman vied for the right to have Grace on their shows. Grace's parents made it clear whenever interviewed by a journalist from the Doylestown newspaper that they would refuse future interviews with any representative of a television show, newspaper, or news magazine if they badgered Grace at any time. They realistically knew that this statement wasn't going to alter the media's frenzy, but just maybe a few would back off to some degree.

Grace's words were misquoted on a regular basis, but the printed accounts sold out as soon as they hit the newsstands. Grace went on the Tonight Show first, accompanied by Ryan, mainly for support, and to confirm what they both had witnessed when in the wooded area. This show wasn't chosen because it was the favorite of her parents, it was simply because it won out when Grace chose from A or B, and when it was B, it was The Tonight Show with Jay Leno. Grace's innocence and genuine appearance, and Ryan, in his noticeable protective role, caught the attention of all that tuned in, and the rating for that time slot went through the roof. Grace was extremely shy and quite adorable, wearing a long, colorful dress, seemingly tight around her neck, and full of soft colored flowers. She was full of information, explaining how the creature, when first seen, made her think of Bigfoot. She went on to explain the creature's horrific appearance and its peee-uuu smell. As Grace said peee-uuu, she scrunched up her facial features and pinched her nose between her thumb and index finger. This description brought unsolicited laughter from the audience, and, in turn, from Jay Leno, and subsequently, Grace. Ryan, like Grace, was quite shy when introduced, and when questions were directed his way, he often looked to Grace, and vice versa, for support and assurance. It was quite evident that here were two children that were being raised with principles; they were mannerly, respectful, and were trustful of one another.

These aforementioned traits were once the norm in our society, but unfortunately, a high number of kids at this time in America have very poor language and behavioral skills. For instance, and as a realistic example, on any number of streets in Philadelphia, there is trash strewn in the street, and that trash is similar to the verbal trash that is emitted from several of the kids that live here. Sexual slang is loud and commonplace, coming from kids that are directly in front of their own row homes. The parent, or parents, are within earshot, but give this abusive language none of their attention. They too get loud and verbally abusive, and are teaching these kids by their example. These types of kids are a direct example of many of the city neighborhoods throughout this once great nation.

Grace brought the attention back to a serious note when she spoke of compassion for the creature. She went from laughter and then set the tone for concern, sadness. She said, in a voice that was just barely heard, "The creature is all alone; it is so sad." Jay Leno attempted to change the emphasis back to laughter, but Grace's sense of compassion had a tremendous grip on all that were listening. Realizing that Grace's statement had piqued the audience's attention, Jay asked Grace how it was that she knew that the creature was alone and, at the same time, sad. It was now that many in attendance were actually seen sitting nervously upon their seats, anticipating Grace's response. "Somehow, I felt that the creature communicated this to me." Eventually, the show ended and all were able to envision the creature in a more sensitive light. It was still a creature, but it was alone and lost; reportedly an alien, from a galaxy unknown to mankind, but was it a monster? Could it be that this creature was indeed an alien; an alien on a mission to create peace between mankind and life that exists somewhere beyond the planet Earth. The reasoning behind this trend of thought was that the creature continuously displayed a nonviolent approach during its capture, and subsequently, to this point in time.

Now that it had been captured and was being safely housed in its mobile cage, the media's speculations ran rampant regarding the federal government's plans.! What would our government find out about its most celebrated prisoner? And what would be divulged to this world, as we know it? Was it the government's plan to experiment upon this creature surgically, and other endless ways? And when having no further use for the creature, what would they do with it?

Chapter 30

FOLLOWING THE SPOT WITH Jay Leno, Grace and Ryan went on Late Night with David Letterman, and the ratings actually exceeded those of the Tonight Show. Following this show, Grace and Ryan appeared on numerous other talk shows. Of all the programs that Grace and Ryan had been on, they were equally impressed by their two favorites; Oprah and Montel. These shows were recognized as their favorites because of the hosts and their crews; both showed a more genuine concern for Grace and Ryan, and treated them with an obvious caring, for the children that they were. Both found this approach to be genuine; it was as if they were family and it was important that these kids were supported and protected. When questioned as to why these two hosts were the kid's favorites, the gist of what they shared was that they felt more at home with Oprah and Montel. They were treated with an age related communication, and this was more important than to sensationalize their situation as the reason for their appearance.

Oprah and Montel had Grace and Ryan's parents on the set with the kids, and this created a family environment. Both hosts treated the kids as children first, and after discussing their family, their friends, and their home areas in Maine and Doylestown, it was only then that the sensationalism of their situation became apparent.

Grace and Ryan were on additional shows and it became

apparent that these other hosts learned some valuable lessons from the authentic approach of Oprah and Montel. Immediately after being on Oprah, the family was asked if an additional show could be done, not here in the studio, but within their home. This idea brought astonishment and smiles from all in the family, and all were in agreement that this was a great idea; an upfront and personal touch. Highlighted on this show would be the interior of their home, the elementary school that they attended, the location where Grace first encountered the creature, the site of its subsequent capture, and hopefully the site where the creature was now being held. Doylestown, and its quaint surroundings, could possibly be highlighted; it was agreed upon, that any other addition to this show would be discussed, prior to being incorporated into the special program.

Chapter 31

DEEP WITHIN THE EARTH, the youthful underground creatures went about their learned behaviors, following what was considered to be basic maneuvers. Whenever the creatures felt a need to satisfy a want, then they chose to satisfy that want immediately, or wait till later. Two of the creatures learned behaviors were that they slept during the human's daylight hours and hunted the earth's surface or roamed their intricate, yet extensive catacombs, when night became apparent, a time when the human race slept. These two functions were very important to the creature colony, for the creature's food gatherers, or hunters, were safer hunting while humans slept.

The ultra-revered bear that had recently been killed, and subsequently had its huge amount of flesh and potent blood stored within the chamber, was paid further tribute by the members of the colony due to the impact of the kill. The homage was initiated when one sent a voluminous sound vibrating throughout the extensive habitat, and when it was deemed time to end this ceremony, another volume of sound was universally heard and understood.

The bear, more massive and so much more deadly than any other animal, was beneficial to the colony for many reasons, and as previously noted, was seen as their kindred spirit. Its flesh and blood content had the most importance, and its skin and hair had tremendous value, in their own right. Since the vats were already lined and were no longer porous, the skin from an occasional bear could be used for something different. This is when it was realized that this skin and its thickened coat of hair had another valuable asset. The hair was thick and soft, and so very warm for these creatures that lived in such a cold, damp, inhospitable habitat. After being recognized for its warmth, and as protection against the dismal environment, the creatures searched the chamber, trying their best to find any previous bear skins that may have been stored as a surplus. They entered the sacred chamber and began their search. Any time the creatures were in the chamber, they risked tripping over items that were newly deposited upon the ground. The dark environment was one thing, but the various scents seemed to amalgamate, very similar to the stench that could have lingered within an abandoned slaughter house.

The creatures moved here and there, and finally, after sensing that they were in the direct vicinity of a huge mound of flesh and blood, it was understood that several pelts were strewn about that area. Many skins were discovered to be large enough to be worn, and these had various amounts of hair, while a few others were smaller and dense with hair. Finally, among the pile were the much sought after skins. The skins, with fur like hair, were scarce; while those with finer hair were more plentiful. These had been separated from the bald skins and placed into a different pile. Then, that pile was separated into two different piles; one pile for skins with fur like hair, and the other with less dense, coarse hair.

The food gatherers were notified of this find, and all moved in the direction of the sacred chamber. Once within the chamber, these elders, according to their status, were rightly given the pick of the bear skins. Any left-over bear skins were stored and reserved for a creature that may become celebrated as a future food gatherer. The skins with hair were then distributed to the other's that had status, for one reason or another. The bear skins gave great comfort to all who had them. Each held great value when hunting, as an insulator against the cold and dampness of their habitat, and when experiencing the surface's winter months. Some of these were worn as vests, while others covered one's body, hanging almost to the middle of a creature's thigh. It would be a crime to overlook what these covers meant to those that had them. Initially, when placing a full length bear skin onto one's body, and wrapping it around to close in front, the food gatherer's experienced a novel sensation. Before having a bear skin, and living beneath the surface of the earth, each colony member always felt the cold, but after obtaining a bear skin, the cold was no more. At times, the skins caused perspiration.

Over time, they acclimated themselves to the warmth of the bear skins and hardly ever took them off. Occasionally, the more aggressive hunters that had the body length skins would temporarily swap with those having the shorter skins because the shorter ones were better when physically hunting, and especially attacking an animal as formidable as a bear. It was further realized that the warmth of these heavy skins could be used as a body covering when choosing to sleep in the chamber's environment. New resources recognized by the food gatherers and specific others placed the bear in a higher place of reverence: the bigger the skin, the better, for when a food gatherer wore the bear skin, there was a tremendous sense of worth and accomplishment.

Some of the food gatherers experimented with the skins; some wore it with the hair against their heavily muscled body, while others wore it with the hair on the outside. Eventually, it became apparent that the bear skin was at its warmest when worn as the bear did; with the fur-like hair on the outside. This was also better for another reason, the bear's hair hardened with time, and when worn with it against a food gatherers skin, it caused an itchy rash. It was also recognized that the bear skin became more pliable and the hair more resilient when worn on a regular basis.

Much like a notorious motorcycle gang, the skin size was the bearer's colors; their emblem of distinction and pride! The others also wore their hairy skins, similar to that of the food gatherers, and found that the skin protected them from the elements, but their skin with hair was slight compared to the one with fur-like hair. Those without a skin were quite envious of those that had one. They became anxious whenever the food gatherers would deem it necessary to leave their protective setting, and venture upon the earth's surface in search of a kill. These others were even more anxious when it was realized that the food gatherers had returned from the hunt, and that the carriers were struggling with a cumbersome weight while moving in the direction of the chamber. Although the others would have preferred a bear skin, they also recognized that these skins were primarily for the elders or food gatherers, and they learned to appreciate skins of less revered animals. These lesser valued skins were always coarser and less desirable in many ways, but the real importance was its ability to keep one warm, as these creatures continually attempted to become acclimated within the depths of the earth.

There was still a great mound of flesh, and the vats were close to full with rich coagulating blood. Enough flesh and blood remained so that the food gatherers wouldn't have to leave the habitat, to roam the earth for another large kill. For more than a century, the hunters have been leaving these hidden passageways to secure the flesh and subsequently the blood of animals. At least one-hundred years of hunting and searching for sustenance, and not once having been seen by its arch enemy, the human.

Possessing limited eyesight was their main drawback, but they managed. Within a radius of five miles were many ranchers that catered to huge herds of livestock. Each rancher had enough acreage so that the livestock were fenced in throughout the night's weather conditions. Though when too extreme, the ranchers brought their cattle from the distant pastures, thus herding the livestock to the barn and the variety of corrals where they could be semi-protected.

Keeping the cattle in the pasture was an advantage for the ranchers and unbeknown to them, an asset for the creatures. Since the cattle and other herds were normally in pastures, this made animals accessible to the food gatherers. Throughout each and every year, these beefy animals were stalked and killed with little difficulty. These kills were hardly ever recognized by the ranchers due to the enormous numbers in each herd; occasionally, there was the suspicion that an animal was missing, but since there was no physical evidence found, it was suggested that the animal had somehow been stolen.

The Cattleman's Association organized a meeting in order to

create a plan to catch the suspected thieves. When the topic was addressed, it was realized that each and every rancher, from time to time, had lost at least one animal from their huge herds. A plan was organized to catch the thief, or thieves, but they had no luck; they made several more concerted efforts, but still no luck. All of the lengthy footage of fence was thoroughly checked, but there was never any recognizable damage. This was utterly confusing, while it was certainly true that the ranchers were losing livestock, it was impossible to understand how the thieves were removing the cattle from within the six-foot high fences; there wasn't the slightest bit of physical evidence that thieves were the actual culprits. Confusion reigned throughout the ranchers thought processes and in the end, they expressed hope, that sooner or later they would solve this mystery. It was suggested, and quickly dismissed as folly, that the cattle were being abducted, and removed from the earth.

As the decades passed, the food gatherers memorized the directions to the various ranches and their subsequent pastures. They knew where to go for hogs, cattle, or for additional sources of flesh and blood. They also realized where they needed to travel to come into contact with wildlife.

To witness the sacred chamber was a site that was quite unnerving. The decaying flesh and vats of steamy, coagulating blood emitted a mind boggling stench, causing one to want to immediately evacuate that area. Among the animal's flesh and blood was another source of food that was now bringing volume to the fleshy mound. However, this source was initially difficult to accept, and subsequently, difficult to stomach. Within time, the creatures learned to adapt to their newest of food sources, for this was the creature itself, and cannibalism became an additional part of their survival. As these creatures aged and eventually died off, were mortally wounded during a hunt or in a fight for dominance, their remains were stored among the other forms of sustenance. At the time of death, the heart, liver, and kidneys were removed from the body cavity and were immediately eaten by the few that were given that privilege. After digesting these body parts, it was then that the head and outer skin were cut free, along with its sexual parts and bowels. Only the fatty innards were kept, along with the muscles, intestines, and whatever blood could be salvaged. These, in turn, were thoroughly washed with the saved blood of the body, and then were dipped into the blood vat before being placed among the ever growing mound of flesh. The only things of value that remained were the talons and the horn-like extensions. They ended up being utilized as tools and weapons.

Close proximity to the rancid flesh and blood gradually desensitized one's sense of smell. However, nothing was as damaging as the smell that emanated from the birth membranes, whenever they cracked from dryness or when the bloated stillborn burst, freeing a deplorable mixture of gases.

Chapter 32

THE CREATURES CONTINUED TO tend to their daily routine and then, all of a sudden, there was an unmistakable sound that pierced the consciousness of every creature within the catacombs. The sound was their recognized, universal plea for help, and all the creatures could clearly hear it, but not one recognized where it was coming from. One thing was clear though. The sound was not coming from within, it was coming from somewhere on the earth's surface. "How could this be possible?"

Questions dominated every creature's thought process and bewilderment ran rampant throughout the catacombs and chamber. The elders assembled as soon as possible, and it was recognized that all were present and accounted for; could it be possible that one of the creatures had broken the colony's coveted law and had entered the earth's surface without being sanctioned by the elders? Even worse, could this creature be alone, or with others, and be injured or, the worst of all scenarios, could it have been captured and held somewhere by the humans?

The elders, rigorously and meticulously, had all of the layers and lengths of the various catacombs checked; the entire living space was searched, and the finding was brought back to the council of elders. One of the youthful creatures was gone. In fact, this missing creature had been missing for over a period of several days. Upon further investigation, it became clear that this youthful creature had surfaced alone, alleviating the fear that more than one was on the surface. Fear, terror, and anxiety ran rampant throughout the catacombs. For, if this creature had been found and captured, then the humans had the knowledge that the colony had survived the human's annihilation plan. If this was the case, then all of the creatures had reason to fear for their lives, their very existence!

If the wail was sent through the air waves as a signal of helplessness, or capture, then the elders had to prepare an emergency plan. A battle plan against such a formidable force as a human would be totally useless, and although the creatures could use their size, superior strength, talons, and oversized teeth and jaws, they were at a tremendous disadvantage when going up against the numbers, and the weaponry of man. It was conceivable that the catacombs and chamber would be found and destroyed, and along with their habitat, their lives, culture, and history.

The elders organized and came up with the unified decision to construct an escape route. The route would extend far away from their present habitat and would gradually surface some seventy-five yards beyond what was presently seen as the far end of their habitat and close by the sacred chamber. Their plan was to begin the exhaustive labor of digging a tunnel at the furthest point from the place where their historical presence began. This place was where, when drugged and manipulated, they were escorted through an extensive maze, until they entered the room that was to be their burial site. As with all of the tunnels in the past, this one went straight down, down further than any other, so as to slow down any pursuit by the humans.

Approximately sixty feet straight down and at the very bottom, the creatures began to construct a catacomb. This escape catacomb was constructed for a distance of seventy-five yards. As the diggers worked, sacks were filled with dirt and rocks, and as the catacomb lengthened, the carriers returned the heavy loads back to the base of the tunnel. Along the ascending tunnel's wall, at ten-foot intervals, there was an additional carrier waiting to take the previous carriers weighted load, place it upon its own back and shoulders, and then carry the load approximately ten feet higher, to the next carrier. To witness these exchanges, and the strength that it took to carry such heavy loads, was without compare. This kind of work hadn't been done by the vast majority of the creatures that now inhabited the catacombs, but it had to be completed well in advance of the human's discovery of the creature's habitat.

All of the diggers and carriers were massive and thoroughly muscled, but this labor seemed as if it was life threatening, especially for those creatures that were carrying their load straight up. These carriers had the massive weight of the dampened soil and rocks in skin sacks lying upon their upper shoulder area. The remainder of the weight put tremendous strain down their spine, exhausting the totality of the muscle mass of each extremity. Each carrier needed both of its upper extremities free for the climb, so it was the strength of its jaws, teeth, and neck that came into play.

The fastest way to get this weight to the next carrier was to place the bag high up on its shoulder, and to firmly grip the topmost, closed area of the sack within its massive jaws and boulder-like teeth. Of course, this method freed up the creature's upper extremities, so it didn't have to use one to hold the sack, but the muscles of its neck quickly fatigued and would often spasm.

Implementing this method, the creature made calculated moves, digging the talons of its upper extremities deep within the sides of the tunnel. As it pulled its massive weight upward, it rotated its lower extremities, following the direction of the upper ones. The initial carrier climbed straight up the tunnel's wall and stopped when slightly above the next waiting creature. At this point, both of the carriers sank the talons of all four extremities deeply into the earthen wall. They now were straddling the opening of the tunnel, above and beneath them, and having the talons of all four extremities sunk deeply into the sides of the tunnel, they were prepared to make the exchange.

It was at this tenuous point that the carrier with the sack released the talons of its closest appendage to the waiting carrier. The carrier with the sack thoroughly secured it with its set of talons and then allowed the sack to be released from its boulder-like teeth. At this point, the sack was maneuvered to the shoulder area of the waiting carrier, and subsequently held in place by that creature.

After the exchange, the weight was entirely upon the shoulder area of the waiting carrier and this creature hefted the sack until the heavy weight was slightly above the next receiving carrier. This tenuous process continued until the topmost carrier hefted its sack, with its powerful jaws and shoulder, and laid it onto the level area that was the catacomb directly above. It was at this point that the sack, which had been originally lifted from the floor of the tunnel, had now been hefted to the topmost catacomb, and would be transferred to an additional carrier who'd carry the sack along that topmost passageway for quite a distance. This last, in the chain of carriers, transported the sack, containing wet earth and stones and then set it down at its destination. While the carrier hefted the sack along the catacomb, the tunnel carriers returned to their designated positions along the tunnel's wall. After the payload was finally emptied at the maze, the carrier sauntered back to the topmost area of the tunnel and communicated a warning that the emptied sack was about to be dropped to the tunnel's floor. As you can imagine, when in an environment absent of light for more than a century, communication was important.

Along the twists and turns of the escape route, the diggers dug out several additional catacombs, each extending thirty feet. These dead-end passageways were meant to frustrate and confuse the human in the event it discovered the tunnel entrance to the escape route. At the same time, these passageways would allow the creature's additional time to safely relocate their entire colony.

As the diggers and carriers performed their assigned tasks, it was evident that they indeed had a purpose. As the escape catacomb, and the variety of dead-end passageways took their final form, these workers began to experience physical and emotional fatigue, beyond what their memory previously had known. Their physical pain and anguish were, at times, overwhelming, but thinking that the human may, at any time, swoop down and wipe out their culture was reason enough to keep them diligently working. Sack after sack after sack was hefted and carried to the farthest area from each new digging site. Dirt was dug and carried hour after hour for days as the escape catacomb was being constructed, and it gradually took its planned form. On occasion, the less formidable creatures relieved those that were noticeably spent, and took over the role of either a digger or carrier. These less formidable creatures met the physical requirements to dig or carry, but were not nearly formidable enough to heft the heavy loads straight up the tunnel.

Each creature worked with an extreme purpose because they did not want to experience their own demise, or that of their colony. As the diggers penetrated the catacomb's length, they'd drive themselves beyond their known endurance when recalling the eerie, alarming sound that came from somewhere upon the earth's surface. The elders knew that they could not leave their habitat in search for the Lone Creature that they sensed was stranded, or for whatever reason, was unable to return to the habitat. They also knew that searching the surface for this stranded one could be a devastating blow to their entire colony. If they went out searching, and this became known by the humans, then there was the possibility that their habitat would be without its necessary leadership and the escape route would not proceed at its regular pace. This reasoning kept the elders at home, leading and encouraging the others to work harder, until every passageway located in and around the escape catacomb was completed. Days of strenuous work ensued, many tons of dirt removed, and this, in turn, began to block the lower tunnels and passageways that were far away, and in close proximity to the original entrance. Eventually, a few of the catacombs were closed off with dirt and stones that were carried from the escape catacomb. If humans did, in fact, enter the habitat, then they could not venture beyond the maze and experience the vast and lengthy catacombs, for many tons of dirt fully blocked their way. Unless the humans recognized this blockage for what it was, they would be unable to move beyond this point, and then could not become aware of the habitat beyond. It was still possible for someone to enter the cave-like opening, descend the lengthy passageway, and eventually experience the ancient maze and the burial chamber. Upon a more extensive investigation, it could be discovered, just at the entranceway to the ancient maze, that there was what appeared to be a newly formed blockage. Finding that the blockage was, in fact, recently constructed, the investigating team could find their way through, eventually finding what appeared to be several tributaries. Each of these tributaries would then be investigated and each would take a considerable amount of time; bringing with it a great amount of frustration due to the fact that each and every tributary had a dead end. Being frustrated when these tributaries ended abruptly, the investigating team would probably put all of its energy into the initial passageway. Each individual, being highly trained, would probably find it necessary to put their minds together upon realizing that the lengthy passageway also ended abruptly. After giving this situation considerable thought, it would undoubtedly be concluded that the blockage at the end of the passageway was put there to slow down an intruder's progress. The evidence that would enable investigators to come up with this conclusion rested on the fact that the soil at this blockage point had two forms of composition. Surrounding the blocked area, the soil was compact, and appeared never to have been disturbed, but, within the blockage, the soil had the composition of being displaced, and being deposited there in the very recent past.

The initial entry was presently open to movement, but only as a precaution until the escape route was completed, and while the creatures readied themselves to move en masse to a new habitat. While the others, and a few of the elders, remained behind to coordinate the colony's eventual move, designated elders stealthily departed the habitat and traveled the surface as one unit for quite a distance, searching for the site that was to be their new habitat. It was during this search that frustration began to take a tightening grip upon the elders. They began, one at a time, and then as a group, to evaluate the tremendous upheaval that the Lone Creature had caused the entire culture and colony.

Eventually, they did find the right location, and using the darkness of the night as a means to camouflage they began their return trip to the habitat. During their lengthy return, the sun was on the verge of showing its brilliance, so the elders knew that they would have to remain within their habitat's protective environment until night came. While in the habitat, their entire population was made aware of the move. It was then that important segments of the move were laid out; to ready the chamber's contents and to leave nothing within this entire site that could give evidence as to where they had gone. Throughout the daytime hours, these creatures moved everything, that wasn't dirt and rock, to the bottom area of the sixty-foot tunnel, and lined it along the escape route's passageway. Once the move was readied, most of the colony slept until darkness covered this section of the east coast. Again, using darkness as their friend, the diggers and carriers traveled cross country, until they were introduced to a descending cave-like structure that was to be the entrance to their new home. Luckily for the creatures, the passageway of the cave twisted this way and that, as it descended deeper and deeper into the earth. With each step came inner jubilation, for each descending step meant that sacks of dirt and rocks would not have to be loaded and carried to the surface. After what seemed to be eighty feet, the twisted passage stopped descending, leading to what continued as a narrow passageway, and now the strenuous work began.

Fortunately for the diggers, the composition of the earth was less rock than their previous habitat, and for this they were extremely thankful. While the sacks were filled, and then were being carried towards the earth's surface, the diggers maneuvered onto their backs and used all four sets of talons to clear away a wider passageway and ceiling. The carriers would then heft filled sacks to the cave-like entranceway, and momentarily wait until the guard signaled that it was okay to move the dirt to the surface, along a designated path, and then unload it, creating an ever-growing mound. Other than when these creatures slept, they were hard at work, widening the length of the initial catacomb, as it slithered along, much like a snake. This process continued for several days, and eventually there was enough space for the creature population to relocate everything to their new habitat. The cave's entrance was somewhat camouflaged by an overgrowth of wild grass, large shrubs, and several bushes. Just off to one side was an ancient tree that had a multitude of limbs and branches, some so heavy and lengthy that it caused the ends to nearly touch the earth's surface.

The eldest of the creatures, who were the slowest afoot and somewhat feeble, were extremely saddened at the realization that they now were being forced to leave the only habitat that they had ever known. This home was truly dismal and dungeon-like, but the eldest of these creatures had personal experiences that the majority could not know. Although the eldest of these ancient beings, they weren't mistaken as members of the elite group known as the elders. A few of the eldest took extreme pride in reminiscing about their culture's history, its evolution, about the construction of the catacombs and tunnels, and some of the changes associated with their existing sacred chamber. Knowing that they had to relocate, tears welled within their eye sockets, streamed down along the many time-deepened cracks in their faces, and in and around the scales of their muscled necks. Sadness dominated initially, but this gradually changed to anger; anger toward the selfish Lone Creature that had broken their forbidden law, and whose inability to abide by their laws meant that It would be put to death when found.

On occasion, the diggers and the carriers would find themselves working longer than usual, and likewise, needed to return to their original habitat without the cover of their much needed friend, darkness. Each time this happened, the creatures would become emotionally upset, fearing that their new location could be jeopardized, and then the colony could experience annihilation by the human, in one felled swoop! Their bodies ached from the amount of stress related solely to the foolishness of the Lone Creature.

Despondency and discomfort dominated the diggers and carriers whenever they exited, en masse, from their new home, heading in the direction of their original habitat. They did everything they could to avoid detection, and subsequently were not seen, but the amount of stress associated with this jaunt was truly overwhelming. The stress did dominate, and was truly painful; but these creatures often worked into daybreak; anxiously awaiting the opportunity to travel across, and at the same time to witness, the landscape of the earth's surface.

The diggers and carriers were not food gatherers, so they had never been on the surface during their lifetime, at least to this point in time, and they found this experience to be exhilarating, actually enlightening. This feeling engulfed them, but they had an important responsibility; sure they had to construct the beginning stages of this new habitat, but they also had to recognize the way of their travels and the ensuing landmarks. The landscape was very important, for the colony needed camouflage, along with the cover that the darkness afforded while moving between the sites.

Each time the diggers and carriers returned to their existing catacombs, they apparently had an aura about them, for these others displayed an energy that gave the impression that they anticipated this special time to actually travel upon the earth for the first, and possibly the last period of time. It was understood that once the move was complete, it would be then that the laborious work was to begin! There would be a multitude of catacombs constructed, and a spacious chamber would have to be carved into the earth below.

To further protect their anonymity, a plan was created to eventually dismantle their cave-like entrance, and to then create a new entry point. Eventually, it came time for the stored flesh and coagulated blood to be moved to the new habitat. During the camouflage of night, most of the decaying flesh and the stored blood were to be carried; the flesh and blood were placed into the skin sacks, and with each step, there was an obvious squishing sound. Also, when the decaying flesh and blood reached the earth's surface, the putrid and vile smell seemed to be more pronounced then when within the sacred chamber.

While the carriers moved the two substances across the landscape, they encountered little in the way of obstacles, that is, until their first roadway was apparent. It was here that the flesh was moved easily, but the blood was a vastly different story. With the slightest movement, the volume noticeably sloshed; so as to prevent excessive loss, the movement was much slower, in fact deliberate. Eventually, all of the flesh and a majority of the blood moved across the narrow roadway, and the carriers found their trek to be reasonable.

The trek continued to be this way until they stopped just prior to entering the shoulder area of a busy highway. This was so much different than the previous roadway; traffic sporadically traveled by in both directions. It became noticeable when the creatures, that were not carriers, would become guards and move to the distant ends of the highway, while still remaining in clear sight. While the carriers remained hidden, the others timed the movement of the automobiles, with the assistance of the distant guards. As was the case with the previous roadway, the carriers of the flesh were the first to go. When the faraway guards could not see oncoming headlights, from further away than where they were situated, they signaled that it was safe to cross the highway. As in the past, the flesh carriers safely crossed into the ensuing forest, without encountering a problem.

The blood carriers wished that this could also be their fate. They found themselves becoming anxious whenever the traffic passed in both directions for extended periods. Occasionally, both of the guards simultaneously gave their okay to move the blood, but occasionally one guard would give its okay while the other would not. This happened repeatedly and caused much frustration. Finally, both guards gave their okay, at the same time, and these carriers stepped onto the hardened surface. As these carriers moved onto the highway's asphalt covered surface, they realized that the inability of their talons, to gain purchase, caused piercing pain to their feet. Experiencing this excruciating pain caused these carriers to lose their balance, and subsequently they had to pay more attention to their movement. While the pain unnerved them, it was only a short-lived problem. Being forced to slow their movement frightened these carriers, for they were aware of the potential traffic, and that if they were forced to move faster, they could spill large amounts of the nutritious blood. It was impossible to keep the blood from sloshing and even though the carriers were cautious, spills did occur. All went well until the carriers reached the far shoulder, and the foggy presence of headlights could be seen in a distance. It was at this point that the carriers needed some additional time to enter the camouflaged countryside, but there was no guarantee, for the lights were no longer foggy, and were heading directly toward their location. Just as an automobile was approaching, all of the creatures had gotten beyond the shoulder, and were now hidden by the forest. Stress continued to mount though, because the driver of this auto all but stopped, and then for some reason, sped away. One of the last carriers to cross went back to see if he could recognize why the driver had all but stopped. There, on the highway, were large spills of blood, hopefully giving evidence to the driver that a rather large deer could have been hit, and possibly killed.

The creatures moved a considerable distance, and then they were introduced to their new home. While it was true that traversing the earth's surface was exhilarating, upon entering their habitat, the creatures were deeply thankful. There was still enough darkness remaining, so the food gatherers and the few carriers planned their return to their old habitat for one last, thorough search.

When this group was sufficiently prepared, it was then that these creatures traveled to their original habitat, thoroughly searched it, and buried the exit way, and some of the initial passageways, with tons of falling earth. Having completed their tasks, the food gatherers and the carriers, being loaded down with a few hundred pounds of excess flesh, left the only home that they had ever known. The elders now recognized that this situation could happen, at any time, and now that it had, they vowed that they would never be left unprepared again!

The elders, along with the others, were livid with the Lone Creature. They held him responsible for all of their present problems. While it was true that the Lone Creature had sent out a warning with its soulful wail, it was also true that it would never be permitted to rejoin their colony. It was truly a Lone Creature now, and forever more, and it was exiled to a life among the humans upon the earth's surface. It was possible that the pain heard in the creature's wail was partly due to its recognition that it now was, indeed, an alien. It was alienated from all other forms of life upon, or within the earth: This was the law of the elder's.

Chapter 33

THE LONE CREATURE AWAKENED within its cell-like cage, feeling differently than when it had dozed off. Still quite sleepy and also lethargic, it found movement difficult, as if it were trudging through mud. It attempted to put all of its weight upon its hind legs, but found that it was necessary to use all four appendages to gain any resemblance of balance. This youthful creature held itself on all appendages, but then felt its strength ebbing; it remained balanced for a short period, but then it began to tremble. The creature wobbled some more, and then before realizing it, its appendages gave out and it was upon its side, its head colliding with the flooring. Unbeknownst to the creature, it had been the subject of several tests and experiments while anesthetized. Prior to the medical work-up, but completely influenced by anesthesia, the creature was moved to an oversized operating table, and once situated correctly, its body was thoroughly secured. There was always the chance that this Lone Creature could awaken, and if this was the case, then it could raise havoc within the hangar.

When the x-rays were developed and the MRI and EKG were ready to be analyzed, the various top-notch specialists were summoned. The x-rays were truly mind boggling to all that read them; what they witnessed was a creature that had the skeletal make-up of a human. Could this creature be an alien and also have human characteristics within? This possibility went against all that had ever been published or was known to science. More than mind boggling, was the information derived from the Magnetic Resonance Imaging test. The MRI gave direct evidence that the creature could have evolved directly from a human being. It had a brain very similar to that of a human's and the EKG revealed activity that was far superior to that of any known animal, and this included extensive testing upon chimpanzees. The variety of tests lent evidence to the fact that the creature may still be an alien, but that this alien had the interior design of a human being. Further tests would have to be done, and if identical results were obtained, then abduction could be a real possibility. The scientists were on the verge of a discovery that, to this point in history, had never been verified. Television shows and movies lent credence to the abduction theory, but here was the actual possibility of proof. Had a human been abducted by an alien life form, spent many years away from earth, and now had returned as this horrific creature?

Could this event actually be happening? If this information was factual, then how was this to be accomplished? The creature had weakened sight, and had not communicated with a human since its capture. Therefore, it was transferred to the abandoned military site, at the intersection of Bristol and Newtown Roads. The only sound that had come from this creature was the loud, elongated soulful one, seemingly as a plea to some faraway place.

Roswell, New Mexico, came into one's thoughts at this time; it was here that aliens had supposedly crashed, and that one alien survived. It was, as the story goes, moved to a secure government site, Bldg. 51, by personnel, along with the UFO material that remained from the crash. Other than being depicted in a movie from time to time, neither these aliens, nor their craft, were ever seen again.

If the creature was at one time a human and was, indeed, abducted, then how and why had a human evolved into this horrific creature?

Chapter 34

GRACE AND RYAN CONTINUED to receive unprecedented news coverage, but now the coverage had been stepped up due to a government leak that the creature may have been abducted as a human child and was now returning to earth as this horrific creature. The proof that this creature was, at one time, human, supposedly was proven by its skeletal, brain, and organ similarity. What did this human (?) encounter while experiencing a distant galaxy that could have qualified it for this unique appearance? There was frenzy around Grace and Ryan whenever they left their house, and now their parents, John and Kathleen, had additional concern for their children. Could this deluge of reporters and paparazzi have a negative effect upon their children? The only way to protect these kids from this onslaught was to keep them home from school and activities. This was tried, but their home was not only a scene for media personnel, but a place where an element of the public came to gawk.

Grace and Ryan, and their parents, were invited by the President of the United Sates to visit with the First Family at the White House, and of course, they were thrilled. They were told that a government limousine would be at their house, accompanied by a government security escort, and that the family would be away from their home for the following week. What a god-send, a break for the entire family from the monotony of the media. After the acceptance of this kind offer, John and Kathleen called their respective employers, only to find that the White House personnel had already tended to the necessary arrangements, and that the government would be responsible for the parents pay for that week. John walked over to the home of the Hengy's and spoke with Jack and Jill; he brought them up to date on their upcoming visit to the White House and asked them to keep an eye out for the safety of their house. Jack and Jill were good Christian people, and although they had no children of their own, they treated Grace and Ryan as if they were their own. Both of the Hengy's were supervisors at their respective jobs; Jack, at the nearby B.C.Y.C. and Jill, at the HealthNow insurance company. Both had always been helpful to those in need and when asked, they said that they would be more than happy to keep an eye on the house. If it be the case that a problem arose, in which they deemed it necessary to enter the house, then Jack was given the key to the back entrance.

The visit was arranged without the knowledge of the media, and when the day came for their departure, all media types within the perimeter of the house were awestruck as the two limousines arrived, along with its smartly dressed security force. The driveway was cleared of reporters and all other media, and the limousines were then backed in until they both stopped; the walkway led directly to the rear door of one limo. While members of the security kept the driveway clear, others entered the house and returned with several suitcases. These were placed into the trunk and, in turn, the trunk was secured. It was then that the security force notified the family to exit their home and to get into the limousine. Once inside, the doors were closed and the entire entourage departed the area, leaving the stunned media wondering what had just happened.

Grace and Ryan turned in their seats and watched the bewildered media as the limousine moved further and further away; the further away they got, the bigger the smiles appeared upon the children's faces. This had the potential of becoming a great week!

Chapter 35

NOW THAT THEY HAD surfaced and traveled across what seemed to be many miles of countryside, paved roadways, and a highway, and were now in the process of constructing their new habitat, the creatures felt that they were safe. As always, they stayed within the earth's surface during the daylight hours, and knew that this, being their second night, would be laborious. They realized that their entranceway would have to extend approximately one-hundred feet before beginning their first catacomb. During the hours of darkness, the diggers worked aggressively while the carriers exited their new habitat, tirelessly emptying sack upon sack of dirt and stones.

The creature's massive strength came into play as the descending passageway was finished faster than what was considered possible, and now the initial catacomb was begun. The diggers and carriers worked endlessly, and in a matter of days, the catacomb was quite lengthy. Now came what all the workers dreaded, the construction of the initial tunnel. At first, the strength needed was equal to that of constructing the catacomb, but as the tunnel deepened, the strain upon a carrier's musculature was almost unconscionable. The deeper the tunnel, the harder the work! And once the workers were within the tunnel's depth and far beneath the catacomb, the carriers had to maneuver their heavy sack. With the sack high upon their dominant shoulder, the carrier had to grab the twisted opening, with its powerful jaw and boulder-like teeth, and then climb the tunnel until its sack was level with the catacomb. At this point, another carrier sliced its talons through the sack, took the weight from that tunnel-climber and proceeded along the trek until finally exiting the catacomb and climbing to the earth's surface.

The tunnel climb was relatively easy during the first twenty feet, but all that changed as the tunnel gained significant depth. The diggers continually penetrated the tunnel's base and its surrounding wall, and the carriers continued their laborious work until the tunnel reached a depth that was too deep for a lone carrier; it then needed assistance. Carriers positioned themselves, as in the past, and hung on at ten-foot intervals, so the sack could be transferred to each after being hefted straight up the interval. The tunnel depth was completed at approximately eighty feet, and at that time, work began on additional catacombs.

The second catacomb, somewhat below the level of the first, extended for approximately two-hundred yards. Then, a second tunnel dropped forty feet, and here is where an additional catacomb was dug. This type of construction went on throughout the hours of each night, for several weeks, and then the creatures realized that they were making considerable headway. The diggers stripped the earth from what was to become walls, floors, and ceilings. The carriers hefted these sacks for longer and longer jaunts, and deposited the displaced dirt onto the earth's surface. Eventually, there were several passageways, and these extended for about one-half of a mile; each intersected with other catacombs and indirectly led to the entranceway of the sacred chamber.

Finally, the sacred chamber was finished, and at this time the flesh and blood was moved within that location. The mound of flesh was quite voluminous and oval in shape; deep vats were constructed to safely house the rich, nourishing, and coagulating blood. When these newly dug vats were ready, the excess animal skins lined them, and then the sacks of blood emptied into these deep, nonporous containers. Mixed in with the mound of animal flesh were the skeletal remains of creatures that had died during survival fights, and food gatherers that had been mortally wounded while on a sanctioned hunt.

To make the skeletal remains of creatures and animals tastier, the lengthy skeletal bones were broken and crushed into shorter segments, and then submerged into the vats of blood so that over time, the marrow would become saturated with the blood's nutrients. The skeletal pieces that remained submerged became softer than the newly added bones, and this made the bone mass easier to chew. Eventually, it got to the point where the creatures would not eat these skeletal remains unless they were, indeed, saturated and softened.

The elders took heed from what they had learned by this Lone Creature's defiance. During this next generation, work would be done to create an escape route, so if they were forced to hurriedly move, en masse, then they could do this in a timely manner. These newly constructed catacombs, and the sacred chamber, gradually picked up the stench of the creature's body odor, the putrid smell of the long decaying flesh sources, the stored animal skins, and the pungent smell of the stored blood. Add to this the stench of the stagnating feces and urine, and one could only imagine the uninhabitable living conditions of these creatures, that is, all because humans born with leprosy were forced by relatives and other community members to lose their human rights, much like the plight of Native Americans when the white man chose to annihilate the Indian Nations.

Chapter 36

WHILE IN CAPTIVITY, THIS youthful creature longed to be home and realized, as it had after colliding with the tree and upon losing track of its home location, that its destiny had drastically changed. It was now without a home! The creature, after gathering some of its secluded thoughts, remembered bringing to fruition its desire to explore the earth's surface, much like the food gatherers had. However, the Lone Creature imagined that it would have been able to do this more extensively. It fantasized that being on the surface would be different, for the creature was not there to specifically gather food, but to explore what it had never experienced. The creature envisioned, within its vivid imagination that it would explore, from time to time, and then gradually share this experience with the others. It realized that this sharing could be dangerous because the elders had not sanctioned the journey, and since the journey had not been sanctioned, it was breaking the colony's most valued law. Coming back to reality, the Lone Creature wondered why it had felt the need to run so swiftly, faster than its thought processes could handle. If it would have just moved at a slower pace, then maybe it would be home, not just maybe, it would be home, planning its next trek upon the surface of the earth. It was, instead, captured, and at the mercy of the human; the one thing that all underground creatures had been taught to fear the most!

The media reported and newspapers continued to sell at a record pace. An excerpt of the story went like this:

The creature that was recently captured within the countryside of Bucks County was initially thought to be some kind of a being; possibly of this earth, such as the fabled Bigfoot. It was then given creditability as a creature from a distant galaxy. After its capture, its living area was found and subsequently investigated. There was strong evidence that the habitat was constructed only one week prior to its capture. This led investigators to believe that this creature was indeed an alien. Upon information obtained from x-rays and MRI's, it was ascertained, by the top experts in their specific fields, that this so-called creature, or alien, could be both, for it had a horrific appearance, unlike anything known to the human race. This creature could also be thought of as an alien because after finding its crudely built habitat, and realizing that it was constructed only a week prior to its capture, this information gave creditability that the creature was most likely an alien. Furthermore, and up to this present time, the year 2002, it was now conceivable that the creature, and, or alien, was abducted as a human child, and had lived with an alien life form for most of its human years.

Until a week ago, the creature was not known to exist. *According to a reliable source that prefers to remain anonymous, this being had creature-like attributes and characteristics. At this time in its life, it is approximately seven to eight feet in height, may weigh as much as one thousand pounds, and is extremely thick from its chest area to its back. It is heavily muscled from head to toe, and the muscularity of its upper and lower appendages is truly grotesque. It has long, hard, and pointed talon-like extensions that take the place of a human fingers and toes, and appears to be heavily clad with hard, thick, armor-like scales, or plates. The description also includes the possibility that the creature may have difficulty seeing, for its eyelids, both top and bottom, have limited movement. The upper and lower lids are heavily encrusted, and this waste appears to have forced the lids apart. It is projected that once the lids became encrusted, they remained apart, allowing light and air to constantly affect the eyes, over time damag*ing* its sight.

There is the distinct possibility that other creatures do exist, but at present, there is no actual proof of this reality. If there is more than one creature, then it might be that the captured creature is the exception, and others possess different characteristics and better sight. The captive creature had sores over its entire body and these sores were open, crater-like, and emitted continual, putrid smelling ooze. Furthermore, this alien, and/or human life form has a very large mouth that is filled with boulder-like teeth, and has super-strength in its jaws. What is even more disturbing to this reporter is the fact that this life form has two, very large, thickened claws, each extending approximately a foot from each side of its enormous head, and that each crab-like claw has a certain amount of mobility. Where has this alien, human life form been? Is it truly returning to earth? Where has it come from, and how long has it been away?

Chapter 37

THE PRESIDENT OF THE United States, the First Family, and the Lightcaps sat down to a superbly prepared meal. The entire meal was served to all by eloquent waiters and the Lightcaps realized what it was to be a guest at the White House. They had arrived earlier that afternoon and were shown to their spacious suite where the parents and children had adjoining but separate bedrooms. Within the children's rooms were various game systems, even some that were not yet available to the general public. Each room had a plush, featherbed mattress, and the pillows felt as if they were the fluffiest thing that they had ever rested their head upon. It was as if they would be sleeping on a cloud.

Each bedroom had its own adjoining bathroom; each child's room had pictures and posters of their favorite personalities. If you wanted to witness an elaborate setting, all you had to do was enter the suite for John and Kathleen. Once inside their living quarters, they found themselves short of breath; a gasp if you will, for their eyes beheld an inspiring remarkable site. Elaborate frames surrounded great paintings, with artist's names that had only been seen in art museums or history books. Gorgeous plush furniture stood majestically upon marvelous marble flooring and the marble was covered, in specific areas, with eloquent area rugs. Along one of the walls was a masterpiece; a fireplace that appeared not to have an equal. It had a very large, open face, and surrounding the opening was a setting of unique, eight inch square tiles, commissioned directly from the Mercer Tile Works, located in Doylestown, Pennsylvania. The tiles told a story as one followed them from the left base of the fireplace, on up to the topmost portion of the opening, across the huge open face, to the other side, and then down that side, to its base. The facing continued with brilliant dark green colored granite that had black lines penetrating it, and these appeared to spread in certain areas. The mantle was also made from granite, and its color was nicely coordinated with the colors of the other granite and tiles. Inside the fireplace were thick, dried out logs, piled high, resting upon a grated iron holder.

John, Kathleen, and the kids walked around this spacious room, obviously amazed, and recognized that there were two adjoining rooms. While Grace and Ryan waited within the living room area, John and Kathleen entered one of these adjoining rooms. "Wow" was all they could hear each other say upon entering the bathroom. White marble encased the entire room; beautiful mirrors and gorgeous embedded lighting seemed to be everywhere. In one area was an extended Jacuzzi tub that had more depth than was the norm; there was also a toilet and a bidet. When Grace and Ryan entered their parent's bathroom, their eyes roamed the room. Graced questioned why there were two toilets and this brought a genuine smile to her parent's faces. Kathleen's answer was somewhat confusing, but both of the kids seemed to accept it.

Off to one side was a large shower that could alternately be used as a steam room or sauna. The towels were plush and softened, and scented soaps and body washes were there. Along one of the walls was a stereo unit, and an assortment of easy listening CD's; a pleasant fragrance constantly permeated the bathroom and seemed to be activated when the door automatically closed upon entrance. After leaving the bathroom, John, Kathleen, and the kids entered the bedroom, and again were mesmerized. The bed appeared to be fluffy, and above the mattress area was a canopy of layered, lacy material. Beautiful furnishings, which included a plush area rug, partially covered the marble flooring. Along one of the walls was another fireplace; wood was stored off to one side and the fireplace had several logs within, readied to provide a euphoric environment. This was truly their heaven on earth. After witnessing the attractiveness of the living areas, bedrooms and bathrooms, the family met in the living room once again.

There was one remaining room that they had not investigated, and so they entered it as a group. To this point in time, they had truly felt special, and this feeling continued as they allowed their eyes to lead them into the next room. This, without a doubt, was the entertainment center. As their eyes investigated the room, it became quite evident that they would not have to leave the White House to be entertained. They all had smiles on their faces as their sight settled upon a smaller rendition of a movie theatre. On a portion of the extended front wall was a movie screen that measured approximately twelve feet in width by eight feet in height; to the forefront of the entire screen was an open area, and then there were continuous rows of large, plush theatre seats. The closest row to the screen was at floor level, and each row, from that point backward, was elevated until the last row was situated against the rear wall. Every seat gave those in the audience an opportunistic view of the screen. Not far from this area, and close to the entrance, was a categorized movie chart; there were classics, mysteries and dramas, horror, sci-fi and more. This selection could challenge even the most celebrated of collectors; movies from the past, present, new releases, and movies that were presently being run in theaters, nationwide. This last category could be viewed if the guests agreed to critique that particular movie.

A notice appeared below movie chart that explained how to operate the personal movie theatre. After reading these instructions, the Lightcaps continued to be amazed; the entertainment center had an extremely large, flat, plasma type television. This was separate from the theatre screen, and had an elaborate cable hook-up. Every imaginable channel, a VCR hook-up, and both sound systems had theatre and surround sound. Close by the VCR was a large cabinet that housed thousands of DVDs: movies, documentaries, specials, and instructional videos. These were also categorized so that if you wanted to watch a specific movie, all you had to do was to look up its title. The videos were in sequential order so when you found the proper number, there would be the corresponding movie that you could view. Along with the VCR and the 'plasma' television was another smaller screened television that offered games. Also, there was a music center that was surrounded by a circular wall with speakers seemingly built within the walls and ceiling; the sound came from every direction and floor, completely filling the room. Any CD that was played had the impression of being performed live and in concert. This room was definitely entertainment and acoustics to the max!

The family stopped exploring so that they could give themselves plenty of time to prepare for dinner. At six that evening, there was a knock on the door and a distinguished butler asked them to follow him to the dining room, which they enthusiastically did as their day thus far had made them all feel extremely hungry. They were met in the dining room by the President, the First Lady, and their daughter. They all sat at a long, narrow table, and once ready, a prayer was said by the President. He gave thanks for many appropriate things, and gave additional thanks, seeing that John and Kathleen, and their children were here to partake of this bountiful harvest; for this is what it appeared to be, and then some. Waiters served each individual from a tray of assorted appetizers, and at just the right time, the entree was served. Tonight's main course centered upon vegetarian lasagna which, by the way, was superbly prepared. Everyone totally enjoyed this meal along with the assortment of desserts. After the meal, the First Family gave their guests an intimate tour of the White House's various rooms, without dominating the tour with excessive banter. When the tour was complete and pleasantries were exchanged, both families wished the other a good night's rest, and then went to their respective living quarters.

The Lightcaps were thoroughly enjoying their stay; they were very glad that they were away from the monotonous harassment of the media. They graciously accepted what the White House had to offer and the food was exquisitely prepared. Prior to Wednesday, they were told that they, along with The First Family, were flying by helicopter to Martha's Vineyard. While at Martha's Vineyard, the exquisite food continued, along with more much needed rest and relaxation. During their three day stay, they were occasionally permitted to take a stroll on the beach. These were three days full of sun, various types of seashells, driftwood, and a variety of brilliantly colored pebbles. The entire group eventually returned to Washington and spent a few hours reminiscing the past week with The First Family. Part of the discussion centered on how privileged the Lightcaps felt by being rescued, and the safety that they felt here in Washington and Martha's Vineyard. They said that they wouldn't forget the President, First Lady, or Chelsea for their kindness, warmth, and caring. Warmth and intimate words were exchanged, and this pleasant conversation continued for a while. It was then that everyone hugged and said their heartfelt farewells. The Lightcaps boarded the limousine and off they went to their home in Edison. Throughout the past week, their visit received considerable press, though there were no interviews or direct quotes. It was during their stay that Ryan and Grace looked at newspapers form around the world, and the more Grace read, the more she felt sympathy for the plight of the captured Lone Creature.

Chapter 38

THE SMELL THAT WAS emanating from the creature's body was putrid, overpowering, and it permeated the entire hangar. Anyone within the building could easily see that the sterile suits and head coverings were not enough to ward off the horrible stench that emanated from the creature. This was evidenced whenever the scientists excused themselves and hurriedly moved in the direction of the bathroom facilities. While moving in that direction, some stopped to convulse, but most made it without delay to their much wanted destination. Those that didn't were a sight better off not seen! The scientists that didn't get sick empathized with their colleague's plight.

Following an extensive meeting, the professional group made a decision. The creature would again be sedated and then, when totally anesthetized, its scale-like skin and crater-like sores that oozed the deplorable stench would be thoroughly analyzed and evaluated. Soon after coming to a conclusion, the creature was sedated and was transferred to a nearby operating table; there, the doctors assembled and the creature was anesthetized. Now their plan was put into action; the surgeons systematically removed scale samples, filled vials with the slimy ooze, and then placed samples from the lining of the open sores into sterile containers. During this exploratory work, the surgeons found something that was understandable, but something that they did not expect. Within the open sore were parasitic larvae that apparently had been living off this being during the majority of its lifetime. These samples, and those of the larvae, were taken to the lab to be examined. Following the examination, the results were printed out and given to the surgical team. At first, the findings disturbed the team, and were thought to be a mistake; the DNA make-up of the skin, the blood, and the substance within the parasitic larvae closely paralleled that of a human.

The open sores contained impacted dirt from earth; the dirt, when analyzed, showed that it had been within these sores for years. Known bacteria were also discovered, and this led the team to believe that this creature had been on the earth for a whole lot longer than previously thought. Again, there was indecision as to the origin of the creature; had it been abducted as a child by an extraterrestrial? Was it an alien, but yet it possessed a human's internal structure? Or could it be a human being?

The tests results, to this point in time, gave creditability of two possibilities: (1) It may have been abducted as a child by an extraterrestrial, or (2) it may be a human that was born here and somehow had remained since birth to the present. The team strongly leaned toward the first possibility, not so much from the collected evidence, but more so because the creature's so was uniquely horrific. Nothing known to science even came close to its description.

Not knowing the being's age piqued the scientist's interest, but not as much as the evidence that this being, or creature, was human and had evolved into this grotesque thing. If they could somehow determine the age of this being, then just maybe they could somehow uncover the lineage of its existence.

If this creature was born of a *Homo sapien*, then how was this possible? Born indicated that the creature came from a source other than itself, and the test results of its interior and exterior indicated that the creature most likely was born of a human. The scientists kept this observation on 'A Need to Know Basis,' and in time, allowed a purposeful leak to trickle down to the press. With the leak, the headlines read:

Scientists Decide upon #1 Choice:

Creature Abducted as a Child!

The grotesque creature that was first witnessed on the outskirts of Doylestown, Pennsylvania, and since has been captured, is being held by the government for ongoing observation. Subsequently, this creature has had a battery of tests, all resulting in the belief that the creature is of a human origin. Furthermore, this horrific creature is said to have been a normal child, born of human parents at some past time. However, how long ago is not known at this time. How did it evolve into this horrific creature?

Taking into consideration its size and horrific features, the consensus of the scientist's opinions is that this creature was born of a human, abducted, and then raised by some alien life form. Furthermore, it is their belief that this creature spent an undetermined number of our earth years experiencing a different universe, and after evolving to this point, has returned to earth.

Scientists, and members of the surgical team, collaborated on the medical findings that culminated from samples of skin, blood work, x-rays, MRIs and an EKG. After this complete battery of tests, the team came to the conclusion that the creature is an alien when comparing it physically to any other living being upon our earth. There has never been a human being that possessed such horrific features, as does this so-called creature; internally it resembles you or me, but externally it is nonhuman, simply grotesque! DNA=Human Being. Further testing will be done during the next few days and this reporter will bring the public those findings.

189

Additional tests were administered, and rather than having leaks occurring sporadically, a forum was set up where there would be a specified scientist meeting with the members of the media, on a daily basis, to keep them informed of any new findings.

The professional staff got together and decided that they would begin the healing process so that they could, given the correct circumstances, heal the creature's body and make it as healthy as possible. They began by disinfecting the creature's epidermal layer of scales, utilizing sponge baths, and then attacked the laborious process of cleansing and repairing the crater-like, open, and the ever oozing sores. These horrific sores were imbedded into the crevices, where the scales joined one another, practically covering the creature's entire body. Almost every day the creature was sedated, carefully placed upon an oversized litter, wheeled to the oversized operating table, and transferred to it from the litter. Here, the creature was methodically checked and when ready, it was anesthetized and the laborious work began. The scientists, with the assistance of the surgeons, hoped that this work would offer them further insight into the origin and previous life experience of this creature.

The disinfectant sponge baths had little effect at first, but following several applications, the stench began to dissipate. As these crater-like sores were being cleansed, the dirt, which had pitted deeply into the crevices, along with infectious material and larvae, were removed and saved for testing. One by one, the depth of these sores were meticulously cleansed and internally repaired; then, a portion of each crater-like sore was surgically removed. The wound was then closed and sutured with the type of material that decomposed in time, and would eventually disappear. With the removal of the diseased portion of each crater-like sore, the stench lessened and the creature gradually became more tolerable to one's sense of smell.

The work was quite tedious for the surgical team, for they had to open the already festering, inflamed sores and allow the healthy blood to flow freely. As the fresh, nutritious, and healthy blood flowed, it washed through the bacteria, carrying the infectious matter and waste out and away from each sore. This once infected area gradually became cleansed and was at the point where it could be considered healthy. The surgical team then closed one incision after the other, using heavy, yet self-decomposing material, to suture the variety of wounds. It was then that the team removed the unhealthy segment of each encircling crater, cleansed the wound, and sutured the area so that when the healing was complete, evidence of the horrific sores would no longer be evident. When the disinfectant sponge baths were finished and all of the wounds were fully attended to, the creature was transferred back to its cell-like setting.

Once the creature was secure within the cell-like enclosure, the professional teams departed the sterile enclosure, undressed and showered, and dressed in their civilian attire. Then, the professionals met in a private office to thoroughly go over this entire day's work. Surgical notes and procedures were communicated, compared, and the progress was evaluated. The initial emphasis was placed upon the enormity of the creature and its distinguishing features. Each surgeon and scientist assisted one another when it came to the extreme musculature of the body, especially in the areas of the neck, shoulders, upper back and chest, and the massive muscle mass of its upper and lower extremities. The creature was in a class all its own, as far as musculature, but then came its weaponry; its upper and lower appendages each had a set of five talon-like curvatures extending for approximately seven to eight inches. Each talon was composed of a hardened substance and these appeared to be unbreakable. When sponging them, it was found that each was razor sharp, and at the tip of each was a needle type point. Protruding from the left and right side of the creature's head was a very thick claw; it extended approximately eighteen inches and gradually narrowed as it protruded further and further from the side of the head towards the front center. At the furthest point from its head, the claw extended in a circular type motion, stopping within an inch of touching each other. It was evident that this creature did not find as much use for the set of head claws as it did for its talons; for the claws were dulled in comparison. On the first day of captivity, its weight and height were taken and the stats came in at ninety-four inches in height and seven hundred and ninety-four pounds in weight. The creature was huge…beyond huge, and deadly, especially when comparing it to the likes of 'Bigfoot' or any other powerful being.

Chapter 39

UPON AWAKENING, THE CREATURE realized that he was famished, and subsequently picked up the scent of an enlarged slab of raw beef lying in the corner of its cell. The beef was oozing blood and unbeknownst to the creature, had been injected with antibiotics and an abundance of vitamins. Off to one side of this forty pound slab was a container of fresh blood, also fortified with nutrients. The creature stealthily moved and soon hovered over the raw meat and without the slightest bit of hesitation or inhibition, it ripped into the pure meat while securing it within its upper sets of talons. It was quite scary to watch this creature devouring this enormous slab of meat. It also captivated one's attention when observing the creature gulping the blood. It practically buried its head into the depth of the vat-like container and brought out a large volume of blood with its thickened, curled tongue. While curling its massive tongue, the creature ladled a great volume of blood into its mouth; whatever it didn't swallow flowed from its mouth and saturated the hairy area below its lower jaw. After inhaling and swallowing this volume of blood, its tongue came into play as it attempted to catch whatever blood that was falling toward the surface below. After eating and drinking its fill, the creature, as in the past, lay in a fetal position and fell into a deep, yet disturbed sleep.

To watch this creature devour the large slab of meat, and

drink fully of the blood, well this made the scientists and surgeons wonder how a human being could acclimate themselves to this type of diet. They wondered whether this would be by choice, or could this diet have been forced upon the creature. There have been stories about humans thriving upon the drinking of animal blood. In the slaughterhouses around the country, it is believed that the men who do the actual slaughtering thrive upon the consumption of the warm blood of these freshly killed animals. Then, there are the legendary stories of humans that take the form of vampires, and drink the blood of animals and humans alike. When given adequate thought, the deduction was that this diet could become essential when there is no other food source available. To think that a human that has always had the luxury to live upon the earth's surface and to consume its endless supply of foods chose the creature's diet was difficult to stomach.

Imagine yourself in the Lone Creature's situation: In galaxy light years from Earth and not knowing how to return to this planet, do you opt to die? Or, by chance, you find yourself born somewhere within the earth's surface, having no opportunity of escape; do you look toward your only recourse with a plan? You recognize that the room you are in is void of light, quite large, and that your food and water supply is limited and dwindling. You organize those that are without and begin the journey of a lifetime, believing that, for the time being, living beneath the earth's surface, and learning to adapt to the environment, is your only option.

You also recognize, and believe, that any attempt to return to the surface could be met with deadly force. Along the way, you must find a way to return to the surface even though you've recognized that the gravest of dangers awaits this decision. Remember that you are in a pitch black environment and subsequently cannot see your hand directly in front of your face. You constantly search for the path through the maze that you recently encountered, and when facing despair, the path is finally discovered, eventually bringing you to the surface during the night. You realize, in finding the surface, that you now have a place to deposit the soil that is dug to form passageways, but that this work has to be done under the camouflage of darkness; when humans sleep and pay little attention to the night. The major fear is the realization that the Lone creature's inability to see clearly may, over a long period, become a permanent thing rather than temporary. It is realized that, if the earth's surface is found, that this is the time when possible blindness could become evident. If this pitch black environment eventually causes blindness, then the experience beneath the earth, could, indeed, become life threatening. If totally blind, how could a creature realize that it was on the verge of entering the earth's surface; and if it somehow found the surface, what resource would they have to remain safe from the detection of the human?

The fear that they became blind overwhelmed the entire colony, and this fear created so much stress that several of the creatures lost their consciousness. The elders displayed why they were given this title; somehow they calmed the entire population and convinced all that the inability to see was, at this time, temporary, but if the surface was not found, then two things were inevitable. First and foremost, if the surface was not found, then the interior of the earth could not be excavated, for there would be no place to take the excavated dirt; and if this was the case, then their eventual demise was a guarantee. Second, the longer they stayed in this pitch black environment, the stronger the possibility would be that it would perpetuate their blindness. To survive, it was absolutely necessary to keep searching and to find the earth's surface. To calm the colony's stress level, the elders promised all that the earth's surface would be found, and found sooner rather than later.

Chapter 40

ON THE FRONT PAGE of a national newspaper there was a different kind of story, but it was directly related to the Lone Creature.

Creature? Alien? Human?

Much has been written relating to this creature that possibly had its origin as a human being and may have been abducted as a child by an extraterrestrial. This may be true and we, as members of the human race, have a right to know the results of the government's testing. It has become public knowledge that this creature, internally, at least, has the same skeletal form and organs that humans have, and that prior to its discovery, it dwelled in a crudely built habitat that was constructed a week before its capture.

Where was this creature prior to a week ago? Is it violent? Has anything been reported showing it to possess an aggressive nature? The answer to these questions is no. If you, the reader, give the creature some of your undivided thought, you will recognize that the creature was first seen by a schoolgirl while waiting at a school bus stop very early one recent morning. According to a previously reported story, this child said that she noticed the creature from a distance, and that it gradually moved closer to where she was standing. She went on to say that this being eventually stopped, stood motionless, and then disappeared from her sight. This reporter actually saw the creature when it was captured outside of its wooded location; it is truly immense, and its appearance gives one the impression of being ferocious. I contend that it ran away because its nature is nonviolent. Since its subsequent capture, the creature has not shown an aggressive trait and therefore I submit to you, the American people, that when the testing and surgeries are completed, that we, the people, petition our government to place the creature within a protective setting; a setting that will show our concern and compassion!

The battery of testing continued and the public forums were held twice each day. It was announced that the scale-like epidermis had been disinfected, and that surgery had removed much of its crater-like, infected sores. The announcement went on to say that these sores had been surgically removed and that the skin, at the base of the sores, had been surgically repaired; vastly improving the appearance and health status of the creature. It was stated that further testing had to be performed because the soil that was found pitted into the side walls of these infected craters did not have the same composition as that found in its crudely built habitat. More importantly, the pitted soil had its origin from our planet Earth, so where was this creature prior to being captured, and for how long?

Evidenced by the composition of the pitted soil, the tests revealed that particles of this soil had been imbedded within the interior walls of the cavernous sores for many, many years. This was real evidence that the creature had lived amongst us, on, or within the earth, for years; very possibly somewhere in Bucks

County. If this is indeed a fact, then where had it lived, why is there no record of it and what did this being eat to sustain its life?

The creature's eyes were examined by a variety of specialists from the world renowned Wills Eye Hospital, and the results were made public, "A surgical team of eye-specialists thoroughly examined the creature's eyes and the surrounding tissue. Initially, but yet tediously, the lids of both eyes had the imbedded crust removed, giving them freedom to move, and while the lids were held open, the right eye was examined. The result of this extensive testing was that this eye had experienced an intolerable amount of trauma and offered little opportunity for sight, and further evidence supported that finding. It was very possible that the creature had lost the majority of its sight, in this specific eye, due to its living conditions; it just may have spent its lifetime within a dark, cave-like environment, and if it ventured out of the cave, it did so under the cover of darkness. However, the testing of the left eye showed that it may be salvageable. After an extensive examination, the left eye was somewhat healthy and had partial sight; while additional eyesight may be recovered, we, as a group, believe that only a slight improvement will be the result. The surgery will be performed tomorrow, and the public will be given the results as soon as we know anything definite."

Fortunately for the surgical team and for the creature, a well-respected surgeon formally on the Wills Eye Hospital staff had recently returned from his homeland in Chile. This doctor had relocated his practice to Chile some fifteen years ago and now had returned to the Philadelphia area on a sabbatical. Being a specialist in the field of corneal surgery, when approached, he enthusiastically agreed to join the team.

While the specialists prepared for surgery, the lab technicians worked feverishly to delve into the soil that was removed from the interior walls of the crater-like sores. Following hours of tedious work, the results confused all that read them. The tests were redone and the results were the same; the soil particles were of this earth and were from various levels, far below the surface. It was confirmed that these soil particles had gotten into the open sores somewhere other than the earth's surface; to further stymie and mystify the scientists, the results gave undeniable proof that these soil particles had their origin some seventy-five to one hundred feet beneath the surface. It was also determined that none of these imbedded particles had their origin from the surface. Furthermore, the crudely constructed cave-like structure, where the creature was first found, was indeed a recent and temporary dwelling. Now, the educated personnel really felt motivated, though anxious for more answers. "Where did this creature come from and is it alone?"

After two weeks of testing and qualifying the results of each test, and the related surgeries, the creature was considered to be a product of our planet Earth, and not a creature that obtained its appearance while living within a culture of another universe. "There is no evidence that supports the alien theory! This creature, or being, is what many feared. It is human! But, how could this be possible?"

Chapter 41

AN EXCAVATION COMPANY FROM nearby was contracted to come to a site where housing developers were already in the process of preparing the land for their own construction. The excavation company had the specified task to create a large opening in the earth, and then to go straight down, through the earth's layers, for approximately one-hundred feet. This excavation company that had its heavy equipment yard in Chalfont, Pennsylvania, gathered all the machinery that was necessary, and transported it close to the site. The team was given their responsibilities by the coordinator, and the designated excavation began. When the opening reached a depth of ten feet, a soil sample was retrieved and labeled accordingly. This process continued in increments of ten feet until the depth of one-hundred feet was realized. Once the hole was one-hundred feet, the team was given the hand signal to shut it down. The team did as was instructed and then waited in the immediate area while soil samples were collected from a variety of levels. Every sample was taken and properly labeled, and then the excavation team was signaled to wrap it up, that is, to refill the hole completely.

At the lab, the soil samples were laid out according to their specific depths, and then the soil obtained from the creature's crater-like, infected enclosures of the then oozing sores was compared with the soil from each depth. While these professionals were hoping to get a match, they were quite satisfied when they hit pay dirt! The soil that was pitted and infectious, and was subsequently removed during the surgery, had come from various levels, but the majority of the infectious soil came from a depth of more than fifty feet. Now that this finding gave valuable evidence that the creature spent the majority of its lifetime fifty feet, or more, below the surface, the question that was paramount in the professional's minds was, "How did something this size maneuver to such a depth? Furthermore, since it evidently did, why did it? How?"

Although there was physical evidence that the creature was the only being that had inhabited the crude, cave-like structure, the discovery lent creditability to the possibility that there was more than one of these creatures somewhere within the confines of the earth. The reason for this deduction is the fact that it would take many creatures, given this individual's evident strength, to dig and carry the weight of the soil to a dumping site (Remember that the earth was solid and supposedly had no vacant areas within). This finding led the professionals to believe that there had to be a population of these creatures somewhere within the earth; possibly at a depth of fifty feet or more, and possibly in the immediate vicinity of where this lone creature was captured. This information was given to the press in bits and pieces, but it was only enough to whet the appetite of Bucks County's residents, and of the interested people from around the world.

Rancher's that had large herds of cattle and other livestock such as sheep, hogs, and pigs, including those who raised chickens and similar sized animals, were now clearly heard whenever or wherever a community meeting was held. As evidence mounted, it supported the belief that there was more than one creature; ranchers and others from all over Bucks County now sought a government subsidy for the livestock that had disappeared over a period of several years without the slightest trace. History supported the fact that livestock had mysteriously disappeared for as long as anyone could remember. The most popular locations for those discussions were after church services, at a diner, a restaurant, or when families visited with one another. What was considered during past decades as an unaccountable loss, now had meaning among these hard working ranchers and farmers. It was now a distinct possibility that there was more than one creature, and possibly many, roaming the countryside of Bucks County. These creatures may have killed and eaten all of the missing livestock, perhaps utilizing these animals as the main source of their sustenance.

These businessmen can remember targeting a variety of minority groups for the continual loss of livestock, but nothing ever was found to be factual. They can look back at a variety of those situations, and be thankful that they did not go off half-cocked and harm those under suspicion. To this point in time, nothing has been officially blamed on this creature, or creatures, but there is a very strong possibility that the creature was the culprit. If indeed it can be proven that there is more than one, and possibly many of these horrendous, horrific looking creatures, it could become a reality that they are responsible for the loss of all livestock. The question lingered as to where these creatures had originated, and if they were, in fact, of this earth. Why weren't they seen from time to time, prior to the capture of this Lone Creature?

Chapter 42

A TEAM OF EYE surgeons from the nationally known Wills Eye Hospital gathered the following morning and shared their game plan. The plan was to operate first upon the left eye to give it as much sight as possible. They knew that this eye was severely depleted, but believed, for whatever the reason, that it would regain some amount of sight. The surgery was extensive, and when completed, the surgeons were pleased with the results. It was determined that this creature had lost all but a small amount of its sight and that this was due to its complete lack of use. The muscles associated with the eye had little discernible strength. This discovery piqued their interests. One of the specialists concluded that this meaningful lack of musculature indicated that this creature had spent its entire lifetime in complete darkness. Assuming this to be factual, the surgeons surmised that the cotton eye patches would have little or no effect upon the creature.

Upon awakening, the creature did as was hoped. It paid little attention to the bandaging. The Lone Creature had no further surgeries while it recuperated from the eye surgery. Therefore, it wasn't taken from its enclosure for several days. When it finally was, it was sedated and eventually anesthetized before evaluating the results of the surgery. Once moved from its cage and placed upon the oversized litter, the creature's huge head was immobilized. At this time, the wrapping was unrolled; eventually the adhesive tape and the enlarged cushion-like gauze pads were all removed. Now all that remained were the soft, cotton eye covers. These covers were slowly removed, and although the creature was under a heavy sedation, it appeared to react to the florescent lighting. The lighting was dimmed and the tediousness of the work continued. The surgeons were extremely pleased with the results, and so they cleaned the residue beneath the covers and the creature was then returned to its enclosure. Now, they simply had to wait and see.

It was now time to bring the members of the media up to date, and so an official press conference was held. Unexpectedly, there were media personnel from states other than Pennsylvania, and even a few representing foreign countries. There was standing room only as a scientist stepped to the podium; he introduced himself and then proceeded. "Two weeks have now passed since the Lone Creature was discovered and captured in the nearby countryside of Bucks County, Pennsylvania. After experiencing a battery of tests, and some sensitive surgeries, the creature has been found to be a product of Earth. Furthermore, it has never been to another universe. In fact, there is undeniable proof that this creature lived its entire life, until recently, within the darkened depths of our earth."

"When captured it had severe injuries to its external and internal structure, and internal bleeding supported this finding. There is speculation that this creature recently ventured upon the earth's surface, and while roaming the countryside, lost its way. While searching for its underground habitat, it was seen by a child who imagined this creature to be the legendary Bigfoot."

"At that time, the creature disappeared, but was discovered days later in a makeshift, crudely constructed, cave-like enclosure. A thorough investigation of this cave-like enclosure revealed that it had been recently constructed. Therefore, it is believed that this creature's main habitat could be somewhere within the vicinity of Bucks County. It is not known, at least at this specific time, if this creature is alone, but it is surmised that it has lived within the earth for many years. This being the case, it has also been speculated that this creature may just be one of a colony. Following its capture, the creature's wounds have been repaired, and are healing nicely at an undisclosed location. At present, it remains at that site, undergoing further testing, and there is an extensive search to discover the colony's underground dwelling."

Chapter 43

USING A PUBLIC WEBSITE, http://www.govtcreature.com, a Bucks County historian e-mailed the site, promising information that may just be the answer to many of the creature's unsolved questions. The historian, a Ms. Ann Laughlin, took the time to contact the website.

Eventually, an e-mail was sent to Ms. Laughlin and a meeting time was set. Prior to leaving her home, Ann wished love to her first adopted child, Marie, as Ann secured her into the transportation seat of the specialized vehicle that was to take Marie to The Overbrook School for the Blind. Christopher, her adopted son, anxiously awaited by Ann's side until his school bus arrived. As he boarded the bus, both he and Ann exchanged heartfelt goodbyes and then the bus departed. Kenny, Ann's foster child, was temporarily away from home due to a problem that affects the entire family. If Kenny gets his long awaited therapy, then the family could be reunited. Ann saw Marie and Christopher off to school, and then prepared herself for the thirty-minute drive to the prearranged meeting place. She was forced to rent a compact car because her extended-van that she primarily uses for book fairs and for around town transportation was being repaired for the umpteenth time.

When ready to leave her house, Ann got into her shiny rental, and then drove through Valley Forge National Park, eventually arriving at the rendezvous point that was only known to her, government personnel, and a number of others. Once inside the meeting room of the restaurant, introductions and pleasantries were exchanged; soon after, a nice breakfast was served.

When these formalities ended, the tables were cleared, leaving the hot coffee and various pastries. A podium was wheeled into the immediate vicinity and the microphone was checked for its proper working order. The podium sat off to one side of an enlarged movie screen and an adjoining over-head prompter. This meeting was brought to order and Ms. Laughlin was introduced as an official Bucks County Historian who may direct the government officials to the actual site where the leper colony was disposed of, some one-hundred and twenty years ago.

Ms. Laughlin gave an in-depth history of the leper colony and how the then political structure of that community had taken it upon themselves to annihilate the grotesqueness of these human beings. "Approximately one-hundred and twenty years ago, a large leper colony lived within the town of Edison, Bucks County. At that time, these humans were seen as oddities because of their grotesque appearance; their leathery type skin encased a multitude of tumor-like growths. These growths were apparent to an observer for they were bulbous and pushed forcefully against the leper's epidermal layer, causing enlarged lumps to dominate the surface. To watch closely was to evidence these lumps in a slow, perpetual motion; pulsating, as if each tumor had its own individual heart."

"These lumps encompassed the leper's skin, even within their neck, face and scalp. At first, the majority of the Edison's community, who were not afflicted with the disease, quarantined the lepers to a particular location quite distant from those within the community proper. Subsequently, the community's leaders were forced to come up with an alternative plan, for these lepers became more and more grotesque, and their pain filled moans could be clearly heard throughout the day and well into the night. It was as if these lepers never slept. In time, a pungent, putrid odor that had been restricted to the leper colony became evident along Edison's boundaries."

"The farmers, ranchers, and homeowners of the community

began to verbalize their fear that the presence of the colony could greatly diminish their property values, and worse yet, the disease would eventually spread to them or to their eventual offspring. The community found these lepers to be a slight and a threat against the health and welfare of every healthy individual that lived in the immediate vicinity. Although it was inconceivable by the minority, a plan was instituted to rid the area of these grotesque beings. After many lengthy discussions, the group reached a unanimous decision. Not far from Edison, the community, as one, prepared a site for the creatures to live, but more importantly, to expire."

"Tunneling on a twenty-five degree angle, a passageway was dug far into the earth, and a maze-like construction was then completed, spilling into an additional passageway, and eventually into a large, connecting room. Kerosene lanterns were placed along the route from the surface of the earth through the intricate maze, and then were placed upon the surface of a second passageway that eventually led to a spacious room below."

Ms. Laughlin paused, gently cleared her throat, took a sip of water, and then continued. "The Historical records of Bucks County indicate that it was found to be necessary, in order to keep the entire leper colony within their underground burial chamber, to construct an intricate maze of lengthy and shortened passageways. The maze had many entrances and dead ends, and upon its completion, it led to an additional, ever descending passageway. This descending passageway would, in turn, empty into the spacious room. It was the assumption of those not afflicted that when the entire leper colony were led, en masse, through the intricacy of the formidable maze, and brought to the large room, it would be virtually impossible for them to find their return route to the surface."

"Realizing that the leprosy had limited the lepers sight, and the fact that the passageways, maze, and room below were in an environment void of light, it was believed that the lepers would become bewildered, oppressed, depressed, and die off in due time. Although it is believed that ranking members of the Edison, Doylestown community organized this planned exodus by drugging the leper's water supply, there is no historical mention of the specific community members who are responsible for the organization and completion of this deplorable act. The records merely state that these lepers were heavily drugged and led into the depths of the earth. They were given a two-week supply of food and water, and then were left there to fend for themselves. Although it was conceivable that these lepers were led to this room to die, and to rid the community of the colony, there is no further entry as to what actually happened. There is no evidence that the entire leper colony died off; this is as true as there is no evidence, whatsoever, that the lepers ever found their way to the earth's surface. They were never seen again, so it was the community's assumption that the entire colony had succumbed."

"Within the records is a description of the area where the entrance was dug, but that area's landscape, no doubt, has changed considerably. At this time, it was wrongfully written, and subsequently recorded, that the health of the immediate community, and its outlying areas were in jeopardy of a plague. Somehow, this condition was wrongly categorized as being highly infectious and an epidemic disease of high mortality, causing severe pain and eventual death." All in attendance listened intently, and seemed stunned when they heard that these lepers were wrongfully labeled, subsequently drugged, and then placed deep within the earth's surface as a means of ridding the communities of Doylestown and Edison of a health hazard. A hand was raised within the audience and Ms. Laughlin signaled for that person to identify himself. The individual, an elderly man in the back of the room, got right to the point, "Can it be assumed that this leper colony, prior to being led to the depths of the earth, were, at one time, members of the Edison Community?" Several people in attendance saw this question as being redundant and frustration was sensed. Then, this elderly man finished his question with a blockbuster. "Is it possible that the leper's fate was chosen by not only members of their own community, but by blood relatives?" This was the first time that the inevitable came to light. Until this point in time, no one had ever taken responsibility for a blood connection to the lepers or their plight.

There were two distinct cultures that were evident within Edison;

those that were not, and those that were afflicted with leprosy. Ms. Laughlin, addressing this belief, said that this was an interesting observation and she would delve into its possibilities. She finished up by saying that such a form of planned extermination is equaled in this present age to when toxic waste is dumped and buried deep within the earth and seas, eventually entering our water supply and contaminating the planet, much like what occurred in Ecuador due to Chevron's corporate delinquency. As Ms. Laughlin reclaimed her chair, all applauded, showing their support and appreciation.

It was now that a landscape expert was introduced, and this person used the overhead prompter to show surface and aerial views in the Bucks County landscape, past and present. He gave a short overview of his credentials and then showed realistic close-ups that portrayed the landscapes of Doylestown and Edison. A member of the audience voiced a keen interest because he too had done extensive studies relating to the land formations dating back to the time in question, one-hundred and twenty years ago. Members of the audience were entranced as they witnessed their community's on-going changes during the one- hundred and twenty year period. Ms. Laughlin recognized this man for his valuable input and observations, and a considerable amount of discussion ensued. Due to the length of time that was being considered, Ms. Laughlin said that she could only speculate on the possible locations for the leper habitat. At this time, a voice in the room interrupted. "Please excuse this interruption, my intention is to offer valuable insight that will shed light upon the investigation. I believe that I can pinpoint the exact area where these lepers were taken to, in effect, to die off. My name is Joseph Leone, and my family history dates back beyond the time when these human beings were placed within the earth. Two of my ancestors were part of the leper colony, were treated as outcasts, and were removed from the earth; they were, in fact, denied their human rights and were murdered!"

This word murdered caught the undivided attention of all people present. Following a short pause, Mr. Leone continued, "I will never be able to forgive those that made the decision to, in fact, exterminate the leper colony, and subsequently, my relatives." Again, the audience could be heard, only this time they appeared to be aghast at what they were hearing. A pause, and then Mr. Leone went on, "This land mass has been surveyed several times during the last one-hundred and twenty plus years, and if you'll indulge me, please display the land masses in and around Edison one additional time." This request was begrudgingly shown, decade by decade. When brought up to the present, one of the so-called experts said, *displaying considerable frustration*, "The landscape remains the same. What is your point"?

Mr. Leone disregarded the question and continued, "My point is that the land mass is not the same; it has shown considerable change when comparing the earlier decades with that of the very recent past and present." Mr. Leone was now using a laser pointer to aggressively display a specific area on the visual screen, and simultaneously asked if that area had been surveyed within the last few days? "I ask because it is of paramount importance." A voice from the rear of the room said: "I have no idea where you are headed, but as you requested, we will indulge you, please get to the point!" It was at this time that another person rose from his chair, and was recognized by Mr. Leone. John Parker acknowledged that he had his own company and that just a few days ago, he and a co-worker surveyed the area in question. He also stated that the most recent land mass in question was the same that he had been specifically requisitioned to survey. Mr. Leone collected his self, and then continued, "Thank you Mr. Parker, please take notice of the land mass in the earlier decades, and then with this most recent one." All were of the same area, and a few in the audience remained stymied, but the majority was now ooohhhing and ahhhhhing! There was a significant change! "Just prior to the time when the leper colony was exiled to live, and subsequently die within the earth, the majority of the land mass was documented to be flat, except for a few large, rocky hills. Other than the rocky hills, there was an abundance of trees and shrubs, and a variety of bushes; this land mass was inclined to be flat. The next documentation, of this same area, depicts small mountains where there were none previously." To further the evidence of change, Mr. Leone pointed out, "Since the time that this so-called creature was found to be living in its crude cave-like home, which was a little more than two weeks ago, do you all remember the report that it vocalized a loud, far reaching soulful sound? Well, just after that cry was heard, the land mass significantly changed again. It is my contention that the leper colony somehow survived their intended demise, and during the last one-hundred and twenty years, they miraculously adapted, evolving into these hideous creatures. In reality, this creature that is being held in captivity, and is being extensively studied, is not alone! And by nature, it is human! I realize that this is somewhat implausible, but it does put considerable light on the recent occurrences."

Everyone said that they were enthused by this summation, and Mr. Leone was applauded for his informative insights. The meeting was adjourned and soon afterward, only the leaders reconvened to discuss the relevancy of Mr. Leone's findings and their potential strategy. **L**and **M**ass **T**echnicians were immediately brought in, and again, the change in the surface appearance was brought to light. The **LMT**s agreed with Mr. Leone's finding; they observed a variety of maps, and eventually settled upon one. Certain coordinates were written down; they were where the surface had the more dramatic change. It was evident that such significant change could not have occurred through nature alone, especially in such a relatively short period of time, the period of one-hundred and twenty years. It was also evident that nature had had extensive help, most probably in the form of Intelligent and physical intervention. Confusion reigned, once again, throughout the meeting. There had been an evident comfort level, but now there was an air of intense anxiety. The targeted land mass could be populated with an additional number of these creatures, and if this were indeed factual, then that area had to be secured, preferably without anyone being injured or killed.

Someone within the meeting room got recognized and offered what many in the room considered to be an obvious blockbuster. This scientist addressed, and therefore captivated, his audience. His summation was spellbinding for he revealed there to be a high degree of probability that the captive creature was actually an evolving leper, human. And that the previous one-hundred and twenty years could have given life to hundreds, if not thousands of these creatures, somehow thriving within the earth's abyss. Eventually, all agreed that the colony could be vast, and because of this possibility, their previous anxious demeanor changed to one of major concern. The meeting was brought to an end, and each contributor within the audience was personally thanked. The audience departed in an orderly fashion, and once those people were out of the building, the scientists and military specialists remained behind. These people convened their own meeting and the topic was the capture and relocation of this potential, but probable, colony. A considerable amount of time elapsed. In the end, much had been accomplished. It became understood that once the suspected land mass was considered factual, their plan would be put into action, orchestrated in order to capture the entire creature population.

The most difficult variables associated with this capture were considered. It is unknown how many creatures would be encountered but, it was conceivable that the captured creature was only one of many offspring that have evolved from the original colony. How extensive is this colony's habitat? Are all of these creatures limited when it comes to sight? Since there is a high degree of probability that the entire habitat is beneath the earth's surface, and that it has an environment void of light, what will a surveillance team encounter? Is the area dangerous? Do these creatures have weapons? All of these issues were delved into extensively and when the meeting ended, all were in agreement that they had a workable plan. Numerous members of the military's special forces were flown into this area and then were introduced to the creature that was being held within the airplane hangar. Having heard and read so much regarding this creature, and not knowing how much was accurate, the team became overwhelmed when directly introduced to the creature's formidable size and obvious strength.

These highly trained team members were obviously taken aback as they surveyed, and imagined what they might be up against when encountering the creatures in their underground habitat. The special forces team was highly trained and experienced personnel, all having a minimum of ten years in the field, but none had ever experienced anything of this magnitude. These individuals were finely tuned fighting machines, both mentally and physically, but now realized that no previous training had prepared them for this type of encounter. After witnessing the creature, they worked on a formalized strategy and eventually were primed to execute that plan.

LMTs diligently surveyed the map coordinates, and using helicopters installed with **T**hermal **I**maging **E**quipment, found electrical signals indicating that life forms were at various depths within a specific area. The signals were weak, which indicated that the battery-operated mechanism had a weakened energy source, or that these life forms were beyond a depth that enabled them to be clearly identified. The coordinates were notated and then the flight navigator landed the chopper. The LMTS departed the helicopter and assembled with the special forces team so that a final, formalized plan could be construed, and the immediate vicinity could be completely reconnoitered. The surveillance team's responsibility was to search the perimeter of the coordinates and once the entrance to the underground dwelling was discovered, it was then that the surveillance team would prepare to enter the underground habitat.

Each team member wore a specialized type of lightweight ceramic-composite body armor designed by a company that has established itself as an international leader in innovative safety systems for occupant protection in military and commercial aerospace and defense markets. Founded in 1975, the company introduced the first military crashworthy crew seat for the modern day helicopter. Since that time, the Applied Technologies Division has continued to differentiate itself by introducing cutting-edge technologies in energy-absorbing seating, personnel and vehicle armor, and inflatable restraint systems. ATD provides its customers with complete product development and manufacturing capabilities for bringing innovative, best-value, lifesaving products into the field.

Each team member also had the use of a product that was not directly linked to the safety conscious company. Unlike the bulky, loose fitting helmets that were common to past wars, each team member wore a new, experimental type of headgear. This was state of the art and it fit one's head similar to that worn by a professional boxer during a sparring session. Therefore, the person wearing this type of headgear was no longer hampered by being forced to hold the experimental headgear while running, as it used to flop upon one's head. It fit comfortably, but yet snugly, it had a lining that included electrical stimuli that could receive and clearly transmit wireless messages, and it had a retractable facemask that was shatter and bulletproof. Along with the state of the art body suit, and the experimental headgear, each team member was outfitted with a minute television monitor which was hardly noticeable, and also had night vision equipment. The television monitor allowed the special forces personnel the opportunity to observe, and to be observed, while their images were continually transferred to personnel manning a centralized monitoring system within a control site. The night vision equipment afforded the team the opportunity to enter the habitat, thoroughly investigate the creature population, and hopefully leave without being detected. The team was led to the designated entrance by the LMTs, but the entrance was found to be blocked.

The **Land Mass Technicians** used their specialized gear, which included the **Thermal Imaging Equipment**, and after an extensive search, found that the blockage extended approximately twenty feet. Beyond twenty feet, the blockage ended, revealing an extended passageway, but there was no sign of life in that specified area. Also found was a passageway that appeared to be unrelated to the first one, and this extended away from the recent blockage, heading in a totally different direction.

An excavation team was brought in and was given all relevant information. The blockage was cleared and a passageway was then established. With the blockage removed, it revealed that the walls and ceiling of the descending passageway had been fortified with planks of wood, and six by six inch structural supports. This was seen as strange, and thus the work was temporarily halted. A specialized team was brought in to observe the construction and to investigate its relevance. As each plank and its supporting timber were removed, new creosoted timber was used to replace it.

At this time, the helicopter was once again activated. The team's mission: to survey the surrounding area of the passageway's entrance. The **T**hermal **I**maging **E**quipment indicated that the blockage was only a matter of yards in diameter and that below, beyond, and surrounding the blockage, there was an extensive passageway configuration. These passageways continually descended, and horizontally snaked throughout a variety of depths. At the far end, and well below the blockage, there was a passageway, and this appeared to end abruptly, revealing the presence of skeletal forms. The sensitive equipment indicated that at a time long since gone, there were life forms resembling that of a human being; and that these skeletal remains were all within the same limited area.

The pilot hovered over this area, giving personnel time to document the specific location. Then, the helicopter tilted to one side and flew off in another direction. There was a loud vibrating sound as the chopper sped off, but as it leveled, a ticking sound became quite evident, similar to that of a Geiger counter. Eventually, the agitated sound reached its peak, and this location was duly noted. The helicopter returned to its landing site and the newly acquired coordinates were communicated. It was believed that this agitated sound indicated that life had been present in this location in the distant past. The agitation was similar in volume to the sound that emanated from the other side of the blockage. Believing that there were no creatures present in this specific area, a team of scientists were brought in to investigate the variety of information.

The **T**hermal **I**maging **E**quipment was activated, but as the chopper hovered, there was no evidence of a live presence. The team of scientists, after reviewing all relevant information, entered a passageway that was just to the forefront of the blockage. While it was true that it was just to the front of the blockage, the scientists had to descend the lengthy passageway to arrive at their destination. Carrying large lamps which thoroughly lit their way, the scientists found that there were two distinct tunnels entering the earth at similar locations, and therefore it was surmised that there was a connection between the two. These scientists carried a smaller version of the **T**hermal **I**maging **E**quipment and began their trek.

In the initial tunnel, the **TIE** signaled a slight evidence of human presence. Although there had not been evidence of a human presence in this area for more than a century, the **T**hermal **I**maging **E**quipment was able to pick up what was thought to be the actual remains of a human. The team followed the path of the presence and they were led through a maze of shortened, intricate passageways. The team tried a variety of other passageways, but was somewhat dismayed, or thwarted, by eventual blockages. They returned to the maze entrance the **TIE** was activated to the highest position. The **TIE** led the team through the maze's intricacy, and as a precaution, items were laid along their pathway so they could avoid frustration upon their eventual return.

The team got through the maze and found that their trek descended as it went further and further into the bowels of the earth. What they found to be interesting were the indentations that appeared deeply inset within the lengthy passageway; one deeply indented, identical continuous track on each side, three to four feet apart. Another thing that caught their interest was that once the team reached the maze, it took on the appearance of a mining shaft. Sturdy, upright, six by six inch supports held the wooden planked walls and ceiling in place, and this type of construction continued as the team exited the maze and descended deeper within the earth. Not knowing what to expect, as they proceeded further into these bowels, the team was surprised to find a spacious room at the extreme end of the passageway. This room reminded them of a tomb; a tomb, within the Egyptian pyramids came to mind. Within this room were several rusted pieces of metal and a few fully assembled human skeletons. Due to the erosion of the room's ceiling and walls, it was at first difficult to see the skeletons, for the only remains that were initially visible were pieces of bone. These bones extended towards the ceiling, and got their height from a lengthy bone extending upwards, as if an arm was being raised for recognition after death. The team cautiously unearthed the bones and eventually found skeletons that lay within the room's earthen floor. They dug deeply, searching for additional bones and artifacts, and found additional bones and a number of skulls, along with pieces of metal. In time, the team members agreed that there were no more artifacts. It was then that all of these remnants were gathered, labeled, and securely placed within storage bins. The team, carrying several of these bins, returned to the earth's surface and their findings were analyzed. One of these scientists made a mind boggling and significant find! Initially, however, the caked dirt attached to the skeletons was gently and thoroughly removed from the bones.

One of the scientists, Dr. Eric Cordes, took a different approach; unlike the approach of the others, he found an interest in the caked dirt. If it were not for this interest, then the origin of these dead souls might have never been unearthed. Due to his approach, bacteria were found to be living within the dirt particles, directly attached to and penetrating the skeletal remains. Dr. Cordes found that bacteria were using the composition of the bones as a parasitic host. He dutifully shared the significance of his find, scraped the bacteria into a Petri dish, and then put a sample from the container under the high powered lens of a microscope. As Dr. Cordes examined bacteria, an excited gasp immediately escaped his lips. He swiftly gained control of his excitement, and without telling the others of this specific find, he asked them, one by one, to view the specimen. When all had done so, it was concluded that there was more than one bacteria present, and that the dominant bacteria was that of leprosy. Many of these scientists could be seen rubbing their scalp, or with their cupped hand covering their mouths, displaying a body language of one being in deep thought. What Dr. Cordes had discovered, and that the other scientists had witnessed, was the fact that leprosy dominated; this disturbed them deeply and profoundly. Was it possible that these skeletons were now revealing their own personal travesty, and if so, who was responsible for their demise? Was the elongated, elevated bone, actually a forearm, and the slender extensions, actually fingers, that extended towards the heavens, a plea for recognition? For justice? Is it possible that these unfortunate souls came in contact with one, or more, of these horrific creatures, while trekking within the bowels of the earth, and that this is how they met their end? Or was it a possibility, as grotesque as it could be, that these leprous skeletons were actually a part of a colony that were exiled, and subsequently driven from their earth community into these deep recesses?

The team knew that these options were a stretch of the imagination, but the creature's existence was also a stretch until it was witnessed, and subsequently captured. For whatever the reason, the team surmised that the community of Edison would not have gone to so much trouble, nor would they have worked as hard as they obviously did, to remove these few lepers from their community. The team further deduced that there had to be more lepers here within the earth, but since they were not with these skeletal remains, could it be that they adapted to their life crisis? Could they, over time, have somehow evolved into creatures similar to the one that was in captivity? These scientists, and those present at the renovated hangar, eventually put their minds together, and only after looking at all of the facts did they finally come to a conclusion. It took a while to decipher everything that was relevant, but in the end, it was universally agreed upon that these skeletons met their deaths through natural causes, that is, they were not murdered. The thorough and painstaking effort revealed that none of the bones or skulls had evidence of foul play. They had died because they could not cope with the changes that were deemed necessary for survival. There was further evidence that these lepers had died in close proximity to one another, perhaps because they could not adapt to their circumstance, and environment. It was apparent that the lepers that had the fortitude to adapt did so, and gradually, over a period of decades, had somehow evolved into horrendous creatures, such as the one that was presently being held captive at the hangar.

Chapter 44

THE SPECIAL FORCES PERSONNEL, moving in a direction away from the passageway that led into the maze, found themselves descending an entirely different passageway. These men cautiously moved forward until one, who was slightly to the forefront of the others, found himself performing a balancing act, teetering on the edge of an opening. Fortunately for this man, he was grabbed by another team member, and pulled back to safety. Eventually, the team refocused and moved cautiously forward, until they were once again at the brink of the drop- off. Upon further investigation, it was discovered that there was a solid wall on the other side of this opening. In fact, the tunnel descended abruptly and unexpectedly. The team, not knowing the actual depth of the chasm, made the proper adjustments, and then repelled approximately fifty feet. At the base of the chasm, they encountered several off-shoot passageways, or catacombs. At this point, the members of the team entered each of these catacombs, and this, in and of itself, put each man in a precarious situation. Alone, and not knowing how far these individual catacombs extended, or if they could encounter a multitude of other off-shoots, they realized that their lifeline was the personnel within the control center.

The control center personnel were continually monitoring the trek of each and every member through video. Recognizing this as one of their lifelines, the team members were now being instructed to increase the volume of their audio equipment. This was an additional lifeline, and one that made each member feel more secure. It was one thing to video one's movement, but the team found it more important to freely talk and listen to each other, and to be able to communicate with these personnel within the control center. This feature was something they thought that they could do without in order to avoid possible detection, but now it became apparent that this option was indeed a necessity.

All of the special forces personnel were eventually in separate catacombs, but none recognized any physical sign of a creature. All reported that they were amazed by the crudeness of the construction. However, suddenly, there came the sound of alarm from a team member. Everyone halted in their tracks and stood perfectly still, listening intently. Then, they were advised by this specific team member to stand perfectly still and to slowly, but diligently, check their ceiling area.

Everyone had abruptly halted and felt that they should prepare themselves for a life form. Several types of exclamations were offered, but none had much volume. Without further ado, the team did as they were advised. Slowly but surely, they brought their lamps up, along with their weapons, until the indirect beam lit the ceiling. Still unnerved by the urgency of the plea, the team members attempted to discover the significance of each and every ceiling. At first glance, the ceiling appeared to be different; maybe a darker brown, or blacker than previous areas. Feeling less secure, but yet purposeful, one of the team gradually brought more direct light upon the ceiling. A strong gasp was heard as he found himself witnessing movement along the denseness of the ceiling. A whisper was clearly heard, with the gist being that the ceiling was somehow alive. All of the team members instinctively ducked and crouched low to the ground. Once they were relatively assured that there wasn't an attack, the communication focused on the movement along the ceiling. What did this mean? Gradually, it became quite clear that this blackness shrouding many of the catacomb ceilings was thousands upon thousands of mature-sized bats. Upon further investigation, it was evident that there was a multitude of these bats skeletal remains strewn throughout the matter that made up the walkways.

The team continued their search, communicating with one another that they found it odd that they had not encountered any of the creatures. As they searched, they all expressed gratitude that their facial apparatus shielded and protected their faces from what their eyes were witnessing. Even with this elaborate and specialized protection, their sense of smell was only being partially attacked by a putrid, foul, and musky odor from this environment. It was evident that these creatures had no central location for their waste; their fecal matter and urine were everywhere one stepped. Initially, this was thought to be mud, but upon closer investigation, it became evident that the mud was, in fact, bodily waste.

The catacombs continued to penetrate the earth and endlessly run parallel to the surface. After hours of searching, the result was the same, no creatures! These seemingly endless catacombs brought the team back to one main source, a centralized abandoned sector. Though this centralized catacomb was crudely built, it was evident because of the sheer number of these catacombs and the tremendous amount of waste that there had to be quite a large number of creatures somewhere. But where?

The search continued, and as the team proceeded, it appeared as if there were no more tributaries. Finally, the team exited their location and the special forces personnel reassembled. They moved in unison to what seemed to be a void; all were warned to be on extreme alert by those manning the control center. They slowed their pace and diligently searched as they moved onward. One member sensed an elevation in another's breathing, but soon recognized that this breathing was due to his own stress level. Many of the unit had been specially trained for any type of encounter; but had never actually had a reason to use it. They were physically and mentally ready! With the tributaries behind, they were now into a more spacious area. These highly trained individuals realized that nothing, and I mean nothing, could have prepared them for what they were focusing upon. There were signs of death everywhere, and it was apparent, upon an in-depth investigation, that these creatures had, at some time, resorted to what appeared to be cannibalism. As they moved, they continually communicated their awe inspired sightings to the control center. Still, no creatures. It was apparent that they were gone or perhaps in hiding.

The highly trained individuals remained alert, though as a team, they felt less apprehension regarding an attack. They continued their search of this spacious room. As one thing eclipsed another, these men saw a wide area of spattered and puddled blood. Further away, their lamps shone on an extremely large pile of what appeared to be animal skins. It became obvious that the skins had their flesh removed and it was also evident that the majority of the skins were from cattle, hogs, pigs, and deer. Off to either side of this pile were large piles of discarded bones, of which there seemed to be an occasional bear skull, and remnants of antlers. Upon a more thorough investigation, there was no evidence of bear skins, so it was presumed that these creatures purposely avoided the mighty bear, or found a use for them, possibly for body warmth. Putting their minds together, the special forces and the personnel manning the control center came to the conclusion that the creatures may have abandoned this site. It seemed evident that this had been their habitat for many decades, possibly for more than a century, probably right up to just a few days ago. So how did they know that they should move? The team continued within this spacious room and realized that it unquestionably had a special meaning to these creatures. It was extremely warm in comparison to the temperature within the other parts of the habitat. The night-vision equipment picked up an apparent moisture-laden steam emanating from the floor which continuously developed throughout the room. This appeared as an endless cycle, but it was not apparent in any of the other catacombs. If these creatures had indeed moved to avoid capture, why was so much left behind?

Were these things left behind because the creatures could not carry more than what they took with them? A further search of the room revealed a deep vat lined with various animal skins. The vat contained what was the remainder of a much larger volume of thickened, steamy, brownish-red blood. The vat was close to empty, revealing evidence that it was cone-shaped, approximately six feet in depth and was crudely encircled, having a six foot diameter at the topmost area. Close by this blood vat were large puddles, and these led to another rather large mound of flesh.

Upon further investigation, it was concluded that the puddles were the direct result of blood that had seeped from the flesh that once was piled high atop this present mound. Unbelievable as it may seem, there was further evidence that the creatures had evidently resorted to cannibalism. This became factual when human body parts were found strewn throughout the mound of animal flesh. By chance, one of these investigators slipped on an area of blood and inadvertently fell head first into the vat. He tried to remain steady, but the vat's lining was too slippery, and subsequently down he went. Instinctively, he protected his head with his hands and forearms, and these, in turn, collided unexpectedly with items at the bottom of the vat. Everything happened so very fast that it was impossible for any of the others to come to his assistance. Instinctively, the man used his arm strength to immediately remove his head from the pool of blood, and no sooner had he begun to scramble, when he felt his legs being tightly held, and subsequently, he was pulled out and away from the vat. Now, lying at the topmost area of the vat, and gasping for breath, the investigator tried to steady his nerves. As he began to wipe his facemask, he immediately became aware that several of his fingers and his wrists were giving him intense pain. Canteens were removed from waist belts and the water washed most of the blood from the investigator's headgear. As this was being done, he complained of pain. It became evident that his fingers, hands, and forearms were bruised and cut. Without pause, he convinced the others that his injuries were not that serious, and that he could continue with the investigation. After regaining his composure and being repaired, he went on to say that he felt that he had encountered more than blood when falling into the vat. In fact, several items appeared to give and snap due to his downward force. The team removed the remaining blood, and there, to their surprise, was a cache of fragmented bones at the bottom of the vat. These were taken from the vat, and by their obvious weight, it was easy to recognize that the marrow had become fully saturated with blood. Recognizing that the vat was for the most part empty, it was believed that this vat not only housed the creature's nutritious blood source, but most probably a multitude of fragmented, saturated, softened bones. The softened, saturated bones were documented, and, like all other discoveries, placed in bins and eventually transported to a lab. Furthermore, it was generally believed that this amount of blood and bones was an indication that a much larger volume, of both items, had recently been removed from this spacious room. The obvious question surfaced. Believing that their trek had failed to uncover a single creature, other than the multitude of bats, were the creatures somewhere up ahead or had they chosen to abandon this venue in favor of another?

Not knowing what form of surprise could lay ahead, the surveillance team separated, each taking responsibility for what turned out to be a seemingly, endless array of catacombs. Upon returning to the starting point, each revealed their findings, but surprisingly, tunnels were discovered along each catacomb, and each presented a void far below what their headlamps revealed. The team reassembled, and acting as one, temporarily departed the spacious room. They repelled tunnels, and in doing so, investigated one catacomb after another, only to find that each hadn't a creature, and was subsequently was free for trekking. Still, having no way of knowing whether or not the creatures may be waiting, it was decided that they would investigate as a team rather than as individuals. The more thorough the investigation, the more amazed were the team members; miles and miles of catacombs appeared to be trail endlessly beneath the countryside, the city proper, and the huge acreage of Bucks County farmland and ranches. These interlocking catacombs, with additional tributaries and tunnels, were mind boggling. However, what gave this expedition its uniqueness was the fact that some of these tunnels would drop straight down, farther than others, revealing layer upon layer of off shooting catacombs. Upon further and more extensive investigations, it was discovered that there were varying degrees of catacombs, either allowing the creatures to ascend or descend from one catacomb to another without having to use the direct route of a tunnel. These findings caused one of the unit members to remark that these passageways, tunnels, and the many tributaries reminded him of a city beneath a city. Adding to this observation, it was generally stated that there had to be quite a large population of these creatures. The team spent many stress filled hours searching the ongoing vastness of so many tributaries, but found that when they had exhausted their energy, they had not witnessed what could be considered to be an end of any one catacomb. Finally, being totally spent, they returned to the spacious room, or what could be recognized as a chamber.

The team took a much needed power nap and then continued their task. The search of this enormous room continued and the next find was what they later learned to be the most significant, with the exception of the actual creature. They encountered several objects that were very similar in shape and size, and though each was the size of a seedless watermelon, its outer covering seemed to be opaque and quite pliable. This area of the chamber seemed to be the warmest, for the unit noticed that their bodies were dripping with perspiration. It was communicated from the control center that they should get close to these objects and examine their composition. One of the personnel that was a short distance away firmly said, "Come over here." In unison, the team moved and found that one of the objects had a widened crack, and that the shell like cover was hard and brittle. Upon a closer investigation, it was discovered that within this oversized bulbous item, was what appeared to be a decomposing fetus. The team felt the surface material and indeed found it to be hardened, and reptilian in appearance, much in contrast to those that lay huddled nearby. The team concluded that this cracked object was indeed a birthing device for the creatures. They shone their light source directly upon the crack, and the streams of light, in turn, illuminated the enclosure. It was then that the decision was made to separate the hardened enclosure into two halves. They did so and observed the fetus within. It resembled the creature's appearance, but also had characteristics of a human baby. This being had leprous sores and lumps that disturbed its skin. This baby was surely disturbing, but that was not what upset the team. What astonished them was the reality that this being had the facial characteristics of a human, and had webbed fingers and toes rather than evident claws and talons. It was taken for granted that this fetus would be disfigured, but it definitely had human characteristics rather than that of the creature that was presently in captivity.

A member of this team respectfully picked up the stiffened decomposing fetus and before placing it in a cushioned storage container, discovered that the fetus was obviously a female. After placing the fetus into and securing it within its transportable container, the team gathered the remaining enclosures. It was sensed that there was a real possibility that these fetuses were alive and could be nearing the time when they would be leaving their membranes. The descriptive word membrane was now coined rather than enclosure because one of the team members saw the enclosures to be more like membranes that housed reptiles. These membranes were counted and totaled four; as team members applied a light amount of pressure upon the membrane's exterior, they could feel an active presence from within each one. It was then that the unit shared their discoveries with those within the control center; this communication was essential so that immediate preparation could be made to house and to adequately nurture these birthing membranes when back at the hangar. Each membrane was pliable when comparing it to the hardened exterior of the cracked one, but being pliable did not necessarily mean that they couldn't be safely relocated. Of utmost importance was the fact that to transfer these birthing membranes, they had to be kept extremely warm. Why were these membranes left behind? There were several ideas, but what made sense was that the colony had not yet had the resources to duplicate the original chamber's hot and steamy environment. Realizing that the cold climate on the surface would kill these fetuses, it was concluded that the colony's plan was to return for them at a time after their birth. The team realized that they were in the same predicament as that of the creatures but, unlike those beings, the team had several options and a vast number of resources. The team's plan turned out, in the long run, to be ingenious; specialty vehicles of the four-wheeler type were transported to the area. These vehicles had insulated enclosures mounted and secured directly behind the front seats, and each container was densely packed with aged composted materials. These enclosures were individually packed prior to their departure to the chamber so that the composted materials could more than adequately heat each and every container. It was at this time that the topmost opening was closed off, thus retaining the majority of the composted heat.

These specified foul-wheeler types arrived at the location of the original habitat and were removed from the flatbed. Each vehicle was placed by the catacomb's excavated ceiling and then lowered by crane to its flooring. The last four-wheeler was still attached to the crane's cables, so its driver could then mount its seat, and in turn, the driver and vehicle could be lowered simultaneously. When all of the four-wheelers were mounted and lowered within the catacomb, their ignitions were activated and the vehicles were ready to proceed. Believing that the composted heat within each and every container adequately resembled the amount that was necessary to safely transfer the membranes, the vehicles were then driven toward the chamber. Each container had clear glass paneled, frontal access doors; it was decided to keep the access door at the top, but to place the membranes into the containers using the frontal vantage point. It was also believed by doing it that way that it would allow the team more availability to recognize when the membrane was thoroughly encompassed, both above and below, within the compost.

With their headlights on high beam, the vehicles were driven along the designated route and eventually were stopped by the chamber. The four-wheelers arrived at the spacious chamber just as planned, without the slightest hitch, and each membrane was diligently placed into its assigned container. Now that all of the membranes were within their assigned container, each was quickly swathed and thoroughly cushioned with straw and compost, and then each set of doors was sealed shut. Throughout each container, there were several steam outlets, and each container had a thermostat that would automatically activate a release valve whenever the composted material got to be too hot. There was also an abundance of the softened, composted material beneath each membrane, thus enabling them to experience cushioned warmth during their entire transport. Once completed, there would be similarities between the previous birth chamber and their present composted one.

Now that all of these containers were secure with their very special contents intact, the operators moved toward what would be considered the rear of the four-wheelers. Once there, one could see why these vehicles were considered to be state of the art. Here, was an additional windshield, steering wheel, ignition area, a collapsed driver's seat, and an automatic transmission setup. In fact, this end was identical to the other end. Each operator sloshed through the fecal/urine waste, and then mounted their vehicle, paying special attention to first kick off the excess waste from their boots. These four-wheelers had oversized terrain tires due to the depth of the waste, and to guarantee a safe ride, all of the tires were deflated somewhat and the treads were deeply set for traction. These operators placed their keys into the designated ignitions, activated the motors and shifted their vehicle so that it moved ever so slowly in the direction from whence they had come. Luckily for the drivers, and subsequently for the fetuses, these four-wheelers had specialized shock absorbers, therefore allowing the vehicles to ride smoothly, even though the catacomb was noticeably uneven and somewhat treacherous.

The vehicles were driven very cautiously until they returned to the location where they had been lowered. Each of these specialized vehicles had enough room for one membrane container. Once these vehicles arrived at the mouth of the underground dwelling, a group of four cables, each being the same length and having identical hooks at their lowest point, were lowered from the crane to the corners of the waiting containers. The hooks, in turn, were connected to each container and they were then lifted from the four-wheelers and transferred to a five-ton military truck. Once secure, all of the membranes were transported to the sterilized section of the hangar where the Lone Creature was being kept. Eventually, all of the four-wheelers were maneuvered into one single line, whereas the driver of the first vehicle got the crane operator's attention. Responding to this request, the drivers and their machines were brought to the surface where the drivers departed. Once departed, it was then that the four-wheelers were moved by crane to a flatbed trailer. These motorized vehicles would soon be secured, but at that moment, the most important thing was to continue with the preparation for the membranes transfer.

Prior to the membranes arrival, a section of the hangar had been partitioned and large incubators were put in place, along with all the necessary personnel and equipment so as to afford the fetuses every conceivable possibility of life. The membranes, presently within their composted containers, were now secured within the five-ton truck. It was then that the containers were covered with a specialized type of insulation for their transport. Then, the four-wheelers were lifted out of the catacomb and loaded onto an additional flatbed trailer. While the membranes were in transit, so were the elaborate, motorized vehicles. These four-wheelers would arrive well in advance of the five-ton trucks, so as to be prepared ahead for the eventual arrival of the fetuses. As soon as the membranes arrived at the hangar, each composted container was uncovered, transferred, and secured onto a waiting four-wheeler vehicle. The containers were then, one by one, transported into the hangar. Once inside, the containers would soon become acclimated to the hangar's warmth, and each membrane was again checked thoroughly. The operators then dressed in their proper gear and drove the four-wheeler and the membrane into the sterile complex. Once inside, the membranes were very carefully removed from their containers and placed in a hot house that was somewhat identical to that of their previous birthing area, their chamber. Incubators were there just in case one or more of these babies broke through their membrane before its designated gestation period had elapsed. If this would be the case, then the newborn would have the appearance of being premature and consequentially be transferred to an incubator. Each membrane was carefully removed from their container, and was immediately transferred to a clouded, semitransparent type of enclosure so the researchers could keep abreast of the fetuses' progress from outside the enclosure.

Chapter 45

GRACE, NOR HER BROTHER Ryan, had been to see the creature since the day it was captured, and, in turn, its capture brought a kind of celebrity status to the children. Everywhere they went, with the family or as individuals, they got mobbed and were asked their opinion regarding the creature. Reporters and journalists from every imaginable media type bombarded them as soon as John or Kathleen parked the family car and began walking toward a desired location. Occasionally, a store manager would not charge them for their purchase because their celebrity status brought so much attention and business to that specific store. The Lightcap family was always tolerant and pleasant toward the people asking the questions because this type of behavior had been a learned reaction. Stories were written about this tolerance, while reporters openly admitted, given the same situation, that they may have been quite irritated and possibly explosive. The family had learned to prepare themselves for the media's onslaught prior to leaving their home each and every day. When going to and from school, both children were interviewed, independent of the other, and also when together.

Almost two weeks had gone by since the capture, and the emphasis was changing from stories directly related to the children and the creature, to stories relating to the creature and the recent, sensational find: the membranes! Each membrane was believed to contain a live fetus, and the significance of the fetal corpse that somewhat resembled a creature, but more so, a human baby. The family never yearned for this celebrity status and was always bowled over by the extent of the attention. The main positive attribute to all of this was the opportunity to visit Washington, D. C. and t*he First Family.* The status thing got old, real fast; it had disturbed their normalcy, and had thrown an unwanted wrench into their lives. After the first few days, this new exhilaration turned into total exhaustion. Upon their return from Washington, the parents found that it was not as easy, as they thought it would be, to return to their jobs; Ryan and Grace found that the students and teachers wanted their time. At bedtime, they often found themselves saying their memorized prayers, and when nearing the time that they would rise from their knees, they made a special and direct plea to God for the media to leave them alone. Their lives were in disarray, and their internal clock was not working properly; sleep came intermittently, and Grace often wished that she wasn't the one to have initially seen this creature. After a matter of days, the media began to target the creature's habitat, and at the same time, de-emphasize Grace and the family; the Lightcaps, one and all, began to sense relief. They had come here from Maine to start a new life and to be with their extended families and in-laws, and then this catastrophe happened. It was far too much upheaval in such a short amount of time.

A writer for a lesser newspaper in Bucks County, and who formerly worked for the Intelligencer, wrote an editorial regarding the woes of a family put under the spotlight of human interest, and how such a situation can have its affect upon them. The journalist took it upon herself to show compassion to a family that was put under a microscope; the parents and the children.

So You Want to Be a Headline?

The Lightcap Family recently moved to the Doylestown area of Pennsylvania to pursue the American dream. After spending the previous thirteen years in Maine, the family pulled up their stakes and moved, lock, stock and barrel, to the big city life of Doylestown, Pa. They purchased an old country home that fit their dream and moved in soon after. Their children were enrolled into elementary schools while John, the father, began his new job in excavation; Kathleen, the mother, began her job as an elementary school teacher. The family could not ask for a smoother period of transition. The family members experienced this change without any major disruption, and then Grace, the younger of the two children, saw what she envisioned to be Bigfoot. It was at this point that their life as they knew it took on a totally new concept. Two weeks have passed since Grace first made it known that she had seen Bigfoot in the countryside near the small town of Edison, just on the outskirts of Doylestown, Pa.

Grace had been waiting for her school bus, accompanied by her brother Ryan who is three years her senior. Ryan, being twelve years of age, and a sports enthusiast, was also waiting for the bus, but he never noticed Bigfoot; he was, instead, totally absorbed by the super hero within his comic book. Once the media got its teeth into this sighting, the family's woes began. Did they ask for this notoriety? No! But like the majority of us, this attention made them feel special, that is, in the beginning. A few days and nights of endless bombardment became a wish for all of this to cease. The family's life was not their own any longer. Grace and the creature were now sharing equal time and eventually the family was more than willing to give full time status in favor of the creature. Two weeks since the discovery and its subsequent capture, and now the media turned the majority of their attention to the trials and tribulations of this creature. The family was grateful for this opportunity to step out of the spotlight, while they attempted to reconvene, what was once a simple, enjoyable, and productive lifestyle. Oh sure, Grace will never be without some sort of recognition, especially now that the creature may be moved, and possibly viewed in zoos around the world. To some, this may be wrong since it is believed that this creature was once a human afflicted with leprosy. However, what can be done with such a hideous being? It cannot simply be set free to roam the earth. At one time, that is what it did, and the collective thought was that it needed to be captured. At least in a zoo, it will be cared for, and protected against the violence of our human nature.

Chapter 46

WHILE THE MEMBRANES WERE situated, the Lone Creature was now stirring, awakening from its extensive sleep that was influenced by the anesthetic. All of the scientists, surgeons, nurses and other personnel watched the creature to see what effect the operation had upon its left eye. Understandably, the creature awkwardly moved about until it sensed that something was different, its eyelids were able to open and close without the slightest difficulty for the first time in its memory. At first, it was the creature's brain that began to wonder if this had happened in the past, but its recollection enabled it to realize that this was something completely new. The creature blinked several times, and those watching its reaction most likely thought that it was realizing its new found sight. It continued to blink and, without willing it to happen, moisture enveloped both eye cavities. This sensation alarmed the creature, but then it realized that the moisture actually soothed its eyes; it continued to blink, and the moisture intermittently occurred.

The anesthetic was steadily dissipating, and as it lost its grip, the creature's present situation became a reality. It now realized that its thought processes had been in a dream state, unlike this present reality. Prior to awakening from its dream state, the creature roamed the catacombs and chamber during earth's night-time hours, and slept through the hours of daylight. The food gatherers had just returned from their hunt without a kill. The disharmony among the food gatherers was more than evident, for this had never happened before. One of the food gatherers, experiencing an unruly attitude, picked a fight with a lesser, and noticeably weaker creature. Before any of the food gatherers could intervene and come to the aide of their compatriot, the viciousness of this fight began. There was no parrying for the position of a strike. There was just the ferociousness of each creature, out of control, growling and snorting as they charged one another, their head claws spread widely, and their talons outstretched and straining! Using every ligament, tendon, and muscle fiber, they attempted to dig deeply into their opponent's body, and rip at it repetitiously until one or the other was mortally wounded. At this point, there was no indecision or compassion; the victorious creature would go for the jugular and viciously rip its opponent's heart from its chest. The other and the food gatherer swiftly moved at each other, over and over again. An observer, feeling unnerved by the viciousness of the combatants intent, would think of the food gatherer as having the advantage since he was the experienced hunter, but this may not be the case! The food gatherer attempted to catch the other off guard by vaulting forcefully toward its opponent, its talons and head claws outstretched, seeking a mortal blow. The food gatherer evidently thought that it could dig its upper and lower sets of talons deep into the other's thickened chest and muscular lower abdomen. It became evident that the other had sufficient fighting skills, for it parried, avoiding the intended onslaught, and the food gatherers momentum took it well beyond the other. As it was swiftly passing by the other, this being took full advantage of its opportunity. Using its own vicious power, it slashed a set of lengthy deep cuts into the food gatherers side.

No sooner had the other struck these slashing cuts when the other swiftly responded to its advantage, completely turning the tables on the food gatherer. The other vaulted its own self with outstretched talons and claws upon and into the upper back and hind quarters of its adversary. The initial talon cuts caused the food gatherer to cry out in surprise and pain, and a subsequent, obvious fear for its survival. This fear immediately turned to dread when the other, continuing its ferocious attack, mounted the food gatherer's upper and lower back. These additional wounds were deeper than the original slashes, and now, the talons were being forcefully implanted deeply into the hunter's muscled back. As the other continually fisted its talons deeper and deeper, gripping the muscled back, it created a permanent hold above and below. What happened next is often witnessed at small town rodeos; the already fisted talons and the head claw clamped tightly into the food gatherer's thickened neck caused tremendous pain and irritation. The food gatherer did everything within its power and imagination to throw the other forcefully from what could be considered its death grip.

The food gatherer bled profusely from the slashes along its one side, but these were not extensive, or thought of as life threatening. The food gatherer, feeling the other's talons ripping into its shoulders and lower back, found it necessary to jerk its body this way and that, vaulting itself into the air. Immediately after coming back to earth, it purposely crashed into the wall of the catacomb and violently assumed an outstretched position, trying desperately to release the other's grip. Finding that this strategy was not working, the food gatherer reared itself onto its lower appendages, and while standing upright, attempted to reach backward beyond its shoulders and around its sides and forcefully grab the other with its own extended talons.

The other, recognizing the food gatherer's apparent urgency and frustration, and realizing its own dominant position, blocked and continued to ride the food gatherer. The other was thrown and violently jerked in every conceivable direction, but its stance was strong and fast. While holding on, the other found that its advantageous position began to reap rewards. In time, the body jerks became noticeably less; the blood was pouring freely from the aggravated slashes and from the areas where the upper and lower talons had their own death grip. Believing that the food gatherer had been mortally wounded, the other lessened its talon holds. Sensing this as a sign of the other's over-all fatigue, the food gatherer recognized that this would probably be its final opportunity to free itself from the death grip of the other. It was now that the food gatherer summoned all of its remaining strength and swiftly threw itself as forcefully as possible, in every imaginable direction. It reached back toward the other in every conceivable way, talons snapping, opening and closing, with all the force that could be mustered. Still, the other held on and rode the food gatherer; blood spewed from every wound, and it was quite evident that the food gatherer's spasmodic body indicated that it was experiencing its death throes. As the slashes, cuts, and any other wound no longer spewed blood, there was less and less resistance from the food gatherer. The aggressiveness of the lengthy fight caused the extension of the other's lower talons to slash and sink deeper into the hip joints, ripping all of that muscularity, and thereby disconnecting ligaments and tendons, thus disabling the food gatherer's mobility. Recognizing this to be to its advantage, the other began to feel some compassion for its adversary. Time elapsed, and with it, the cramped muscles that supported its hold began to relax, allowing the other to gradually loosen and slowly remove its talons. Therefore, its head claws, which had also been deeply imbedded in the food gatherer's neck, spread and eventually released their hold. As the other gained the response of its upper talons, it then was able to slowly release the grip of its lower ones. Upon the realization that the lower talons caused the most debilitating blows, the food gatherer appeared to be in awe of the other's fighting ability; it began to display evident signs and symptoms of its defeat. Having absolutely no further ability to be the aggressor, the food gatherer, with blood seeping from various wounds and its innards protruding from the ever widening slashes, finally succumbed, breathing its final breath as it crumpled heavily to the base of the catacomb.

The elders or food gatherers had to choose one of the others to replace the mortally wounded food gatherer and, at first, the consensus was to choose the victorious other. Given time to reflect, however, the elders thought that this other may use its physical power and attitude to dominate, and therefore disrupt the group that was presently intact. The elders searched their resources and finally elected the Lone Creature. It finally got its break, and now would be able to roam the earth as a food gatherer. Its desire had come true!

As the reality of its present situation sank in, that is, its elevated status to that of a food gatherer was no more than a dream, the creature crumbled to the floor, exhibiting an obvious deflated and depressed state of mind. The elevated feeling of status power became a feeling of total despair. Globs of moisture ran freely from its eye sockets and seemed to saturate its facial area, as well as the growing size of the puddles that had been created upon the floor. This reaction confused everyone. They realized that the creature was aware of the mobility of its eyelids, but was this increased moisture a reflection of that reality?

The creature's mood continued to be melancholy, and then it began to blink excessively, as if focusing upon its eyesight for the first time. The tears clouded whatever vision the surgery had afforded the creature, and this confused it. As it continued to blink, the focus gradually cleared to the point where it could make out its immediate environment. While its head was still lowered, the creature saw sets of talons that were extending from its lower limbs, and then it brought its upper appendages within focus. Suddenly, and without warning, the creature cried out with such a volume, as if it was in tremendous pain, apparently recognizing that its fingers and toes had been replaced with unsightly talons. The creature had often wondered what it looked like, and now, having an increased level of sight, it wondered why it did not previously have the ability to see this clearly. With its head still lowered, its gaze caught sight of a large puddle, and while staring into it, the creature was seemingly mesmerized while turning its head slowly to the left and then to the right, as if it was seeing its reflection. The creature seemed to be in amazement by what appeared in the puddle as it continually moved its head in one direction and then the other. While studying its appearance, the creature could be heard making long drawn out sounds. It would be quite a stretch to think that these sounds were reminiscent of a human's response; it continued to marvel at its body parts in the stillness of the puddle, and when finished, balanced upon its hind quarters and swiftly blinked several more times.

The creature's body language was that of disbelief, of discouragement, but within a short time, colors flooded its environment and something shone brightly from above. The creature found that by shutting its eyelids that this voluntary movement provided a sense of comfort for its eyes. The creature opened and closed its eyelids several more times, and then found by doing so, the light and colors gradually became tolerable, in fact, more comfortable. And by doing this, it was enabled to keep its eyes open for extended periods of time. It raised its head slightly so that it appeared to be looking straight ahead; what it saw were smaller creatures that did not resemble itself in any way. They did appear to be overly wrinkled, and they had strange facial features. There were several of these smaller beings surrounding its location, and all appeared to possess a commonality in appearance. The creature extended its head backwards and sniffed long and deeply, searching for some type of recognition. There was none. Absolutely none!

The creature's discovery, and subsequent notoriety, had truly been spellbinding, but with the discovery of the membranes, life on earth had taken a giant historical step forward. The main point of interest was the fact that through the creature's evolution, these evolved human fetuses had somehow done what no other human form had done before. The creatures had somehow become independent and self-sufficient, without the need of an umbilical cord while within the membrane-like shell resembling that of a reptile. Although this creature was born as a leprous being and had skeletal characteristics that strongly resembled that of a human, it was now evident that through its evolution, it no longer found the need for a physical connection to the mother. There is no indication as to when the colony severed itself from the umbilical cord connection, but the fetus within the membrane had no physical evidence of once having a cord. There was absolutely no indication anywhere on or within its body. As previously noted, these reptilian type membranes were the size of a seedless watermelon, and each pliable enclosure held a fetus, totally encompassed by a life sustaining fluid. After these membranes were transported to and placed within the constructed birth chamber of the hangar, they were, in turn, quickly examined. All of these membranes were given the thumbs up and subsequently, each individual hot house was closed and secured.

These membranes were continually observed and monitored by nurses that had previously worked with crack addicted and other high-risk babies at specialty hospitals in and around Philadelphia. These exquisite nurses were selected to maintain the monitors and to keep a daily vigil upon the membranes, twenty-four hours of each and every day, while the fetuses continually matured toward their eventual birth.

These nurses were truly special, and it was through their skill level and expertise that they afforded an addicted, and often prematurely born, baby the real opportunity to survive and to thrive given their deplorable predicament. Some of these nurses, on temporary leave from Bryn Mawr Hospital located in a suburb of Philadelphia, found themselves feeling truly comfortable while working with this type of newborn. This was a norm at the hospital, and it carried over while they monitored each hot house and its variety of gauges and other mechanisms.

The scientists and surgeons, upon the realization that the membranes and their enclosed fetuses were in good condition, turned their attention to the fetal corpse that was discovered within its cracked membrane. As all eyes were set upon this fetus, it was easy to recognize the distinct differences from the creature that was in captivity.

This unborn fetus was obviously a female, and although its skin was leprous and showed obvious signs of tumor-like lumps, it was noticeably different. This female had little or no recognizable muscularity, had webbed toes and fingers, facial characteristics resembling that of a human, and there was little evidence of head claws. These features caused a stir among the scientists and surgeons, and their speculations gave an initial creditability to the idea that the females held a specific responsibility; to become impregnated and to bare the offspring. However, why no talons or head claws? Was it a possibility that a mature female never achieved the appearance or status of its male counterpart? If, through time, a mature female could be discovered, captured, and examined, then an important emphasis would be placed upon the discovery, if possible, of how these females adapted from experiencing pregnancy with access to an umbilical cord and then live birth, to that of a membrane's independency.

Chapter 47

GRACE HAD BEEN EXPERIENCING a strong desire to visit the area where the creature was being kept, but did not know who she was to contact. Her parents, relatives, teachers, and friends had kept her and Ryan abreast of the creature's situation; it continued to have the majority of the media's attention. Newspapers were selling less than when the story first broke, but the site of its captivity was congested by television trucks from almost every locality throughout the United States. Almost all of these trucks had large dishes mounted upon their roof, and a multitude of elaborate, attached antennae. Occasionally, there was a reference as to where the being was going to be placed once the government's scientists and others had no further need to seek understanding.

Kathleen came up with an idea and discussed it with John; they then agreed to telephone the President and ask him to assist their daughter in getting the necessary permission to visit the government's site. John and Kathleen sat with both children and let them know that John was going to call President Clinton in order to get permission to visit the site that presently housed the captive creature. John went to his study and made the call, a dignitary answered and, after verifying who was on the line, promised to relay John's request to the President. A few hours later, the phone rang and John answered; someone from the White House identified herself, saying that the President wanted to speak with Mr. John

Lightcap. John responded accordingly and then the connection was transferred to the President. Pleasantries were exchanged and then John was advised that the family had an open invitation to visit the site. They simply had to notify those at the installation prior to their intended visiting day and then they would be given a specified date and time. John was notified that the call was to be put on hold, and that the President would be returning in a matter of minutes. Eventually, John heard a sound, and following a short pause, President Clinton advised John that he and his family were invited to visit on this coming Saturday at ten in the morning. After some cordial words, the President asked if Grace was home and if he may speak to her. Grace picked up the receiver and from the other end, she could hear, "Grace, Is that you?" And Grace responded that it was she. The President said that she, Ryan and her parents would soon be seeing the creature and wanted to know if she was excited. Grace said that she was very excited. They talked to one another for approximately five minutes and then goodbyes could be heard. Grace felt good about the opportunity to visualize the creature once again, only this time it would be in a controlled setting.

On the following Saturday morning, the family sat down to breakfast, but Grace was too excited to eat. Eventually, the entire family got into their car and was on their way to the government facility. It was approximately eight miles to the site, so Kathleen asked Grace if she remembered what the creature looked like. Grace responded, saying that she had little recollection of the creature's appearance because she was so frightened at that time, and that she only saw the creature for a matter of seconds. Grace also said that she did remember thinking that the creature was possibly Bigfoot. Addressing her mother's question further, Grace said that she was, indeed, looking forward with great anticipation to witnessing the creature again. Ryan, although having never seen the creature, said that he too was very excited. As the drive brought them closer and closer to the compound, it was easy to hear and to visualize the excitement within the entire family.

Upon their arrival, credentials were verified and then they were directed to drive beyond the double set of gates and to park in a designated location. The facility's chain linked enclosure was entirely visible from where they were and they couldn't help but notice the seemingly endless number of television trucks and vans parked next to the perimeter's fence. Upon further investigation, it became apparent that there was an additional chain linked fence within the original one, and between the two were extensive spools of shiny razor wire.

It was virtually impossible for an interloper to enter these premises. The only conceivable way was through the double set of gates or to use a helicopter. These possibilities were indeed conceivable, but without the proper authorization, all but impossible. Military police manned the gates and intermittently patrolled the immediate interior of the entire compound. These men and women were heavily armed and were on watch twenty-four hours a day; also on-call were fighter planes from the nearby Willow Grove Naval Station, which could be at the compound within seconds.

After exiting their car, the family was met by a uniformed official and all were led to the hangar. They entered and passed several security personnel, and then were led to a conference room. Once inside, they were asked to take a seat and upon doing so, another officer entered. He introduced himself and then went over the important ground rules. He said that his main objective was to insure the creature's safety, and that he was well aware and confident that no one in the family would intentionally want to upset or harm the creature. He went on to say that cameras were not permitted; that, to this point in time, the creature had never been photographed by anyone other than military personnel. He went over a few more precautions and then said that the parents would be required a wear sterilized suits and attached face masks while within the creature's enclosure. The children were permitted to enter without wearing anything additional; it was believed that the suits were not necessary because since their first encounter with the creature, neither child nor the creature had shown any sign of sickness or disease. It was believed that children were immune to anything that the creature could pass on, and vice versa. Therefore, children didn't have to wear anything additional. John and Kathleen went through the process, and once dressed appropriately, entered the enclosure accompanied by military personnel.

Upon recognizing their parents in their sterilized get-ups, the children were overwhelmed by the need to laugh, but stern looks from others in the immediate vicinity soon ended any merriment. As the family proceeded toward the creature's enclosure, they were asked to halt. At this time, they were notified that very recently, several live fetuses were discovered and that each was enclosed within its own membrane. Hearing this, Kathleen blurted out, "Do you mean that there is more than one creature?"

The entire family, upon hearing Kathleen, mouthed her words, but did not speak out. The family received a quick synopsis of the last few days, and then was promised a debriefing upon the completion of their stay. It was at this time that the family's attention was directed to a certain area within the enclosure, an area that was a short distance from the creature and most likely was the birthing area for the membranes. Their suspicions were correct and when they got close enough, it was evident that these membranes were larger than but similar in shape to that of a reptile's membrane egg. Ryan was smiling from cheek to cheek, and was heard to say, "They are really awesome," and Grace said, "Yea, they are." As Grace was watching, she noticed what she thought were intermittent pressure points against the outer wall of a membrane. She gasped. This was met with an official confirmation that the fetuses, in fact, push against the membrane's enclosures. Now, there was a tremendous amount of excitement exuding from Grace, and after a few minutes, the family members were urged to move away from the warm enclosure and directed in a completely different direction. As they walked away from the membranes and crossed the room, they headed in the direction of the largest cage-like structure that they'd ever seen. When they got within a few feet of the elevated structure, they were asked to halt once again and remain very quiet.

They immediately stopped and their gaze fell upon an extremely large mass that was lying within a huge clump of hair, actually in the fetal position on the floor of the cage. Immediately, Grace felt a rush of emotion swell her entire self, and for whatever the reason, tears began to flow from her eyes, down and over her cheeks; her breathing became noticeably labored. As she reached up to wipe the tears away, her mother asked what was wrong. Grace said that she wasn't sure, but that she felt so much sadness seeing the creature in this way. Ryan put his arm around Grace's shoulders, and said that everything would be okay. The tears continued to flow, and Grace responded, "No, everything is NOT going to be okay."

As everyone's attention was absorbed by Grace, they failed to recognize that the creature was beginning to stir. That is, everyone except Grace. She was not looking at the creature, but somehow felt a connection with it as the tears welled up and burst from her eyes. She felt its presence and was heard to say, "The creature had lost its way, and that is why it was captured." Grace brought her eyes to the creature as it began to rise from its fetal position, but everyone else was still looking at Grace, in wonderment. Where did this information come from? Was it thought out before she said it, or was it simply a spontaneous statement? Kathleen asked Grace what she meant by what she had just said, and Grace told her mother, and all that were listening, that what she had just said was what the creature had just told her. Everyone that had heard her had questioning looks on their faces. Kathleen explained that it was impossible, that the creature's mouth did not move and that no one had heard the creature make a sound. Grace said that she had not heard the creature, but felt its words. Spontaneously, Grace then said, "Shhhhhh!" A few seconds elapsed and time seemed to be endless. It was then that Grace spoke again. "The creature is very sad and wants so badly to return to its home." Ryan asked Grace if the creature could hear and understand her, and Grace said that she did not know. Grace then tried talking to the creature; she spoke loud enough and said that she was sorry that it was so sad, and that she hoped that it could return home soon. After saying these words, she looked at the creature anxiously, anticipating some sort of response, but there was none. At this point, Grace began to wonder whether or not she had simply imagined that the creature had, indeed, communicated with her. The family was led to a group of chairs not far from the creature, and they sat, in awe, as they observed it. The creature's putrid smell was all but gone, but it was even bigger than portrayed by the media, or what Grace could remember. It was absolutely huge, and this was a fact that could not be disputed.

As the creature sat upright using its lower sets of talons for balance, it was easy to hear the tips of its talons scraping across the metal floor similar to the screeching noise when chalk is misrepresented on a blackboard. As the creature balanced itself, it maneuvered its rump onto the floor, and steadied its balance. At this point, the creature was staring directly at Grace, that is, not in her general direction, but directly at her!

Chapter 48

THE ANGER GREW WITHIN the colony when the creatures realized that it was inevitable that they had to move from their present location and construct a new habitat. Leaving behind their entire history and starting over was a chore that none of them envied! Also, since the Lone Creature had been captured, it was inevitable that the human would eventually investigate and discover that their colony does, in fact, exist. In turn, their habitat could, and most probably would, be discovered, and what had always been sacred as their culture could be thoroughly dissected and demeaned. Worst of all, it would become an integral part of the human's history. All of the back breaking hard work and the ingenuity that went into their initial adaptation and subsequent survival; their evolution, to this point in time, would no longer be their own.

At first, there was confusion among the colony, then anger and extreme hostility began seething from the depth of each creature's heart and soul. The anger festered and grew with every revelation that their individualized culture could become insignificant; a small segment in the history of the human race. Anger gradually became rage as many of the creatures communicated their want to capture and annihilate the enemy of their colony and its survival, which was now threatened.

Strange as it may seem to a human's way of thought regarding capital punishment, these creatures, using every conceivable means to survive, found it necessary to consume their dead, and therefore considered themselves to be cannibalistic. This cannibalism initially came into play when they shared information regarding the severity of this Lone Creature's punishment. Upon its capture, the creature would be taken to the sacred chamber, and once securely staked and pinned directly to the ground, each and every creature would take its designated turn. As each creature approached this traitor, they'd purposely distance themselves from any previous knowledge, kneel down, lean forward, and while paying strict attention not to touch this evil being, they'd take a small bite from its flesh. After taking its bite, and holding the piece of flesh between its front teeth, making sure not to swallow, this creature would then forcefully spit the piece of flesh onto the ground, as a sign that it did not want to be associated with this mortal sinner. This continued for as long as these creatures kept this enemy alive. When it was determined that the enemy was indeed lifeless, the pieces and the rest of the remains would be buried rather than ingested as a sign of their respect.

Prior to this Lone Creature's mortal sin, no other creature had, according to the knowledge of the eldest creature, ever been disgraced by burial. There were, however, stories handed down through generations of creatures that were buried prior to the time that the culture resorted to cannibalism. These were the initial underground inhabitants that were unable to adapt to their life sustaining change. One by one, these creatures, also referred to as humans with leprosy, lost their will to live, and once deceased, were buried as a sign of reverence.

Chapter 49

WHEN THE ELDERS AND others moved from their original habitat, they realized that they had to leave the membranes behind. The reasoning for this decision was due to the chill factor related to the area's weather. The elders were well aware that if they attempted to transport the membranes across the open land, without affording them more than adequate warmth, all would perish. The elders also knew that it was a common occurrence for birth to occur in one of every two membranes under normal conditions, let alone in this degree of cold.

The elders plan was to create the necessary warmth within the new habitat's sacred chamber and then to return once the weather warmed in order to retrieve the membranes. They believed that moving the membranes, one at a time, from their present location to that of the new habitat could be accomplished without detection. As a back-up plan, the elders were aware that they could wait until early spring. By that time, the fetuses would have freed themselves by breaking through their cracked, decomposing membranes. The decision was finally made to retrieve the membranes before they cracked. Time elapsed, and eventually the elders organized this important journey; their plan was then put into action.

The initial catacomb had been completed and eventually connected to the distant chamber where various supplies had been transported and were now in storage. The supplies included piles of animal skins, an enlarged mound of decaying flesh, a deep, skin-lined vat of coagulated, darkened blood, and a variety of other things that were previously kept within the original chamber.

Once placed within the new chamber, these items seemed to replicate what the original chamber, and it was the mainstay in the colony's continual battle for survival. During a period of many months, the warmth within the recently constructed chamber gradually escalated, and when it was sufficiently heated, the journey began. There wasn't a moon this night, so the creatures were in luck. The elders recognized that without the moonlight, the night would be darker and therefore would make it safer for their trek. The selected creatures moved stealthily across the land, and as they approached their old habitat, they sensed that something was seriously wrong. They felt the uncanny presence of the human being, but not the intensity of the fear that regularly accompanied that presence. The old habitat was approximately fifty yards further from where they had first picked up the scent, so they huddled and gave their point of entry some thought.

The elders communicated among one another and it was decided which of the creatures would be the first to move to the opening of the previously constructed escape route, and that, when on the verge of entering, it was then that the one chosen would be the first to enter. They realized that this entry point would lead them along the passageway that would eventually bring the group to the base of the escape tunnel. As the group moved closer, they found themselves feeling extremely anxious, but this anxiety seemed to be coming from an internal source. They were within five yards of the entrance and they could still sense the human's presence, but this presence had not increased as the distance lessened. Their fear was that the human had been there since their previous escape, and if this was a reality, then the human's may have found the membranes. If this was indeed a fact, then what would the Humans have done? Would they remove the membranes or would they destroy that life?

This fear elevated the elder's anxiety, and the chosen one was urged to quicken his entrance to the tunnel and subsequently to the chamber. Upon its entrance, the lead elder knew that with each step it was moving deeper and deeper within the earth. It remembered that this opening was recently constructed as their escape route, that is, an escape route that would be used if it be the case that they needed to flee as an entire colony due to the human's attack. The elders remembered the tremendous amount of catacombs and tunnels that led back to their elaborate and distant maze and the fact that it was constructed to thwart off any and all humans that were pursuing creatures by way of the original entrance into their habitat.

When the chosen elder moved along the escape passageway, and finally found itself at the bottom area of that tunnel, it realized that its trek had brought it closer to the chamber. The group was not far behind the chosen one and it was their choice to assemble as a group at the base of the tunnel. At this point, they could still pick up the scent of the human, but were confident that there wasn't a threat within the general vicinity.

Although none of the elders communicated their fear, they all hoped and prayed that the humans had not discovered the membranes. The chosen elder waited until all of the remaining group were accounted for and then began climbing the tunnel. Using its talons and extraordinary strength, the creature propelled itself upwards, passing other interconnecting catacombs and scaling the tunnel's wall for approximately seventy-five feet, until it was on the level of the passageway that led to the sacred chamber. Once upon that level, the elder notified the group and in groups of three they easily scaled the wall and assembled on the level of the chamber. When comparing this original habitat with the newly acquired one, it was quite easy to separate the two simply by using ones sense of smell. The original overwhelmed the senses, though at the same time reminded the creatures of home. It was easy for them to realize just how far they had to go to bring the home scent to their newly acquired habitat.

The elders realized that it would take some time to acquire the home smell, but also were well aware that a debilitating scent was already set into motion. They eventually found and entered the chamber only to find that the membranes were gone. Was it possible that the fetuses had already broken through their individual membranes, and were somewhere within the chamber, or worse yet, dragging their membranes throughout a catacomb?

The elders were stressed and this was evidenced by their need to continue moving while not venturing far from where they stood. They gradually calmed, but remained anxious due to this attack against their normal behavior. They grunted and growled and in doing so, it was recognized that if it were the case that the fetuses had been born, then their discarded membranes would surely be here, in the direct vicinity of the chamber. The reality that the humans had found the membranes and had removed them was something they all were trying to ignore, but it was evident that the human had been in the chamber and had taken the membranes from the habitat.

The suspected carnage was too much for the elder's emotional makeup to bear. Taking their cue from an elder that unsteadily stood upon its lower limbs, this being began a pain-filled cry, similar to the fear of a full grown alpha wolf when stepping on the trigger housing of the jagged jaws of a well hidden, formidable trap. While similar to a soulful wail, this sound was different. This elder continually spread his upper extremities and extended its clacking talons as far to the heavens as they could reach! With its upper extremities raised toward the heavens, the cry that emanated was far reaching and quite primal; a painful bellow! As if taking their cue from this elder, the remainder of the group took on the same posture and let out their far reaching cry that added considerable distance to the initial sound. Now, more than fifteen miles away, the captured creature clearly picked up on this primal wail, as did all living things in the vicinity of the hangar, and beyond. The vibration, which traveled along the airways and into the captured creature's sterile enclosure, was truly spellbinding. The eerie, needful sound was not coming from a radio, but instead, purely from an original source; the group's pain-filled hearts and frustrated souls. The Lightcaps, the scientists, the surgeons, the nurses, and all assembled within the hangar were well aware of this soul searching sound. Feeling that this was directly related to the Lone Creature, all attention was directed to its cell.

Grace impulsively said, "The membranes are missing and are

feared to be dead." Simultaneously, the captured creature rose unsteadily from its seated position, put all of its body weight upon its lower limbs and extended talons, and while spreading its massively muscled crooked upper appendages out to its sides, realized that the incoming soulful wail was in some way directly related to it. Next came what many humans would consider an out of this world experience; the captured creature, while continuing to expand its chest cavity, evidently drew in a tremendous volume of oxygen and created its own prolonged wail. This appeared endless, and as though it were a reply to the initial cry. The captured creature's soulful sound displayed an increased amount of pain and was tumultuous. Evidenced by the creature's appearance, it was understood that this being was responding with its entire physicality and soulful self to one of its own kind somewhere within the area. Everyone within the hangar, and those that resided along its immediate perimeter, were stunned by the creature's voluminous response. When the Lone Creature finished its lengthy, mournful and primal wrenching, it became evident that the exertion left it totally spent. At this point, as if in slow motion, the creature began to slump heavily toward the floor of its cell-like structure. It became evident that it was no longer necessary for those that were in the direct vicinity of the enclosure to shield their ears from the volume of the sound. As Grace, Ryan, and their parents looked at each other, they began to remove their hands from their ears, and this is when they realized that they had considerable pressure upon the sides of their heads. With their hands removed, they sat motionless, not knowing what to expect next, if anything. They did not know how long they had remained in this position, but as they adjusted, they found their eyes fixated upon the slumping creature. Its body appeared to be, for the most part, limp and unconscious. As its momentum picked up speed, it was falling helplessly towards the floor, its upper extremities freely flailing. As the creature helplessly collided with the floor, there was no noticeable resistance, thump, and then an additional thump, as its head forcefully bounced off of the metal floor, and then it bounced again, and again, until the creature's entire body lay motionless. With its entire body completely still, it was easy to recognize that its muscularity was steadily pulling at its own body parts, until the creature lay in an exaggerated fetal position. It was also apparent that the creature was experiencing a deep sleep or that it was possibly unconscious. After its body parts jerked this way and that, it became frozen, and its breathing seemed to be shallow and noticeably labored. There was concern throughout the entire hangar for the creature's well-being. All of the medical team feared that the creature's life was in jeopardy. Also, the medical team was now acutely aware that they did not have the time to sedate the creature, and even if they did, they realized that sedating it at such a critical phase would probably kill the pain-filled being.

A decision had to be made immediately by the members of the medical team. It was now necessary for one, or more than one, to enter the creature's cell-like structure to save its life. What made this setting even more life threatening was the fact that Grace clearly stated, "The creature is dying!" The people in Grace's immediate area could see that she was in some sort of distanced mental state when saying these words; that she may have been experiencing a sort of trance-like state of mind. Recognizing this and the fact that she seemed to have had a telepathic contact from the creature, the words, "The creature is dying," were given serious creditability.

A doctor specializing in gastroenterology had opted to work with the team on this day. Dr. William Battle, celebrated in Philadelphia Magazine's 2001 annual section as the gest gastroenterologist in the region was watching the creature while listening intently. Without the slightest bit of hesitation, Dr. Battle announced that he would enter the creature's structure to administer any and all medical aid. Recognizing that he needed additional support, a pediatric nurse, Judy Miletto, threw caution to the wind and volunteered to assist the doctor. All of this happened within a matter of seconds, immediately after it was realized that the creature had slumped heavily to the floor, its head bouncing freely against the floor's steel plating. This, along with the trance-like utterance from Grace, caused the following series of events to occur.

As Dr. Battle and Nurse Miletto were making their final preparations, the locks were simultaneously being removed from the metal door. This entrance door was solid steel, measured ten feet across its base, and twelve feet in height; the length of the structure was thirty feet. The lock was removed and as a precaution, the door was ever so slowly opened. There were no heroics at this time; concern for the creature's well-being was paramount. Several personnel could be seen with their hands clasped tightly together as they mouthed silent prayers. There were previous times that Dr. Battle had been within the sterile enclosure; times when he was a part of a team effort to rid the creature's body of extensive sores and infections. At that time, he diligently worked with the team of other accomplished doctors to disinfect the creature's scaled skin and to prepare the numerous crater-like sores for surgery and their subsequent removal.

It was quite possible that a sort of bond had been created between the medical team and the creature. This bond appeared to be a type of trust, if you will, that often becomes apparent between a doctor and his or her patient. It appeared as if minutes had elapsed, but in fact, it had only been seconds after the collapse that Dr. Battle and the assisting nurse passed through the entrance and cautiously approached the injured creature. As soon as they were beyond the entrance and clearly within the structure, the door was closed and the lock was replaced. Although the lock was closed, it was purposely left unlocked. As Dr. Battle and nurse Miletto apprehensively approached the fallen creature, it was evident that there was something seriously wrong. The creature's eyelids were fluttering; its breathing was labored and quite shallow. Dr. Battle immediately knelt by the creature's side and made his initial decision; he purposely laid his latex covered hand upon the creature's shoulder as a sign of connection, compassion, and concern. Next, he planned to check the creature's vital signs. When checking its blood pressure, Dr. Battle had to improvise because the cuff of the monitoring apparatus wasn't long enough to extend around the creature's massive bicep area. Realizing this, and the immediate need to get an accurate reading, Dr. Battle retrieved an ace bandage from his bag and used this to secure the blood pressure cuff to the creature's upper arm. Considering the creature's size and physical make-up, the doctor believed that the improvised reading was excessive, but that it was close enough to being accurate. He believed that the collapse and the subsequent unconscious state of the creature was due to a tremendous amount of stress and anxiety just before trembling and colliding heavily with the metal floor. It was strongly suspected that the creature was experiencing a stroke or some type of similar affliction. Its collapse may have come from a total loss of feeling on one side of its body. It was also possible that the creature recognized this critical loss, but was unable to recover before falling, henceforth, colliding heavily with the floor.

Dr. Battle immediately turned to his assisting nurse and summed up what he recognized as the problem. He asked her for a syringe and a vial of a specific serum. Nurse Miletto, known for her exactness among co-workers and physicians, got the necessary syringe and serum, and handed them to Dr. Battle, who, in turn, used the serum to fill the syringe to the amount that he deemed necessary. Dr. Battle then held the syringe upright and squirted a small amount of the serum from the tip of the needle. As soon as he was satisfied that the syringe was working properly, he placed the needle point into a crevice between two of the hardened scales and pushed the needle's tip into the leathery skin. With a popping sound, the needle penetrated the epidermal layer, and once it was fully immersed, Dr. Battle injected the serum. Once the syringe was empty, the needle was removed and after a few seconds, it was apparent that the serum was affecting the creature. Meanwhile, Dr. Battle turned his attention to nurse Miletto and explained that this serum would most likely restore the creature's physical stability and regulate its blood pressure. He also made it clear that there was no immediate danger to them when the creature began to recover from its lethargic state. He went on to say that the creature's physical make-up had been dealt a terrific blow and that it would awaken extremely weakened.

Nurse Miletto, being the consummate professional that she was, realized that this would probably be the creature's response, but listened respectfully for the reassurance that came from Dr. Battle's words and caring demeanor. He also took the time to say that he was proud of her for risking her life in such a dire and potentially dangerous situation. Several seconds elapsed after the injection, and then a positive sign was witnessed from the fallen creature. Its breaths seemed to be fuller and appeared more vibrant. As the creature stirred, Dr. Battle wrapped his creative blood pressure cuff around the creature's massive upper arm and rechecked the gauge. The blood pressure had slowly, but surely, moved into a safety zone, and now rested at an acceptable level.

The professional personnel, off to one side of the cell, recognized the physical changes associated with Dr. Battle's facial features and realized that the creature was responding favorably. At this point, Dr. Battle looked directly at Nurse Miletto and shared the good news with her.

The creature remained upon the floor, in its same position; Dr. Battle, being positively assured by the results of the second set of vitals, examined its head for any cuts or abrasions. He did so being fully aware of the creature's size and probable strength, and the fact that he and the nurse were in no real danger. There was noticeable bruising upon the upper side and toward the rear of the Lone Creature's head, and most likely, severe hemorrhaging and trauma to the same area. Neither Dr. Battle nor nurse Miletto were situated at a vantage point where they could see the creature's face, and therefore did not see that its eyelids had recently blinked a few times and were intermittently open for lengthy periods. While lying upon its side, the Lone Creature appeared to be searching the immediate vicinity of the structure. With its eyes finally settling upon Grace, the creature's gaze seemed to be glued upon her. Grace watched the creature with great anticipation, attempting to pick up any message, but none seemed to come. As Grace intently watched, the creature struggled to free one of its arms from underneath its thickened, upper body. Over time, the arm was freed from its impending weight and the creature physically struggled to slide its outstretched appendage so that its talons lay just below the bars that encased it. Everyone was intently watching the doctor, the nurse, and the creature.

Without being noticed, and possibly not being in charge of herself, Grace had gotten up from her seat, and leaving her family, walked confidently and stoically in the direction of the cell-like structure. When a few feet from the outstretched talons, Grace's physical movement was caught by her mother's eyes. Impulsively, Kathleen stood up and got everyone's attention by succinctly saying, "Grace!" Kathleen was horrified by what she imagined Grace was about to do. At that precise moment, Kathleen's fear became a reality. Grace's fingers connected with the tips of the creature's talons. It was as if these two had always been kindred and cosmic beings! Simultaneously, there was a gasp from all in attendance, for Grace was so tiny in comparison to the creature's height, weight, and massive musculature. What happened next was visibly apparent on everyone's face; without a doubt, a great sense of urgency and concern flooded the room. Grace continued her physical contact as she began to lightly stroke one of the Creature's lengthy talons, back and forth, with a noticeable tenderness for what seemed to be, in Kathleen's eyes, an eternity.

Dr. Battle noticed that Grace was by the side of the creature's enclosure and recognizing that she was touching the talon, sensed that Grace and the creature had a connection. He also felt that his diagnosis and subsequent treatment were correct, so he and the nurse took this opportunity to gather up the syringe and vial, blood pressure cuff and monitor, the ace bandage, any debris remaining from the syringe, and placed everything within his satchel. At that point, he and the nurse backed away, one deliberate step at a time, preparing to leave the structure. As they looked toward the exit, the doctor signaled the attendant to remove the lock. The supervisor surveyed the situation, and upon recognizing that Grace and the creature were still connecting, gave the verbal okay for the lock to be removed. This was done and Dr. Battle and Nurse Miletto steadily closed the space between them and the exit. The lock had been removed and the metal door was slightly ajar. A few more feet, and they would be safe and sound, on the outside of the structure looking in. Now, their gaze returned to the creature. Suddenly, they were physically and mentally caught in a dilemma, and a decision had to be made whether to flee the final few steps or become motionless. The creature had evidently picked up on their departure and apparently most of its attention was now upon them. Dr. Battle and the nurse ceased all movement. "Do not move!" For what seemed to be an eternity, there appeared to be a stand-off; it was more than evident that no one could get a read on the creature's demeanor for it simply stared intently, securing the medical team's full attention.

Grace made the decision for all involved; she compassionately moved the warmth of her tiny hand beyond the talons and was now touching the creature's palm. It was as if beauty was claiming the heart and emotions of the beast. The creature gave no more attention to the doctor or the nurse, and gradually lowered its head until it was, once again, lying upon the floor, its gaze totally captivated by Grace.

Dr. Battle and Nurse Miletto exchanged glances, and it was at this time that they were prepared to leave the structure. Dr. Battle asked "Are you alright?"... "Are you able to move slowly until we are out of this enclosure?"... And finally, the most significant question, "Are you ready?" Nurse Miletto responded affirmatively to all of these questions and did so quietly, always readying herself for their departure. Both professionals removed themselves from the structure and once beyond the exit, the lock was replaced and secured. Grace continued to rub the creature's palm, and it was more than apparent that this was the first time that a human being had ever compassionately touched this youthful being. It was also apparent that this was what the creature needed in order to fully recover; its physical mass was slowly, but surely, moving from the rigid, constricted form to that of being prone and eventual tranquility. Both Grace and the creature had dispensed of their defenses and were now emotionally connected, for what could be the remainder of their lives.

Chapter 50

WITHIN THE STERILE ENCLOSURE, there had been an evident calm, but now the creature was moving, stretching this way and that, here and there, as if preparing to change its physical position. The creature and Grace were locked in what appeared to be a stare down, and then Grace was no longer soothing the creature's emotions. For whatever the reason, she began to move away from the creature and in the direction of a nearby computer station. As Grace got closer, it was clearly evident that she intended to use one of the many machines. Grace's intention was clear to all in the immediate area, except to her parents. They knew that Grace had no formalized computer training. Nevertheless, there she was, sitting in one of the chairs that was situated directly to the forefront of a monitor. Once situated, Grace appeared as if she was awaiting someone's instructions, but it was then that Kathleen quietly said "Grace," but Grace did not respond. She merely sat there staring, as if in some kind of a trance. Kathleen, although approximately fifteen feet away, could clearly see the monitor, and was in amazement as she saw words beginning to fluently appear, forming one sentence after another. At this point, Kathleen verbalized a sound that resembled a gasp and then found that she was totally astonished. She noticed Grace typing while viewing the monitor screen, as if it was second nature. Grace was zipping through the sentences and soon there was a paragraph, and then

262

another. In any case, Kathleen found her eyes off of Grace and now focused upon the creature. Amazingly, it was staring directly at Grace, as if being responsible for Grace's most recent actions. Grace continued to type, and she did this for what appeared to be a while. All present were watching the monitor, and through word of mouth, other professionals became concerned; they began walking from their own workstation, as if mesmerized, to that of Grace's computer. Finally, Grace stopped typing and could be seen sitting in front of the computer, seemingly relaxed, with her hands lying in her lap. Again, Kathleen, having a mother's instinct and concern, quietly said, "Grace?"

Kathleen purposely moved to her daughter's side and began lightly rubbing Grace's upper back. "Grace?" Grace seemed to be extremely distant, but all of a sudden, as if she had been snapped out of a trance-like state and appearing visibly weakened, she quietly responded by saying, "Mother." At the mention of this, Kathleen swept Grace off of the chair and hugged her tightly, tears welling in Kathleen's eyes and streaming down her cheeks.

Feeling emotionally spent, Kathleen felt her legs begin to weaken, so she brought Grace with her as she found chairs for them to recuperate. While mother and daughter were headed toward the chairs, John, being the caring husband and nurturing father, immediately moved to Kathleen's side, assisting her and Grace.

Dr. Battle, you may recall, had recently exited the sterile enclosure, and without the slightest hesitation went directly to Grace to check her vital signs. John and Kathleen felt secure relinquishing Grace to his care, and Grace's vital signs were checked. Following a quick evaluation, the doctor concluded that there was an appreciable amount of disorientation and rectified this with a proper and immediate medication. He then turned his attention to Kathleen, found her blood pressure elevated, and also corrected that situation.

A senior official waited until Grace had cleared from the computer station and then directed security personnel to keep everyone from that immediate area. This specific area was secured and then the senior official printed out several pages that Grace had typed, and also burned the entire document to a disk. After making sure that all of the information was indeed saved, this official was instructed to delete the information from the hard drive. At that time, the information was deleted and then the printout and the disk were then placed in a sealed envelope and hand-delivered to the Pentagon. The envelope did arrive as intended, and was considered to be of the "highest priority." It was opened and read by personnel that had been thoroughly familiarized with the situation within the area of Buck County.

The document was much more than anyone could have ever expected. The lengthy printout read as follows, "I am from a large community that began more than a hundred and twenty years ago within the confines of Bucks County, Pennsylvania. At that time, the members of our community were envisioned as human beings, much like yourselves. Slowly but surely, leprosy changed the lives of the entire community. The lepers were sporadically born into various families and subsequently, when found, they were singled out and ostracized. Our population grew to the point where we were forced to live apart from the community, living as a colony of lepers. Completely separated from our family members, years passed and our lives became more difficult, but no one believed that our situation could actually get worse. The colony was manipulated and forced to either die off, or adapt to a life deep within the recesses of this earth. Some of us could not adapt and subsequently died off, but the majority did adapt, and to this day are thriving as an unknown entity. When comparing myself to your size and questionable strength, it is easy to see why I am envisioned as a creature, a monster, if you will allow me that freedom. The evolution of our species was a gradual process; our history began through an abuse of power when we were unknowingly removed from the earth's surface, en masse, and expected to die off within a matter of weeks. This happened more than one-hundred and twenty years ago. We acquired a human disease, unique at that time to our over-all community, but acquired by no fault of our own. We were then forced to live separately from our families and those that were not afflicted continued to live, as they always had, in Doylestown and Edison. The dreaded disease changed our appearance and I, considered a worker with the designation of digger, am just sixteen years of age. I am huge in size and muscularity due to our evolutionary process and diet."

"In the beginning, we saw ourselves as human beings first, and then as human beings with a disfiguring affliction and disease, namely, leprosy. The changes that our bodies experienced saddened our unaffected relatives, but in time, these same relatives saw us as despicable and grotesque, and sought, with the assistance of others within the community, to annihilate us once and for all. Without tools except for empty cans and their ragged tops, and being hampered by the pitch black environment, we began the arduous task of creating our habitat. Eventually, these tools were misplaced within the darkness, and so our diggers had to use their own hands and feet. Before long, the room where we were initially led began to fill with the displaced soil; it became imperative for us to find our way to the earth's surface."

"It took a lot of work and subsequent luck, but eventually the surface was found. A deer had somehow entered and found its way into our work area. In its frenzy to escape the maze and find its way back to the surface, it became disoriented and unable to escape. We killed the deer and used its flesh and blood for nourishment. Its scent enabled us to follow a trail through what was believed to be some kind of elaborate passageway. Following the scent, it led us to the surface."

"We formed a kind of council and called them the elders, also known as the food gatherers or hunters. This council made all of the laws that we lived by and created the number one law. No leper was permitted upon the earth's surface, at any time, without the expressed sanction of the elders. Over time, these lepers evolved into creatures."

"To this point in time, our diet consisted of tubers and whatever life form we could find tunneling to our depth. The killing and subsequent eating of the deer was the exception, but this kill whet our appetite for larger game. The tubers were usually bitter and distasteful, but did help to sustain our lives; the burrowing animals that we killed taught us to accept the taste of the raw, bloody flesh. Years went by and we continued to adjust; catacombs lengthened and through the use of tunnels, additional levels of lengthy catacombs were able to be constructed. We were always looking for additional food sources because we needed greater amounts of raw meat and blood to sustain our physical size, and ever-growing population. While mingling among other creatures, another food source was recognized, and this was evident by vibrations felt to be overhead; a steadfast presence seemingly attached along the catacomb's ceilings. Fortunate for the creature population, this vibrating presence became a constant food staple for all leprous creatures; adorning the ceiling area of finished passageways were thousands upon thousands of vibrations, that is, bats. With one fell swoop, a small meal could be had by one of our kind. These bats became our staple because they were found to cover every foot of specific ceilings. In time, we depended upon them so we left large areas of catacombs uninhabited, believing that the bats would continually return, feeling a sense of false security. No matter how often we went to their area and no matter how many we killed, thousands always returned! At that time in our evolution, we appreciated these creatures because they were our staple source for food and blood. We also drank of the water that found its way through a variety of vein-like cracks as it dripped enlarged droplets from the ceilings. This water was usually cool and often plentiful, but we had no way of storing it. We tried a variety of methods, but whenever we went to the cache, it had always transformed into a muddy paste."

"Our greatest and most important achievement was finding the difficult path that led us to the earth's surface because with the fear of being annihilated by the human came the realization that we could now hunt, though only under the camouflage of darkness. The food gatherer's did become more organized, and over time became successful at killing large animals and we used the flesh and blood to sustain us further. We saved and utilized the animal skins as carrying sacks, clothing to keep us warm, a lining between ourselves and the cold earth; and even more importantly, a nonporous lining for the vats that held the supplies of blood and water, which now could be stored. The longer the blood remained in the vats, the more it coagulated and became a true elixir for our lives."

"Using our hands, we continually penetrated the earth, and by utilizing the sacks, we were able to carry the dirt and stones to the earth's surface, causing ourselves great pain and anguish. Over many years of digging and carrying, our appearance was ultimately forced to experience undesirable change. The diggers gained muscles upon muscles, and began their path toward a more grotesque appearance, adding to the already leprous effects. Along with the extreme muscularity came the gradual disappearance of our fingers and toes. The massive digging effort continually reduced the length of a digger's fingers and toes to the point where they became mere nubs. Mercifully, these bloody nubs quickly changed and subsequently calloused, thus becoming talon-like, similar to the claws of a fully-grown grizzly bear."

"These claw-like talons were likened to that of a grizzly bear's claws, but during the digger's maturation process, the curved talons grew to become quite a bit thicker and longer than that of a grizzly. These talons enabled the diggers to work harder and the food gatherers to hunt more efficiently. The carriers interchanged with the diggers at times, and in doing so, also lost their fingers and toes, creating their own sets of talons. The deeper the tunnels and the further the catacombs penetrated and extended throughout the inner-earth, the further the carriers had to heft the weighted sacks upon the return to the earth's surface. Decades elapsed during our massive habitat construction and its eventual completion. The end result was miles of catacombs at various levels, well below the earth's surface in the immediate vicinity of Edison, the town from which we were so abruptly removed, as if a speck of waste."

"The food gatherers hunted by night, using the camouflage of darkness to afford them this necessary opportunity. Initially, our quarries were chickens, dogs, cats; although cats afforded us little flesh and were, for the most part, avoided. Recognizing the need for a more abundant source of flesh and increased amounts of blood, the hunters killed more frequently and began storing the excess flesh and blood of an occasional pig or hog. During these hunting excursions, we eventually found that it better met our needs to kill cows; cows were somewhat similar to the smaller animals. They had little resource to offer and thus we sought cattle and horses. As it turned out, the killing of a steer rather than a cow provided an ample supply of meat and blood for our entire colony. The carrying of an animal, the size and weight of a full grown steer, from the site of the kill to our distant habitat further testifies to the size and strength of the food gatherers. These massive creatures could alone carry the weight of a fully grown steer or bull upon its own shoulders, but two workers often shared that responsibility."

"The food gatherers then turned their attention to other types of wildlife, such as deer, which were more than plentiful in that region, and to that of an occasional, fully grown, black or brown bear. Due to the wildlife being plentiful, the meat and blood eventually stockpiled, and these larger animals fully sustained our needs."

"Throughout our evolution, the fetus carriers continued their somewhat human appearance, experiencing little outward physical change; other than the obvious effects from leprosy, the females possessed a limited amount of a male's muscularity. Their responsibility was to be receptive for the sexual needs of the massively muscled males, that is, the diggers and the carriers, and to further our species. It was often the case that whenever a male was in the direct vicinity of a fetus carrier, then the fetus carrier could be envisioned as taking an immediate submissive role, squatting deeply and then leaning extensively forward with its head down, until the fetus carrier rested its arms, bent at the elbow, upon the earth below its feet. Being in this position, it was easier for the fetus carrier to elevate its reproductive area as high as possible, giving off a unique receptive odor. The fetus carrier was now prepared for the initiation and eventual completion of the sexual act. It was not always the case that this positioning would bring about a sexual act, but it was the case that the fetus carrier had felt the need to prepare. Due to the unique evolution of the males, and not the females, their thickened, massive muscularity, excessive size and the fact that there had been little change experienced by the fetus carrier, the sexual process was extremely painful and unfulfilling for the female. The sustained grunts appeared to be signs of stress release and pleasure for the males, while the pain could be heard at quite a distance emanating from the female. The male had a history of being forceful, pulling and powerfully thrusting its sexual member deep within the female's smallness. The act itself was short-lived, but the pain far outlasted the slightest air of pleasure for the fetus carrier."

"Somehow during the evolutionary process, the fetus carriers took on a different response to the abusiveness of the sexual act; the pregnancy and delivery, unlike the norm of our predecessors, changed considerably. Where the pregnancy could and did happen anywhere within the habitat, the eventual birth always took place within the sacred chamber. For whatever reason, as mentioned above, the umbilical cord was no longer used during our pregnancy and birth process. Instead, the fetus spent months in an independent, yet pliable, reptilian type membrane, similar in size to a seedless watermelon. It was believed that this significant change was brought about by the size of the male's sexual member. Over time, it punished, bruised and severely damaged the entire sexual make-up of the fetus carrier. When the female was ready to give birth, the membrane slowly slid along the fetus carrier's vaginal canal, and was laid ever so gently upon the surface of the warmed and steamy sacred chamber. A period of months would elapse and then the newborn would gradually crack through its ever hardening membrane, beginning its life-long, independent struggle in complete darkness. We no longer have parents as we once did, as you, the human still does. We eventually lost that opportunity at some time during the early years of life, evolving within our habitat. Upon birth, our change brought with it independence, and subsequently, we possess an inner guidance mechanism for survival."

"**Upon t**he completion of our habitat, the catacombs extended for miles and at a variety of levels. While the tunnels gave us access to the upper and lower passageways, our lives continued to be a perpetual struggle. We found ourselves constantly limited by the darkness, and our real, intense fear of the human. Throughout the decades, it was always our ultimate fear that our survival would be discovered and that we would be annihilated by the weaponry of our far superior enemy. Our entire colony strictly adhered to the elder's laws. Only the food gatherers were permitted upon the surface, and that jaunt was limited to the hunt and only under the camouflage of darkness. Although it was felt that others wanted to venture upon the earth's surface, it was never a known fact that any other creature had actually broken the law, that is, until I ventured away from our habitat. I was eventually captured, and for that selfish action, I am sentenced to be executed if, or when, I return to the colony."

"During my trek upon the earth's surface, I encountered the child and soon afterwards, I lost all sense of memory. During the time that I have been at this site, my thought processes began to return, and the time that had elapsed began taking a visual form. I remember visualizing the child and, at the same time, I believe that the child actually saw me. This was the first human to have ever seen one of us in approximately one-hundred and twenty years, since the time that we were exiled to die within the earth. I was terrified by the child's presence and chose to run as swiftly as I could, but something happened that intensified the danger of my predicament. I found myself out of control, moving swiftly, faster than ever before. Running at that excessive speed caused my chest to tighten and my breathing to become labored. As I ran, I lost my balance, and just as I dug my talons deeply into the earth's surface, I collided with something, knocking myself unconscious. Upon awakening, I was extremely cold, externally and internally injured, and temporarily without a memory. I was a stranger in a strange land and had no recollection. I struggled and subsequently survived, but my survival, along with its loss of memory, most probably caused my eventual capture. "

"I am the cause for the colony to have become known to the human, for the capture of several impregnated membranes, and for a massive undertaking; the effort it will take for our colony to relocate to a safe haven. For my dastardly act of defiance, I will face death."

The preceding document was read by one of the Pentagon's chief officers and shared with a handful of other government, supposedly within the strictest of confidence. However, nothing could be further from the truth. Within a matter of hours, two of the most prolific newspapers within the United States would cause the government to understand its predicament. While Grace and the creature were communicating through a kind of telepathy and Grace simultaneously typed, words appeared on the computer's monitor, paragraph after paragraph. It was entirely unknown to our government's homeland security division that a computer hacker had broken into the government's computer system. This was not the first time, though it was seemingly more significant than any other. As Grace was receiving and subsequently typing the words that were being transmitted, a hacker was receiving this document at exactly the same time. While the document was expediently being hand-carried to the Pentagon, the same document had been secretly purchased by The New York Times and The Los Angeles Times for the total amount of $500,000. Prior to the sale of this document, there had been a contract written and signed by all relevant parties, stipulating that each newspaper would keep the story's source, this specific hacker, confidential. The only way that the government could obtain the hacker's identity was if the hacker would opt to turn him or herself into the respective authority. This document was then faxed back and forth until all parties were satisfied with its composition and all signatures were intact. Anything and everything was accomplished through the power of the internet.

Chapter 51

THOSE SITTING FAIRLY CLOSE to the creature's structure, including the Lightcaps, were very concerned for its welfare. Once Grace was able to regain her composure, she then said: "The creature isn't talking to me; it seems to be aware that the membranes are here." Again, her family and the few government personnel that were close enough to hear Grace's words were concerned by what they were hearing. All of the officials within the chain-linked site now had what they considered to be proof that there was, in fact, more than one creature. It was now evident that there were more creatures within the adjacent countryside, more than the captive creature and the membranes.

Chapter 52

THE NEWS MEDIA CAUGHT wind of the telepathic connection between Grace and the Lone Creature, and they were fast to act. Newspapers across globe directed the attention of the reader to the developing story.

Creature and Child Use Nonverbal Communication!

When the celebrated creature was first seen by the young child, Grace Lightcap, it was thought to possibly possess an aggressive nature. While waiting for the school bus with her brother one morning, Grace sensed a disturbing smell and found herself overwhelmed by what she envisioned to be Bigfoot. Within seconds, Bigfoot moved closer to the now traumatized child, but when she nervously looked away and then back again, Bigfoot was gone. Initially, Grace's recollection related doubt in many people's minds, but following a thorough investigation, it was her strength of character that won out over those that doubted her convictions. Grace, along with her brother's help, stumbled upon the area where the creature was discovered and then captured. This specific location was in the direct vicinity of

> *the Lone Creature's crudely built habitat within the countryside of Edison, PA, one of the many intriguing communities within Bucks County. There was a great amount of speculation and suspicion by the media that this creature's horrific appearance and putrid smell gave creditability that it had been an alien with a life force, that is, not of the planet earth. After considerable thought and an in-depth investigation, it was concluded that this creature was closer to mankind than previously assumed, that is, a human.*

Initially, there was suspicion that the courier had leaked the story to those respected newspapers, but there was some doubt as to this being the reality. In the past, this specific courier had always been honest and completely trustworthy, but there was speculation that he had somehow prospered prior to reaching the Pentagon. The courier was then whisked back to the Pentagon and questioned at length. After answering many questions, there was absolutely no evidence that the courier was guilty of any wrong doing.

Now, the question was *who had* leaked that information to the press? Internal Affairs interrogated every individual that had been present at the compound the day that the creature telepathically communicated with Grace. Again, and much to the chagrin of the government, they came up empty! Frustration was now rampant! How the hell did these two newspaper giants get this 'Top Secret' information? Government personnel picked their brains until it was surmised that a hacker had likely penetrated their computer system. Whenever a hacker broke into any government computer installation, there was a message that awaited this person. This message was similar to the warning that could be found when a civilian chose to copy a movie on video. However, the difference between copying a home video and hacking into a government server was vast. This was the United States Government, believed to be the most powerful government in the world! If this hacker was eventually found, then he or she could count on spending some serious time in a federal penitentiary, possibly a lifetime.

Government personnel were sent to the two newspaper's front offices and the chief editors of both were advised to give up the source of their story. These two media giants are extremely powerful, in their own right, but were mindful that these people represented the United States Government. It just so happened that the source of the information had never been seen; that all communication and subsequent transfer of funds was anonymously executed. It seemed that the government had hit a snag. Just how secretive had the hacker been? Had that person shared the exploits with another person? If so, then the investigators could possibly use their resources to unearth the culprit expediently.

The government opted to show its power by notifying the American public via national television spots that the government's security had been breached by a hacker, possibly someone, or more than one, bent on potential terror. What followed was meant to catch the attention of all that were paying attention. The various TV spots led up to an official statement, broadcasted nationally, announcing that the government would guarantee the payment of $500,000 to the person that would step forward and identify the hacker that had sold confidential information to both The New York Times and The Los Angeles Times. New stories followed for several days and there was an abundance of anticipation, but then the document's importance lost some of its significance. It became evident that no one was willing to give up the source, or that the hacker had acted on their own. Frustration ran rampant throughout the Pentagon and within every government office related to this issue.

Chapter 53

THE ELDERS, IN OBVIOUS discontent, understood that their missing other was indeed alive and somewhere within the vicinity of their communicative space, likely being held captive along with the membranes.

Believing that all were safe, the elders recognized, as painful as it may be, that it was time for the colony to return to their new habitat without the membranes and get on with their lives. It was now that these creatures could identify with the struggles of their cultures survival. This singular catacomb, and its connecting chamber were large enough to temporarily house and protect their population, but space within the passageway was limited. Other catacombs had to be constructed, and with this construction came a great amount of work. When considering the extensive amount of digging and carrying that would have to be done, the others realized that the work may just exhaust all of their abilities. They had not done this type of labor for decades. The immediacy of their situation found the elders forced to enlist the services of all, old and young, male and female. The work was difficult for all, but not as difficult for the offspring of the muscular diggers and carriers, for they found that their natural physique and their stamina was a product of their genes, passed on from one generation to the next. The fetus carriers experienced the most pain and discomfort for the only physical work they had ever accomplished was during the term of their pregnancies and the subsequent safe delivery of each membrane.

Eventually, one of these fetus carriers, experiencing unrelenting aches and pains, refused to further involve herself. Because of this refusal, she soon found out that this decision placed her into an unforeseen and dire situation. Considering the immediate need of all creatures to be involved and the reality that there was an abundance of fetus carriers in their community, the elders recognized that this fetus carrier would have to be used as the example, one that would clarify the elders stance on rebellion! The elders were well aware that other fetus carriers were struggling and could very well choose to follow this individual's lead, thus causing a needless slowdown of the work's progress. The elders were aware that this refusal could spread like wildfire and cause the less physical specimens to also refuse their necessary workload. There was a tremendous amount of work yet to be accomplished; building extensive catacombs, tunnels, and increasing the size of their venerable site, namely, the sacred chamber.

The elders had a decision to make and realized that this decision was made somewhat easier because this troublesome fetus carrier had little use as a worker. The decision was made to make an example of her, thereby instigating great terror and anxiety in those that may want to follow in her footsteps. In order to create this fear, the elders needed to find this disgruntled fetus carrier and create a significant ruckus, bringing mass recognition to this form of discipline. The elders began their search, and since the colony was so congested within their only catacomb, it didn't take long to locate their target.

None of the elders took the lead. Instead, they moved as one dark cloud and attacked the fetus carrier. They immediately and efficiently sliced, ripped, shredded, and bit into this disgruntled female, causing those in the immediate vicinity to recognize this for the ferocious, frenzied, and vicious attack that it was. What remained lay unrecognizable in a large pool of blood. The creatures that were in the immediate area quickly dispersed, thanking their lucky stars that they weren't the intended victim, and thus panic and worry ran rampant throughout the entire colony. Needless to say, there were no further incidents related to being a slacker when it came to work. The lesson was surely learned and subsequently stamped deeply within the memory bank of all creatures.

As the passageways were being constructed, every fiber of the digger's and carrier's musculature experienced tremendous amounts of fatigue. There was wonder and astonishment among the working force regarding how the old habitat was eve. The creatures knew that through their evolution, they had changed from leprous human beings to the present massive creatures, with horrific features and super strength. There was no recorded history, so these creatures had to seek out the oldest of the others and be totally dependent upon their recollection. Considering the length of the intertwining catacombs, the number of levels, the multitude of tunnels, and the tremendous size of the sacred chamber, it was estimated that it took approximately fifty years to complete the totality of their labyrinth.

The majority of the creature population assembled, and being completely aware of the elders disciplinary way, concluded that the work pace needed to be slowed; not drastically, but slowed. A proposal was presented to the elders suggesting that the creatures work in shifts. If they continued at the present pace, several would eventually die, thus depleting the necessary work force. After contemplating the proposal, the elder's response was heard: "Taking into consideration the colony's ever-increasing population, it is evident that the new habitat needs to have many more catacombs, tunnels, and possibly an additional chamber. To slow the construction is risky, for it is clear that the human is now fully aware that there are more of us. Due to the physical pain and suffering that the workers are experiencing, they need time to replenish their systems with food, blood, and a recuperative sleep!" The elders considered their options, and then decided that the shift approach made the best sense. This was presented to the work force and the entire colony agreed.

Now that it was evident that the humans were well aware of the creature's existence, what was the course of action that these creatures could or should take? The increased awareness by the human added a new dimension to their lives, and along with this awareness, an additional amount of fear and anxiety; the human was closer than it had ever been in more than a century. The creatures, one and all, could feel the intense anxiety exuding from their bodies as they passed one another in the catacombs; nervous energy abounded and the foulest of odors increased and escaped from their pores.

The elders, realizing that the Lone Creature had left the safety of the catacombs without their sanction, knew that its inexperience and lack of knowledge of the earth's surface could be a definite threat to the culture's existence. Initially, the real fear was that after being cautious for such a very long time, and taking it for granted that every other creature valued its anonymity, this Lone Creature was not just bold, but also foolish, impulsive, and reckless, that is, a real danger to the entire colony. This Lone Creature had taken it upon himself to venture onto the earth's surface and therefore break the most coveted of laws. It was evident by this individual's impulsive behavior that it placed its own desires ahead of those that were thought to be universally observed and sacred Fear, anxiety, stress, and a real sense of anger flourished throughout the hearts and souls of the entire culture. The elders were well aware that this Lone Creature had been aware of their universal law. The Lone Creature may have roamed the earth in its past, but there was no evidence, according to the elders, that this had ever happened. It may have roamed the earth just prior to this past time, and returned without being recognized, but It made the costliest of mistakes some two weeks ago, not only for itself, but for the entire creature population. Being so selfish would definitely bring it death, whether freed or if it escaped from its present captivity, or was found and then returned to the catacombs of the new habitat!

One hundred and twenty years! And in just a matter days, their world had been turned upside down and inside out, all because of a self-centered individual. "This was so very disgusting!" The creatures not only lost the only habitat that was cherished as their home, but they also lost a major segment of their history and a significant part of their next generation. The membranes, which were found by the government and transported to the hangar, were no longer seen as offspring, but human property. Pain, severe emotional sadness, and an unidentified stress level brought many of the mature creatures to the point where previously unheard primal sounds now emanated from deep within their being.

Grace and her family, as well as everyone else within the enclosure, were sitting or standing with their hands cupped over their ears as they attempted to lessen the volume of the creature's primal wail. This was such an amazing sight and sound! The creature seemed to be more massive than words could describe. Its chest continually expanded until an observer thought that it might burst, and then it steadily roared with such volume, such profound pain. It was as if this was the sound of someone pleading for another chance when it already knew that there was not another chance to be had.

Chapter 54

THE HISTORICAL SOCIETY OF Bucks County was instrumental in finding the connection between the creature and the leper colony that had its roots within Bucks County. Around that time, these unfortunate beings found themselves being ostracized by those that lived a normal existence, those that were not afflicted in any conceivable way by the disfiguring, disabling disease. It was as if these beings were on the earth to be singled out among those that made up the population of the human race. Besides their disgusting smell and horrific appearance, they also had internal tumors that pressed upon the surface and were the size of baseballs. There was also a multitude of visible lumps that protruded from the top of their lumpy heads to the skin that covered their lower appendages. To witness one of these creatures was, for all intents and purposes, to witness the appearance of all males within the colony. One's normal reaction when visualizing a mature male was to gradually lower one's head, involuntarily moving it from side to side, wondering, "Is there a God?" Ordinarily, one would not find it necessary to question his or her faith, but in this instance, the question could be heard coming from within: "Why would God have allowed this to happen to anyone or anything?"

While the creature and the membranes were being held captive and were constantly being monitored, there were two things that the present community of Edison and the community in the area of the hangar were experiencing. Both things were odd. At first, these occurrences happened with little recognition, but when the media caught wind of a connection to the creature and the membranes, there was a frantic race to see which of the reporters could arrive first upon the scene. Firstly, and just as important as the second, was the fact that a significant amount of government personnel had returned to the area where the membranes had been discovered. These people were intent upon using specialized equipment to take photos of the catacombs, tunnels, and the rest of the site that seemed to be the home, birthing location, and storage area for the creature colony.

The creature, membranes, and their previous habitat, along with the general location of the hangar continued to be the number one story. Newspapers, news magazines, television news, the internet, and shows such as 20/20 and 60 Minutes had, what seemed to be, unlimited expense accounts. This belief was given creditability at various times, but especially when a story, appearing to be factual, was written in a major NYC newspaper and in The Los Angeles Times. The story, while lending itself to creditability, also employed sensationalism, and the significance of the story, if found to be true, most probably could be extremely costly to two powerful newspapers. The stories were centered on specialized government personnel who were officially investigating the extensive catacombs and tunnels, and especially the creature's chamber so that dimensions could be taken of the original habitat. There was a proposal to relocate the entire creature colony from its present site to the seventy-three acre government site bordered by Bristol Road. The proposed habitat was to be the location where the captive creature and the membranes were presently being housed.

Through further media investigation, it was found that there was, indeed, a large constituency of military specialists at the previous creature habitat, and that the specialized four-wheelers that were previously used to search this habitat were now being brought back. There were several of these four-wheelers already at the site, and a crane could be seen lowering them below the surface. Since the ceiling covering was excavated to allow the four-wheelers to be lowered, it was clearly evident why all personnel in this immediate vicinity were wearing full body protection. This body suit was securely attached to a protective head gear and, in turn, was connected to a canister of oxygen. While this gear was worn, it was impossible to be invaded by the slightest amount of bacteria, and incredulous odors became all but nonexistent.

Everyone was ordered to wear this form of body gear, and once these investigative personnel were lowered to their designated four-wheeler, it was easy to understand why. With helmet lamps directed toward the flooring, or wherever their eyes brought their heads, these investigative personnel felt okay to put their full body weight upon their boots. If they would have only looked at their designated four-wheeler, instead of taking the surface for granted, they would have noticed that the floor was falsely represented, that each four-wheeler was submerged approximately fourteen inches below what had appeared to be the catacomb's flooring. Furthermore, if they would have been able to smell their immediate environment, then they may have had suspicions regarding the flooring. As their boots came into contact with what was assumed to be the floor, they were immediately thankful that they were still connected to the crane's semi-taut cables. As these investigators put their body weight upon their boots, you may be able to recognize their immediate reaction. Down went their boots, for as they submerged, neither got a solid purchase. Eventually, both did find ground, but not before sinking deeply into the accumulated body waste.

There were other personnel upon the earth's surface, and they too wore the protective gear. All of these personnel watched as each investigator was lowered toward what was considered to be the catacomb's surface. All were startled when noticing the frantic behavior of the lead investigator, and subsequently motioned for the crane operator to stop the cable. The operator, upon recognizing the directive, immediately neutralized the crane's power. Upon doing this, the gears could be heard as they rubbed one another, making aged metal to metal sounds, and the cable became taut. The crane operator descended the lengthy ladder and then jumped the remaining three feet, landing upon the earth. The operator, fearing the worst, walked hurriedly to the opening and looked toward the bottom. He had expected to see this investigator standing on the passageway's surface, already detached from the cable. What he actually observed was that the investigator, for some unknown reason, was in a position with his boots being held slightly above what appeared to be the catacomb's surface. It was at this point that the crane operator spoke loudly to the investigator, asking about the problem.

The investigator responded, and an explanation followed. Soon after, it was evident that the crane operator climbed the ladder and within a few minutes, the investigator, via the crane's cable, was returned to the earth's surface. At that time, it was decided that this investigator was to be the go between for the crane operator and the other investigators. The operator understood that what appeared to be the surface was not. This surface was merely a porous composition of waste that had been deposited throughout various catacombs during the lifetime of the species.

The go-between investigator was to use hand signals in order to communicate with both parties, ensuring that all were safe. That was done without a hitch, and soon afterward, all of the investigators had unhooked their cable connection. It was then that these men found themselves struggling while sloshing through the waste to the location of their partially submerged four-wheelers. It was at this point that the go-between was finally lowered to the earthen floor; he too unhooked, and subsequently found that walking through the waste was exhausting while proceeding to the location of his assigned four-wheeler.

The machine's headlamp was turned on; this lamp had been specifically mounted onto the frontal area of each four-wheeler, between and above the headlights and it produced a tremendous amount of critical, softened light. This light source afforded the investigators a clear view of the walls, ceiling, and the waste that leveled itself just below the vehicle's headlights. Even more importantly, since these catacombs were, for the most part, an unknown, this lamp illuminated the area a great distance to the front of the vehicles. Securely mounted above and just slightly to the rear of the lamp was a video camera; rather than limit this excursion to an occasional picture, there was adequate justification for continual recording.

During a previous reconnaissance performed by military specialists, it was discovered that a large number of catacombs and connecting tunnels existed, and because of the tunnel's depth, only lightweight four-wheelers were to be used. Unfortunately for these investigators, maps were not drawn, and therefore the exact location of the tunnels wasn't definitive. Directing their four-wheelers this way and that, the investigators occasionally got caught up and were in complete awe when considering the precision of these catacombs. They found it to be astonishing that the catacombs were constructed within the complete darkness of Mother Earth's depths. It was when these men had finished their investigation and back upon the surface that one shared a thought with the others. He said that he had been raised on the east coast and when a child, his parents would take the family to the Jersey Shore two weeks of every summer. While vacationing, he remembered going to Wildwood to experience the variety of exciting rides. He went on to say that one of the rides, the haunted house, reminded him of the time that he had just spent driving along the expanse of the catacombs.

When traveling along the rickety track of the haunted house, one would inevitably remember the darkness that was encountered. All of a sudden, and without any warning, a gory scene with several mannequins would become brightly illuminated just off to one side of the passenger car as it turned a corner. It was inevitable, whenever this happened, that children would scream while others raised their arms and hands to protect themselves. The ride continued, and the riders were continually caught off guard until heavy wooden doors opened, light appeared, and the end of the ride was at hand. The investigator said that this ride, along the expanse of the various catacombs, brought back those distant memories, and that he half-expected to witness an illuminated, gory monster at one time or another as the trek took him along the various passageways.

At the far end of the lamp's illumination, there appeared to be something odd. The closer the team got, the more aware they became of what they were witnessing. They had been proceeding slowly through the lengthy catacomb, but when their eyes fell upon something odd, they immediately downshifted, and moved even more cautiously. They then reported to their headquarters' personnel who, in turn, were intently watching their monitors and observing that something up ahead had caught their undivided attention. Eventually, they were within a short distance of what appeared to an expanse to their immediate front at floor level, measuring approximately ten feet in diameter. At this point the four-wheelers were turned off with the emergency brake set. Each investigator dismounted and stood, knee deep in waste, utilizing the lamp for illumination while they peered into what appeared to be a bottomless void. They came to the conclusion that it would be best to attempt a measurement.

The depth of this tunnel was measured to be fifty-eight feet, give or take a few inches either way, and that is when the forethought of utilizing these more costly, lightweight machines came fully into play. Each machine had a thickened rope knotted at each of the machine's four corners, and then these four ropes were joined at an equal length in one chain approximately ten feet beyond the machine. Just prior to maneuvering the machine over the lip of the opening, there was a considerable amount of apprehension as to whether or not their total body weight would be enough to control the weight of each four-wheeler when lowered to the tunnel's floor. As an added safety feature, a precaution was decided upon: attach the farthest end of the gathered rope around the three remaining machines and secure it there. The team made sure not to allow enough slack to permit the machine to free-fall and subsequently be destroyed. As it was, the machine was to be halted approximately five feet above the bottom of the tunnel.

Apprehension and stress ran rampant as each machine was maneuvered so that it rested in a level position just beyond and below the top edge of the tunnel. These men were thankful that they were cautious, for they realized that these machines were even lighter than they had imagined. The investigators were on the rope, much like the alignment for a tug of war, and the one closest to the edge found that a lengthy board came in handy to keep the machine from digging into, and getting caught, at points along its descent. Once a machine had reached the bottom of the chasm, one of the team lowered himself to it, unknotted the rope, and then drove the machine along that level of the tunnel's connecting catacomb. After shutting down the machine, he then returned to the rope and shimmied up, as if it was a normal occurrence. Although the final machine was more cumbersome and challenging, it did get to the bottom without any major difficulty. While the heaviest team member held the rope securely, the others individually descended the rope swiftly and with ease. The remaining member bundled the rope, tied it off, and then slung it around his shoulder. He then made use of the tree climbing equipment that had been previously stashed on his four-wheeler; he attached the metal spikes securely to each boot and utilized a small pick-ax in each hand as he safely descended the tunnel. The team followed this same regimen at each tunnel, and once the four-wheelers were safely aligned at the bottom, it was then that the search continued.

Eventually, the entire habitat had been videoed, or so it seemed, and the trek brought all of the machines to the topmost area of what they hoped would be the final funnel. The machines were lowered just as they had been at each previous tunnel, but as they drove along, it became apparent that the team was gradually ascending a passageway. This passageway was far, and I mean far, extending along the lowest level of all the catacombs. Up, up, up they continued their gradual assent; the catacomb had a variety of off-shoots, but eventually it ended. It was now obvious that they were at the topmost level, for as it turned out, the surface area of this passageway was directly adjacent to that of the chamber. After thoroughly investigating and filming this room, the machines were driven along until they came upon another tunnel. They stopped and thought that they would have to proceed on foot, but fortunately, a team member noticed planks of wood lying against a wall. Upon further examination, the planks were found to be just what the doctor ordered, and they were then laid across the tunnel's opening. This procedure continued at each tunnel location; after traveling along what apparently was an endless catacomb, the team was finally, and joyfully, at the location of the entrance. The crane operator was awakened from what he described as a cat nap, and then the machines and the investigators were brought to the earth's surface.

Chapter 55

MEANWHILE, AT THE PREVIOUSLY abandoned federal site where the creature and the membranes were being kept, there was an extensive excavation initiated. A seemingly endless line of oversized dump trucks, starting at the entrance to the compound, went down the roadway as far as the eye could see. Within the security conscious compound were different kinds of those heavy equipment machines with gigantic tires. It was evident that there was a huge excavation planned for this area that had been uninhabited for at least fifteen years. Little was known about this location, especially among the civilians that resided in this section of Bucks County. At least three-quarters of the landmass was flat; there was an airplane hangar, a few other large buildings, and smaller ones that resembled military barracks. All of these buildings were located in the same vicinity, while off to one side, and far from any building, there were several acres of dense, lush vegetation. Within that specified area, there were a large number of tall, thickened trees, and each was fully covered with leaves.

Hours turned into days, and days into weeks, and still the main emphasis was placed on the ever-continuing removal of tons, and then more tons of earth and rocks; even boulders. This process went on as if forever; deeper and deeper the excavation went into the depths of the earth. The joke among the workers was that the target was China. As the work penetrated deeply, huge steel plates were continuously trucked in, removed from the flatbeds, and stacked one upon the other. The cache of steel plates was stored just within the entrance gates where the surface would remain untouched by the excavation. Specialized flatbeds came and went and when they stopped coming, the heightened stacks of steel plating could be seen from a distance. Exclamations of astonishment could be heard among the nearby homeowners as they observed the many towering stacks of the enormous steel plates. People communicated their wonderment as to the tremendous amount of plating; could it, in fact, be too much for the project?

Among the huge machines there was a towering crane, the kind that was often seen when skyscrapers were being built. This type of crane was unique, for its operator, who could have been Larry White at a time in his distant past, had to climb a one-hundred and fifty foot ladder and, being this far above the ground level, had to walk a precarious horizontal distance until he entered the operator's enclosure. All of the necessary shifters were within, and Larry would have had the ability to view the majority of the work place below. Its height made the crane extraordinary, and along with its height, the crane had mobility. It had the ability to move, ever so slowly, along extensive tracts; to the left, right, forward, and backward.

In the same area as the crane there was a mammoth earth mover. This machine was also advanced in size and had a very large bucket that had the ability to deeply penetrate the massive landmass. Considering its massive size, the term earth mover made a lot more sense than to continually describe the machine as a steam shovel. There were also immense bulldozers and a large number of roller types.

For fifteen years, this entire area laid dormant, boring, and quiet for the most part. Now, without the slightest warning, there appeared to be a dramatic change. Diesel-powered engines were constantly laboring and their tractor's smoke stacks billowed huge puffs of blackened clouds. The neighbors of the surrounding community could be seen on their front porches and lawns, observing and intently listening to the powerful roars of the heavy equipment.

It was a fact that the media, which had been continually covering the story related to the creatures and the membranes, were in the right place at the right time. While these journalistic types were checking out the information regarding a massive excavation, they just happened to witness the flatbed trucks as they continually delivered the tongue and groove steel plating. Each plate was seen as huge and extreme, and measured twenty feet in length, fourteen feet in width, and four inches in thickness. These were stacked high on the flatbeds, and were secured so they had little or no movement. One flatbed after another, these steel plates were delivered without incident and the very powerful crane moved the plates to their designated stacking areas. There were two distinct areas, each having its stacks of steel plating; one area had a multitude of rectangular plating where all were tongue and groove. The other area had steel plating that was rounded with no tongue or groove along one of its lengths, but was tongue and groove along its corresponding length and widths. The steel plates that were rounded at the corner and along its extended outside length were to be utilized as some sort of finishing touch to the topmost lengths and at the cornering portions of the towering walls.

The excavation continued from the very early morning until the last remnants of daylight, five days each week and until four o'clock in the afternoon on Saturdays. Once the work was begun, the endless supply of dump trucks seemed to move continuously. Being loaded with large mounds of dirt and covered with a tarp, the trucks moved slowly, but with purpose. Every gear seemed to come into play while transporting the dirt, rocks, and boulders. Truck, after truck, after truck, the earth was removed from this immediate area; while watching from the bordering homes, the designated surface area began to disappear. Where the earth movers were previously seen loading the multitude of dump trucks, none of this equipment was now visible. It could be heard, but couldn't be see. Soon after, one could hear these laboring machines, but within the adjacent community, the distinct puffs of blackened smoke seemed to be the only thing evidenced. Upon a drivers return to the excavation site, it became more than clear that a tremendous amount of dirt had been removed, and as unbelievable as it may be, approximately ten times that amount remained to be dug and removed. Roadways passed by the site and when a first time observer peered across the vast expanse, it was difficult to see clearly from one side to the other. This was, without a doubt, a magnificent place for the colony's habitat. Landscapers had previously been there, and had done all of the necessary planning, so that the trees, bushes, and shrubs could be safely uprooted and then their life sustaining roots, along with an abundance of rich soil, would be wrapped within large swathes of burlap. When the date of the uprooting came, it was then that the landscapers returned to the site. The landmass that directly encircled the trees was removed, and while the trees still stood tall, a smaller crane was maneuvered so that its topmost area was directly above each subsequent tree, bush, and shrub. A cable was gradually lowered and one at a time, the cable was securely attached to a tree's upper trunk. As if these were miniature trees instead of the fully grown ones that they actually were, they were slowly elevated so that their roots became unattached to the soil. This process consumed a large amount of time, though finally all of the vegetation that could be saved was, and all of the roots with their adjoined soil were preserved within the burlap swathes.

Extended flatbeds were driven to where the vegetation lay after being prepared for a short term of storage, and this is where a formidable crane hefted each tree and secured all upon the specialty flatbeds. Once all of the vegetation had been loaded, these flatbeds exited the area of the habitat and waited until all were to be replanted.

The dump trucks could be eerily heard whenever their operators attempted to get the transmissions into their lowest of gears, and then, moving ever so slowly, the laborious shifting was heard until the gear was finally set. The trucks seemingly struggled with their massive loads, but before a truck was seen, several elongated, powerful puffs of blackened smoke were witnessed as the gear was changed, and the truck's accelerator moved the weight forward. Much like the chain that drives a Harley Davidson motorcycle or possibly a Can-Am cycle, these trucks had huge linked chains which made a smooth, wrrrrring sound once the truck was driven along the road surface in a higher gear. The trucks left the excavation site, filled to the brink, and each payload was covered for a safe transport. Eventually, they would return emptied, and at that time the chain wrrrrrred noticeably because there wasn't any labor involved. These enormous trucks could be clearly heard as they moved along the roadway that led to the gates, but the sound was noticeably changed, muffled, if you will, as they descended the roadway that gradually led to the bottom level of the ever deepening excavation site. One of the drivers was truly surprised; he had previously seen the size and towering height of the crane, but now realized, from a distance, that only half of it could be seen above the earth's surface…unbelievable!

What appeared to be a lengthy amount of time was probably just that, but as astonishing as it may seem, all of the earth that needed to be displaced was, and now it was being leveled and prepared for the laying of the steel flooring. The engineers were hard at work, and with the assistance of the multitude of machine powered rollers, the packed earth base was measured to be as wide and as lengthy as was needed. It was at this point that the tongue in groove, rectangular sheets of steel began to be connected, creating the formidable flooring for the creature's new habitat. Now, the cranes were the only pieces of heavy equipment that remained within the excavation site. The excavation company had an extensive storage yard, and this is where the dump trucks were emptying their heavy loads of dirt and stone. After a period of time, the storage yard no longer had huge mounds of earth, but in fact, had transformed the area into a small mountain range. Two earth movers were at that location, and as the dirt was trucked in, the earth movers spread the payload; it was then that the dump trucks headed back to the excavation site. It was truly unbelievable how much dirt, stones and rocks had been moved from the new home for the creature population.

Chapter 56

THE MEDIA WERE KEPT at bay and newspaper sales were dropping off; finally, there was a substantial leak, and the public's attention piqued once again. Neighbors who lived in a close proximity to the site were interviewed, and their stories adorned various sections of a wide variety of newspapers. These stories appeared to be more along the lines of sensationalism, but were interesting and therefore kept the attention of subscribers as far away as New York City. These stories turned out to be the tip of an iceberg!

The story that followed these headlines differed slightly throughout the U.S. and abroad, but the emphasis was always the same. The federal government site that was being partially used to house the captured Lone Creature and nurture the membranes was to become the new habitat for the creature population. It was the government's plan to use helicopters containing state of the art, high-tech equipment to locate the colony. Once located, the plan was to capture the entire colony and relocate them to the new habitat. While the habitat was in the process of being constructed, it was estimated as to when the finished product could be expected. This is when the plan for capture would be disclosed to all relevant personnel.

The engineers gathered all of the information that had been acquired when the military specialists had used the four-wheelers to survey and video the entirety of the old habitat. When this investigation was completed, it was then that these specialists, and their high-tech four-wheelers, were removed from the habitat. All of the man-hours that went into the investigation and discovery of the creature's original habitat brought a great reward. Within the hangar, but outside the sterile transparent chamber, plans were laid out on tables; several blueprints of what were envisioned to be the creature's new home. While the engineers checked the specifics of these prints with the construction supervisors, the heavy equipment moved as if it was in perpetual motion. Indeed, there was progress; one by one, the steel plating was tediously maneuvered by the crane's operator. The steel plates were lowered to the point where construction teams could handle them; it was then that the plating was ever so slowly lowered and maneuvered into their proper placement. These men used walkie-talkies and hand directed the crane operators, steering the plating so that the tongue and groove continually connected and were precisely interlocked. Once the inspectors gave their okay, it was then that those specific tongue and groove plates were spot welded, thus remaining that way for evermore. Plate after plate were laid in place, connected, and welded; this process moved along nicely, and one of the smaller crane operators maneuvered his rig along an extended track that now lay upon an expanse of the plated flooring. This work continued throughout the week, and as the flooring covered more space, the crane gained a better purchase upon the original set of tracks. Again, plates were laid, and finally the base was completely installed. The curved ended plates fit perfectly into the outlying section and extended upwards so that the walls could begin to be constructed. The four corner curvature plates had to be the most exact, for each corner was the mainstay for all of the enclosure's walls.

With the flooring complete, and the sides, ends and corners curved and facing upwards, it was now time to begin constructing the walls and eventually the topmost corners. Just like the flooring was connected and welded, so were the curved sides and corners. All curved base plates were more securely welded, mainly because the habitat walls would initially have little support from within and without. With the complete base intact, the walls began to take form. The crane was used to manipulate each wall plate to its proper placement; it was then securely connected and welded. This same process continued for several more weeks and then the walls and corners were to the point where the entire enclosure could be seen by those living in the neighboring homes.

There was an air of elation among the excavation and construction crews, for more than one-half of the work had been completed. It was Saturday, and being off Sunday, they decided to celebrate. The entire crew was from areas within the County of Bucks, so they decided to party somewhere close by. Representatives of the crew made the necessary arrangements so they, their wives, and significant others could meet at the Cock & Bull, located in Lahaska. This restaurant would be the perfect eatery for anyone interested in nearby tourist attractions, such as Peddler's Village and New Hope.

The crew had a banquet room that could easily service seventy to one-hundred people. Dinner was buffet style and was nicely laid out; there was also the opportunity to visit the bar. Everyone had a fantastic time; the men that were single and had come without an escort; well, these men had the opportunity to venture into the bar area and mingle after the dinner festivities were completed.

The crew enjoyed their gathering and was well-rested following the long weekend; it was now very early Monday and everyone showed up for work. The weather was changing, but still it was somewhat brisk and chilly, as this was the norm during this early hour.

Chapter 57

WITHIN THE STERILE ENCLOSURE, the nurses were keeping their diligent vigil over the membranes within their sterilized setting. More than two months had gone by since the membranes were found and brought to this site. Several times, on a daily basis, the membranes had an ultrasound and each time the results were promising. There was apprehension, however, for those doing the ultrasounds were well aware that they were dealing with an unknown entity. At this point in time, there appeared to be similar amounts of fluid remaining within each of the membranes, which was an indication that all of these membranes began their gestation period around the same time.

The various doctors and nurses went over the findings and came to the conclusion that the fetuses were all at similar stages of development and that all appeared to be quite healthy. The only major change and main consideration given to all of the membrane's development was the fact that a small amount of the fluid surrounding each fetus had already been consumed. This factual observation was noted and would be further observed during ensuing ultra sounds. There was also a note of interest discussed by all personnel that were present. Could it be that when the majority of this encircling fluid was gone that the membrane would become susceptible to dryness, and its subsequent birth? The doctors and nurses agreed that this was a logical conclusion and considerable thought was now given to where the fetuses would be kept following their departure from the membranes. It was estimated that there were several months remaining before the births would take place, but a plan had to be devised if it were the case that the births happened sooner. A member of the team that had investigated the original habitat was summoned, and was requested to bring a copy of the habitat video with him. This was done and then viewed; the decision was to construct a small version of the chamber and it was to replicate the creature's original chamber. Within this enclosure, there would be a pile of animal flesh and a vat of blood. The scientists were hoping that the continual ultrasounds would give them enough information so a calculation could be deducted, projecting the month of birth. Once this was done, the flesh and blood could be readied and stored; awaiting the new births.

Chapter 58

AT THE CONSTRUCTION SITE, the crane operator was maneuvering the steel plating so that the assemblers and the welders could effectively do their assigned jobs. One layer after the other of the steel plating continued to enclose the emptiness within until all of the walls were capped off at forty-five feet above the surface. At this point, the topmost area curved inward and hung over the emptiness for approximately eight feet. This extension of overhang was meant to assure the outlying communities that these creatures would not be able to escape their habitat. At the topmost area of the encircling wall, there was a mirror image of overhang, only this overhang extended eight feet toward the roadways and homes. This overhang, when observed from above, formed a type of widened 'V,' and laid within this configuration were bundles of extended and connected razor wire. As a safety precaution, the razor wire entirely filled the widened 'V' and was tack welded to the steel plating at locations all the way around the entire enclosure, thus guaranteeing that no one would ever gain an entrance, or an exit, by scaling the walls and going over the top.

New notices adorned the outside walls stating that this was a federal government site and that no unauthorized personnel were permitted within twenty feet of the enclosure. The walls, razor wire, and the notices were to assure all that no one was permitted within the walled enclosure without an authorized security clearance. At the far end of this habitat, closest to the entry point, there remained an opening that separated the wall's width by twenty feet from the earth's surface to the top of the enclosures height. It was also at this height that a twenty-foot wide section of the razor wire was temporarily removed. This opening was intentional, and would be closed off once the new habitat was completely finished. Each of these plates that were intentionally missing had their tongues purposely removed, all the way around, so they could be placed securely within the slot and then tack-welded at a future time. At that time, the plates were not in place because the dump trucks needed an entrance and exit while returning tons of dirt within the enclosure.

Now, this ground floor for the habitat's prefabricated catacombs, tunnels, and storage chamber was filled in and leveled several feet above the steel-plated base. To an observer, anywhere between the storage yard for the dirt and the site of the new habitat, it was seemingly clear that there were dump trucks from all over Bucks County being utilized to return the dirt to the government site.

Along the truck route, there were several intersecting roads and streets; at these locations, flagmen were present and were directing traffic through the intersection, but not allowing regular traffic to enter onto the truck route. Throughout the first day, this was hectic, but the second day brought with it calm; those civilians that had experienced the frustration the day before, now sought out alternative routes. The trucks snaked back and forth along the route for more than a week, and finally there was enough dirt to construct the lowest level of the creature's catacombs. These catacombs were state of the art, and once installed at their level, it was easy to recognize that each level of extended catacomb was an intellectual configuration.

The bottom of each passageway, or catacomb, had a perforated mesh that would give a little under the weight of the heaviest of these creatures, and this mesh was an intricate part of the habitat; a health factor for the creatures, and also for the people living in the surrounding communities.

Beneath the mesh, there was an enclosed conveyor belt constructed of a state of the art material. The conveyor belt was as wide as each catacomb, and it was aligned with a multitude of indentations, similar to an oversized egg crate. These indentations had the ability to capture and transport any or all of the creature's body waste and subsequently move it towards a machine that would dispose of it. A state of the art forced water spray was attached intermittently along the mesh, and subsequently would come on, power wash the waste off the mesh and onto the conveyor, thus maintaining a healthy environment.

𝔉orbidden
𝔓art 2

THE CATACOMBS, TUNNELS AND chamber were constructed of a material that had its interior temperature maintained by the temperature of the creatures that would be living within. It was as if this novel habitat was centrally heated and cooled, dependent upon the weather conditions and the creature's over-all body temperature. The mesh had a lifetime warrantee and was guaranteed not to stretch beyond a distance that could interfere with the movement of the conveyors below. Two other reasons, besides the lifetime warrantee, were factored in before the webbing was purchased. The fact that the mesh material would remain nonstick and had elasticity, thus allowing the waste to continually fall through to the conveyors, and when a creature's weight was no longer on a webbed section, it would spring back to its original position; the conveyors would only activate when there was enough accumulated waste lying upon and within the lengthy widened receptacles.

A power washing steam attached intermittently above and along the wall, and throughout the mesh cycle would become activated and thoroughly power-wash the waste. The power washing mechanism caused the waste to break away from the mesh and fall down upon the waiting conveyor, thus enabling the habitat to maintain a much healthier environment than what the creatures had previously experienced.

Each conveyor was extremely sensitive and when a certain amount of weight rested upon it, it was then that the conveyor would become self-activated, moving independently toward its catacomb's centralized waste station. Once each conveyor was a few feet from the area of its waste station, it would by-pass its normal route, thus entering its specified waste station and simultaneously had its waste removed. As if not losing a beat, the conveyor was completely cleansed, disinfected, and then air-dried. The conveyor then left the area of its waste drop and traveled its return route, until the cleansed area realigned beneath and along the pathway of the catacomb from which it just bypassed.

Chapter 59

EACH CONVEYOR'S HOUSING, BEING abnormally wide, was placed upon the outlying galvanized bolts that were embedded, and ran along the top of the cement-guided tracks. These were then secured with doubled galvanized nuts and spot-welded. The bolts were purposely protruding above the spot welded nuts so that a hard, rubberized material, resembling that of a fat donut, could be placed on top of the nuts, acting as a buffer between the catacomb's base and the conveyor above. The bolts extended through and above this buffer, and therefore were used to attach the catacomb to the top of the elongated conveyor. Once the buffer was between the lengthy catacomb and the cement guide-way, it was then that the catacomb's base conveyor was encased within a type of protective insulation. The insulation was indeed protective, for it had been thoroughly tested and found to prevent burrowing animals, sharp objects, dirt, and water from entering the conveyor mechanism, and possibly interfering with the smoothness of its operation. The catacomb extended for several thousand feet, snaking to the left and to the right, giving the appearance of being interconnected. In fact, it was separated by tons of dirt and stones.

Each catacomb had its own waste drop; the waste that was collected at this point was then deposited onto a type of dumb waiter platform that moved the waste up and to a centralized, elaborate waste station that was situated upon the earth's surface. It was here that the waste was decomposed and eventually vaporized.

Chapter 60

THE TUNNELS WERE BEING lowered vertically, one by one, using the tall crane that was now purposefully situated work along lengthy tracks centralized within this initial catacomb. There was plenty of room for it to travel the length of the catacomb and still be able to avoid contact with the inward snaking of the passageway. A cable was attached to the topmost part of each tunnel, and once the tunnel was freely hanging, it was hand-maneuvered until it hung straight up and down. These tunnels were constructed so that they all were the same, for the most part, and were curved inward at the two ends, resembling the curvature of the smoke stacks upon the larger troop carriers.

The circumference of each was somewhat smaller than that of a catacomb, for these were to be used as the creatures ascended and descended from one catacomb to the next. Tubular in shape, there were many, and each had the same diameter as the next. Sleeves projected from the tunnels and also from the connecting catacombs so that they could be interconnected to one another. Once these sleeves were solidly connected and welded, it was then that tons of dirt was placed between the catacomb and its plated wall. There were also openings facing inwardly along the catacombs, but these were some distance from the outer ones. One by one, all of the inner and outer openings were aligned, sleeve to sleeve with their designated tunnel. Then, their individual cap or covering was released, removed, and then the sleeves were connected and securely welded.

It was then that truckload upon truckload returned from the storage yard laden high with what seemed to be an endless supply of dirt and stones. To save time, each truck unloaded its payload into the area that was at the bottom of the excavation so that it could then be transferred by the crane's gigantic clamp-type shovel.

Eventually, hundreds of tons of dirt were placed between the surrounding walls and the entire exterior of the initial catacomb. The protruding sleeves of the initial catacomb were checked one final time and then each tunnel's lowest of the four sleeves was connected and welded. It was at this point that additional tons of dirt and stones were distributed until the only things visible were an earthen floor, four individual towers, cranes, and the vastness of the enclosure's wall.

The entire length and width of the initial catacomb, plus the snaking of its lengthy passageway, was now completely covered with dirt and stones. It was time to replicate the initial catacomb, and all of its intricacies with that of the other three and eventually the chamber. Approximately forty feet of packed dirt separated each horizontal layer of catacomb and off-shooting paths, its connecting conveyor and an accessible location for each and every connecting tunnel. This tonnage did not just cover the aforementioned object. Instead, it raised the entire surface to a certain height, save the area where the crane and its tracks were positioned.

The dirt and stones continued to be trucked in, deposited, and then it was distributed via the cranes throughout most of the enclosure. After enough dirt was tightly packed and leveled throughout, it was realized that there was, as planned, an additional forty feet over and above the first and now the second tier. Before each tier of catacombs was locked in by the weight of the deposited and packed dirt, it was imperative that the connecting sleeves of the catacombs, and of each and every tunnel, be properly aligned and welded.

Ultimately, the third catacomb tier and its many necessary, connecting parts were properly attached and intermittently welded, and then its grouping was then readied for the topmost catacomb and the all-important chamber.

As the preparation was being finalized for the installation of the fourth and final tier, it was then that one of the workers was heard to be thinking out loud. It was easy to hear him talking to his self, followed by his raucous laughter, and this laughter caught the attention of others within the immediate area. He laughed so hard that his eyelids were squeezed shut, and while joyful tears ran down his cheeks, he finally took a break from the laughter. He regained some of his composure and remarked to anyone that was willing to listen, "Do they plan on burying the cranes along with those cylinders?" As his laughter erupted again, others were heard to chime in, the merriment snowballed until most could be heard, attempting to talk while laughing.

A supervisor was drawn to the group's laughter and eventually became aware as to the reason for the merriment. He waited for the laughter to subside, and it eventually did, most likely due to witnessing his stoic presence. Not known for being the life of any party, the supervisor, while slowly turning his head to the left and right, asked, "Have any of you given any thought as to how we are going to retrieve the cranes from where they are?" The men, feeling somewhat slighted, admitted that none had given this their undivided attention. The supervisor was then heard to say, "That's why we are paid the big bucks; it's called cleverness!" He went on to say, as if giving an explanation, "There was a time when a group of men continually, day after day, used their picks and shovels to dig an elongated trench which became deeper and longer with each passing day. It just so happened that on a specific day, the heat was practically unbearable. While the men were hard at work, their supervisor, wearing a clean, pressed white shirt and pressed pants, came by to check on the crew. Seeing the supervisor at the top of the digging site, one of the men took a break and climbed out of the trench. This laborer was somewhat disheveled and was immersed in sweat; he drank a ladle full of cool water, and then approached the supervisor saying, "We work hard each and every day, year round, no matter what the weather, and go home dirty, tired, and totally exhausted. You, on the other hand, come to work clean and spiffy, never touch a pick or an axe, and leave when you want, appearing the same as when you arrived! And you get paid a lot more than us. Why is that?"

Their supervisor took a step back and then said, It's intelligence! The laborer then asked, "What is this intelligence and how do I get it?" The supervisor then said that, rather than to explain what it was, he would rather take the time to show the laborer. The supervisor motioned for the laborer to follow him, and told him to bring a shovel. The laborer retrieved the shovel and followed the supervisor to a nearby tree. It was here that they stopped walking and the supervisor placed his opened hand very close to, and just to the forefront of the tree, about head high. The laborer looked at the supervisor and then the placement of his open hand. The supervisor then said, "You are about to witness intelligence; I want you to take that shovel, get a mighty grip and hit my hand just as hard as you'd like." The laborer had had disagreements with this supervisor and now saw this as a way of getting even. In his amazement, the laborer said, "You mean that it is okay for me to smash your hand?" The supervisor emphatically said, "Yep, go ahead! As hard as you can!"

The laborer spit onto his palms and rubbed them briskly together, creating the necessary friction; he then picked up the shovel, got a good grip and stared at the hand, zeroing in on it. The laborer took a powerful stance and let go with the mightiest of swings. **BAMMMMMMMMMMM!!** The shovel collided forcefully with the tree, causing the handle to snap, and the laborer's body to visibly shake, as if he were convulsing. When the laborer settled down he looked at the supervisor and noticed that the hand was not injured. The laborer was confused, and on the verge of being angry when he vehemently said, "You moved your hand!" His supervisor moved a foot back and then replied; "Now that's intelligence!"

The supervisor continued his explanation. The laborer then walked away from his supervisor, took another drink of the cool water, settled, and then returned to the trench. He picked out another shovel and got back to work. One of the other laborers asked him where he had been for so long, and he told this man that he was talking with the supervisor.

Eventually, that supervisor told the laborers to take five. While they drank water and sat together the supervisor 'thing' was mentioned, and that specific laborer said that he found out why the supervisor made so much more money than they did, wore nice clothes, never picked up and pick or shovel, and left work whenever he wanted. The other laborers, almost in unison asked, "What's the reason?" The laborer kind of smirked, and then saw his chance to do some teaching of his own. He responded that it was due to intelligence. As if in turn, the co-workers did just as the teacher had previously done. They were emphatic, wanting to know the meaning of 'intelligence'. He picked out one of his co-workers and said, "Rather than tell you, let me show you; pick up your shovel and make sure that you have a mighty grip!" The 'teacher' then put his opened hand in front of his own face and emphatically said, "Use your shovel and hit my hand just as hard as you want!"

So much for intelligence!

Chapter 61

THE FOUR TIERS OF catacombs emptied into the various tunnels and the topmost catacomb had a capped passageway that faced toward the center area of the construction, curving away and bending toward the closest end of the habitat. When the crew was ready, they had the catacomb extension lowered from the surface. Ever so slowly, the lower end moved closer to the capped area of the catacomb; with the extension held in place, the crew uncapped the entrance and thus the two cylinders were joined and welded, becoming one.

The flooring of the extension was webbed, as were the other catacombs, but slightly below the webbing of this ascending passageway was a permanent, nonstick surface. Beneath this webbing, the surface was slanted, motionless, slippery, and encouraged any kind of waste to slide freely, speedily, below the webbing until it landed in the pockets of the weight sensitive conveyor. It was at this point that the nonstick webbing would be power steamed, whether it was necessary or not.

Along the final and topmost of the continuously snaking catacombs, there was a passageway that led away from the main catacomb and headed in the direction of the habitats outside wall. Upon entering this outwardly curved off-shoot, a person could walk a few yards only to be halted by an additional capped sleeve. This section was at the furthest end of one of the habitat's sides and although the capped sleeve headed in the direction of the corner and subsequent walls, there was a large, vacant area in between. Previously, there had not been any noticeable work done in this area, but there could have been, for this area was quite a distance from the entrance.

The area had been leveled, and with the cap removed from the off-shoot, it was noticeable a distance away from the end of the off-shoot that there were several huge galvanized bolts, intermittently located, in a designed pattern. Upon further investigation, it was evident that each bolt was an inch and a half in diameter, and that each was solidly encased in a block of sunken concrete. While the crew finished up their investigative work, their attention became centered upon a noise in the distance. A minute went by, and as it did the noise gradually became louder. Eventually, the womp, womp, womp, womp, womp became recognizable; some kind of helicopter could now be seen high above the wall. As this flying machine got closer, it became evident that lengthy cables were hanging from its undercarriage, but whatever was attached was not yet recognizable. Closer and closer the helicopter came, and then it was evident that the cables were connected to a prefabricated structure. Womp!,Womp! Womp! Womp! Womp! It was now that the helicopter hovered above the location that held the secured bolts in place.

The cumbersome blades caused the dirt to swirl, but no damage was done below. Slowly but surely, the helicopter descended, and in a matter of time, the prefabricated structure was hand guided so that the sleeves could connect and be welded. While the welding would keep the connection intact, the structure was steadily lowered, maneuvered, and it eventually sat solidly upon the readied bolts. The helicopter continued to descend until there was a noticeable slack in the cables. It was then that all of the cables were detached, interconnected, and then the helicopter rose somewhat, took a slight nosedive to the left, and sped out of sight.

With the helicopter gone, the construction crew gathered and began securing the prefabricated structure to its mounts. When that job was completed the crew was instructed to move to the location where the operator of the crane had already lowered a huge bucket. This container was usually used to displace tremendous amounts of dirt, but now it was, for the most part, empty, and the operator waited for the men to climb aboard. Although these same men already had the opportunity to previously ride in the bucket, they had always opted to keep their feet on the ground.

When considering the amount of work that had been completed that day, and the reality that they had no access to the inner working of the catacombs and tunnels, they now realized that they must climb into the bucket. Some of the men found this experience to be exhilarating, while others had to be coaxed to climb aboard. At least one of the men was heard to say, "Oh, my God," as the bucket lifted off. Once off the ground, the bucket rocked forward and backward; this simply caused too much anxiety and so a couple of the men found themselves huddled in the bottom most and backward area of the bucket. For these two men, it seemed like an eternity before the crane maneuvered them to safety, but in fact, it only took a couple of minutes for the bucket to reach an area that was off to one side of the walled-in site. The two men were weak-kneed, but were able to climb out of the bucket and gather with their co-workers.

Chapter 62

IT WAS NOW TIME to remove the cranes from the great divide that was completely encircled by the four levels of catacombs. Mechanics from the motor pool where the cranes were unusually stored and maintained drove a truck or two to the location of the huge machines. Upon their arrival, they gathered the tools and equipment necessary to disengage the lengthy sections of the cranes. Much like removing a flat tire from a car, the men went to work.

A supervisor, using his cell phone, contacted the Willow Grove Naval Station and asked for the helicopter to be returned to the habitat site. This action was confirmed and within a matter of minutes the womp, womp, womp sound was recognizable again. The mighty helicopter hovered over the crane while its lengthy cable swayed back and forth along the air current.

One of the mechanic's noticeably removed his tool belt, and did something that raised the spirits of all that were watching the subsequent removal of each crane. The mechanic, without the slightest bit of hesitation, scooted up one extension after the other, as if he were an islander shimmying up a coconut tree. Rather than opting for the ladder, he was now approximately one-hundred and fifty feet above the surface, and moved as if he was walking upon the earth's surface. The topmost horizontal section was then connected to the helicopter cable and was all but taut as the mechanic loosened the connecting bolts to the section below.

The pilot was given his instruction and when the topmost horizontal extension was freed from its mount, it was flown away and placed outside the steel-plated walls. The mechanic looked to the heavens and pumped his fist toward the sky, much like one of the characters might have done in the celebrated Rocky series. At the time when this worker vigorously pumped his fist, there was an instant applause, and much whooping, hollering and loud whistling; smiles registered on everyone that watched this event. Each of the smaller cranes had its topmost section removed, in a similar fashion, and then the helicopter landed.

Before returning to the cranes, a thickened, lengthy cable was attached to the formidable helicopter. It then lifted off, and eventually the cable was connected to the topmost section of the towering vertical apparatus. With the helicopter high above and the cable being almost taut, the mechanic shimmied down this section until he was at the next connection point. The mechanic removed all of the bolts and in a split second, the cable became taut and could be seen to slightly vibrate. It was now that the topmost vertical section was held in place, solely by the formidable strength of the helicopter and its attached cable.

The uppermost section, being the narrowest of the four vertical parts, was permitted to slide down and within the section below it. It was now that the cable hook was removed and then attached to the second highest component. As was previously done, the next lower section had its bolt removed, and in turn was permitted to slide down within the next lower component. This scenario happened one more time and then the three topmost sections were resting within the largest and the lowest of the four components. While remaining above the now compacted crane, the helicopter pilot lowered three additional, attached cables toward the collapsed crane below.

These four cables were then attached to the now compacted crane and then the pilot displayed the true mechanical power of the helicopter. The ground crew watched, in obvious awe, as the cables began to strain. At this point, there seemed to be a stand-off between the helicopter and the crane's weight. As the four cables became taut, the crane was seen to move and then to elevate; at first, a few inches and then a foot or two. Eventually, the crane was above the steel-plated wall and was transported to an area close by the location of its previously placed, horizontal section. Back and forth, the helicopter traveled until all of the crane's parts were compacted, and then moved to their temporary location. It was now time to fill the void that remained since the cranes were gone!

Chapter 63

IT WAS NOW THAT several additional helicopters were utilized; they were significantly smaller, but still quite formidable. A cable hung from each, and a bucket attachment was connected to the lowest end of each cable. The buckets had a half-ton capacity, and a door at the base of each could be triggered to open upon command, thus allowing its payload to fall freely in the direction of a targeted location. When the bucket was emptied, the helicopter would then return to the storage yard to be continuously refilled. Mountains of dirt still remained and the earth movers were used to refill each and every bucket until the great void was no longer evident. Dirt continued to be flown in, one half-ton after another, and finally there wasn't any evidence of the habitat's construction other than the waste station and the encompassing, steel-plated walls.

The fill finally reached the predestinated marks along each interior wall, indicating that the dirt was twenty feet above, roughly leveled over the catacomb and that it was time to stop the dirt delivery. The dirt was now above the planned configuration, but of course within and far below the top of the habitat's walls.

Extensive forethought had gone into the placement of the wall that was closest to the chain linked entrance gates that were situated in the same place along the perimeter. From the habitat's surface, all of the way up to and including the razor wire, these twenty by fourteen-foot plates were tongued but not grooved. The connecting permanent plates that immediately bordered the entrance and exit only had grooves, thus allowing the center plate to easily slide up and down. The centralized plates were aligned, and seeing that there was no complication, the plates were laid off to one side.

One of the crew came up with the brilliant observation that the removable plates could be laid flat across and along the opening, thus allowing the trucks and other vehicles to utilize them as a temporary device to drive on when entering and exiting the habitat. All were in agreement, and so the plates became the temporary roadway into and out of the habitat. Utilizing those connected plates, several bulldozers entered the site and began to distribute the dirt so that when finished, the huge piles would be broken down and moved, giving the impression that the complex covering was leveled.

Coincidentally, one of the bulldozer operators was Jeff Fischer, the same Jeff Fischer that had been the operator months ago when the bulldozer broke through the earth's surface. He had thought that he had done damage to a sewer line, but in fact, he had likely caved in the ceiling of the creature's sacred chamber. No one knew that had happened because Jeff was able to maneuver out of the hole, repair it, and then go on with his work. No one knew then and no one knows now, most likely, not even Jeff.

Indeed, the dirt appeared to be level within the expansive walled enclosure, but its actual height was, indeed, two feet above the amount previously intended. As far as the engineers were concerned, this difference was right on target; out went the bulldozers, and in came the massive steamrollers. It appeared to be fun as the operators drove this way and that, similar to the fun that children and adults had when riding bumper cars on the entertainment pier in Wildwood, New Jersey. The subsequent packing and leveling of the dirt continued for days; their only restriction being the waste station and the entranceway to the habitat. It was evident that this expansive land mass could eventually be seen as monotonous work, so to liven things up, each and every operator received earphones and a Walkman. The rollers were definitely the right choice, for their tremendous weight easily compacted the dirt and stones, ultimately aligning the level inside with the ground surface that lay on the other side of the plated walls.

The landscapers returned with the previously uprooted trees, bushes, and shrubs. All had been cut back so they could be easily transported when the time came. While doing their work, the landscapers kept in mind that the entranceway to the habitat was fourteen feet in width.

It was previously decided to replant all of these removed items in the vicinity of the habitat's entrance. All of the vegetation's roots and dirt had been wrapped in burlap and now that it was time to do the replanting, they were thoroughly examined and found to be healthy. The landscapers used the necessary means to replant the trees and the other kinds of vegetation so that the entrance was well hidden, completely camouflaged when viewed along the surface or from the sky above.

One flatbed followed the other until there appeared to be an entourage, each carrying many pallets full of rolled sections of sod that were a vibrant green in color. Each flatbed transported its own forklift attached to the rear end, and these were used to unload the pallets. It took days, but eventually the habitat surface had an appearance much like any other uninhabited area of the countryside, save the massive walls and razor wire.

The ground level had been prepared for the sod and once it was ready, every available person entered the habitat's surface and began to push the huge rolls of sod, one roll connecting with others that were previously laid. With one huge roll after the other being laid, it was easy to visualize that a dent in the work had been accomplished. The work went on and on, and finally someone was heard to say that they could actually visualize the green vastness that lay within the steel-plated walls. When entering, it was easy to sense the forty-five foot height of the walls, but when looking from a distance, it was harder to imagine that the configuration at the far end of this complex was actually that far above ground.

Once a flatbed was empty, it was driven to the location where the sod had been harvested. Here, prepared pallets piled high with the rolled sections of newly cut sections of sod were readied to be loaded onto the flatbed. After the load was thoroughly secured, it was then returned to the site of the new habitat. This routine continued and finally the habitat had a wall to wall grass surface. The sod that remained unused was reloaded onto flatbeds and was driven out of and away from the habitat. It was hard to comprehend that the habitat and all of the work that went into its construction was finally finished.

If Wilton Wilbur Little Sr. was piloting a Cesena from a nearby airfield, and were to fly over this location, he would see a huge tract of green surrounded by a high wall. It would appear to Wilton as if the walls had been completed, but that the land mass within had not been disturbed. This walled-in site would be given little thought by most, and perhaps slightly more by others.

Chapter 64

THE INTERIOR CONSTRUCTION OF the habitat, its catacombs, tunnels, and its chamber were heated or cooled depending upon the season of the year. The degree of heat or cooling was contingent upon the outside temperature reading of a computerized system, plus the generalized body temperature of the creatures within this state of the art habitat. With the use of computers and chips that were imbedded throughout its interior walls, the habitat was kept at a comfort level that was previously unknown to these creatures; what a significant change this was to be.

During the past one-hundred and twenty years, the winter months, more so than the summer months, took a great toll on the creatures. The bone chilling temperatures and the freezing cold water seeped through the earth above, finding its way into their catacombs. The freezing cold water constantly dripped upon these creatures as they roamed throughout the catacombs, and was often experienced during their fit-filled sleep. The creatures endured and gradually came to accept these disturbing factors, but it was impossible to understand this as normal. The other seasons could be as equally suppressive, especially the summer days and nights that produced consecutive, unbearable, and sweltering heat waves.

When the habitat was finished, there were four layers of catacombs and each was a duplication of the one constructed below, with its concrete guide, buffer, conveyor, and webbed walkway. All were enclosed within a specialized insulation and protection, with the exception being the topmost catacomb which had an off-shoot leading away from the passageways and eventually ending at the creature's most sacred chamber.

Try to comprehend, if you will, the feelings that the food gatherers would recognize when, during the height of the winter season and for the first time since living in their newly acclimated catacombs, they would come to the earth's freezing surface for the hunt. This could be the first time that these creatures found themselves strongly preferring their acclimated habitat to the bitter cold of the surface. Each of the four layers were warmed and snaked through the expanse of the walled-in enclosure, sometimes extending straight for more than one-hundred yards, and then gradually they'd weave this way and that, passing a variety of tunnel openings.

Seemingly endlessly, each catacomb eventually reached the place at which it began, much like the continuous track of a roller coaster. Each catacomb traveled along and eventually bypassed its own waste station, processing any and all waste that lay upon the pocketed tracks of each conveyor.

Chapter 65

THERE WAS A TREMENDOUS sense of accomplishment among all that took part in the construction of the habitat; all were eager to enter and to experience whatever part they played in its creativity. Finishing touches were applied and then minuscule, but extremely powerful and durable video cameras were installed at specific positions throughout the entire habitat, especially within the chamber.

There were many cameras and each was practically invisible to the naked eye; each had specialized lenses and when viewed as one, they showed the entire length and width of the four catacombs, from top to bottom and from one side to the other. These video cameras would clearly show the creatures within their softly lit environment, and would help with our understanding of their colony. Each camera was approximately two inches in height, one inch in width, and four inches in depth and completely silent while operating twenty-four hours each and every day. Each camera was, for the most part, concealed within the porous texture that lined the catacombs and tunnels, and all were wireless and high-tech. Being the best of the best, each camera's view was beamed directly to its own screen which was part of a gigantic monitor housed within a temporary tracking station.

The tracking station was presently within the site that housed the captured creature, but would eventually be moved into a completely new facility once the membranes were reintroduced to their colony. These cameras would receive their first major test when the creatures found themselves, for the first time, relocated within the hazy, softly lit environment. It could be quite interesting to watch them as they acclimated themselves to all of their new and subtle changes. How long would it take for them to adapt? Could these creatures behave in an uninhibited manner, much like they had when in their previous environment? How much would their intelligence and instincts come into play?

Once the creatures were discovered, captured, and readied for their relocation, the plan was to deliver the membranes to the sacred chamber once the ultrasound revealed that all were beginning to harden. Hopefully that same day, or on the following day, the creature population would be delivered to the habitat and soon after the most risky of moves was to take place; the captured creature was to be reintroduced to its colony. There was tremendous fear associated with this precarious move, but it had to happen.

Chapter 66

UNEXPECTEDLY, THE FEDERAL GOVERNMENT was contacted by Mr. John Malher, a man of prominence living in New Jersey. Mr. Malher requested a meeting with one of the government's representatives, and this, in turn, took place at a prearranged site in 'The City.' As it turned out, Mr. Malher and his family had been quietly following the news regarding this Lone Creature since day one. He said that what piqued his and his wife Nancy's interest in this ever-increasing and very interesting saga was the fact that the news articles centered on the small town of Edison.

It was at this meeting that John, accompanied by his wife, said that he, his wife, and his children had been relentlessly following these stories with special interest. John went on to explain that his great, great, grandfather, and other members of the Malher Clan, lived in Edison approximately one-hundred and twenty to one-hundred and seventy-five years ago. John went on to say that he believed that Jedediah Malher, because of his status, was likely instrumental in the town's government. He went on to say that he believed that his grandfather was partially, or more prominently, responsible for the town's decision to drug the lepers and eventually abandon them deep within the bowels of the earth, hoping that they would swiftly expire.

Mr. Malher paused and then continued, stating that there was written documentation within his family's historical records that these lepers could have survived, but that suspicion lost consideration when no evidence of life was ever discovered. That remained the case for more than a century, until recently when this celebrated creature was discovered and captured!

Mr. Malher said that he had quietly built a financial empire and wanted to be instrumental in righting the wrongs that were done to the leper colony. He felt a responsibility toward them and wanted to know the cost of the newly constructed habitat. Hearing this, these high level government officials were caught off guard and completely stunned!

Immediately following this meeting, Mr. Malher changed what was his usual character. He had made it his lifelong goal to positively change many people's lives, and in doing so always accepted little, or no recognition for his generosity. Sometimes misunderstood for this or the nature of his gifts, he always felt that being recognized was not necessary; for whatever his reasoning this had always been John's nature.

This time though, John chose a different tact, and the reasoning for this change, according to his wife, was due to the circumstances surrounding the habitat. John asked, and was given permission, to be escorted to the original habitat and was afforded the opportunity to drive a four-wheeler that was to be lowered into the previously opened end of the habitat. On the day of the drive-through, John was up early, as was his entire family; they were all excited by what this day would offer. John was chauffeured into New York and once there, he entered a building; he then rode the elevator to the roof's heliport and was escorted to the waiting helicopter. His escort made sure that John kept his head down while they approached the already opened door. John climbed aboard, buckled in, and passed on a "Good Morning" to his regular pilot. His escort closed and secured the door, and then tapped the door prior to returning to the hotel. The flight's destination, located on the grounds of The Willow Grove Naval Station, was about a twenty minute flight, but was glorious compared to drivers that were experiencing the morning bumper to bumper traffic. It was early, and luckily for John, the weather was still cold and brisk. In what appeared to be a matter of minutes, he and the pilot set down upon the heliport at the naval station. John departed the aircraft and was escorted to a building. Once inside, he was instructed as to what he was to change into, and why. This immediately brought to mind a constant that occurred in news stories relating to the original habitat, namely, the entirety of the passageways had produced such a foul and putrid smell.

John put on the suit, boots, and headgear and found himself feeling claustrophobic, though soon after he adjusted and learned how to use the oxygen canister that securely hung from the side area of the attached headgear. Once fully acclimated, he was then further assisted with the sterile suit; extensions were interconnected between the headgear and suit secured by Velcro. The neck section of the headgear was thoroughly zippered and completely closed. Now John was fully attired to enter the habitat.

John Malher was then led from the building and assisted into a waiting military jeep; once seated, he was securely strapped in. It took a few minutes for John to acclimate himself to his gear, but he found that he could actually relax, even though the suit and headgear were quite cumbersome. It was surprisingly light in weight, and John was surprised at just how comfortable he felt after a matter of minutes. After a few seconds, he recognized that the jeep was in motion. While riding along, he and the driver exchanged words, and eventually the driver introduced himself as Staff Sergeant Walter Hinojosa. After a few more minutes, Walter raised his hand, and recognizing that he had John's undivided attention, told him that the habitat was in the direct vicinity. The area was noticeably off the beaten path and this section of the landscape had no visible roadways. Eventually, the jeep came to a full stop and the emergency brake was set. Sgt. Hinojosa got out of the jeep, went around to the other side, and addressed John, saying that it would be best if he remained in his seat for approximately ten minutes. To be perfectly clear, Walter said that he was going to accompany John during the habitat trek; he went on to say that in a matter of moments, he and John would be lowered into one of the habitats catacombs and that John would be driving one of the four-wheelers that awaited them. Furthermore, Sgt. Hinojosa said that he would return to John once he was assisted with own gear.

Finally, Sgt. Hinojosa did return and since both he and John were fully attired, they were led to the original habitat's entrance. Bright lamps lit the opening so that John and Walter could be lowered to the catacombs surface; it was then that Walter told John that he had already driven throughout the entire habitat and that John would be extremely thankful that he was wearing such an excellent quality of protective gear.

Walter was the first to hook up to the crane's cable and was slowly lowered to the flooring. Once upon the solid surface, he unhooked from the ring on his sturdy vest and the cable end was raised up to John. Walt mounted his four- wheeler and familiarized himself; he then moved the vehicle forward and waited for John to be lowered into the catacomb. John was also lowered slowly and in doing so, watched as his boots sunk deeper and deeper, inch by inch, into and beneath what appeared to be the solid surface, until the boot's foot area was no longer visible. John thought that if he were alone, then this experience would have been stressful. While still being lowered, John looked ahead and noticed that Walt was already upon his designated four-wheeler; this reassured John that his boots would soon find a solid purchase within this lumpy, porous mess. John did not know, for sure, what he was standing in, but suspected that it was not mud. He sloshed his way to the other four-wheeler and before getting in, he kicked as much of the waste from his boots. Once situated, he turned his attention to the operating mechanism of his machine. John became familiar with the various knobs and turned the ignition key until the motor began turning over; once, twice, it continued methodically, until the steady hum became a quiet roar. He revved the motor with several short bursts, and then secured himself within the seat before turning on the headlamps. Slightly ahead, but still within plain sight, was another four-wheeler, being operated by Walter.

These were Polaris Sportsman 400, 4x4 all-terrain vehicles, with Blackwater XT tires (these specific tires were chosen because they would propel the vehicle without splashing the surface matter). Walt was dressed in the identical gear to that of John, and John, remembering Walt's words, was indeed thankful that he was wearing the protective gear. John noticed a cable hanging freely in his immediate vicinity, and found himself wondering why it was there.

Before placing his machine into drive, he gave this cable some additional thought and was glad that he had. Trying to behave as if he had been aware of his chest harness, he unhooked the cable and let it dangle in close proximity of Walter's. John, feeling somewhat embarrassed, found himself inwardly smiling at the thought of the cable yanking him off his seat as his four-wheeler moved away from the entrance without him. Trying to give the impression that he was in total control of the present situation, he signaled Walt with the thumbs up sign. The two cables continued to hang freely and remained at their depth, so that when the two men returned, they could reattach themselves and be hoisted up and out of the catacomb.

John raised his bowed and shaking head, and saw that Walt was motioning for them to proceed. John put his machine into gear and proceeded at a slow speed, following Walter's lead. As they proceeded along, John realized that he was experiencing the complete evolution of a species; creatures that were, at one time, considered to be human. They traveled slowly, going this way and that, and fairly straight for lengthy periods. It was evident why they were proceeding slowly, for the bodily waste might be overly disturbed if they went too fast. There was also danger within these darkened catacombs because tunnels have been documented to suddenly drop straight down, at least to a depth of fifty feet in a variety of locations.

The dangers had been stated to the two men prior to entering the habitat, though Walt was well aware of these because he was a member of the team that first entered and thoroughly investigated these catacombs. (This fact was taken into consideration before Mr. Malher was given the clearance to enter).

As they proceeded along, John could sense an unknown presence, and this fact unnerved him. It was John's understanding that no other person would be within these catacombs while he and Walter drove through, that they would remain alone until they returned to the site where they first entered.

This presence was either not recognized by Walter, or if it

was, it held little or no significance. Continuing to feel unnerved, John began to feel increasingly anxious and subsequently looked more thoroughly at his surroundings, but there was no sign of life. Suddenly, and I mean instantaneously, John was completely taken aback and frightened when a slight amount of motion was sensed; this presence came from the area above Walter's vehicle. John slowed his vehicle and in doing so, his eyes were now focused upon the ceiling area; he slowly rolled his head backwards and to the left and right, allowing his eyes to canvas the ceiling above Walt and continuing backwards to his own location.

John's headlamp softly illuminated a specific ceiling area, and after a few seconds, several animated movements were apparent. Walter looked back in the direction of John and, thinking that John was concerned about their movement, got his attention and gave John the sign indicating that everything was okay. John's eyes went from Walter back to the ceiling. Upon doing so, he realized that the blackened area was not the catacomb's ceiling, but was, in fact, thousands upon thousands of hanging bats. It was not easy, but John accepted Walt's decision; he then lightly pressed the accelerator and moved forward until both vehicles were once again a safe distance from one another.

While they moved steadily forward, John found himself more attentive to his surroundings than to the direction of Walt's vehicle. After traveling approximately thirty-five yards, John found it necessary to put immediate pressure upon his brakes. His vehicle was sliding and when it finally came to a stop, it was a few inches from Walt's. Being visibly upset, it took a few minutes for John to gain his composure, but upon doing so, he said, "Sorry about that!" Walt got off his vehicle and eventually arrived at the driver's side of John's four-wheeler. Walt gave John the once over and feeling certain that he was, indeed okay, he said that there was something to be aware of in this immediate vicinity and that John should shut down his vehicle.

John did as requested, expecting to be hearing about the bats, but that had nothing to do with the reason for Walter's decision. John was motioned to get off of the Polaris and to be extremely conscious as he walked. Walt shone the way with a powerful, large-lens flashlight, and after walking a few feet, John felt a hand upon his chest, restricting his forward motion. Not knowing what to expect, but feeling increasingly anxious, John halted. His eyes followed the light as it moved away from the two men and steadily forward, upon the waste below. When the light was a short distance away, it became noticeable why it was so important for the two men to be motionless. Directly to their forefront was an opening similar to that of a mineshaft. It was circular and dropped straight down, too far for the powerful light to depict its bottom. As the light beam was ever so slowly brought back up from its furthest depth, small holes became evident set deeply into the circular wall. It was communicated to John that these were holes created by the lengthy talons of the creatures when ascending or descending the tunnels.

As John crouched upon the outskirts of the rounded tunnel, he gained a vision, actually a feeling of complete understanding, as if he were seeing one or more of these monstrous beings scaling the circular shaft. That vision seemed to be too realistic, and John found himself visibly shaken and blinking repeatedly; with one final blink, the vision was gone and his anxiety lessened considerably. Talking loudly so that his voice could be heard through the headgear, Walter told John that the wide, temporary planks that connected the one side to the other were placed there to avoid the danger associated with the tunnel's depth. Walt continued, saying that he and John were going to use the four-wheelers to travel along and across these planks because the chamber was on this level, and that it was imperative that John had a chance to witness that site. Walt's four-wheeler crossed the planks without difficulty and to John's surprise, he too found the tracks wide enough to cross with little apprehension.

Onward they went, and eventually Walter turned directly to the right and was out of sight, that is, until John came to the same location. Feeling apprehensive, John slowed considerably and eventually came to a stop; Walter had halted and his Polaris was silent. Walter was off his vehicle and motioned for John to shut down and follow. This was done and then John walked ahead as he followed the light stream of his and the lead vehicle's headlamp; off to the right, the catacomb gradually widened, spilling into a spacious room. This room was enormous and Walter explained that this was the creature's sanctuary, their birth and sustenance chamber, and the actual place where the membranes were discovered.

The two men followed the lengthy beam of the four-wheeler headlamps, and the room was further illuminated by John's flashlight, plus the brilliant light handheld by Walter. The headlamps gave a general view of the room, while the handheld lights enhanced specifics. As the room was being checked out, John's light fell upon a variety of debris and what appeared to be a miniature sized skull. John picked up the skull and placed it into a bag that was hanging from his waist; he then went about his continuing search, without giving the skull any additional thought. A near-empty vat containing what remained of the coagulated blood was found; there was also a small amount of decaying flesh, a few animal skins, remains of discarded membranes, and a multitude of adult human skulls and skeletal remains.

John found himself in amazement as he quickly recollected the distance of the intertwining passageways that they had just driven, and it was mind boggling to realize the time and effort that went into creating just this one level of the various catacombs. Here and there, within this chamber, were the skulls of a variety of land animals, and John surmised that the larger skulls were that of cattle, bears, horses, and deer. Although the skulls were evident, there was no evidence of these animal's skeletal remains; John thought of this as being odd and placed it in the recesses of his mind.

As if being able to read John's mind, Walter said, "John, if you look closely, you'll realize that there are many skulls of animals, and of a few humans, but it is rare to find skeletal remains." At this time, Walter walked to the lined vat that held what remained of the coagulated blood; he knelt down, and with John holding tightly to Walter's belt, he reached deeply into the blood that still remained in the vat. Luckily for both men, Walt was able to find and scoop up a few lengths of fragmented, saturated bone. He scooped several pieces and, in turn, brought them to the surface. While doing this, he explained that the skeletal remains of both the animals and humans had been saturated with the blood and eaten, and that this is the reason only the skulls remained.

Although the four-wheeler headlamps were on during their trek to the sacred chamber, and the motors had echoed within the closed environment, very few of the bats retreated from their purchase; it was as if their time was accurately set upon daylight. The two men were now finished with their investigation; John was advised to remount his vehicle at its opposite end. He did this, and then waited until Walter sloshed his way to the end of his. John realized something that Walt already knew, that each vehicle was identical at both the front and back, and was fully operational from either end. They activated the motors, turned on the headlamps, shifted to the proper gear, and headed back to the place where they had initially entered the habitat.

After shutting down their four-wheelers, they reattached their harnesses, and then were slowly lifted, one after the other, to the surface. Once standing upon the surface and at a safe distance from the habitat's entrance, John luckily heard Walter say, "Brace yourself!" It was now that John experienced something that he hadn't expected; a military person had a nozzle within his hands that was attached to a narrow fire hose, connected to a portable power-washing machine. The initial blast of the cleansing solution was indeed forceful, but an instant before the solution hit John's suit, he remembered Walter's warning and thus was prepared. The suit and headgear had been more than adequate, but even with their state of the art protection, there seemed to be a lingering smell of fecal matter, and an equally bad smell of urine. When both suits were completely washed, disinfected, and air dried, they were removed. Then, both men found themselves standing on the earth's surface, free of their harnesses. They stepped away from their gear and, in doing so, John remembered to get the pouch. They entered a waiting limousine; this time, both men attached their own seatbelts prior to being driven back to the naval station. During the return drive, John found himself reminiscing the past few hours, and then he realized that he was daydreaming. The limo came to a full stop and John opened his eyes. The limousine was at the entrance gate to the Willow Grove Naval Station, and the entranceway was manned by a smartly dressed officer. Proper identification was shown and the driver took the two men to a specific building; there, they could be more thoroughly cleansed and disinfected. Eventually naked, each man walked beyond a doorway and was sprayed from a mechanized shower nozzle until completely engulfed with a multicolored foam. As the foam layered itself upon the men, John, for whatever reason, had a flashback to his days at Roanoke College, located within the Shenandoah Valley of S.W. Virginia, between the Blue Ridge and the Allegheny Mountains. John had met Nancy, his wife, while attending Roanoke, though the flashback likely stemmed from a distant memory of his playful antics and storied fame.

The two men remained within their shower stall for a few minutes, and then the foam automatically changed to a clear, warm water spray. This spray lasted for approximately two more minutes, and then the men were air dried. They exited through another mechanized doorway, and when the door closed behind them, there was an evident, comfortable temperature and pleasant fragrance.

Chapter 67

JOHN COULD NOT WAIT to compare the newly constructed habitat with that of the original. Soon after being cleared to leave the naval station, John returned, via helicopter, to New York City. Once in the city, he was driven to his New Jersey estate. While being driven, John rested his head upon the seat and within seconds was fast asleep. He dreamed of the original catacomb experience and when awakened at the estate, he actually believed that he had already experienced the new habitat as well. John cleared his thoughts, and after realizing that he had been dreaming, exited the limo and found that he was anxious to share the adventure with his family.

John's wife, Nancy, and their seven children were equally anxious to see him, and to receive an in-depth explanation of his once in a lifetime experience. The family entered the living room and was given a storybook type description. When John had finished, his eldest son, Sandy, said that his father's adventure would probably make a good book. The family agreed, and then John told them that he was to return in a few days to witness the newly constructed habitat. All were joyful and visibly excited, but not to the extent of John, for he was going to experience this innovative habitat first-hand. He would be one of very few that would ever enter the new habitat, that is, other than the construction crew and eventually, the creatures. He went on to explain that this time he would not need a four-wheeler, or any other kind of vehicle. This time, he could simply take all the time that he wanted to explore the entire complex.

It had been previously explained to John during his most recent visit to the Bucks County area, and especially to Edison, that, for the most part, each of the four levels of catacombs was identical in construction. Furthermore, he was advised that the topmost of the four possessed the only marked difference, that being the entrance and exit to the habitat. He also became aware that this was the level upon which the chamber was situated and last but not least, the waste station was strategically connected to all catacombs, with its main component sitting upon the surface.

After dinner, there was ongoing excitement focused upon their father, and unbeknownst to the family, he had made an all-important telephone call. During that call, he was given the okay to bring his wife and children when returning to the new habitat. The family made a concerted effort to awaken and have breakfast with their parents. Even though all were pumped and wanted to see their father off, the children were witnessed to be in some type of temporary funk as they sauntered toward the kitchen table.

During the night, John had kept his news from everyone, even Nancy. Finally, everyone was at the table and the food was served. At times, the children found that food disinterested them, and today was one of those times. The cook had prepared a delicious breakfast, but it wasn't the food that was causing their disinterest. It was, however, their envy of their father's most recent trip and now this return trip to the Bucks County area.

John made a point to thank everyone for getting up at this ungodly hour to see him off. This was a special day for all, but especially for John; he thanked them for their kind gesture, and also said that he really appreciated their concern. It was then that the children, along with Nancy, began to further question John in regard to this trip. What was scheduled? Could he take pictures? Would there be any interviews? Was there a possibility that he could actually see the Lone Creature?

John was making a concerted attempt to be coy, and to his surprise, he was pulling it off, that is, until he turned his attention to Harley and Dakota. They, in turn, recognized the slightest of smiles coming from their dad's face. Nancy also witnessed this and said, "What's going on here?" As if embarrassed, John's face flushed, and at the same time he began to quietly laugh. Now, he told them that he wanted to share some great news that he had, in fact, made a call after arriving home yesterday and was given permission for the entire family to come with him to witness the new habitat. Communication was common at their meals, but the whooping and hollering that immediately followed his announcement was not the norm. Nancy pulled John aside and told him she was feeling such warmth within her heart, all caused by his amount of caring; that she and the children were so excited and beyond thrilled!.

The entire family finished their breakfast and then prepared for the drive to the heliport. Once in the city, they all boarded what appeared to be an extremely large military helicopter and then off they flew toward Willow Grove Naval Station. Everyone was really exited upon their arrival, and soon after departing the helicopter, they were led to a building where they were briefed about the new habitat.

During the briefing, Harley quietly leaned toward her father's ear and when John leaned toward Harley, his daughter said, "Dad, is this where the lonely creature and membranes are being kept?" John responded that the naval station was not the location, but that they were all going to that location in a few minutes. When the briefing was finished, John and Nancy entered separate limousines; Sandy, Clark and Tim got in with John, while the younger group of Nora, Dakota, Harley, and Wyatt got in with Nancy. Everyone, including both John and Nancy, were now feeling electric! Chills were shooting through their bodies as the limousine's doors were closed. The vehicles were driven from the naval station, traveling north on Route 611, and eventually made a right turn on Bristol Road. The entourage traveled along Bristol Road for a few miles and then the family members were told that the habitat was just ahead. Eyes strained as the youngest of the children pressed their heads against the various windows, and finally there it was. WOW! The closer they got, the higher the walls appeared, and when they were along one side of the habitat, where Bristol Road bordered the site, the steel walls appeared as if they were touching the heavens above.

The drivers purposely drove around the entire perimeter of the complex and then pulled up to the entrance. The family's hearts were now racing, somewhat out of control, as the limousines traveled beyond the security gates. The family members were advised that the building straight ahead and to the right was the site where the creature and the four membranes were being kept and subsequently monitored. This information further excited the entire family, and upon witnessing this, the driver, who had been previously authorized to advise John that if he and the family had the time after viewing the habitat, they were authorized to enter the hangar area to get an up close and personal view of the creature and the membranes. The family members were beside themselves with a heightened enthusiasm as the limousine drivers were now prepared to take the family into the steel enclosure and then across a wide expanse, until they arrived midway between the compound's entrance and that of the new habitat.

Chapter 68

WHEN JOHN HAD RETURNED home from his initial habitat visit and had spoken with the family regarding the dismal living conditions that he had witnessed, everyone was overwhelmed and saddened! This information was clearly within everyone's memory bank as they got out of the limousines and were collected by the drivers. Each family member had been previously given a helmet that fit snugly and had a headlamp attached that increased their scope of vision. The entire family was led by the two military personnel along the vast expanse of grass and an abundance of trees, brushes and shrubs. Initially, the group only saw the green expanse, but when looking toward the one end, there seemed to be something different. The group walked a distance and finally was brought to the habitat entrance. Here, the family periodically rested, and in due time found themselves being led along a lengthy, descending passageway. This passageway was quite large and circular in shape; being approximately ten feet in width and maybe eight or more feet in height. As the family members moved along, their nervous systems began to calm.

No sooner had they entered the descending passageway when all of a sudden it was sensed that the floor was moving, lightly giving way to each person's body weight. Sandy made the initial mention of this and one of the military personnel said that the flooring was a new concept. It gave, as it did, so that the creatures could walk and experience a limited amount of stress and impact to their ankle, knee and hip joints. The family also recognized that they had to be careful walking because the floor construction had an innumerable amount of openings, all being uniform in size. Wow! What a strange sensation! It was at this point that John contrasted this habitat to the original one, explaining that the old habitat was void of light. He went on to say that the original site had such an awful, foul, and putrid smell throughout, while this new habitat would remain clean and offer the creatures a far superior quality of life.

At first, the youngest of the children, Dakota, Harley, and Wyatt, found themselves being more risky than the others; their smaller stature came into play when they attempted to walk along the perforated webbing. These three seemed to be the most anxious, and because of these feelings, moved ahead too swiftly, displaying less concern than was necessary for their safety. All three had been fortunate enough, while moving ahead of the group, to find the necessary foot purchases upon the strands of webbing, but eventually, their lack of caution caught up with them. Each child found themselves recklessly placing their feet where there was no eventual purchase, and subsequently their feet and legs went through the webbed openings. At this point, synchronized yelps could be heard, and the three were seen dropping, as their legs and feet dangled freely below the mesh.

While sitting upon the webbing, the three leaned forward until their hands came into contact with the strands of mesh. John and the other two men moved cautiously to assist the kids, and got to them without succumbing to a similar fate. The three kids were somewhat frightened, but fortunate; they had a few bruises, but did not incur any serious injury. The three men reached toward the boys and, as they did, the boys were already struggling to get upon their hands and knees. They maneuvered their legs and subsequently their sneakers up and through the mesh, and used their leg strength, along with the men's assistance, to steady their balance while standing, once again, upon the webbing.

Before receiving the necessary assistance, Dakota attempted to right her precarious situation. She used her athleticism to push her upper body back from the mesh, and while doing this, instinctively extended one of her legs for support; in doing so, her foot inadvertently pressed against the conveyor, activating the forward motion of its belt. This movement frightened the jawoozies out of her, and she instinctively jerked that same foot upward. The conveyor's motor, now without any stimulus, immediately shut down.

The family members were stunned by this occurrence, but were immediately reassured by the personnel that everything was okay. The men got to the shaken child as she was standing upon the mesh with her two siblings. Now, with their body weight fully upon the elasticity of the mesh, the children felt assured that they were indeed safe and secure. Dakota was overheard to say "Whew!" and Harley and Wyatt, said, almost in unison, "You got that right!" The group reassembled, but now they remained together; they walked along, paying strict attention to the webbed flooring, and could easily smell the newness of this setting. John temporarily lost his balance and inadvertently reached toward one of the walls for support. In doing this, he experienced an additional surprise; his force caused his fingers to penetrate the wall of the habitat. Due to the wall's composition, John's fingers went slowly, but surely, into its surface, followed by his palm, though the penetration stopped once his wrist had been engulfed. As his hand penetrated, it was as if it was held in place by the material; John got his feet under him and gradually gained his composure and balance, but while still exerting strength, found that his entire hand remained securely in place. Once standing with his legs and feet securely beneath him, his hand and fingers began to relax. The more that John's hand relaxed, the more the material gave freedom to his hand. It was as if the material had also relaxed its grasp, allowing John to easily remove his purchase. One of the personnel told the group that this wall material was recently created specifically for the habitat and had not been fully tested, but that it met the needs of the colony.

Sensing that he had their utmost attention, the speaker went on to explain that the majority of the creatures were believed to be huge, heavily muscled, and extremely powerful. What once were their fingers and toes, were now long, curved talons. The ultra-sharp talons would need a somewhat porous material that would not tear or cut, but would allow talon penetration, especially in the tunnels when traveling from one level down or up to the other. The material's composition seemed to be quite tough, and one of its main selling points was that when the talons were removed, there was, within seconds, no visible indentation or sign of entry.

The speaker went on to say that the material had been found to be too tough for bats to get a purchase, and that this material also lined the ceilings in order to maintain its healthier environment. The bats were a limited food source since the food gatherers had met the challenge of supplying a staple for the entire colony, and the bats tended to add tremendous amounts of needless waste and foul odor to the interior of the original habitat. That waste and putrid smell was acceptable within the original habitat, but this new location was only a short distance from civilian housing and that foul smell was totally unacceptable.

Chapter 69

JOHN DID NOT REALIZE it, but he was thinking aloud; one of the other men responded saying, "John, that's a good question." This same person continued, "There was considerable thought given to the installation of brighter lamps throughout the habitat. The decision not to install those was due to the creature's limited eyesight; the brighter lamps might do further damage to their already weakened eyes. It is estimated that these creatures lived for the most part in a pitch black environment. Actually, they lived that way for more than a century. It is also important to know that these dimly lit lamps do not get hot and will never 'blow out.' They are imbedded within the surface lining of the walls and, believe it or not, are an energy source. If everything goes as planned, these lamps will never need maintenance. If, by chance, one or two stop working, they will not affect the others; they operate independently of each other. If enough of these lamps cease working, then a plan will be initiated to replace those that have been damaged. It is also believed that dimly lit lamps will not add additional stress to these creatures, a stress that is better off avoided."

The family members and their guides intermittently discussed several topics as they continued their trek, and as they found themselves growing tired, one of their guides alluded to the fact that they were now close to the entrance way, that is, they had practically come full circle. One guide told them to be careful, as they were now closing in on the area that bypassed the tunnel, and rather than exit, he wanted everyone to witness the chamber.

"What was this chamber?" This question was on the mind of each and every family member as they moved further to the right and away from the catacombs exit. It was their understanding that the chamber was close by. John, having had the opportunity to witness the original habitat's sacred chamber, looked off to his right and questioned, "Is that it?"

Bordering the catacomb was an entranceway that spilled into an enormous room. It was easy to recognize that air was circulating from a source within, and Nora was the first to recognize this. As her eyes searched, her head lamp directed them to a large pool of liquid, and to her surprise, she was informed that the liquid was coagulated blood. "Ewwwww" was emphatically heard from Nora as her facial features contorted, and she then said that she could only imagine what this would smell like if there was no circulating air. The group, after witnessing the vat, began to search the room more diligently. Almost in unison, the group let out a gasp that was easily heard as one set of eyes after another fell upon a tremendous cache of freshly killed animal flesh, and subsequently upon a large pile of fur-lined animal skins. This time there was more than one "Ewwww" succinctly heard. In a far off corner of the spacious room, and a good distance from the chamber's entrance, there appeared to be a smaller room within the main room measuring approximately twenty square feet. This was pointed out to be the birthing zone, the specific location where the membranes would soon be brought. The floor area had a constant warmness, and the warmth also emanated from below the mesh, constantly circulating.

The cavernous home was simply overwhelming, and in fact, futuristic. John, being the only family member to have witnessed the original habitat, felt a certain warmth from within himself, a feeling of complete satisfaction. John knew that every dollar that he was investing in this new habitat was well worth it, and he was thankful that he and his family were involved.

The entire group exited the chamber and then walked along the meshed webbing until this assent brought one and all to the earth's surface. The guides led the entire group to the renovated airplane hangar, and once inside, they were led to a specified room that all entered and were asked to take a seat. Here, they were briefed by another uniformed soldier, and then were readied to witness what few people in the world had actually seen in person, that is, the Lone Creature.

The Lone Creature was lying on its side in an evident fetal position, seemingly asleep. The Malhers approached, and as they did, it was easily seen that what was in a fetal clump, was huge. All of the family were taken aback, and were utterly amazed, except Wyatt. He was the youngest, and for whatever reason, he seemed to empathize with the creature, much like Grace had, as soon as he focused upon its massive presence. Wyatt was indeed the youngest, but he had overcome a severe sickness, and that just may have been the reason why he and the creature experienced a connection. Just as Grace had done in the past, Wyatt, without his family's knowledge, approached the creature, seemingly without the slightest amount of fear. As the other Malhers were finding a seat, Wyatt was steadily approaching the cage. The Lone Creature, sensing the approach, began to move, and in doing so, kept everyone's attention riveted upon itself and completely away from Wyatt.

Indeed, the creature was moving; it turned over and situated itself so it was eventually in the position where it was able to focus upon Wyatt's approach. Wyatt was now a few feet from the side of the enclosure, but kept moving forward when something unexpectedly happened. As if reaching out for contact, the creature allowed its talon laden hand to lie beneath and beyond the cell-like bars; its palm up. Several people were instinctively moving their eyes toward the tips of the talons, and were now able to glimpse Wyatt's presence.

"Oh my God" was heard, almost in unison, as people imagined themselves running to the aide of Wyatt, though these same people were too far away to prevent what happened next. Wyatt placed his small and seemingly fragile hand within the creature's opened mass. Very soon after this initial connection, it appeared as if Wyatt's touch brought the heaviest of tears to the creature's facial features. Wyatt's outstretched hand lay palm down upon the creature's palm, and then the Lone Creature closed its talons into a kind of fist, securing Wyatt's hand totally within. All that had instinctively moved to assist Wyatt were now motionless, not knowing what to expect or what to do. All in the room gasped, and remained completely still, quiet.

You would expect a mere child to be frightened in this situation, but Wyatt appeared composed, as his face and body language gave the distinct impression that he was safe with the creature. A few seconds passed, but these few seconds seemed to last an eternity for Nancy and John. They held one another while remaining still, and then found themselves instinctively reaching out in the direction of their other children. During these few seconds, the creature and Wyatt seemed to be communicating, but their mouths were closed. Their eyes were locked upon each other's, and neither blinked... not even once. Then, the creature made an eerie, mournful, yet soulful sound.

The sound was audible, but had little volume. It seemed to come from the depths of its being as it slowly opened its clenched fist, releasing and allowing Wyatt to remove his uninjured hand. Those that were watching expected Wyatt to remove this hand immediately, but he didn't. He very slowly and with purpose lifted his hand from the creature's palm and began to lightly stroke the palm and wrist area. As was the creature's demeanor when encountering Grace's touch, it appeared to be soothed. It seemed as if the Lone Creature appreciated a child's innocent touch, as it absorbed all of the love that it could. Wyatt then stopped stroking the creature's emotionally starved presence and turned to face Harley.

Harley, Wyatt's sister, being close in age and demeanor to Wyatt, was watching from a distance, and was overheard to say, "Wyatt said that the creature is extremely sad and fearful, that its life is coming to an end." Harley was overheard by a scientist and, as if in turn, the scientist said, "What is going on here?" No one's mouth is moving, but messages seem to have been communicated."

Chapter 70

GRACE AND RYAN HAD returned to what could be seen as a normal lifestyle, normal in the sense that they had returned to school and their celebrity status had diminished to the point where they appeared to be one of the regular students. Life for the Lightcaps returned to the point where they all wanted it to be. Occasionally, a journalist would make an appointment to interview Grace, but that occurrence had lost much of its appeal. Kathleen had returned to her teaching position and John aligned himself with his responsibilities at Geppert Brothers. They had experienced what few families had, and they had come to the conclusion, one and all, that given a choice, they would prefer being an observer rather than the specimen under the scrutiny of the public's microscope. There were times when John and Kathleen found themselves somewhat stressed when leaving the house for work. They expected to see the same hoards of journalists, crowding one another to get 'The Story.' Reality immediately came rushing to the forefront and the Lightcaps were thankful that their vision was merely a vivid memory and nothing more. This was the time when both parents had the opportunity to take a step back and give thanks, for that period of their lives had ended. Although that experience had ended, the Lone Creature would re-enter their lives with more force and influence than they could have ever imagined. Their journey was far from over.

The population of Edison was fully aware that something was in the works. The womp, womp, womp, womp of the helicopter blades were now being heard throughout the community. It seemed as if helicopters were everywhere, as if their pilots were in the process of observation, possibly searching for an escapee from the nearby prison. The great swarm of helicopters made some of the homeowners extremely uncomfortable, for the sight and sound of these military helicopters brought back pain-filled memories to the residents that had served their country during Vietnam. The government personnel knew that this could be of significance and had justified their use so that the creature colony could be discovered without delay. Hours went by and anxiety began to flourish among several of the homeowners. Telephones rang off the hook at the Doylestown newspaper, at a variety of the surrounding township police departments, and at the headquarter locations of the area's politicians.

The search continued and finally the **T**hermal **I**maging **E**quipment zeroed in on the creatures and their subterranean habitat. The land coordinates were documented, and it was evident that the TIE had found its designated quarry. The TIE found the colony huddled closely together, for the habitat was only in its beginning stage of development. With the colony now located and documented, the helicopters, in unison, flew from that location and returned to the Willow Grove Naval Station.

Chapter 71

WYATT GRADUALLY MOVED TO what could be considered a safe distance from the creature's enclosure and was met by his mother. The creature remained in the same position, with its talons and palm extended, still below the cell's steel bars. The Lone Creature was visibly subdued and its eyelids noticeably fluttered; its eyes were barely noticeable. Nancy embraced Wyatt and held him firmly; she then escorted him to the location of the family. The Malhers sat together and gradually settled themselves; there were several questions directed toward Wyatt, but he did not understand all the commotion, and explained that he did not know what motivated him to touch the creature.

Recognizing that Wyatt was yet a child, several military personnel were instructed to interrupt the questioning and to whisk Wyatt and the other Malhers into what could be considered a safe room. It was here that the family found that they eventually calmed and collected themselves. After becoming unruffled, they asked if it was still possible to see the membranes. They were given this opportunity and just prior to viewing the membranes, the family was given a brief, but complete, history.

As a special gift, the Malhers were permitted to place their hands onto parts of the membranes and to feel the exterior composition of all four. Everyone took advantage of this privilege and each recognized that movement was within all of the membranes. As

348

each person felt the movement, it was easy to recognize the excitement within each adult, but what was really thrilling was the exuberance displayed by the younger of the children. The family eventually regrouped and following a standard debriefing, were escorted to the limousines and driven to their waiting helicopter. The family eventually returned to their home in Rumson, all the while knowing that their life would be forever more enlightened and enriched by the experience.

Chapter 72

BREAKFAST WAS ALWAYS A special treat for the Lightcaps; they were fully aware that Kathleen went to great lengths to make sure that the food was tasty and nutritious. Ryan was the first to the table and displayed an eagerness to eat the homemade sweet potato pancakes topped with real maple syrup, turkey sausage, and a glassful of the most flavorful and yet the healthiest drink on the market today. Orange juice, with all of its goodness, was now a drink of the past. NuVim was simply the best; it came in half-gallon containers and had a thickened consistency. The Lightcaps found it difficult, when shopping, to simply choose a single flavor as they were all beyond delicious. Ryan had already consumed some of his drink and was now eating, though Grace was still a no-show. Eventually, Grace wandered into the kitchen, sat down heavily and hardly touched her food or drink. Grace's behavior naturally brought the attention of her mother, who asked, "Grace, are you not feeling well today?" What happened next added fuel to the fire. Grace behaved as if she had not heard her mother and used her fork to play with her pancakes. Kathleen, this time more emphatic, said "Grace, did you hear me?" Grace stammered and then acknowledged her mother, "I don't know, I guess I am; I'm just not hungry."

Grace was urged to drink her NuVim, but even this delicious treat seemed to be too much for her to manage. Needless to say,

Kathleen was concerned; she laid her opened palm upon Grace's forehead. Kathleen, feeling that Grace was probably okay, told the kids to wash up and prepare for their walk to the bus stop. Kathleen placed lunch into each child's pack, hugged them and kissed each upon their forehead just prior to pressing her cheek against theirs, and out the door they went!

Kathleen watched with apprehension and noticed that her friend, and neighbor, Jack Hengy was sitting on his deck, obviously drinking a steaming hot mug of coffee. Today, the scent of the toasted coconut coffee momentarily took Kathleen's thoughts away, but her precarious situation came rushing back. As Grace and Ryan walked and were nearing the bus stop, Kathleen walked over to Jack, greeted him and exchanged pleasantries and then explained her concern regarding Grace. Jack offered Kathleen a coffee, which Kathleen courteously declined, and then he said that he fully understood. Since he was not scheduled to work that morning, he would keep a close eye on the kids while Kathleen departed for her teaching position. Kathleen continued to watch the kids, but then went into the house, and after a few minutes, she was seen waving to the kids as she drove by.

Jack set his mug on a table and walked towards the bus stop. Grace and Ryan, as usual, were the only kids at this specific stop. Once Jack arrived, he squatted, much like the position of a catcher in baseball, and leaned back against one of the many trees. Jack was often friendly with both kids, most probably because they were so pleasant and normally well-mannered, and both enjoyed various types of athleticism, either as a player or fan. Jack was heard to say, "wazzupppp?" Ryan found this approach quite amusing and said "Hi Jack!" As upbeat as Ryan was, Grace was, uncharacteristically, the complete opposite. She did not look up, nor did she respond. Jack said, "What's going on Grace?" Being normally vivacious, but noticeably in some sort of funk, Grace appeared to be numb. Jack backed off, but noticed that were tears were welling up in Grace's eyes. Just then, Ryan was heard to say, "There's our bus." As the bus approached, its warning lights were flashing; the stop sign could be easily seen as it swung away from the driver's side. Ryan began to move toward the steps, but Grace was still lethargic.

Ryan, noticing Grace's mood, took her by the hand and urged her to enter. She did, and found a seat close by the entrance. Ryan continued to hold her hand, finding that Grace's hand was very cold and clammy. Being the brother that he was, Ryan moved closer, cuddling her with his arm around her upper back and shoulders. Grace was whimpering, so Ryan pulled her closer and hugged her tightly, asking if she knew what was wrong. She responded, "I don't' know, I'm just so cold!"

Before closing the door, the driver acknowledged Jack, and then with all of the safety features returned to their rightful place, the bus rumbled down the road and Ryan knew that they would be at their school in a matter of minutes. The other kids that were on the bus were upbeat, readying themselves for a variety of school activities. As time went by, Grace appeared to be more and more despondent, and more dependent upon Ryan's grip. She was noticeably huddling into his side, her head tilted downward and her eyes tightly closed.

The bus was now at the school and Ryan could still feel the cold emanating from Grace. It was uncanny! At this point, Grace was trembling, and her lips were blue and quivering, indicating that she was shivering. Ryan assisted her from the bus and practically carried her as they walked in the direction of the nurse's office. Grace appeared to be possessed; she was mumbling and when outside the nurse's office, she removed her backpack and slowly slid down the wall into a seated position. Once upon the tiled floor, she hugged herself ever so tightly and again said, "Ryan, I'm so cold!"

Ryan was frightened and tried to enter the nurse's office. Finding the door locked, he began to pound on it and yelled at the top of his voice, as if totally out of control! The nurse had not yet arrived, but fortunately for both children, she was walking down the hallway, approximately twenty-five feet from where Grace was seated. She noticed that Ryan was in a state of agitation and called out, "Is there an emergency?" Ryan turned toward the voice and noticing that the person inquiring was the school nurse, he immediately said, "Yes there is! Something has happened to my sister." The nurse then said, "Has she been injured?" Ryan responded, as if agitated, "No! She's very cold and clammy!" Now, being very close to where Grace was seated, the nurse came to a conclusion and while doing this, she spoke soothingly to both children. There were eventually other teachers in the immediate area because they had responded to the commotion. The nurse wanted to give Grace her undivided attention, so she asked two of the teachers to escort Ryan to his first class. While he and the two teachers walked together, one of the teachers temporarily excused herself and went into a vacant office. While there, she dialed the principal's extension and notified Dr. Joyce Mehaffey of the situation.

Prior to her position as the principal, Dr. Mehaffey had gained considerable respectability during the time spent as a child psychologist. She listened intently to the incident description and decided to walk to the office rather than telephone the nurse. When she was within sight of the office, she stopped walking and evaluated the scene that confronted her. Grace was still seated upon the floor, with her back and head plastered against the wall.

Believing that Grace may be showing signs of depression, 'the common cold of mental illness,' Dr. Mehaffey proceeded to the immediate area of the office and said, "Good Morning". She allowed her greeting sink in and then said, "Let's get Grace up and onto the bed in the office." This was done and the nurse placed a cold compress upon Grace's forehead. The nurse then advised the principal that Grace had expressed the feeling of being quite cold, and that she was sweating profusely. The nurse, reassuringly, told Grace that she wanted her to lay there for a while and that she would be in the adjoining room with the principal. Every so often, the nurse looked checked on Grace, and when doing so, refreshed the coolness of the compress. Each time that this happened, Grace was able to weakly say "thank you" for the kindness. "You take it easy and try to get some rest." The nurse, while exiting the room, repeated herself, feeling that this may be calming," I will be in the next room, call me if you need anything!"

The nurse and the principal were, in fact, in the adjoining room, discussing a plan of action. No sooner had the two adults gotten seated, when they heard an unsettling sound; they got to their feet, but before either could check in on Grace, she came through the doorway.

The compress, having fallen, was lying haphazardly on her shoulder and she appeared to be extremely agitated. Grace was clearly in a state of shock and had no idea of her whereabouts; she shook uncontrollably, had lost the color in her cheeks, and was feverishly scratching her forearms and face. Dr. Mehaffey, being a tall and athletic woman, reached out and was able to fully grasp Grace. While holding Grace firmly, she leaned back against the wall, slid down, along with Grace, and came to a seated position upon the floor. At this point, the nurse entered the room from where Grace had come and returned with a light blanket. She placed the blanket upon the floor, next to the seated principal, and then asked if she could be of some assistance. While holding Grace in the same seated position, the principal asked the nurse to wrap Grace's body with the blanket. The nurse recognized exactly what the principal was doing, for she had studied passive physical restraint and first aid training on a yearly basis as part of the school system's safety regulation. Grace had been expertly placed within the lap of the principal, facing away, in a position where the principal was able to control both of Grace's legs and arms and at the same time, protect her own head from Grace's.

Chapter 73

THE LONE CREATURE CHANGED its position somewhat, and was laying upon the floor of its cell, with its hand-like extremity and curved talons, apparently straining for more human contact. Unfortunately, the only people that had the ability to communicate with the creature were Grace and Wyatt, but neither was there to possibly understand its wants or needs.

Unbeknownst to the doctors, nurses, and scientists, the Lone Creature was spiraling into a very serious, depth defying depression that continued to coil toward an unknown dimension. This was a despair brought about because the creature had experienced an abundance of confusion, turmoil, and trauma since its arrival upon the earth's surface. There was a book entitled, Stranger in a Strange Land, and the creature's experiences personified that title. It lay within its enclosure, in a tightly bound fetal position, giving off the body language of desolation while emitting long, drawn out, pain-filled sounds. As unbelievable as it may seem, no one was picking up on these signs or sounds. The creature, seemingly resting after its encounter with Wyatt, continued to lie in its emotionally starved. They had previously walked through the doorways and out of the creature's sight, much like Grace had done previously.

Were these two humans to be out of its life temporarily or forever, and if forever, what was to become of its quality of life? The creature's body language appeared as if it was trying to signal additional fears and anxieties to anyone that was willing to look its way, but no one did. What the creature was internalizing now took on additional pain; the emotional pain of desperation.

The creature realized that its self-serving choices had brought nothing but disharmony, pain, and suffering to itself and the colony. The bombardments of its negative thoughts were dominating its entire being. The depression darkened and continued to spiral deeper and deeper, taking with it more and more of what was left of the creature's stability. It hadn't made an attempt to move further because its immediate environment was restrictive, and it was fearful that it wouldn't be able to gain enough balance and emotional freedom. An additional factor that caused this decision was the feeling that its entire body was seemingly being drawn by an unknown force far below where it lay. Consequently, the creature made the calculated decision to remain in its tightly bound fetal position, attempting to cope with this unbearable, tear-filled emotional pain.

Chapter 74

BEING OF THE REALIZATION that the ultrasound test had shown a recent spurt in growth within each of the membranes, it was generally understood that the creature population would have to be moved as soon as possible to their new habitat.

The **T**hermal **I**maging **E**quipment was used again to ensure the location of the creature colony, and being assured that the entire population was still confined to the same limited area, it was decided to put them to sleep in the very near future. Putting them to sleep and moving the entire colony, en masse, to their new habitat would be simplified if done soon and done right. One of the military personnel addressed the group, saying that this move could be easily accomplished, but if it were done from the original habitat, with its multitude of catacombs and tunnels, that it would have been very complicated and practically impossible. Everyone present agreed, and then the plan was laid out.

Without having the slightest amount of information regarding the human's plan, the creature population was hard at work, digging and carrying during their long and arduous nights. Then, when the hours of darkness changed to daylight, they ate from the pile of flesh and saturated bones, and washed this down with their blood source.

These saturated bones were the product of the creature's kills, and of those creatures that had met their untimely and sometimes vicious death. After eating and drinking their fill, the creatures would occasionally desire carnal pleasures. However, but more often than not, they'd forego the sexual encounter and fall into a very deep, sound, restorative slumber.

That morning, being like the mornings of their recent past, the creature population had readied themselves for sleep, and could not recognize, among their ever-increasing amount of excrement, any difference in the smell of their interior space. The colorless and odor-free gas was slowly penetrating every inch of space within the temporary habitat and every living thing was slowly, but surely, finding it necessary to lie in a comfortable position while ever so gradually experiencing an extremely deep, exhausting sleep. The gas had been thoroughly tested, and all evidence led to the finding that these beings would be fast asleep for the duration of their subsequent move and beyond. A lone helicopter flew over the dwelling, and having experienced personnel operating the TIE, it was documented that all of the creatures were motionless. Believing the TIE to be accurate, the technicians assumed that all of the creatures were now totally anesthetized, and were, in fact, incapacitated.

Tractors with extended flatbeds were driven to and parked in readiness, from motor pools as far away as military bases in New Jersey and New York. The troop carriers and flatbeds had their motors revving, and their diesel noise, when the accelerators were pressed, was deafening. The entourage drove through the naval station's guarded exit way. In time, all of these trucks were on their way to the slumbering creature population. The entourage maneuvered its way along Route 611 north, and traveled for several miles until a dense countryside was evidenced. The entourage exited the paved highway and traveled about a mile across the terrain of rolling countryside. When the lead vehicle stopped at the designated location, the soldiers disembarked. One truck after another stopped, and when the last truck had its motor shut down, extensive lines of vehicles were revealed. There were now many soldiers milling about the area, and seeing this, the drivers were directed to park their trucks here and there in a military type of order.

Chapter 75

THE MEMBRANES WERE SCHEDULED to have their final ultrasound and if everything went as planned, they'd be transferred to the sacred chamber before the slumbering giants arrived. The nurses went to the birthing containers since part of the overall plan was for them to prepare each membrane for its individualized ultrasound. "Oh My God!" The nurse peering into the incubator stood motionless. Dr. Battle stopped what he was doing, and hurriedly arrived at the nurse's side. He and the nurse were not prepared for what their eyes beheld. One of the membranes was visibly cracked, and lay ajar. Inside the birthing container was a live newborn, noticeably struggling to free itself from its enclosure.

Dr. Battle and the nurse were completely taken aback by what they were seeing. Dr. Battle instinctively reached into the container, carefully freeing the fetus from its shell, and then lifted the newborn; he then quickly handed the newborn to a waiting nurse.

While Dr. Battle was initially lifting the newborn, he paid little attention to its appearance. Prior to taking the newborn from Dr. Battle, the attending nurse had gone and returned with a softened, sterilized bath towel. The nurse took the newborn and cuddled it close as she walked to the warm area where a newborn could be placed while being cleansed and towel dried. The newborn's cry was reminiscent of a human, unlike its appearance. As other nurses got their first glimpses of the newborn creature, everyone seemed to be confused by what their eyes beheld. The nurse, who had cleansed the newborn, wrapped it in the clean bath sheet, and then kept it safe while awaiting the Dr.'s examination. While the nurse awaited the doctor, the other nurses were noticeably excited, but acted professionally, anticipating the newborn's examination and the ultrasound of the other three membranes. Each of the remaining birthing membranes was checked, but there were no additional "Oh My God" exclamations. Dr. Battle examined each and found that the remaining membranes were totally intact. Additionally, it was determined that all three fetuses were male. Dr. Battle then left the nurses with the responsibility of securing the birthing containers, and when finished, they were instructed to join him.

When unwrapping the baby, Dr. Battle was ready for almost anything; what he actually saw was quite disturbing and caught him somewhat unprepared. He remembered that this baby seemed to be different when handing it to the waiting nurse, but the area was dimly lit and therefore he missed what was presently evident. There, lying upon the table was the newborn creature, but upon further examination, what lay there more resembled a human baby girl than that of a creature. "Wow" was softly said by more than one nurse, and nearly in unison. Dr. Battle was speechless. Finally, he was able to vocalize his dismay. "How can this be?"

There were several, very small, oozing sores, from head to toe, but the facial and body skin did not appear to be scaled; it did, however, appear to be toughened, but definitely not scaled. Dr. Battle turned the baby's head to the left and to the right, and the head was definitely more reminiscent of a human's. While the baby lay within the warm encircling air, it gradually calmed, stopped crying and seemed intrigued by the faces. This caused an overwhelming joy to all as the doctor and nurse's faces appeared to glow.

Dr. Battle then said that he was going to do a more thorough exam. He excused himself and retrieved a handheld digital recorder from his brief case. He then returned to the side of the table and pressed play and record simultaneously, documenting the time and date, and what this exam was about to entail. The doctor then began his examination, using words for what he was about to do and for body part descriptions. He then excused himself once again and went to the telephone. He returned in a matter of minutes, thoroughly washed his hands and resumed the exam.

There, lay a baby girl, not a creature. As he examined, his voice carried in the direction of the recorder; he began with the head, noting that the oozing sores were of the same description as those that had been manifested upon the skin of the Lone Creature. Dr. Battle went on to say that the creature's sores were eliminated through surgery and to this present time, there had been no reoccurrence. He then paid special attention to the baby's eyes and found that the lids opened widely, similar to that of a human baby. Other than the sores and the toughened skin, there seemed to be no outstanding differences between the characteristics of this baby and that of a normal human. It was then that the doctor noticed the webbing of its fingers and toes. Again, he documented this, and while doing so, he speculated as to whether or not these differences could be corrected. After finishing the overall body exam, he made sure that all had been documented. Now, the all-important question, that is, what was to be done with this adorable baby who, by the way, was staring directly into Dr. Battle's eyes?

Soon, the membranes would be placed within the newly created chamber and at that time, what would be the plan for the baby? Everyone directly connected with this project knew that it was only a matter of time before the media got hold of this, yet another captivating story. The general consensus among the group was that it would be better to have a news conference rather than allow the media to write their stories. Every type of accredited media was contacted and all acknowledged their attendance for the upcoming revelation. Just how much information was to be delivered into the laps of the media was fully discussed; the result being that the baby's well-being was the major focus.

After a variety of introductions were made, Dr. Battle approached the podium and began to speak into the microphone. He presented a vivid description of the baby, much like what he had documented, and then opened the session up for questions. The media and the doctor continued their banter for a while and it was clear that the focus was upon where the baby would spend its lifetime. One of the reporters asked, "Is there any evidence that the creatures know that this baby is alive?" Dr. Battle addressed this question, saying that as far as he knew, the creatures could have no definitive way of knowing whether or not any of the fetuses were thriving. The same reporter then continued, "Excuse me, if you will, if this is factual, then the baby wouldn't have to be placed with the other three membranes in the new habitat." Dr. Battle said that he saw no reason why the baby would have to accompany the membranes, but that it was not his decision to make. With that said, there were several loud interruptions, though none were addressed as the new conference had officially come to an end.

Every type of news coverage wrote articles, all focusing upon the baby and where it could spend its lifetime...

Chapter 76

IT WAS NEARING THE time for the relocation of the creature population, and the main concern was whether or not the chamber would be warm enough to nurture these membranes once they were moved there. A team investigated and it was believed that the chamber was indeed warm enough. At first, the investigators were suspicious, but as they were exiting, they realized that their individual bodies were immersed in perspiration and that the heat caused their feet to move around within their boots.

All was now ready for the transport of the membranes; they were securely placed within their composted enclosures and secured upon the four-wheelers. Now secure and readied for the transport, they were driven out of the hangar and through the entranceway of the walled enclosure. Once the four-wheelers were within the complex, they were driven across the surface expanse until they were at the habitat's entrance. Each composted enclosure had handles on every side and was outfitted this way so that two men could easily hand-carry it from one place to another. Being ready for transport, each of the three containers was lifted by men that had previously experienced the habitat's webbed flooring. Immediately upon lifting the containers from each of the transports, the men entered the descending passageway. Moving cautiously, they eventually came to the webbing and found themselves carrying the membranes along what seemed to be a level area. While en route to the sacred chamber, these men could not remember their thighs or their breathing being so painful and labored. One of the men thought to himself that this obvious exhaustion had to be the result of walking upon the webbing while transporting the cumbersome enclosures, and they were probably right.

Obviously exhausted, the transporters continued their tedious trek and finally came to the chamber's entrance. Once all of the membranes were within the chamber's designated birthing room, the enclosures were set down very carefully and the men took a break. After vigorously rubbing their thighs and recovering their depleted breath, one of the men made mention that the way he had felt was the way he imagined athletes felt when experiencing the higher elevation in Denver's Mile High Stadium during an NFL game.

Before each of the membrane's eventual removal, the composted cases were given the opportunity to breathe, allowing the intensely heated membranes to become acclimated to their new environment. Time passed very slowly, but then the men were given the okay to remove the membranes. Each membrane was handled with great care, lifted from the interior of their temporary enclosure and all three were placed by the mound of flesh and purposely at a distance from the vats of coagulated blood. Then, the composted material was placed in three different mounds and the membranes were placed within, much like a baby bird appears within a nest. Believing that the membranes were perfectly safe, the personnel secured the metal enclosures and stood there motionless for a minute or more. The men looked at one another, seemingly aware that these membranes would soon encounter an environment that any other creature had ever experienced. The now emptied enclosures were picked up and carried to the four-wheelers, and then all of the men, while looking from the exit way, took one last opportunity to say their heartfelt goodbyes. It was then that each quietly prayed for the creature's subsequent safety, and when finished, raised their bowed heads and drove the enclosures back to the hangar.

The troop carriers and the flatbeds were parked in their designated locations and all personnel were bivouacked, awaiting instructions regarding the relocation of the colony. There was a noticeable amount of anticipation, and this continued until the time when the operation's commander took his place in front of the large group. He had a handheld speakerphone and before getting into the gist of this mission, he asked, "Can everyone hear me?" All personnel responded with a vociferous "Yes Sir!" The OC then began to address the group, saying that what they were about to achieve was of great importance, and went on to say that nothing, not the accounts of the newspapers or the television coverage, could adequately prepare the men for what they were about to witness. "You probably understand that these creatures are huge and powerfully built; that is definitely an understatement in the case of the males, but the females are much smaller in size and have a limited muscularity. You soldiers have been selectively chosen because of your size and incredible strength; many of these creatures weigh in excess of eight-hundred pounds. I want you to understand that your strength is going to be tested, but if you come through as I expect you will, then all of you will receive a week's paid leave, compliments of "Good Old Uncle Sam;" Guaranteed!" What followed could be expected; there was excessive hooting and hollering, whistles and cheers, and the 'higher ups' had no doubt that these men were up to the challenge!

Although these creatures were heavily sedated and would remain that way throughout the operation, they were dangerous in other ways. The soldiers were told to be extremely careful of the razor sharp talons and the ragged claws that emanated from the temple areas of their heads; these parts were spattered and encrusted with infectious materials, such as decayed blood and scraps of flesh. These are just part of the danger that can come from living in such a dismal environment; also, the soldiers were to be aware that there will be fecal matter and urine where they walked. "Please! Please! Please be extra careful to keep the protective gear on your bodies, no matter how uncomfortable it might make you feel."

The plan was to enter the habitat that the creature population was in the process of constructing, and while being careful not to harm any of the slumbering giants, temporary lighting would to be installed in advantageous locations. Once the lighting was in place, then the troops would not have to depend upon head lamps while they labored. Just before finalizing the plan, the men were broken down into groups of four, and were given stretchers that were especially equipped to carry these creatures of such a great size and weight. There were many stretchers, and each had a set of connecting straps that were to be used to secure the legs and arms of each creature. This was seen to be the most efficient means to move the creatures from within their lengthy, over-crowded, putrid area to that of the trucks, and then from the trucks to their newly constructed environment.

Once a creature was securely attached to a specific stretcher, it would remain on that stretcher until it arrived within the new habitat. Each soldier wore protective gear and prior to their entrance into the habitat, more than enough lamps were placed within the singular catacomb and connected to generators. These generators were placed upon the earth's surface, which was beyond the entranceway that led to the singular catacomb; being quite a distance from the slumbering creatures enabled the generators to run at full throttle, and not be a disturbance. Rope-like extension cords snaked along, from each generator to the lamp locations, allowing the entirety of the lengthy catacomb to be easily viewed.

Depending upon how many creatures were found, it was estimated that all of the personnel would be at the site for most of that day and possibly into the evening. Furthermore, an accurate count was to be kept as each drug-induced creature was brought out of the temporary catacomb, and then once again upon its entrance into the inventive habitat. In the beginning, the soldiers found difficulty when walking within the lengthy catacomb because their boots could not find a secure purchase below the waste. These men realized that working where their boots could not gain the proper stability heightened the stress factor in the area of their back and shoulders. Over time, they did adapt to the slippery conditions and, in doing so, found the necessary posture so as to walk securely.

Eventually, the first group of creatures was about to enter the habitat. It was fortunate that the decision was previously made to carry the initial creature, upon its entrance, to the furthest area of the catacomb. It would have been easier to lay the first creature onto the surface after a trek of one-hundred yards, but there was the possibility that one-hundred yards would not be enough room for the entire colony. It was believed that a distance of two-hundred yards was needed so that each creature would have its own separate space once the entire population had been relocated.

One creature after another was brought to rest on its own space, and as the total mounted, there was less and less room in the direction of the entrance. Some of these creatures were noticeably youthful, while others appeared ancient, but all had more than their share of stench that emanated from their being. Those that appeared to be the oldest had what appeared to be a severe skin disease and horrific sores that covered their bodies; these open sores oozed a thickened, fluid-like, rancid and filthy odor. It was extremely difficult to control the urge to vomit. Somehow, the personnel were able to avoid this bodily function.

What the military personnel found to be most interesting was the noticeable difference between the males and females. Some of the males were larger than others, and their muscularity differed, but every male had talons projecting from their feet and hand-like appendages. The larger the male, the larger and longer the talons, and the thicker and longer were the claws that grew from the sides of their heads.

The females were a different story altogether. They had breasts with evident nipples, limited muscularity and their hands and feet did not have talons. What they had was better-characterized as a deformity that slightly resembled webbed fingers and toes. They also had growths emanating from the sides of their head, but these were a hardened material, similar in size to that of a sharks tooth. These females generally weighed in the vicinity of one-hundred and fifty pounds and were a feather's weight when compared to that of an adult male. The female had a less horrific odor and this could be tolerated in comparison to the male; the female also had epidermal areas that weren't dominated by oozing sores and scales.

One by one, the creatures were removed from their horrible living conditions and eventually relocated to the new habitat. In whatever position a creature was found, the side that was against the flooring was smeared with a waste mixture. Several of the soldiers could be seen shaking their heads in obvious wonderment and empathy when they became aware of the living situation.

The count began with one, and then two, three, four, five, and then into the teens, twenties, thirties and forties. The carrying slowed considerable when the count reached in excess of three-hundred creatures. Finally, the relocation was complete when the official count reached four-hundred and eighty-nine, all prone upon the webbed flooring. The musculature of every soldier was severely fatigued upon the completion of this task. Even though all of the creatures were, in fact, within the confines of their new habitat, there was still much left to do. A few of the men were selected to pull a fire hose through the catacomb's length, around, over, and through the colony, as the creatures continued their drug induced sleep. Once ready, a signal was given for the warm water to be released and it gradually filled the length of the previously collapsed hose.

Those manning the hose thought that they were taking a risk, but were assured that nothing could awaken the creatures, at least at this point. No matter how much assurance was given, the soldiers were more than aware of the creature's size and presence. The nozzle was slowly opened and eventually a powerful spray of warmed water was interspersed among the sleeping giants. The longer the soldiers worked, the more secure they felt for the creatures were able to be moved, washed, and subsequently cleansed of any and all waste, without the slightest hint of an awakening. All of the waste and the excessive amount of water fell from each and every creature, creating a continual motion for the conveyor belt. The conveyor and the waste station worked efficiently, as they were designed to, removing all of the waste and its unpleasant smell.

The vast majority of the soldiers that had carried the creatures were now back at the naval station, while those that were chosen to spray and cleanse the creatures were just now leaving the habitat. To avoid any possible danger to the creatures, one of the soldiers instinctively picked up the heavy brass nozzle and hand-carried it while heading to the habitat's surface. While this soldier led the way, others picked up various sections of the hose as it snaked along, as if in pursuit of the nozzle. You could tell by watching these soldiers climb onto a waiting flatbed that they were completely and undeniably spent.

Some of the military personnel entered the hangar that housed the Lone Creature and its sterile enclosure, not expecting to witness the scientists, doctors, and nurses in some type of emotional upset. All appeared to be quite anxious as they sat at their work stations, or briskly walked here and there, seemingly having purpose and direction. An attachment, or bond, had gradually grown between them and the Lone Creature and membranes.

Chapter 77

GRACE HAD CALMED CONSIDERABLY and asked the adults if she could sit on her own. She was physically assisted to a chair and given a cool glass of water; Grace sipped the water and gained more of her composure. With both adults watching, the nurse felt that it was as good a time as any to hear what Grace had to say. She impulsively attempted to get up from her chair, but immediately was aware that her physical and mental capacities were still quite shaken. It was at that time that she found herself slumping back into the chair; overwhelmed, and visibly trembling while in a close proximity to the adults. Tears were flowing, repetitiously, and before either adult could come to Grace's aid she was heard to softly say, "The creature is dying." She softly repeated this phrase, over and over again, each time softer than before. Then, as if she had lost all of her own muscularity and substance, her eyes rolled up and towards the back of her head; as if in slow motion, she collapsed toward the floor. The school nurse and the principal made an attempt to catch her, but her collapse was too sudden.

Luckily for Grace, Dr. Mehaffey's effort enabled her to catch Grace just before her head collided with the tiled concrete, saving Grace from serious injury. It was then that Grace was lifted from behind and carried back to the bed. There she lay motionless, her breaths quite shallow; it was evident that Grace had lapsed into some sort of coma. The nurse checked Grace's vital signs and decided to call 911. All of the relevant information was given and within a matter of minutes, the paramedics were at the entrance of the elementary school. Since this was early in the morning, the students and an occasional teacher were mingling on the school grounds, preparing to enter their classrooms.

As the litter came out of the vehicle, its legs automatically extended and locked, allowing its wheels to freely roll upon the pavement. One of the paramedics, a highly trained technician by the name of Gene Hathaway, placed the necessary equipment upon the litter and proceeded to wheel it into the school. Both paramedics expeditiously arrived at the nurse's office and immediately went into action. It was at that moment that Gene realized that, by coincidence, the stricken child was none other than a daughter of a relative. In a matter of minutes, it was clearly understood that Grace was, in fact, experiencing a type of coma and that she was in great need of their immediate care. Prior to the paramedic's arrival, Kathleen was called and notified that Grace had recently collapsed, and that paramedics would be at the school in a matter of minutes. She was asked to notify her husband and to please wait at her school until the nurse could get back to her regarding any findings. She realized that Kathleen was very worried and said that Grace was most likely going to be hospitalized. The nurse went on to say that instead of making the trip to her office, Kathleen would be better served if she waited for the nurse's return call and then go directly to the specified hospital. This advice made perfect sense to Kathleen and she thanked the nurse for her concern and assistance to Grace. Kathleen went on to say that Grace and Ryan were extremely close and asked if she would locate Ryan and to bring him up to date regarding this happening. The nurse promised that she would attend to this immediately and for Kathleen to consider it done.

Grace was secured upon the collapsible litter and wheeled through the doors and into the circular courtyard; there, she was met by concerned students and teachers. The sounds of concern were evident from all that were in that area. The litter was wheeled to the rear of the emergency vehicle, and then was slid into and along the secured tract that aligned the flooring. Gene Hathaway climbed into the back of the emergency vehicle and immediately began attending to Grace while the other paramedic drove the vehicle in the direction of Doylestown Hospital, sirens singing loud and clear. While en route, Gene was at Grace's side and in continual contact with the ER. Upon their arrival, everything and everyone was in an apparent state of readiness. Grace was wheeled along a hallway and once inside the ER, she was transferred from the litter to the ER operating table. There she was thoroughly examined, and while this was being done, Kathleen came through the entrance, exuding a noticeable amount of anxiety and stress.

Kathleen had, indeed, been notified by the school nurse that Grace was on her way to Doylestown Hospital. Kathleen had then arrived and was advised that Grace was receiving the best care that she could get, and that she, Kathleen, had to try her best to calm down. Nevertheless, Kathleen was in a state of obvious panic, and it was a necessity to give her an injection to smooth her frenzied state. This was done and no sooner had she been injected when John sat down next to his wife. John and Kathleen attempted to calm one another, and no sooner had John sat when a doctor approached them, introduced himself, and said that Grace was experiencing a coma; she had been taken to the Intensive Care Unit. Kathleen immediately asked if they could be with Grace and the doctor responded with a yes. Nothing, and I mean nothing, could have prepared John and Kathleen for what they witnessed when entering the intensive care unit.

Chapter 78

IT WAS ONLY EARLIER today that John had kissed both Grace and Ryan while they both slept soundly as he prepared to leave for work. Kathleen said that she remembered that Grace was not feeling well, but that she did not have a fever. Therefore, Kathleen felt that it was okay to send her to school. John, sensing that Kathleen was feeling apprehensive, reassured her that she had done the right thing and that everything would turn out fine.

Tubes protruded from Grace's nostrils and mouth, and were attached to several other machines; lighted numbers and blinking lights were close by. There was a heart monitor and other gauges; a clear liquid, hanging above, was being administered intravenously. Adhesive tape was placed on her face to keep the tubes in their proper places. This was a sight that they had never imagined for either of their children.

Both parents were obviously saddened by Grace's circumstance, and while looking for a sign that she was aware, a reassuring hand was laid upon Kathleen's shoulder. It was the priest that they had come to know and trust since becoming parishioners at a church near their home in Oreland. He asked, "How are you holding up?" He went on to say that this was an excellent hospital with an exceptional staff and that God would take good care of Grace; that this is when John and Kathleen needed to trust in the Lord. The priest's words were just what they needed, for both parents found themselves calmer, obviously influenced by his demeanor and the fact that they trusted him and God.

The principal chose to keep Ryan at the school until it could be confirmed that at least one of his parents was at the Doylestown Hospital. When this was finally confirmed, the principal offered to drive Ryan to the hospital to be with his family. The other family members were now at the hospital and while John remained at Grace's bedside, Kathleen excused herself and went to a courtesy phone and made several calls to her most immediate relatives. Needless to say, the news was upsetting to all. While Kathleen was returning to Grace's room, she noticed Ryan, accompanied by the school's principal, walking in the hallway. Kathleen called to them, and when they were in her direct vicinity, she wrapped her arms around Ryan and practically smothered him with her love. She eventually released Ryan and made certain to warmly thank Dr. Mehaffey for being so kind. At this point, Kathleen hugged the principal and then Dr. Mehaffey said that her prayers were with Grace and the family. She then looked in on Grace, said a quiet prayer, and left the hospital. A battery of tests was done, but none were conclusive as to how or why this coma had gained its hold upon Grace, or for how long it might linger.

Chapter 79

IT WAS ESTIMATED, GIVEN their height and weight, that the creatures would begin to stir sometime within the next twelve hours. Subsequently, all of the equipment and military personnel were gradually removed from the new habitat. While all of the creatures were moved to their new habitat, the personnel from the hangar watched with great anticipation. They viewed their various monitors within the makeshift control center. The eventual plan was to construct an observation tower just to the outside of the enclosure wall and above it. The temporary control center had all of its monitors centrally located so that one person had complete access to all of the screens and warning signals within the hangar. All of the screens were wirelessly connected to a variety of video feeds placed throughout the interior of the new habitat and at vantage points along the walls.

The creatures were beginning to stir and whatever amount of intelligence they possessed would immediately come into play. While it was true that they had gotten acclimated to their previous environment, it was just as true that they never found themselves to be comfortable. It was also a fact that these leprous creatures knew of their habitat's filth and deplorable smell, along with its accompanying diseases, and always found that their colony hoped to experience a better way of life. Time passed, eventually a century, but the habitat's environment only degenerated. Every catacomb on every level had a stench beyond compare; feces were everywhere and in some places, it was more deplorable than in others. Where there were feces there were also pockets of urine lying within the lumpy waste, and this was most prevalent within the catacombs constructed at the lowest level.

As the drug began to dissipate, the colony felt the warmth and sensed the soft lighting, though initially, neither comprehended by the creatures. Gradually coming out of their drugged state, it was as if each and every creature believed that they were dreaming. No matter how often the creatures blinked or allowed themselves to feel the warmth, the dream was recognized for what it actually was, that is, reality, and the creatures found themselves wondering about their illuminated surroundings. Each and every creature found themselves completely bewildered, as if they were experiencing something new, that was old, and vice versa. None of the creatures trusted what seemed to be in front of their weakened eyesight, and thus remained startled. They had used their eyes before, and feeling mistrust this time around, they began to wonder what their other senses might reveal. One of the elders had sensed the lighting for what it actually was, and realizing its full effect, it allowed its lids to remain opened. This elder then sensed a continuous pleasant airflow. The airflow was indeed pleasing and refreshing, but had a distinct effect within these catacombs; it had the distinct scent of freshness and a misty kind of wetness. It was like heaven on earth; there was absolutely no scent of waste and no disturbing scent that immediately, or adversely, stung one's senses.

It was inevitable that all of the creatures would eventually rid themselves of their stupor. In time, as they further investigated their environment, they would come upon the chamber and there lost membranes. It would be, most assuredly, like a dream come true that the membranes, which disappeared such a long time ago and believed to be dead, were back in the chamber, thriving and awaiting their birth experience. There was no doubt that this would confuse the colony, but hopefully they would be able to adjust and adapt.

Chapter 80

THE NURSES PACKED ALL that was brought with them and were preparing to leave the hangar for the last time; their work being complete. The four membranes had been diligently cared for, and three were now within their new habitat, waiting out their time so that the creatures within could break through their ever hardening enclosures. One of the nurses, by chance, glanced over at the creature's cell-like enclosure and remembered that it appeared to be in the same position now, as it had been when Wyatt touched its talons and opened hand. The Lone Creature was still on its side, with its hand-like extremity open, talons extended, and the extremity was hanging limply out of the cage beneath the barred enclosure and toward the floor. It was now as it was then, the only difference being a few hours and the slab of meat had not been touched. Was there something wrong with the creature?

The nurse found that she was staring at the creature for what seemed to be an eternity and came to the conclusion that the creature hadn't moved during that specific period of time either. Unbeknownst to the other professional staff, the Lone Creature was experiencing a similar condition to that of Grace. It had witnessed the departure of the three membranes and the two children; it was the creature's belief that the membranes were being returned to the colony, but it didn't know the whereabouts of the children. The creature further understood that being in its present circumstance, it would never be afforded the same privilege as the membranes. The creature had been in captivity for several months and initially this was acceptable, but more recently, it had experienced a discouraging feeling, a debilitating presence, to be more exact, that apparently was gnawing at its brain and body; an agitating and frightening annoyance from within. The creature realized that it had the size and the power to thwart off any physical threat, but the humans had a strategy that wasn't recognizable.

Without the slightest warning, the creature began to feel much different, in fact, overwhelmed; tremendous sadness and melancholy had overtaken its entire psyche. With each passing second, minute, hour, and eventual day, the sadness and melancholy worsened; what had been intermittent was painfully consistent. The Lone Creature found that it was fearful of doing anything other than remaining in its fetal position, motionless and sleeping. Being in a continuing negative mind set, the creature was being bombarded and was subsequently overwhelmed by guilt and other unsettling thoughts. Recognizing these to be an absolute truth, the creature found it needing to recapture the boy's touch, and at the same time, spiraling helplessly into depths previously unknown to any living being, at least that is the way it felt.

While the majority of the professionals were giving their undivided attention to the relocation and safety of the membranes, the creature was in the throes of a very painful, scary, and disturbing depression. Deeper, and deeper, and deeper yet, the depression took the creature, spiraling towards an experience that caused its breathing to be labored, tremendous pain escalated within its chest and subsequently within its heart. The Lonesome Creature wanted to cry out for help, but remained quiet; it recognized that it did have choices. One was to be recognized for the pain that it was experiencing and to possibly recover, recover to live a life as an untouched oddity; or it could choose to keep its predicament unknown and hopefully experience its own, swift demise.

The creature, however, did not get the opportunity to make its own decision, for its chest had what seemed to be a massive, pain filled explosion and as the searing pain circumvented each artery and vein, life ebbed from its heart. The creature's entire life force was shutting down. What was to remain would be lifeless and, finally, pain-free.

Chapter 81

THE SAME NURSE THAT had been observing the creature notified Dr. Battle that she suspected something was terribly wrong, furthermore stipulating that she had been observing it for a few minutes and did not see any movement. When notified by the nurse, the doctor found himself doing a double take for his attention had been focused upon the membranes, but was now fully directed toward the creature.

The doctor, realizing that the creature had recently displayed positive signs of alertness and of a willingness to recover, wondered what could have happened since he and the nurse had vacated the enclosure. Dr. Battle went directly to the enclosure, reached through the bars, opened its eyelids, and witnessed what was thought to be a lifeless being. A spontaneous, yet frustrated, "Oh, Damn!" was heard to come for the doctor's mouth. He immediately called out loudly, notifying all present that there was a dire emergency; he needed the entranceway to the creature unlocked. This was done and the door was left ajar. In a matter of seconds, Dr. Battle was within the enclosure and was seen checking the creature's carotid artery; as he did, he could be heard making additional pleas. He then said that it was necessary for the heart paddles and all portable heart accessories to be brought into the enclosure as fast as was humanly possible. Realizing that time was of the essence, Dr. Battle checked the creature's vital signs.

It was obvious that the doctor needed assistance, but nurse Miletto had previously finished her assigned shift and was on her way home. Dr. Battle, appearing somewhat anxious, received the assistance that he needed. Another of the nurses swiftly moved to the opposite side of the creature, she kneeling onto one and then both knees. She emptied her hands of whatever she was carrying and then awaited any and all instructions. Now, both professionals had their hands empty and the necessary pieces of equipment lay a short distance away.

Dr. Battle asked the nurse to assist him in rolling the creature from its fetal position onto its back so that it could be attended from both sides of its then prone positioning. This was accomplished immediately, and the nurse hurried so she was directly across from the doctor; the examination revealed that the creature was alive, but that its heartbeat and breath were barely recognizable. So very weakened were these signs, signaling that the creature was closer to death than to life. Dr. Battle then said, as if talking to no one in particular, "This being has lost its will to live." He then opened his medical bag and took out a container of small white pills; he advised the nurse that he was going to secure the claws, so as to raise the creature's chin, thus opening the creature's airway. The doctor went on to say, and therefore verify, that the small white pills were, in actuality, nitroglycerin and that this medicine was meant to jump start the creature's heart.

As was the plan, the creature's mouth was forced to open widely, with its chin jutting upwards and towards the ceiling of the structure; its mouth hung open and it was then that the nurse took a dry cloth and wrapped it around the creature's swollen tongue. Holding it securely, and towards the roof of the mouth, she then followed Dr. Battle's instructions. Using her unoccupied hand, she placed the pills within the creature's saliva. These pills now lay in a puddle of liquid within the lowest area of the creature's cavernous jaw where the tongue would usually rest. The pills began to break down immediately, seemingly melting into the flesh of the creature's jaw. Upon witnessing this, the nurse released her hold upon the tongue. The nitroglycerin, no doubt, expediently reached the creature's heart, but his reaction was more than mind-boggling.

The nitroglycerin was expected to invigorate and motivate the creature's heart rhythm, thus bringing life back to the now listless body. This did not happen.

While the doctor and nurse were administering the prescribed first-aid, the creature's mind and soul had taken a temporary departure from its physical shell to reminisce the experiences of its youthful past. The creature's heartbeat remained, but only gave the slightest hint that one beat had acquired enough impetus to follow the one before. Doctor Battle felt that death was knocking at the creature's door, but also realized, as long as there was the slightest heartbeat and the sign of a weakened but evident breath, then the creature would continue to live.

Dr. Battle and the nurse removed the equipment from the immediacy of the creature and then moved to a closer proximity, continuing their assistance. After a short wait, the doctor reached into his bag and withdrew a syringe along with a vial of serum. He vigorously shook the vial and while holding it upside down, placed the needle into the vial, filling the syringe to a specific level. Dr. Battle urgently moved to the creature, knelt by its side and after applying some rubbing alcohol, injected the serum fully into the creature's hip area. This serum had a history of being highly potent, especially when a patient displayed symptoms that were presently being exhibited by the creature. Just like its reaction to the nitroglycerin, the creature's heartbeat did not react to the potency of the serum. Unbeknownst to the doctor, the nurse, or any of the remaining staff, the creature's life force was experiencing a sort of limbo between life and death.

In this dream state, the creature envisioned that it was floating, hovering above its physical shell. As its mind continued to reminisce, the creature remembered the law that it so callously chose to break. *All creatures are forbidden to ever enter the Earth's surface, unless this action has been previously sanctioned by the elders; furthermore, if a creature took it upon itself to flagrantly break this law, then that creature, or creatures, would be subject to a penalty of death!*

Still, the creature's soul bounced among the pillow-like clouds, witnessing other past souls that had been experiencing an indeterminate state for such an endless time. Recognizing the pain of its own depression and the limbo of others, the creature drifted, and at the same time wondered why it so callously chose to break the covenant of the elder's laws. Now, the creature could actually envision its mind, and, in fact, its life force appeared to be floating while also separated from the shell. The creature found itself envisioning its initial encounter with the little girl.

For some reason, the memory of this situation and its outcome was much more clouded than any of its other visions; it remembered tremendous pain, internally and externally, and of having an oversized knot protruding from the upper part of its head. From that point in time, its memory was vague.

Chapter 82

THE DOCTOR AND NURSE witnessed the jerking and believed that the creature was in the throes of some type of seizure; they therefore provided creature all of the floor space that was available. The creature's body parts were spasmodic, but no sooner had they begun, when all of the sudden the creature laid still, as if totally spent. Remaining conscious, it looked within its dream state and visualized the turmoil that its irrational decisions had made upon itself and the entire colony. Subsequently, the creature envisioned what it believed to be its fate, a debilitating death. The creature, feeling substantially weakened and possibly hallucinating, experienced a vision of Grace, immediately followed by that of Wyatt. The jerking gradually ceased as the children appeared to be a reality. At that time, the creature's body seemed to be experiencing a totality of calm and solitude. The creature had thought that experiencing the surface was to be the ultimate in its lifetime, but now it realized that being touched by the innocence of Grace, and then, subsequently by Wyatt, made it feel that these two children were, in actuality, each, the left and right hand of God. The creature then envisioned Grace and Wyatt, each taking a secure hold of its individual palms, and subsequently elevating the purity of its life force from within.

Dr. Battle, and the nurse, continued to work feverishly, but the more they did to strengthen the creature's ability to live, the more the creature continued towards its chosen path; its final breath. The creature's facial color appeared to be ashen and realizing this, the doctor rocked backwards; while still kneeling and holding a heart paddle in each hand, Dr. Battle eventually sat upon his heals. He was now exhausted, with his eyes tearing and his chin resting upon the lower area of his neck. Dr. Battle had experienced much since becoming an integral part of this all important medical team that attempted to nourish the creature's existence. However, now, he sensed that the creature was ready to die. He remained in this semi-seated position for a few more seconds, and without having a warning of any kind, he noticed that the creature was slowly opening its glazed and moistened eyelids.

While staring intently at the doctor, the Lone Creature took hold of his forearm and gently squeezed; a full, lonesome tear, streamed from an eye and flowed over its cheek. As the doctor's attention moved toward the creature's grip, he felt what he thought was a strong gust of wind against his face. Looking back at the creature's face, Dr. Battle realized that the gust of wind could have been, and in fact was, evidence of the creature's final breath. Dr. Battle thoroughly checked all of its vital signs, and then, realizing that it had been through enough pain and suffering, announced that the creature was dead.

Dr. Battle then made a mental note of what would be known, forever more, as the official date and time of the creature's passing. Everyone present had witnessed Dr. Battle and the nurse as they did everything that could have been humanly done to save the life of this huge, yet sensitive being. At the same time, most that were present had also been witness of everything that the creature endured since its capture, and understood why it may have lost its will to live.

Chapter 83

MEANWHILE, WITHIN THE INTENSIVE Care Unit of Doylestown Hospital, Grace remained in her coma; not giving the slightest indication that she was aware that her parents and brother had been constantly by her bedside.

It was late in the afternoon, and John decided to get some food items from the vending machines located within the hospital's cafeteria. Kathleen urged Ryan to catch up with his father and help him choose the snacks. Ryan peered at his mother and then at Grace, and feeling okay about the decision, he left the room, running to catch up with his dad.

Kathleen's full attention went back to her daughter, and while clenching Grace's hand, she felt a strange reaction. Kathleen's thoughts were wandering, but now her eyes were fixed on Grace. Her eyelids were moving! Kathleen's anxiety tentatively grew, and continued to grow because she could feel movement in Grace's fingers. It was then that Grace temporally removed her hand from that of her mother's. Kathleen, being too excited to speak and calmly gather her breath, continued to observe; as each split second passed, she recognized additional sparks of awareness.

Kathleen placed her hand upon Grace's, and when their palms connected, it seemed as if this brought Grace out of her coma. Simultaneously, Grace gently closed her hand around her mother's, and then opened her eyes. "Hello Mother...Do you want to know something?" Kathleen replied, "Of course, yes!" Grace said, "I was having a dream that myself, and a boy named Wyatt were holding the creature by its hands, and then we lifted it out of its body. Isn't that strange? We then walked the creature toward a brilliant white light and when we were very close to the light, the creature stopped, removed its hands from ours, and motioned for us to go back. We hugged him for a long, long time. We then began to back away, along the path that we had come, and as we were walking, we both stopped and turned to check on the creature. The light seemed to get brighter as the creature walked into it, and just before the creature disappeared, it looked in our direction, stared for a few seconds and then was gone."

For whatever reason, Kathleen looked at her watch and made a mental note of the time; she then collected herself and pressed the bedside button, signaling the nurse's station. No sooner had she pressed the button, when Kathleen recognized the sound of shoes, moving swiftly, in the direction of Grace's room. Upon their entrance, the nurse's facial expressions quickly changed from that of concern to delight. The nurses witnessed Grace sitting up, looking directly at them. One of them went to the phone and notified the on-call doctor that Grace had come out of her coma, was fully awake, and apparently was functioning on her own. The doctor said that he would immediately come to the room.

Medical personnel were hurriedly coming and going from Grace's room as John and Ryan walked down the hallway. They noticed the hustle and bustle, and were alarmed that something was wrong. Without realizing it, John had lost his grip on a cup of hot coffee and a few snacks; his fear had taken over. Ryan, being more composed, reflexively caught the covered container just before it would have collided and splashed onto the floor. Unbeknownst to all present, this scene was reminiscent of Grace's experience in the school nurse's office. John rounded the doorway, not knowing what to expect, but found a heart rendering scene; the doctor was removing tubes from Grace's nostrils and mouth, but kept the intravenous line intact. Grace was chatting and smiling with her mother and the nurses; at this same time, Kathleen was continually thanking the doctor and the nurses.

Kathleen saw John first and then Ryan, who had just rescued the coffee and picked up the fallen snacks. As they entered the room, Kathleen said, "The doctor said that Grace is okay, but to be safe, she will have to remain in the hospital for observation and most likely will be able to go home in the morning."

John, a man of few words, usually shy and reserved, went completely out of character. He had a smile from ear to ear and crisply said, "That's great news Grace, that's Fantastic!" Kathleen then asked her husband, and best friend, if he would take Ryan home while she remained with Grace. John understood and before departing, he made sure that Kathleen had enough money for the vending machines. He and Ryan then said their earnest adieus, lightly hugged Grace, and subsequently, Kathleen. They then went out of the room and exited the hospital, feeling the 'Greatest!' (Watch out Muhammad Ali)

Chapter 84

DR. BATTLE PROCEEDED TO notify the coroner's office of Bucks County that the Lonesome Creature was dead, and requested that the coroner set up a time and place for an autopsy. The coroner, being aware of the immense size and weight of the creature, said, "Just a Minute," he took the phone from his ear and gave the situation some serious thought. He got back on the phone and after checking to see if Dr. Battle was still on the line, he said "The creature is probably too big, but taking all things into consideration, the autopsy has to be performed at the morgue." He went on to say that there was a lot that had to be done in preparation, and when all was ready, the transport would arrive at the hangar. Dr. Battle said that he fully understood, and would have everything prepared on his end so that access to the creature would be in complete readiness.

After hanging up the phone, Dr. Battle went about his business, preparing for the creature's transport. It was then that one of the military personnel gave the order to remove the blood from its container within the creature's enclosure and to pour it into smaller, capped containers. The order also included the untouched slabs of raw meat that lay on the enclosure's floor; these slabs, plus the meat that was in cold storage and the containers of blood, were to be loaded into a refrigerated truck and taken to the Philadelphia Zoo.

As the morgue's vehicle approached the hangar, there were homeowners milling about, doing a variety of yard work. When the vehicle arrived in the direct vicinity of the compound, it caught the attention of several homeowners. "Had someone died from within the compound?" The vehicle approached the entrance, and as it did, concern began to spew from the neighbor's body language and facial features. One of these homeowners turned off their lawnmower and went directly into the house to notify the news desk of potential front page information. This person had been a writer for The Intelligencer, Doylestown's most prominent newspaper. No sooner had the call come in, when a specific journalist was sent to investigate; upon her arrival, Mrs. Joanie Broskley found that the site was under the status of high alert. Something big had happened!

Mrs. Broskley, being an energetic, sensitive, and caring young woman, attached the clearance badge to the pocket of her blouse and headed toward the entrance door of the hangar. She knocked on the door and, being somewhat impatient, reached for the knob. Before taking hold of the doorknob, she realized that the door was opening. A spiffy attired officer eyed her, her press badge and then requested her driver's license; Mrs. Broskley did as asked and then gained entrance to the area that surrounded the creature's enclosed, sterile setting. Her body language depicted that she suspected something had happened to the creature, and this was confirmed when she was allowed to enter the sterile enclosure without having to suit up. She had heard that all adults had to wear a specialized, protective outfit, and she had expected to experience this happening as well.

When entering the sterile environment, Mrs. Broskley was led toward the cage-like apparatus, and her suspicion was confirmed. Almost immediately, she realized that the door to the creature's cell-like enclosure had been left open and was unguarded. Mrs. Broskley was introduced as a writer for the Intelligencer, and received permission to get all of the information that she needed. She was also permitted to take as many photos as she deemed necessary. Mrs. Broskley was given the official time of death and was advised that the cause, at that time, was undetermined. She walked toward the opened end of the creature's enclosure, and was caught completely off guard upon the realization of the creature's size as it still lay within. She asked if she could enter the cell-like enclosure and found that this was permitted.

Mrs. Broskley then heard someone say hello; she turned, looked, and there stood a casually dressed man. He advised her that that he was from the morgue, and if she wanted to get photos, then she should do so promptly. The creature would be taken to the morgue in approximately ten minutes. She introduced herself and thanked him, and her lucky stars, for it was her plan to take photos after doing interviews. Mrs. Broskley found that she was completely spellbound by the creature. She had heard and read a variety of descriptions relating directly to this being, but she was more than taken aback by what she was presently witnessing.

The creature was indeed huge in every conceivable and imaginable way, shape, or form. She entered the cage, and being within a few feet of this captivating being, hesitated; she knelt by its side and while placing her hand upon the creature's bowling-ball sized shoulder, she closed her eyes and said a few silent prayers. Mrs. Broskley got to her feet, and after verifying that there was a new roll of film within her camera, began taking a variety of angled shots. For whatever the reason, she felt an immediate bond and no sooner had she started taking the photos, when all of a sudden she stopped, stood motionless and felt a generalized melancholy that depressed her mood. Before she realized what was happening, tears were streaming from her eyes and steadily down her face. Now experiencing some form of anxiety and an unsettling nervousness, she struggled, but could not prevent herself from the need to return to the entrance steps. This immediate experience was truly strange and frightening!

Dr. Battle, being nearby, noticed the journalist's unsteady demeanor, collected her at the steps and assisted her to a nearby chair; he then got some cold water from the cooler and upon his return said "I am Dr. Battle, drink this and you'll feel more at ease!" She looked at him, as if ready to ask a question, but he spoke first, saying that it was just cold water. She drank and then followed his directions by leaning forward at the waist and placing her head close to her knees. It did not take long before her comfort level began to normalize. Mrs. Broskley gradually sat upright and then drank the remainder of the water. She purposefully thanked Dr. Battle and looked in the direction of the enclosure. The creature was gone!

Joanie Broskley introduced herself and said that she worked as journalist for the 'Intel.' She gradually got to her feet, and after steadying herself, she said that she felt much better; it was then that she asked Dr. Battle about the creature's destination and what had caused its death? Dr. Battle, being somewhat hesitant due to a variety of factors, especially those that pertained to stories being changed by reporters, looked her directly in the eyes and sensed that she was genuine. He then stated that until the autopsy had been completed, he could only speculate as to the reason for the creature's death. Mrs. Broskley promised that she would be true to his word, printing only his accounts and being careful to not sensationalize the event.

Dr. Battle reviewed the creature's recent history, including the importance of his recollections regarding Grace, Ryan and Wyatt. He went on to say that this creature had been experiencing what could be understood as a very serious bout of clinical depression. Mrs. Broskely found herself listening intently, anticipating, and hanging onto each and every word. "Since its birth, the creature evolved, and adapted, but following its discovery and subsequent capture, traumatic circumstances surrounded both of those occurrences. These involved experiences led the Lonesome Creature toward the gradual and debilitating reality of what was evidenced to be a devastating, ever spiraling depression, the kind of implosion that brings tremendous amounts of emotional pain and turmoil to its host." Dr. Battle hesitated, allowing his words to penetrate Mrs. Broskley's psyche; then chose to continue. "Its leper colony had, at one time, been characterized as afflicted humans; but in time, these lepers were forced to acclimate themselves to an oppressive and depressive environment. Living conditions, restricted to the bowels of the earth, were not worthy of any human's body, mind, or spirit. To experience this environment within the colony's extensive catacombs, tunnels, and chamber was deplorable, at best! Then, to be hunted, captured and held within this form of captivity, and possibly having the knowledge that its colony could have chosen to exile it from their habitat…well, that could have brought on the negativity of complete worthlessness!"

Mrs. Broskley had now gone from being inquisitive to feeling empathy for the creature and its plight. A kind of lethargy eclipsed her over-all being, and noticing this, Dr. Battle asked her if she was okay. This question snapped her out of the lethargy, and after abruptly raising her head, she went on to say that she was okay, and then said, "Doctor, you tell a captivating story; did you ever envision writing a medical column for the paper?" At this, Dr. Battle smiled warmly. He avoided answering the query and then went on to say that it was a possibility that the creature recognized its limited options, and with a dominating surety, spiraled into the unknown depths of a very damaging and mindful depression."

"The Lone Creature may have suspected that it would eventually be relocated to a place, like a zoo or someplace that resembled it, and could remain there without a mate for the remainder of its lifetime." Dr. Battle, then, to better explain the experience of depression, related a personal situation. He asked Mrs. Broskley if she had the time to listen and she said that she did. He then continued and, being totally sincere, said that animals experience severe depressions, as do humans. He went on to say that there was a time when he had a friend who had a cat. It was found as a kitten in the dead of a bitter winter beneath a trash dumpster; it was totally alone and very frightened.

Dr. Battle went on to say that his friend rescued the kitten, but from the time the kitten was rescued until it was a few years of age, it never seemed to thrive. In fact, it seemed to be somewhat depressed. During its lifetime, it had an abundance of complications, one of which was that its hair fell out of its head and from the paw area of one leg. A salve was applied on a daily basis and Sam-Sam, the cat, recovered; after the full recovery, the youthful cat had an ongoing, playful nature. Then, Sam-Sam had a bladder infection and began urinating on a rug, but not in its litter box. Sam-Sam, recognizing that he was out of sync, began to hide in dark places. He would not come when called and avoided his food and water. When found, the circumstance was addressed, but it only worsened. Wherever he was found, it was always dark and at times cold; eventually, Sam-Sam's system completely broke down. His internal organs were not one-hundred percent and thus he was euthanized.

Dr. Battle allowed time for this information to be digested and then continued saying that animals, much like human beings, were known to experience debilitating bouts of depression. Mrs. Broskley found that she was empathizing with the words of the doctor, and before she could speak, he continued. "The creature may have felt disturbed by the realization that humans could be quite insensitive; that they tended to point and gawk at anything that appeared different, or was considered to be an oddity. It is bad enough that there are a variety of animals in zoos and other forms of captivity around the world that are no longer able to experience their habitats. Instead, they are housed in concrete and secured with bars and glass! All of these animals, big and small, and even tiny, lived in the wild. However, today, they are held in captivity and are forced to cope with devastating bouts of depression!"

"The Lonesome Creature possessed what remained of a human brain and had the ability to think and feel like most human beings; it subsequently lost its will to live. So, most likely, it made the choice to no longer fight against its debilitating depression. In more ways than one, it was probably better off accepting its inevitable choice. Surely, its death was not swift. It was most likely emotionally painful, but its life experience, and subsequent death, may have caused each and every human being to recognize a lesson in futility and reality. Everything that lives, either upon or within the earth, or within the vast waters of our planet, has the right to live the life that creation designated for it! It was not and is not created for the abuse of a restrictive cage, bars or glass, or widened ducts of water; animals are not created so that they can be used in experiments to save mankind, injected with disease, or to see if they can overcome various types of cancers or the AIDS virus!"

Dr. Battle's body impulsively jerked and that function made him realize that he must have been rambling, and he said something to that extent. Mrs. Broskley said that she found herself captivated by his story and now had a more inclusive understanding of the creature. She made the initial arm motion and the doctor reciprocated, they hugged each other and Mrs. Broskley voiced a heart rendering "Thank you." Dr. Battle responded, "Oh, you're more than welcome."

She had the makings of a great story and while not having as many photos as she would have preferred, she realized that she had the only ones that were truly up to date. Mrs. Broskley thanked the appropriate personnel and then, while walking in the direction of her car, something became apparent. She found herself mystified that she was the only journalist in the vicinity. She entered her car, drove to the exit, and was given permission to leave the compound. Eventually, she was on Bristol Road and as she drove, she listened intently to the recorder. It was even more captivating now; she could not wait to arrive at The Intelligencer's headquarters. As Joanie Broskley proceeded along, she found herself impulsively peering into her rear view mirror. While expecting to see other cars, she was surprised once again by the vacant throughway to the hangar.

Chapter 85

ALL OF THE CREATURES were now within the confines of their new habitat. Great amounts of anticipation emanated from everyone connected to the project. The door, to and from the new habitat's landscape, was now temporarily sealed. Tractors and trailers were driven into the vast compound and were expertly backed-up to the entrance of the hangar. The driver and his crew got out of each tractor and went to the trailer's rear doors. Once there, they unlocked the double doors, opened and then secured each door to the outsides of each trailer. Metal ramps were pulled from slots beneath the trailers flooring and were secured so that the workers had easy access to the trailer, and to the man that remained in the trailer's storage area, who designated as the packer. There was an abundance of machinery, both from the present undertaking and a variety of stored machinery that had been in operation when the hangar was used on a regular basis, way back when. The operation went swiftly; everything that was supposed to be removed from the hangar was, and two forty foot trailers were packed from front to back and from the floor to the ceiling. If you had the luxury of viewing the finished packing job, no doubt you'd be impressed by the tight appearance of all the items; each was covered by a heavy, protective packing blanket, and every so often, strong elastic bands securely held everything close together. Once the last band was put in place, the doors were swung until closed and locked; the portable, lengthy ramps were then lifted and slid into and along the tract where they remained when unused. It was appreciated that the move went so smoothly. Now, the tractors and trailers were being driven through the habitat's perimeter gates, heading in the direction of the naval station.

Chapter 86

AN INDIVIDUAL COULD ENTER the elevator at the ground level of this newly constructed observation tower and press their right thumb against the highly sensitive glass covered decoder, thus allowing it to accept or deny their specific fingerprint. If the print failed, then the elevator would remain motionless, except for its doors. They, in turn, opened and closed, until the passenger's body weight was no longer an issue upon the elevator's flooring. It was also important to know that the elevator would not operate with more than one passenger at any given time. This information was classified and was only known by those that worked within the observation tower.

If the print was accepted, then, just prior to the elevator's movement, the doors would close automatically. As if in conjunction with the print being accepted and the doors being closed and locked shut, the elevator would then begin its assent to the observation level of the tower. Upon the elevator's arrival, it would stop, an alarm would sound, and the person within would have to re-enact the same process that happened at the ground level. If the second print was accepted, as was usually the case, the set of doors mechanically unlocked, slid open, revealing an impressive array of technological equipment, all appearing to be from a futuristic world! The tower had a tubular design, housing a single elevator, and at its apex, the observation level was easily seen. Just below the observation level was a second tier of offices, and these too were accessible only by way of the elevator.

The observation area, being the topmost level, was twenty feet above the top of the habitat's perimeter wall. When looking at this construction from a distance, one could visualize it to be in the form of a gigantic T. When exiting the elevator, a person could turn directly to the left or right and walk for quite a distance either way along an extension of the observation level, or walk forward for approximately fifteen feet. To the front of the elevator's doors was a grouping of large, outward curving windows, and these extended in both directions along horizontal walkways. Each window behaved as a one-way mirror; these were quite large and kept crystal clear. When standing by the front windows, it was easy to recognize that this tower was built to observe the creatures and their vast tract of land. At this vantage point, the entire complex could be viewed, but when attempting to see movement at its far end, the end where the creatures had their entry, one would need the use of the magnification lenses that were incorporated into the futuristic machines.

The horizontal walkway that paralleled the direction of the habitat's wall below was approximately fifty feet in length, twenty feet being to each side of the base tower. To the forefront of the elevator and just inside the frontal windows were two futuristic machines. Each one had the seating capacity for one adult, and the seats could be electronically adjusted for comfort to fit the height and weight of any individual.

Depending upon the desired room temperature, each mechanism within the lounge type seating automatically reduced or elevated the over-all temperature. In this way, it acclimated itself to the room, but would fine-tune itself according to the body temperature of its occupant. This caused the occupant to be constantly attentive, but yet comfortable. The machine's base was secured within four separate tracts and each machine was available to travel from the center left or the center right until they reached an extension's far end. At that point, the futuristic machine could be electronically redirected so as to return along the same set of tracts. The seating apparatus had been calibrated so that it could rotate quite smoothly upon enlarged ball bearings. After finding a comfortable seated position, it was then that its operator, using a variety of knobs and a centralized joy stick, would cause powerful lenses to come back to his or her face, and subsequently to their eyes, rather than being inconvenienced by leaning forward and into them.

These lenses cold be adjusted up or down, far to the left and also far to the right, all of the time remaining close and comfortable for the person within the designated seat. These lenses were so exact that very small objects, whether close or a great distance away, could be brought into focus and clearly recognized; they were known to have no equal when it came to distance and clarity.

One of the perks of these seats was the shiatsu rollers that were imbedded within the back support. It could be extended to include both the neck and head area, or left intact so its focus was upon the back area. This type of massage addressed pain and discomfort along the entire width of an operator's upper shoulders, all of the way down the entire back, including one's lower back and all the way to the base of the tailbone. The knobs along the sides of each armrest could be easily manipulated so that the eight sets of rollers could target pain points, a variety of stress triggers and other release points.

Slightly overhead and within easy eye access were several enlarged monitors forming a horseshoe pattern. Within each enlarged screen were several sub-screens that allowed the machine's operator to observe any type of action or reaction within the habitat, and be able to witness every movement within the enclosure. Off to the far right of the centralized area and to the rear of the tracts was a typing sound, similar to that of a printer and this sound was intermittently heard twenty-four hours of every day. Every so often, printouts would accumulate, one upon the other, and once they reached a designated height, they would be physically removed and carried to personnel in the offices below. Once these pages were hand-delivered, they were subsequently signed for, packaged, and then readied for mailing to the Pentagon.

Situated strategically along the observation level was audio and video recorders and these could be activated at any given time. If or when an occurrence happened directly related to the creature population, it was then that the tapes would also be sent along with the paperwork.

Chapter 87

MRS. BROSKLEY, WHILE RETURNING to the newspaper's headquarters, pulled off of the paved roadway and stopped her vehicle upon the shoulder area of Bristol Road. She turned off the motor and let out an exasperated steady stream of air, all the while attempting to compose herself. After a few minutes, she found herself calmed and realized that she was on the verge of an extraordinary story, that is, a story that could launch her career. To the best of her knowledge, she had been the only journalist to have access to this story. She knew that it was imperative to get it into print as soon as was humanly possible. While still anxious, she turned the ignition key and the vehicle's motor came to life. She drove directly to the office and once inside the building, she found herself confronted by the editor and several top level executives. Mrs. Broskley was hand-guided into a large and elaborate meeting room. The editor eagerly asked, "Okay Joanie, what do you have?"

Joanie was visibly anxious as she brought out a container of film which was subsequently taken to the darkroom for development. She then placed her voice recorder on the table and activated it. What was heard, and eventually seen, by way of the photos, brought a tremendous amount of excitement to all who were present. The editor, and all present, made it a point to compliment Joanie for a job well done. The next edition was due on the shelves the following morning, but the editor decided that a Special Edition should hit the streets as soon as was humanly possible.

Mrs. Broskley wrote a riveting, informative story, and following a review by the editorial staff, the entire front page had the gist of the story and an elaborate pictorial display.

THE LONESOME CREATURE IS DEAD!

The Nation and the World is in Mourning...

What followed was not in bold print, but was sure to hold the reader's attention. This was an all-inclusive story that brought the reader through the life and times of this creature. It offered a review of various documented stories from the time when the creature was first witnessed by Grace, on through its discovery and subsequent capture. An elaborate description of the habitat and membranes was also featured.

It described the process that led to the realization that this awesome oddity was of human origin, in fact, the creature was found to be nonviolent and quite sensitive. It described how this Lone Creature related telepathically with children, though no evidence existed that it could communicate with adults. It described how bonds were formed between the creature and the scientists, doctors, and the nurses, especially the evident connection between it and Dr. Battle. In closing, the article described how a suspected, ever spiraling depression took this poor soul to a place much more formidable than its experiences when roaming the earth's surface. This written account was so informative, spellbinding, and powerful. Once a reader had completed the story, there would surely be an instant clamoring for more. This was an all-consuming story, and there was absolutely no doubt that the public would empathize with the creature, its colony, subsequent exile and its death.

The special edition hit the streets very early in the morning, via The Intelligencer, and once it was distributed to the newsstands and onto the steps and porches of subscribers, the initial leak was given. Like wildfire, the information reached the entire nation within a matter of hours.

Once it had been verified that the nation had the information, it was then that teletypes were to be heard in editorial offices throughout the entire world. Within a matter of hours, copy of Mrs. Broskley's story and the accompanying photos were gracing fax machines and the front pages of every known newspaper and the news station, even in remote areas of the world. As the copy was read, a kind of melancholy could be evidenced upon the faces of the human race, as the death of the creature began to sink in. The various peoples of the world had been following the written and televised accounts ever since its celebrated arrival, capture, and captivity. Undoubtedly, people identified with the creature's plight. There had been genuine concern regarding its future, but now, any type of future was impossible.

During 1963, the world experienced a shock that seemed to parallel this happening. Now, forty years later, there was a similar jolt to one's system; it was a common sight to witness people hanging their heads in sadness and saying their private prayers. Concern and melancholy had become the world's visible face and inevitable emotion.

Chapter 88

AFTER THE BODY CAVITY was separated, the doctor removed one functioning part after the other, and each was identified, weighed and examined. The examination revealed that the creature, at the time of its death, was in excellent physical health and the reason for its death was an unknown. The doctor, needing more information, contacted Dr. Battle and a meeting was set. What ensued was very informative, and both doctors believed that the creature had died due to a broken heart; its unwillingness to live when being bombarded, day and night, from a depth defying, spiraling depression. Without further ado, the official cause of death was documented as being "natural causes."

Mrs. Broskley wrote a follow-up story which targeted the creature's broken heart and its melancholy; like her original story, people clamored to get a copy. Never before had anyone, or anything, within the documented history of mankind created more interest. What followed was a frenzy to understand the creature, its life experience, and its ultimately death. The sadness surrounding the creature's death continued, and with it became a universal plea that hurriedly changed to a demand. The public desired to be made aware of the burial site. The government made its power play to have the burial at the Arlington Cemetery, but political pressure caused by many within the County of Bucks and the politically correct, swayed the decision makers to bury the creature within the area that it lived and died. The information that sold the decision makers was that the Lonesome Creature was born, experienced its lifetime, and finally its subsequent death in and around Bucks County.

A variety of burial sites were mentioned, but the one that was chosen was the quaint and ancient Neshaminy Cemetery. This was not a large place, but it was located among scenic trees and the rolling hills associated with the county's countryside. It was common to hear birds and to witness squirrels and rabbits scampering, as they most probably envisioned this to be a safe haven. Adjacent to the cemetery, the rippling waters of a creek could be heard as it rolled along the side of Bristol Road, traveled under a bridge and came out on the other side. Headstones of centuries past were weather beaten and adorned with lush vines. This was the perfect place for the creature to share the earth with people that dated back to, and beyond, its colony's beginnings. There was even the possibility that some of those same people were instrumental in the decision to exile the lepers into the bowels of the earth.

A unique landmark adds to the quaintness of this burial site, that is, a small, ancient, stone church is situated close to Bristol Road, and is easily seen as motorists travel along the roadway. It is a one of a kind structure that stimulates inquisitive conversation and is located in one corner of the graveyard, close by the ever-flowing stream.

While the creature's tombstone was being carved, the burial site was being dug by the cemetery crew. It took a while to have everything ready, and since special attention was being paid to the cemetery's history, it took on a very special significance. The County of Bucks governing body prepared the viewing and burial site for what it imagined to be a special occasion. Indeed, this event was swiftly becoming more than colossal! What was about to happen could not have been imagined, let alone understood in the realm of reality.

Many of the world's newspaper offices were deluged with inquisitive calls related to the viewing and burial. Calls repeatedly came into the news desk of the Intelligencer, in Doylestown,

Pennsylvania; the initial influx was understandable. What was not understood was the fact that the phone rang off the hook for several hours. Calls from places that were near and far, throughout the Continental United States, and then intermittent calls came from as far as Japan, China, India, Europe and even Africa. You name it, and there was most probably a call from that area, all for the same information. When and where was the viewing and the burial?

Each and every caller was given the same courteous answer, that is, the viewing was to be held on August 23rd at nine o'clock in the morning and would continue until the last person was given the opportunity to pay their final respects. The callers were further notified that the burial would take place the following day, the 24th, at the nearby Neshaminy Cemetery. The volume of callers caught the county completely unaware; it seemed as if the world wanted to know the directions from the Philadelphia International Airport to the site of the viewing and the eventual burial. Concern grew by leaps and bounds within the government offices in the County of Bucks.

Chapter 89

AS THE CREATURES BEGAN stirring, their drugged state had lost much of its debilitating force, though as they opened their eyes, they were uncomfortable. While expecting to awaken within their rustic, pitch black environment, they gained their focus and were apparently somewhere entirely different. Gradually, their eyes adjusted and in a matter of minutes, they were able to recognize a soft, hazy type of illumination. A few of the creatures still had not fully recovered, but it was evident that most were concerned and bewildered by the light.

At the point where each had experienced the light, the creatures could be seen clasping their hand-like extremities over their faces, blocking as much as possible. Some imagined that they were in a dream, and it took these creatures the longest time to adjust. Others somehow realized that the change was, in fact, a reality, but had considerable trouble adjusting their eyes to what was thought to be a brilliant light. All of these creatures, whether experiencing a suspected dream or accepting this environment as a kind of reality, took a considerable amount of time to acclimate themselves, so that they could gradually remove the entire cover from their eyes.

As of yet, not one of these creatures had changed its body location, but they were investigating their present situation using various degrees of available eyesight. At first, they were concerned that the humans had entered their work site and placed lighting throughout. Could this have been possible while they slept?

Confusion reigned throughout the entire population, and then one of the creatures got to its feet and immediately fell due to the movement of the webbed flooring. The creature that fell remained in its prone position, wondering what had caused its loss of balance. This same creature had naturally closed its eyes when falling, and with them closed, it could feel the sense of light through its eyelids. It also expected to experience waste on the floor, but the stench and composition of such was completely gone.

Because of the light in that area, all that had their eyes open recognized the fall of their comrade. Others got to their feet, but they too collapsed due to the flooring. Bewilderment took over, and with this, not one creature attempted to get on their feet immediately. Watching, as others eventually attempted to stand and remain balanced, it became comical as they also fell. A few chuckled at first, but then most imagined their awkward appearance when falling, and they too began to laugh. Some laughed harder and longer than others, but all recognized that this laughter was something they had never experienced.

While upon the webbing, the creatures began to crawl; this movement was successful, but the webbing upset their hand and knee purchases. For some, this instability brought with it fear, but for those that were more secure, it brought a kind of joy. As the more secure creatures lost their stability, they found themselves rolling here and there while the webbing slightly gave, though this was hardly noticeable. These secure creatures gradually got to their feet, and while several watched, they were able to gain a semblance of balance. Those standing found it necessary to hug a wall as they tentatively moved one foot forward, and eventually the other. Other creatures had also lost their balance, but now none were falling; they knew that they would have to eventually move away from the wall if they were to gain their independence.

In time, they all adapted; this is not to say that there was not grunting, and sounds of anger and frustration. However, eventually, all of these creatures recognized the webbing for what it was. One of them noticed that its talons sank into the surface when using the wall for support. Indeed, the talons entered the wall, and due to the creature's force, the talons and a partial amount of their palm became immersed. Once within the wall, everything that had been absorbed gained a solid purchase and the wall totally resisted the pull of the creature's weight. The creature that first recognized this sensation dug its talons further into the wall, but in doing so, found that the further it reached, the denser was the composition.

After immersing its talons and a good part of its palm, the creature realized that the material did, in fact, bind its extremity steadfastly within the wall. This was surely amazing, though what was more astonishing was the fact that the talons were held so securely that the creature had to use a certain amount of force to release the wall's grasp. In time, all of the creatures adjusted to the webbing and walls, and learned to walk with a certain amount of dexterity; they found that experience and confidence were key.

All learned, some better than others, how to climb up and down the tunnels, and some were adroit enough to jump from the flooring to a wall. The creatures talons, extending and straining from its four extremities and always moving as intended, found comfort in the wall's composition. With ease, the directed sets of talons sank deeply, giving adequate support for their massive weight.

Some of the more youthful, inexperienced, and naïve creatures were noticeably less secure while moving along the webbing and subsequently didn't feel the strength and dexterity of a food gatherer. These creatures used the webbing as kind of a springboard and found themselves eventually connected with a wall. At that time, the youthful creatures slowly, but surely, released their footholds and placed the majority of their body weight upon the webbing. They then apprehensively had their full weight upon the flooring, but were more than ready to reclaim the wall as their necessary savior. As these creatures gained more confidence, they continued to test the webbing and eventually realized that this type of flooring was more than strong enough to hold their massive size. They grew more and more confident, and in doing so, these same creatures could be seen bouncing upon the steadfast webbing. The creatures then moved tenuously away from the walls and towards the catacomb's center. With each step, the flooring gave ever so slightly, though the areas along the centers of the paths gave slightly more than along the base of the walls. The creatures then passed this information on to those that still adorned the walls and that continued to fear the unknown.

Once all of the creatures were aware that the webbing would hold their weight, they wondered where they were and how they got there; these questions dominated the communication. Was it possible that this entire scene was merely a dream of one creature? This possibility was clearly not the case; confusion and apprehension now reigned. The more aggressive creatures began to explore the environment; everywhere they walked, the flooring held beneath their weight and the ever present scent was clean and refreshing. There was an evident flow of air throughout the area, and as their bodies encountered this, they felt euphoric. The air was fragrant and appealing, as if a fan was propelling a constant flow that met with everyone's acceptance. A clean air stream intermingled with misty, soothing moisture. The more hostile creatures were called back and the elders organized a search party; their responsibility was to determine their location. The others were to remain in the area where they had awakened so that the elders could perform a thorough investigation and eventually return to this same location.

The elders departed the area and were gone for several hours. Upon their return, large sub-groups were created and information was passed on. They said that they discovered a total of four lengthy, intertwining catacombs and that each level appeared to be endless. The catacombs had an abundance of room and that each had the webbed flooring throughout. It was also discovered that there were a number of tunnels, each connecting to all four catacombs. There was lighting throughout and along with the lighting, all of the catacombs and tunnels had a refreshing air stream.

The best was saved until last, "One of the membranes is missing, but three have mysteriously turned up in the birth area that is located on the top level." The colony was told that the three remaining membranes appeared to be thriving and that they were nearing the end of their cycle.

There was what appeared to be a momentary lull, and all of the creatures seemed to be completely overwhelmed. The colony, en masse, heard what was said, but none believed that the membranes had survived. As the colony gained their composure, all were apparently thankful and couldn't wait for the eventual births.

"The sacred chamber is similar to the one that our population had in our original habitat, with the exception that we did not do the decades of work. There is a huge pile of raw meat and large vats of what appear to be animal's blood; within the birth chamber are the three membranes, and each has evident movement."

New life was very near, and soon all of the fluid would be gone, leaving the membrane to eventually crack from its dryness. These three creatures were very close to their birth and were about to experience a habitat unlike any other.

Chapter 90

THE CREATURE'S AUTOPSY WAS done and it remained at the morgue, being prepared for its eventual viewing. After the viewing, it would be returned to the morgue until moved to the site of the funeral. August 23rd was fast approaching, and the tremendous volume of calls had finally diminished; the viewing was to be on the land where the creature had been captured. This, being a scenic area, had several different kinds of wild flowers, lush grass and a vast amount of vacant land.

It was now very early in the morning of August 23rd and an enlarged canopy had been constructed to protect the creature from the elements, being either sun or rain. Fortunately, the weather report for that day and the day of the burial called for clear skies, little humidity, slight winds, and a high of seventy-eight degrees. The canopy was of the size that it could fully protect the creature and give adequate coverage to those officially invited.

Chapter 91

DR. BATTLE RETURNED AND was now finishing up his examination of the baby. What happened next caught all in attendance unaware, with the exception of Dr. Battle, for he had made the decision that blood was to be drawn, and in turn, be sent to the lab. A mobile cart was witnessed coming through the double set of doors, being guided by an intern. A white cloth covered whatever was on the cart as it was wheeled to the immediate vicinity of the doctor. The cloth was removed, revealing syringes, and subsequently Dr. Battle explained, "It is my opinion that this baby is much more human than that of a creature, and it is my intention to take samples of her blood to be absolutely sure that she is not lacking in any vitamin, mineral, or enzyme."

"Earlier today, I had a meeting with a colleague about the baby's situation and I was directed to a distinguished nurse in Atlanta, Georgia. I then got into contact with Mary Jane Kennedy, the Senior Research Coordinator at the Emory Health Care Center in Atlanta, and her PKU expertise was quite helpful regarding the baby and the Lone Creature. She alluded to similar information that I had found through my own personal research."

"As soon as the newborn was available to our doctors, the phenylketonuria (PKU) test was administered; a test that is administered soon after birth across the entire United States. PKU is a rare condition in which a baby is born without the ability to properly break down an amino acid called phenylalanine. Without the enzyme, levels of phenylalanine and two closely related substances build up in the body; these substances are harmful to the central nervous system and cause brain damage. Fortunately, for this baby's sake, all of the testing came back negative. Unfortunately for the Lone Creature, he tested positive during a previous surgery. It is probably impossible, but wouldn't it be fantastic if we were able to test each creature following their birth for inadequacies and diseases?"

"I have seen several successful surgeries performed upon the creature and believe that vital surgeries can be performed on the baby to bring about significant change. The webbing between her fingers and toes and the oozing sores, which are intermittently seen on her body, can be removed and healed without scarring." Most present readily agreed with Dr. Battle, at least for the time being.

The vials of blood were taken from the now screaming baby; soon thereafter the tears subsided and a smile was coaxed by those that were in the immediate vicinity.

Later on, Dr. Battle met with a group of professionals, including psychiatrists and surgeons, and his theory was discussed at length. After much deliberation, the surgery was set for a date in early September. During the discussion, an important question was raised; if the surgery goes as planned and there is no reoccurrence of the webbing or sores, is it conceivable that this baby girl could be raised within a human family? One of the prominent psychiatrists from Philadelphia responded in a manner that was short and to the point; "It is a real possibility."

Chapter 92

IT WAS VERY EARLY in the morning and the sun was just beginning to peak above the far off horizon; this was surely a bittersweet time for the farmers, who now had been bought out and found themselves living off the fat of their mother earth. Since the sale of their farms, a few chose to purchase homes within one of the many adult communities for folks that were fifty-five years and older.

These men and women continued to get up at the crack of dawn, but not for work; only to walk the land areas that were still vacant of housing and malls. Cars and trucks were seen moving in one direction and then the other, driven for the most part by young adults who were on their way to various jobs. These men and women had their cell phones plastered against their heads, cups of coffee steaming from various holders, and the driver's eyes focused on everything but the road; off in the direction of never-never land.

The older farmers walked along and occasionally were seen to squat. While remaining in this position, a scoop of darkened soil was picked up and could be seen being refined between a thumb and fingers, pensively. If, by chance, they were strolling with a long time mate, they may eventually be snapped out of the captivity of their deep thoughts.

Early in the morning, one could smell a variety of fragrances and notice that signs of nature still abounded upon the fringes of the ever growing developments. It was every so often that one of these farmers would mentally entertain the thought related to the word progress; a semblance of a smirk would appear, and inevitably, a quiet laugh could be witnessed as his head moved smoothly to the right and then to the left.

It was a peaceful site when nature was at its finest. There were rolling hills and a wealth of gorgeous wild flowers, recently mowed lush green grasses and an abundance of trees burdened with stunning colors, indicating the beginning of a seasonal change. The sky was blue with tufts of white here and there, and the day was pleasantly brisk on this 23rd day of August.

The creature lying within the mahogany wood and polished brass was situated well-beneath the canopy, and to the forefront of the casket were enough chairs for every official guest. The casket's covering was in two parts; the forward part lay open, revealing the creature's head, neck, and massive chest, while the lower half was closed.

Due to the ceremony being held outside, the Lonesome Creature's upper body was covered by a fiberglass shield. Everything was in readiness for whatever presented itself on this day; due to the tremendous volume of calls, worldwide, there was the possibility that this could become more than a viewing. It was sure to become an epic part of Bucks County's history.

Chapter 93

THE ELDERS CONTINUED TO investigate the new environment and realized that this habitat was different. The most striking difference was an evident, constant amount of light, enough to make out images that had never been seen throughout their history. Images that, as it turned out, were in fact, mirrored by themselves. Except for the food gatherers, who had witnessed and subsequently shocked one another during sanctioned hunts, the remainder of the colony had lived entirely within the pitch black environment, never seeing their own appearance or that of another creature. Now, being within the softly lit habitat, all were able to witness first-hand why their appearance could frighten an innocent child waiting for her school bus.

The elders sensed this scene to be enlightening, and with their willingness to venture into parts unknown, they found familiar things; similarities to what was originally the only habitat they considered to be home. When at the precipice of the initial funnel, they recognized that they were at an area that only descended!

These elders, not accustomed to over-using their sight, could now see the other side of this cavernous opening; it was blocked! Confused and bewildered, at least one of these elders wondered why the catacomb's path did not continue. It gave this confusion additional thought, but the blockage remained a real concern. One of the elders offered to spring to the other side, but withdrew the offer when hearing that the depth was undetermined.

Realizing that that investigation could be put off until another time, they decided to back away from this immediate area and to further investigate the catacomb. When completely away from the tunnel, but yet still situated within the catacomb, all were elated for off in another direction was a substantial amount of light that came from a distant source. The group walked forward and in time, the reality was that they were now traveling along an ever inclining path. Closer and closer they got to the light source and in time, it was understood that the light source was not so brilliant. In fact, it was more like the light that shone from the moon. The group finally reached the source and being there, they listened intently, but they did not hear any sound. They continued to listen, and recognizing that it was nighttime, they were confident that they could depart this habitat and wander the surrounding countryside. They eventually found themselves picking up familiar scents; slowly, but surely, and with a certain amount of confidence, they all were able to move away from the security of the exit.

As soon as these creatures were clear of the exit, and now upon the earth's surface, there was an unfamiliar sound clearly heard by the person manning the observation tower. Activated for the first time, this sound caught the observer off guard; he found himself automatically tensing and wondering what the piercing sound meant. He looked around the automated observation board, and upon settling his nervous system, he realized that the brilliant green light and the piercing sound indicated that there was movement upon the surface and furthermore in a designated location.

The observer then did as he was trained; his eyes fell upon the variety of switches and he flipped those to the 'on' position, immediately activating both the audio and videotape. He then readjusted his seated position and gave his full attention to the indicated area. The light of the moon allowed for limited visibility, but this was better than none. Overhead, and off to the right, were several monitors, and at least one had several physical forms moving about within the direct vicinity of the habitat's exit. The observer tried to visualize the creatures and thought that such forms were in the distance, but wasn't absolutely sure; he then switched his attention to the monitors and his job at hand.

The food gatherers, one and all, knew that they had just exited the habitat, but that something was very wrong; subsequently, they began to experience intense anxiety! Messages were sent to one another and as these telepathically bounced back and forth, it was evident that their minds were in some sort of turmoil. They rolled their heads backwards and deeply sniffed the air. At the same time, they listened intently, but surprisingly there was little recognition. While continuing to feel a hint of anxiety, there was little fear, and so they moved further and further from what was the habitat.

The seconds turned into minutes and the further they ventured, the more they experienced things that were unprecedented; for whatever the reason, they felt safe and secure in this unknown environment. They began to move faster, occasionally looking back from whence they came, wanting to have a reference for the return to the habitat. The creature that was the furthest to the front found itself looking back, when all of a sudden it collided with an immovable mass. **THUMP!** It knew that it had come into contact with a static object, but it did not know what part of its body hit the object first. Unfortunately, the other food gatherers were too close behind, and almost simultaneously, they too experienced a similar fate. **THUMP, THUMP, BUMP, and more THUMPS!** It was somewhat comical to hear the collisions that resulted in moans and groans as the creatures rolled here and there, following their collisions with the formidable slab of steel. Completely shaken, the entire group tried to gather what wits remained and attempted to return to their feet and hopefully find access to their habitat.

The elders collected themselves and gradually got to their feet; they sauntered around for about a minute, and then the lead elder found it necessary to take a knee. Rather than collapse from the evident effects of the collision, other elders also knelt, but became noticeably woozy; in this position, they were light headed and unsteady. Eventually, all of the elders moved to a seated position and once comfortable, found that their sight registered a completely new environment. The full moon was evident, but even more so, their eyes caught hold of other lights that were seemingly in an alignment high above the surface.

One of the elders was seemingly over its ill effects and stood. Finding that it was able to walk, the elder moved in a different direction, still away from the habitat's entrance. As it walked, it became completely mesmerized, mystified by the alignment of the lights. While the individual elder walked in that direction, the remaining elders watched and anticipated his progress. When seemingly beneath the lights, the elder stopped and stood absolutely motionless in disbelief. It remained as it was, and was apparently fixated until the other elders moved to the same location. Now, all being in awe, they eventually settled and walked forward until they could go no further; this time none collided with the formidable object that seemed to touch the sky, high above. None of the elders had been seriously hurt, but while continually holding their heads, they found new lumps appearing beneath their hands. As the elders regained their equilibrium and composure, they found the pain lessening and so they decided to return to the habitat. Still somewhat woozy and befuddled by a different reality, they sauntered along and down the passageway, leading toward an area where several of the others waited for information.

These others recognized the food gatherers disorientation, their degree of pain, and questioned what had happened. Through communication, the lead elder informed the others as to the reasoning for the food gatherer's state of mind, and for their bumps and bruises. The information caused the others to feel unnerved, and consequently there was a general state of confusion and uneasiness among the entire group.

The food gatherers calmed the anxious group by communicating that there was no evidence at any time of the human's physical form upon the earth, and that the environment appeared safe, green, and lush. Before continuing, a question was posed pertaining to their evident discomfort. The food gatherers then addressed this by responding that the surface restricted their movement. In fact, as far as they knew, the colony was now within a solid, walled-in enclosure. The elders then said that it was the last happening that convinced them that they were no longer within an environment that was familiar.

It was further stipulated that these same food gatherers would re-enter the surface environment the following night to further reconnoiter and document as much of this setting as was possible. That information helped calm the other's anxiety, and with this amount of ease came a feeling of stability.

Chapter 94

SEVERAL OF THE INVITED guests had clearances to land their helicopters at the Willow Grove Naval Station. Others, such as the Lightcaps, were local and drove to the site, but those from out of Pennsylvania and beyond, flew into the Philadelphia International Airport. Almost all of the invited guests had arrived and were seated. It was then reported that a seemingly endless entourage of cars had been observed traveling north on Route 6II, from as far away as Broad Street and beyond.

The people that had tuned in to watch their variety of programming found an ongoing news break on specific channels; these stations, plus cable news, were directing their commentary to the viewing and the subsequent burial of the creature.

All who attended the viewing got to witness an unprecedented amount of security, and many wondered, silently and aloud, whether the security was more for the President, or for the Lone Creature.

People came from all parts of the world; Bucks County would never be the same again. The viewing was orderly, and like viewings for people of notoriety, the line was continual. Each person was given a similar amount of time to observe the creature, say a prayer, and then move on.

Some of the observers were more stunned than others, and after paying their final respects to the celebrated creature, their attention usually moved on to the seated guests. At times, it was clear that they were trying their very best to visualize Grace, Ryan, and Wyatt, the three children that had the most impact upon the creature's discovery and subsequently, its life connections since being captured. The observers attempted to recount the variety of news articles and photographs that depicted this happening from its beginning until this moment in time.

This area of Bucks County appeared to be chaotic, but in actuality, it was simply deluged by traffic. The inundation was not in just one direction, for many had already experienced the viewing and were now returning to the airport and to their distant homes. The traffic that was proceeding north was, at best, congested, but it was kept in motion by police officers from various townships. The traffic signals continually blinked, enabling the traffic to move when directed by policemen, both north and south.

When considering the amount of people that wanted to stay in Bucks County for this event, there were just too many, and not nearly enough rooms for those that wanted to experience both the viewing and burial. It was unfortunate for those that needed rooms, for the month of August was a major month for conventions in Philadelphia. No matter how one looked at the problem, there were not enough vacancies for that great a number.

When considering the multitude of people that did come, it was fortunate that they had previously received relative information, for without it, there could have been a mass of confusion. Fortunately, for the multitude that came, they had paid attention to the recorded messages and were able, for the most part, to make flights out of Philadelphia on the 23rd, or during the very early morning hours of the 24th.

There were vehicles of every type traveling along Route 611; limousines, rental cars, vans, taxicabs with plates from Pennsylvania, Virginia, Delaware, Maryland, New York, New Jersey, and school bus types adorned with temporary limo plates. All of the visitors had to find transportation to and from the viewing site, with as much comfort as possible, and all of the companies that supplied the transport vehicles realized that these two days would bring in some very serious cash and tips. The foreigners came, viewed the creature, paid their final respects, and then returned to their waiting transport to be driven back to the airport. This procedure happened throughout the morning, afternoon, and evening. Finally, the last person viewed the creature and was seen departing the area. Those that remained found themselves much more at ease. This was best evidenced by the fact that the President, the First Lady and their daughter, Chelsea, walked a short distance to where Grace and Ryan were seated, sat next to them, and exchanged warm hellos. As greetings were exchanged, Grace had an immediate and swift flashback of her visit to the White House, and the sincere hospitality that the First Family had accorded her and her family. Grace found herself hugging the President and saying a heartfelt "Thank you." Pleasantries and greetings were passed among all and then the President announced that he was leaving, and unfortunately he, or the family, could not return tomorrow for the funeral. As the President and family moved, so did his ever tightening security; those people were so adept at their job that an observer would have been led to believe that they were no more than invited guests.

Normally, security made their presence known when accompanying the President, but today, he wanted them to be less conspicuous, at least during the actual viewing. That was the case until the President moved here or there, then the invited guests could be seen for what they were, that is, experts in highly trained positions. They moved with a precision that had no equal, as they went into their 'protect mode' whenever the President and the First Family left their designated chairs. It was more than evident that these people were indeed proficient and totally professional. The President and First Family said their farewells, and once in the limousine, they were whisked away, heading in the direction of the naval station and the waiting military helicopter.

Chapter 95

JOHN AND NANCY MALHER got up from their chairs and asked their children to accompany them to the creature. They were aware of the creature's struggles since first being seen by Grace and the circumstances that surrounded it, from the time of its capture to this present date of August 23rd. The entire family went to the creature and while in its direct vicinity, Wyatt instinctively reached and laid his hand, palm down, upon the tubular covering. Wyatt remained this way, and within seconds, John laid his hand upon Wyatt's shoulder, showing his willingness to share his son's emotional bond. Wyatt eventually removed his hand, as did John from Wyatt, and then John told Nancy that he and Wyatt would be waiting by the limo. Nancy and the rest of the children paid their final respects and after talking amongst one another, they eventually walked toward John and Wyatt.

Indeed, the creature was finally experiencing peace, but it was a shame that a sensitive being had to die within our culture to finally find peace. The creature never experienced the new habitat; here it was, just prior to its subsequent burial, after living its entire life, save a few months, in a pitch black, dank, foul smelling, horrendous environment, all brought about by its initial community's decision and not its own culture.

Nancy and the children joined John and Wyatt and then all entered the limo and were driven to the location of a nearby hotel.

The family members got out of the limo, and while Nancy took the children to the lobby, John made arrangements with the driver for the pick-up time in the morning. Once inside their reserved hotel suite, each family member realized that they were more than spent by the totality of this day.

Now that the President and the First Family had been driven away and most likely had already boarded their helicopter, there was the possibility that they were already experiencing their home in Washington.

Chapter 96

THE LIGHTCAPS GATHERED TOGETHER and they too visited with the creature; Grace found herself reminiscing as she studied the creature's features. John and Kathleen thought that Grace was praying, but really, she was thinking with her eyes gradually closing. While reminiscing, her thoughts flowed and Grace found herself in sort of a dilemma. She realized that when she first saw the creature, that she was overwhelmed by its smell and subsequently by its horrific and frightening features. She remembered that those things alone caused her great amounts of stress and fear. She also remembered being completely unnerved when noticing that Bigfoot was coming closer and closer to where she and Ryan waited for their school bus. Being the intelligent child that she was, she realized that was when the dilemma came into play.

Grace understood that her stresses and fears dissipated as she became acquainted with the creature and its depth of sensitivity. As her thoughts continued, she found herself wondering just how many people in the world would have behaved as she had, and how unfair that type of thinking was. Pensively, her mind wandered, and as it did, she felt an increased sadness. As Grace opened her eyes, the welled-up tears began flowing; she looked deeply into the creature's heart and soul and asked for forgiveness. It was at that time that the tears stopped and somehow she knew that the creature had, indeed, forgiven her. Grace looked at her mother, having a warm and softened smile upon her face. Kathleen, noticing the smile, understood that both the creature and Grace had found an inner peace; Kathleen pulled Grace tightly to her side and momentarily held her there. Grace, Ryan, John and Kathleen gathered together and eventually were within their scenic home; tomorrow was, no doubt, going to be another eventful day. All were subdued while seated around the crackling sound coming from the nearby fireplace insert, in a contemplative state as the heat warmed their faces.

Chapter 97

THANKS TO THE VARIOUS police forces and their never ending professionalism, all went well. It was now late in the afternoon on the 23rd and the creature's coffin had its protective covering removed. It was then that the opened portion of the lid was closed and prepared for its return to the county morgue.

During the night, the creature was kept in the coolness of the morgue; several hours elapsed and now it was August 24th. This morning could not have been more beautiful or more appropriate for the celebrated burial; the breeze was steady and brisk, but not overly cold, and the sun was just beginning to warm the countryside.

The gravesite was prepared and ready. The pall-bearers had considerable difficulty moving the coffin between and around the worn and ancient headstones. These marked the various places where the departed souls finally rested; rested, yes, but also could be roaming about, among old friends and the newest of acquaintances.

The coffin was laid upon its mount and then draped with ceremonial colors; the creature was here and was now in readiness for its ceremony. Unlike the day before, when there were people from all parts of the world, this day, in comparison, had only a small presence. As it turned out, all of the world travelers and almost all people that were from outside of Pennsylvania had made their return flight connections; they were now either home or nearing their far away destinations, having stories to tell their children and grandchildren.

People began arriving; the Lightcaps were the first. The Malher family, Mrs. Broskely and her husband David, the Hengy's, Dr. Battle, the nursing team, the doctors and scientists from the hangar; they all got the opportunity to witness one another, and to renew friendships. Along with the aforementioned people, a few state politicians and dignitaries were present, but beyond the scope of these prominent people, there were approximately a hundred onlookers. The variety of onlookers who hadn't walked to the cemetery from their homes parked their cars, along with others, along Bristol Road and gradually moved close enough to pay their final respects to the creature.

During the early evening of August 24th, the Neshaminy Cemetery returned to its normalcy; the creature had been gently lowered into its final resting place and all of the onlookers were now gone. Invitations to visit were extended to all that were present, but none accepted. Everyone wanted to return to their homes, to reflect on the events of these past two days and to eventually get back to their daily routines. There were handshakes, hugging, pleasantries passed around, and then everyone was gone; a multitude of footprints remained that had just flattened the normally well-kept and thriving landscape.

As Grace approached the carved stone stairway, she turned her head and gave the area one more look. By that time, the casket had already been lowered and it was now resting upon the bottom of the gravesite. No one was in the immediate vicinity. However, believe it or not, a squirrel, a few chirping birds, and a rabbit were visiting the creature. Grace said her final farewell, turned her head forward, and then slowly descended the ancient steps.

Traffic resumed its normal comings and goings along Bristol Road, and one would find it difficult to realize that, just a short while ago, there was a ceremonial burial right in that immediate area. The gravediggers retrieved the necessary tools from the storage shed and then returned to the grave. The two men thought about opening the coffin one last time, but chose not to; they removed the tarp from the large mound of dirt and then began to shovel it around, and eventually on top of the coffin. An hour or more went by and then what was previously a hole, was now filled, leaving a small mound cover at the top. One of the men left and then returned, hefting a small, yet efficient machine. From the storage shed he came and once at the gravesite, the machine was operated to compact the mound of dirt. Once this was finished, the soil was then thoroughly soaked and sprayed with grass seed. One of the workmen hesitated, and read the inscription on the brass plate within the marble grave stone. It read as follows; "Here Lies a Sensitive Being, God Bless!" The work was completed and all of the equipment was then returned to its storage shed; this had been a day where everything had gone as planned.

Mrs. Joanie Broskley would, of course, do a follow up story, and it would certainly sell a tremendous amount of newspapers within Bucks County and throughout the entire United States. The tremendous volume of sales would be due to the fact that now, people worldwide, had a personal connection to the life and the subsequent death of the Lonesome Creature.

Chapter 98

THE CREATURES WERE SAFE and secure within their walled enclosure, and the men and women that had constructed the walled enclosure, and its habitat, knew that this creature colony was there to stay.

Dr. Battle returned to his prestigious practice, and the nurses to their chosen hospitals and other places of employment.

The three fetuses completed their birth cycle, and one by one consumed the liquid nutrition that was responsible for sustaining their lives; inevitably, the membranes hardened, cracked and decayed. Once the liquid was entirely consumed, it was then that the membrane became fragile enough for the newborns to crack the exterior and push through, removing themselves from within. Once their instinct led them towards slabs of raw, bloody beef, and a smaller blood cache than that of the sacred chamber, it was then that the newborns slithered across the birthing area's surface. Eventually, they found themselves at the edge of their nutrients; they gnawed and slurped, making noises that were easily heard and recognized. At this point, they would muster enough strength to thrust their entire heads into the raw meat. Once their fiendish need for food had been appeased, they'd then move to the separate birthing area's vat of blood, dunking their heads into the nutritious staple, drinking and slurping.

These newborns remained within the birth chamber for a

433

month or more, and swiftly grew to a size that allowed them their independency. Ultimately, they began to venture beyond the birthing area, but remained in its close proximity, often lengthening the period of time between their pangs for hunger and thirst. As their size and strength increased, these newborns found themselves possessing an internal strength that made them feel superior to any other living being. Their dependency upon the birth chamber was closing in on a second month; when this was the case, it would only be a matter of days before these newborns would become full-fledged creatures, becoming as self-sufficient as any female and many of the adults. It was at this point in a creature's life cycle that all newborns would somehow know that all of the raw meat and the designated supply of blood within the birthing zone were to be totally consumed before depending upon the creature's regular meat and blood source within the sacred chamber.

Chapter 99

THERE HAD BEEN SEVERAL related studies done while the Lone Creature was in captivity, and they resulted in the supposition that there was enough meat and blood presently within the sacred chamber, and that amount would sustain the entire colony for the thirty days. It was furthermore estimated that the food gatherers would have to hunt once every seventeen to twenty-one days, and one of the studies further stated how much wildlife would have to be brought into the walled compound from places such as Valley Forge National Park and various game preserves within the Pennsylvania State boundaries. Any and all game would then be transported, and be encouraged to run directly from the transports during the daylight hours, directly into the walled-in enclosure.

Presently, several large deer had entered, and most likely saw this setting as a haven. They also discovered a place to go when frightened, a place filled with trees of various girths and heights, and the camouflage of shrubs and bushes. Feeling adventurous, a few of the deer found themselves sniffing a suspicious opening that was located along the border of the vegetation. Having a healthy fear associated to an unknown scent, these animals chose not to enter and then bounded away to play among the others; all were relatively sure that they were experiencing their unexpected nirvana.

The amount of deer and other wildlife would have to be

recalculated from time to time when projecting increases in the creature population, but for now, the raw and bloodied meat and blood cache, which was periodically needed, was believed to be more than enough.

There was considerable thought given to placing an abundance of nonburrowing wildlife within the enclosure, and keeping all of that sustenance supplemented with the vitamins and more; the wildlife would then remain healthy, and in turn would keep the creatures immune systems strengthened. It was also suggested that a variety of wildlife could be brought to this site, and eventually become self-sustaining. If the abundance of deer and other large wildlife became self-sustaining, then there would be a seemingly endless supply for the creatures to hunt, kill, and eat. This idea was tabled till a later date, but was seen as a most viable solution.

Chapter 100

SOON AFTER THE ENCLOSURE was completed and the Lone Creature had experienced its final resting place, there seemed to be a dramatic change in the amount of traffic witnessed along Bristol Road. Upon entering Bristol Road from 2nd Street Pike and heading in the direction of York Road, it was easy to understand why the traffic continually slowed and caused congestion.

Bordering Bristol Road, about three-quarters of a mile from 2nd Street Pike, was the enormity of the creature habitat, and about four miles beyond that enclosure was the location of the historic Neshaminy Cemetery. There were signs evidenced at both sites forbidding anyone to park a motorized vehicle within one-hundred yards of the walled-in enclosure, or within twenty-five yards of the cemetery.

There seemed to be a lot more attention given to the monstrosity that was now the home for the creature population. Like any other newsworthy sensation, this sight grabbed the world's attention. Months passed, and as captivating as the story had been, the creature's experience had lost the majority of its lure. Now, life was slowly, but surely, returning to normal within the quaint, affluent structure of what is the County of Bucks. It was directed, more so, or so it seemed, to the specific towns of Edison and Doylestown, in Pennsylvania.

Epilogue

WHILE IT WAS TRUE that life was slowly returning to its normalcy within the County of Bucks, it was just as relevant that the creature's influence touched all that crossed its path. The creature changed the way many people viewed those with a disability such as leprosy. Life does change, and although change often causes anxiety, it is this change that often creates strength and character. When change does become a reality, it is, more than not, an occurrence that brings about more good than bad!

Sadness has been the prevailing emotion throughout our world since Grace Lightcap first set her eyes onto what she envisioned to be Bigfoot. As time went on, the creature's experiences and how we reacted to them taught us a lot about it, but even more so, about the frailties of the human race; how our power can influence tremendous pain and suffering, or sheer happiness.

While it was true that these creatures were human beings approximately one-hundred and twenty years ago, it is also true that their relatives continued to live, as humans, within the communities of Edison and Doylestown. These same relatives were fortunate not to experience the disease, but it is true that unbeknownst to the leper colony, these relatives were instrumental in forcing the lepers underground. The lepers gradually adapted to their environment, and due to their ungodly circumstances, evolved into what could only be described as a creature, *a monster*, if you will, that had absolutely no resemblance to the most hideous of any other within the human race.

The Lone Creature experienced many physical changes by way of a very competent surgical team and the caring and sensitivity of Dr. Battle, a specialist in the field of Gastroenterology, plus the highly experienced team of professional nurses.

Kept within its sterilized setting and being sedated whenever it was deemed a necessity, the creature constantly received the best of care. Doctors and nurses worked throughout the day and evening hours, and were on-call from midnight until eight o'clock in the morning. Being cared for as it was, the creature experienced continual change; subsequently, it was now readied to be seen by visitors and possibly the public.

Much happened during the month since its capture, and then, during the time of its captivity, it succumbed to its death, viewing, and burial. After the burial, life gradually regained its normalcy throughout the world, but it took quite a bit longer for those living within the County of Bucks.

The day following the burial was refreshingly cool, and for the next two weeks, it sporadically rained, each and every day. Among other things, the downfall was good for the gravesite; the newly laid grass seed had gotten a jump-start on its growth. After the lengthy period of rain, the weather cleared and the cemetery ground crew finally had the opportunity to return to the creature's grave. They knew that the rain was good for the seed, but also wanted to make a thorough check of that immediate area.

The grounds crew expected to find everything much as it had been before the rains came, but they could not have been more wrong. While it was true that the grave marker had not been moved or damaged, it was just as true that the site had seemingly been vandalized. Around the marker and all about the newly laid seed were sizeable punctures, deep within the earth, that had noticeably damaged the site. Where the cover had not been spiked, there was evidence of huge footprints. The crew put their minds together and decided to report this happening to their boss and in turn, the authorities were notified. A team of investigators arrived at the scene and after several lengthy days of communication, the end result was deemed inconclusive. "Could it be that other creatures, similar to those that were presently within the walled enclosure, were also in the area? While the authorities wanted to dismiss this thought as folly, they really did not know what to do. The investigators returned to the site and obtained plaster casts of the indentations surrounding the grave.

John Malher had returned to his Wall Street business, and life returned to normal, at least for the most part. Nancy and the children were back to doing the things that made them the progressive family that they were. Their son, Sandy, announced that he had chosen to study at Roanoke College, Which was exciting news for John and Nancy, who had both graduated from the same college during the early 1970s.

One day out of the blue, John and Nancy were asked to fly to Philadelphia where they would be met by a driver and driven to Saint Christopher's Hospital for Children. Not having the faintest idea what the request was for, John talked it over with Nancy, and they came to the conclusion that it was probably a request for a sizeable donation. Both knew that if, in fact, the request was for a donation, then they didn't have to leave the estate; that an official letter would have been more than sufficient. What intrigued John the most was that both he and Nancy were requested to come to St. Christopher's, where it was the norm for requested donations to come through his name alone. It was later that same day that John returned the call; he stated that he and his wife would be arriving at a specified time and that they would be waiting to be met at the baggage claim area.

All went as planned, and upon their arrival, they were warmly greeted and escorted to the hospital director's office.. Once inside the office, they were asked to be seated, and upon doing so were notified that the director would be with them in a matter of minutes. As promised, a neatly dressed gentleman entered the office and introduced himself as Dr. William K. Soens. As the doctor approached John, he rose to greet him; while extending his hand, he could not help but notice that the doctor was extremely tall and that his weight appeared to be appropriate for his stature. They shook hands, and then Dr. Soens went to Nancy; he greeted her warmly and then thanked them for making the trip. It was at this time that the doctor moved behind his desk, sat down, wheeled his chair forward and upon his desk he opened a folder full of documents. He thumbed through it, hesitated, and remained still, being pensive as he searched for the appropriate words. Both John and Nancy found that they were becoming anxious, but just then, Dr. Soens raised his head and began to speak. "Let me get right to the point; I know that you are familiar with the case of the baby girl that was born after spending many months within a membrane. Well, that baby survived and has continued to thrive here at St. Christopher's. She has been here since very early in her life, and now, more than a year later, she continues to respond extremely well to her surgeries."

"Almost no one, other than our professional staff, knows of her circumstances and I am only informing you for a specific reason. She was born as a creature, but had several human characteristics. Unlike a human, she was born with webbing between her fingers and toes, and no umbilical cord; she also had epidermal sores, and was noticeably heavier at birth than a human infant."

"Since her arrival, she has had surgeries to remove the webbing, and also to remove the epidermal sores. Those surgeries were somewhat tedious, but not overly difficult, and since then, there has been no reoccurrence of either malady."

"Several additional surgeries have been performed during a period of many months, and all were related directly to the baby's reproductive system. As unbelievable as it may seem, our baby endured a unique surgical procedure that had favorable results."

"It just so happened that another baby died in an automobile accident, and subsequently, her mother allowed her baby to be included in the organ donor program. The baby was then rushed to the OR and after removing her entire reproductive system, it was then placed into proper containers and flown to this hospital. The reproductive system was then given a complete examination and was declared appropriate for a transplant. Very early the following morning, our baby was prepped for the surgical procedure and after a lengthy, but successful surgery, our baby was moved from the OR to the recovery unit and then on to our intensive care unit. There,

441

she was constantly monitored and after a few days, she began to thrive and eventually was removed from the ICU. She healed nicely and over time, her scarring was hardly noticeable. The fact is, she is prepared to continue with the rest of her life, away from the hospital, as a human child rather than as a creature."

Both John and Nancy were amazed at what they had just heard Dr. Soens say; it felt like a daydream. First of all, it was simply amazing that this creature had survived its incredible birth, and was, in fact, thriving; as amazing as that was, the transplant of an entire reproductive system was, well, mind-boggling! After hearing all that was said, and seemingly digesting it, John then spoke to Dr. Soens, "Why are we here?"

It was then that Dr. Soens, seemingly perplexed, got directly to the point, saying, "I have been made aware that you both have an excellent approach toward the raising of adopted children; I would like you to consider the adoption of this very special baby." The pros and cons of the adoption were thoroughly discussed during what was to be a lengthy conversation. When all was said and done, John took the initiative to speak. "Dr. Soens, my wife and I will remain in Philadelphia tonight and will discuss the proposal. Hopefully by morning, we will be able to give you some sort of answer."

Nancy, seemingly in favor of the adoption, asked if they could see the baby. Dr. Soens did not hesitate and immediately led them to a room where he stopped in front of a specific crib. He then began to depart, but as he was exiting the room he was heard to say, "You may pick her up if you'd like".

Not knowing what would be the baby's actual appearance, Nancy was more than overjoyed at what her eyes beheld. There, lying in the crib, adorned with many different items and warm colors, was nothing like what she could have ever imagined. The baby was dressed in pink and white, and while awake, hadn't yet noticed either John or Nancy. Caught-up in the moment, Nancy looked at the baby's cover and then returned her attention to the baby's face. It was then that Nancy's eyes met the alerted eyes of the baby, and both smiled warmly. Nancy was heard to say "Ohhhh" as she reached in the direction of the baby's sides. The smiles continued as Nancy held the baby against herself and softly rubbed its back. There were several sensitive sounds, and then another "Ohhhh" as Nancy leaned against John. Before Nancy could ask the inevitable question, John got in a heartfelt let out a heartfelt reverberation. "Wooooooowwww!"

Early the following morning, the Malhers returned to St. Christopher's and walked to Dr. Soen's office. The lights were on so John took the initiative to knock. "Just a minute," was heard, and soon after, the doctor asked John and Nancy to be seated. Rather than go behind his desk, Dr. Soens moved a chair and was then seated in the same immediate area as John and Nancy. He waited and then John said that they had decided, but that the decision could not be finalized until they returned home and had spoken with their children. John went on to say that they did want to adopt this baby, but that the adoption was contingent upon their children's decision. Dr. Soens said that he fully understood and that he would be waiting for the family's decision.

Having an eighth child, and that child being but a baby, was fully discussed. Also of importance was the fact that the baby would require further surgeries, and John asked if Nancy remembered if, in fact, the doctor mentioned whether or not the baby, when becoming an adult, could have children? Nancy said that she was almost sure that he had not mentioned that, but that she believed the previous surgeries created that possibility. *If the decision was made to adopt, then how much are we willing to tell the children?* John and Nancy discussed several different scenarios, and then decided, for the mental health of all involved, that the baby's background would remain a secret; this would be best for the baby and the entire family. If asked by their children, or any other, it was decided to say that the baby's background wasn't known; that she was abandoned.

There were no arguments, just thoughts that were discussed at length, and then, after they had talked with the children, a decision would be made. Before talking with the children, they decided to sleep with their thoughts for a few more days. That first night, they both slept fitfully, but since the following day was Saturday, they found themselves somewhat laid back. Nancy found herself downstairs before John, and she went to the basement to check on the amount of laundry that had accumulated. While by the clothing bin, she fished through this and that, and by chance felt something completely unfamiliar. She picked up a sack and feeling that it had some weight, felt inside. She reached in further and removed the object. Nancy then returned upstairs and finding John, wrapped in a bath towel, asked what the skull represented. For John, that settled the matter of the adoption, for what Nancy was holding was the skull that John had found when searching the original habitat. John then told Nancy that the skull had creature history, and for him, a lot of meaning. He then said that he was agreeable with the adoption, but that he needed to know what Nancy wanted. Nancy responded, as John knew she would, and then they shared the adoption possibility with the children. All of their children had storied backgrounds and were very excited with the prospect of having a new sister; they could not wait to have her for their own.

The baby remained at the hospital for continued surgeries and its subsequent healing process, and while there, Nancy realized that the baby had not yet been given a name. One evening, while the family had gathered in the living room, Nancy told everyone that the baby had not been named as of yet. She went on to say that she had, what she thought, was the perfect name. While all waited in anticipation, Nancy was clearly heard to say, "Tess." This named rolled off of the tongues of each family member and all were in agreement with this splendid choice. Nancy, appearing anxious but happy, then asked, "Can we call her Tess?" John immediately responded, saying, "Tess it is, Tess Malher!"

The adoption papers were drawn-up and finally signed, making if official. John and Nancy were now the parents of an eighteen-month old little girl, Tess Mahler.